EVERYONE'S A LIAR

Books by Alexandra Ivy

Guardians of Eternity
WHEN DARKNESS COMES
EMBRACE THE DARKNESS
DARKNESS EVERLASTING
DARKNESS REVEALED
DARKNESS UNLEASHED
BEYOND THE DARKNESS
DEVOURED BY DARKNESS
BOUND BY DARKNESS
FEAR THE DARKNESS
DARKNESS AVENGED
HUNT THE DARKNESS
WHEN DARKNESS ENDS
DARKNESS RETURNS
BEWARE THE DARKNESS
CONQUER THE DARKNESS
SHADES OF DARKNESS
DARKNESS BETRAYED
BEWITCH THE DARKNESS
STALK THE DARKNESS
SATE THE DARKNESS

The Immortal Rogues
MY LORD VAMPIRE
MY LORD ETERNITY
MY LORD IMMORTALITY

The Sentinels
BORN IN BLOOD
BLOOD ASSASSIN
BLOOD LUST

Magic for Hire
WILD MAGIC
ANCIENT MAGIC
ETERNAL MAGIC
DRAGON MAGIC

Ares Security
KILL WITHOUT MERCY
KILL WITHOUT SHAME

Romantic Suspense
PRETEND YOU'RE SAFE
WHAT ARE YOU AFRAID OF?
YOU WILL SUFFER
THE INTENDED VICTIM
DON'T LOOK
FACELESS
UNSTABLE
DESPERATE ACTS
THE MURDER CLUB
SHE'S GOING TO PAY
EVERYONE'S A LIAR

Historical Romance
SOME LIKE IT WICKED
SOME LIKE IT SINFUL
SOME LIKE IT BRAZEN

Don't miss these Guardians of Eternity novellas
TAKEN BY DARKNESS in YOURS FOR ETERNITY
DARKNESS ETERNAL in SUPERNATURAL
WHERE DARKNESS LIVES in THE REAL WEREWIVES OF VAMPIRE COUNTY
LEVET (ebook only)
A VERY LEVET CHRISTMAS (ebook only)

And don't miss these Sentinel novellas
OUT OF CONTROL
ON THE HUNT

Published by Kensington Publishing Corp.

EVERYONE'S A LIAR

ALEXANDRA IVY

KENSINGTON
PUBLISHING CORP.
kensingtonbooks.com

KENSINGTON BOOKS are published by

Kensington Publishing Corp.
900 Third Avenue
New York, NY 10022

ISBN: 978-1-4967-5549-0
ISBN: 978-1-4967-5550-6 (ebook)

First Kensington Trade Edition: November 2026

10 9 8 7 6 5 4 3 2 1

Printed in the United States of America

The authorized representative in the EU for product safety and compliance
is eucomply OU, Parnu mnt 139b-14, Apt 123
Tallinn, Berlin 11317, hello@eucompliancepartner.com

To my mom, who always believed.
I miss you every day.

CHAPTER 1

New Orleans, LA
Wednesday, June 18th

It was 10:15 a.m. when Livia Benoit stormed into her New Orleans real estate office. Elegantly designed with large glass windows that offered a stunning view of Lake Pontchartrain, the front lobby featured a round table and two leather chairs arranged near the windows, as well as framed photos of famous local landmarks on the wall. The sleek reception desk, angled at the back of the room, blocked anyone from entering the inner office without approval.

A slender man with neatly trimmed black curls and features a breath from beautiful glanced up to study her with a raised brow. As always, Marcel Rivera was impeccably attired. This morning he wore a bright yellow shirt, which highlighted the golden flecks in his dark eyes and the rich gloss of his skin and tailored slacks.

Marcel had been her personal assistant since she opened her own real estate agency two years ago. He was not only her employee, but her best friend.

If she was honest, he was her *only* friend.

Livia was smart, driven, and ruthlessly honest, but her social skills were a disaster. At thirty, she'd finally accepted she would never change. Might as well enjoy her career and the comfy home she'd bought a few blocks from her office.

"Good morning, sunshine," Marcel drawled. "You're late."

Livia's stilettos clicked against the black-and-white tiled floor, her brunette curls bouncing against her shoulders as she stomped to stand in front of the desk.

"Love sucks," she announced in dramatic tones.

"Preaching to the choir, sweetie."

"No. I mean, it really, really sucks."

"I know. We've been saying it for years . . ." Marcel's words trailed away as he abruptly narrowed his gaze. "Wait. I thought you'd switched sides. You know. Everything is rainbows and butterflies. Ain't love grand and all that nauseating crap."

"Jacob Pearson happened."

"Your knight in shining armor? The yin to your yang—"

"Stop."

Livia clenched her teeth. She didn't blame Marcel for his teasing. She'd been vocally anti-love since the age of two. Just after her mother had died and her family had sent her off to a foster family in New Orleans. She'd never wavered in her certainty. Not when she'd gone to college at Tulane to get her business degree. There'd been a few casual boyfriends and plenty of fun nights with friends and lovers, but nothing lasting. Not even after she'd gained her real estate license and opened her agency. There were business acquaintances and casual men who she could call to escort her to formal events, but they barely skimmed the surface of her life.

Until Jacob Pearson.

The thirty-five-year-old financial advisor was her complete opposite. He was tall with the muscles of an athlete. He had short blond hair and bright blue eyes.

Livia, in contrast, was a little over five feet with full curves she emphasized with her hand-tailored power suits. Her dark curls held hints of fire in the sunshine and her skin was remarkably pale, even when she spent time in the sun. Her eyes were a light gray, like the mist that would rise from the bayous in the early morning.

And unlike her, Jacob was funny and charming, with the ability to fit into social situations with casual ease. A confident extrovert.

Still, there'd been an immediate connection from the moment Jacob had strolled into her office looking to buy a house. And for one glorious month, they'd discovered that opposites truly do attract.

Jacob might be outgoing, but he'd insisted that he loved spending quiet evenings at home with her, watching old movies and sipping wine. He hadn't even complained when she had to work late. He said he admired her commitment to her career.

Livia had foolishly started to hope that she'd been wrong. Maybe true love did exist.

Of course, it'd all been a scam.

"Livia?" Marcel leaned forward, his expression worried. "What did he do?"

"He lied to me."

"And?"

"What do you mean, 'and'? Isn't that enough?"

"We all lie, sweetie." Marcel pressed a hand against his chest. "Even us saints."

"You?" Livia snorted. "A saint?"

"Just ask my momma." Marcel batted his lashes.

Livia managed a weak smile before abruptly turning to pace toward the large front windows. "I'll agree you're more saint-like than any other person in my life."

"Okay, Livia, spill the tea." Marcel easily sensed her coiled tension. "What's got your panties in a bunch?"

Livia stared blindly at the sun-drenched parkway that rimmed Lake Pontchartrain. It was almost summer and tourist season was in full swing, filling the streets with happy sight-seers.

"You remember I gave Jacob a key to my house last Friday," she demanded, wrapping her arms around her waist.

"Yes, you were hoping for a candlelit dinner after a hard day at the office, right?"

"That's what Jacob wanted. Or at least, that's what he told me." Her stomach twisted into a knot of betrayal. "It felt a little soon for me, we'd only been dating a month, but he pointed out that I hate to go out to a noisy restaurant after working all day, and if he could get into the house before I got home, he could have dinner waiting and we could enjoy a nice, peaceful evening together." Livia's lips twisted into a wry smile. "How was I supposed to resist? I hate cooking, I hate restaurants, but I love a good meal and a glass of wine after a long day."

"Let me guess. There was no candlelight and no dinner?"

"No nothing." Livia rubbed the goose bumps suddenly coating her bare arms. This morning she'd chosen a sleeveless white silk shirt to match with her black pencil skirt. Summer in Louisiana wasn't for the faint of heart. It was already suffocatingly hot.

"I haven't seen him since the night I gave him the key," she admitted in grim tones. "He texted me to say he was too busy to get together this weekend and that it would probably be next Friday before he'd have time to meet up."

"Putting you off for an entire week?" Marcel clicked his tongue. "Not a good sign."

Livia sighed. Of course it wasn't a good sign. And if she'd taken one moment to question why the man who claimed to be falling in love with her was suddenly MIA, she might have realized something was up. Instead, she'd blissfully gone about her business without a care in the world.

"I didn't think about it until my nosy neighbor—"

"Which nosy neighbor? Betty or Lester or Eva?" Marcel interrupted.

"Betty." She tried to keep the impatience from her tone. It was a legitimate question. Livia lived in a quiet suburb where people-watching was the favorite hobby of her neighbors. The primary culprit was Betty Stonewell, who lived next door. Livia found her poking and prying into other people's private lives annoying, but she kept her mouth shut. In Betty's mind, she was simply being a good neighbor. "She stopped me after I got home last night. She was gushing about my decision to invite 'that nice young gentleman' to move in and suggested it was time he made an honest woman of me."

"Honest woman of you?" Marcel laughed. "She did not say that."

"It was implied," Livia conceded, slowly turning back to meet her companion's curious gaze. "Anyway, I told her that Jacob hadn't moved into my house and asked her why she thought he was living there. She looked confused and said she'd seen him coming and going during the last couple of days."

Marcel folded his arms on the desk and leaned forward. "He was at your house when you weren't there?"

"That's what she said."

"Maybe she made a mistake. You said she's elderly."

"That's exactly what I thought." Livia had gone into her house and tried to dismiss Betty's intrusive probing. The woman had always seemed in her right mind, but who knew? She was getting older. It would be understandable if she was getting confused. "But it bothered me. There was no reason for Jacob to be at the house during the day, but that didn't mean there hadn't been someone else sneaking around the neighborhood. Thieves sometimes creep around an area a few days before they decide where they want to break in." She sucked in a deep breath. "So, I decided to check my security videos."

"And?"

"And they were blank."

"All of them?"

"Yes."

"How's that possible? A glitch?"

"Definitely not. They were deliberately erased."

Marcel released a low whistle. "The thief?"

"Why would a thief go to the trouble of erasing the footage? It would have been much easier just to smash the cameras. Besides, nothing was missing."

"So who was it?"

The question had gnawed at her the entire night. At last she accepted there was no way she would feel comfortable in her own home until she knew who Betty had seen creeping around, and more importantly, who had erased her security videos.

"This morning I was determined to find out. That's why I'm late."

Marcel pressed a hand against the center of his chest. "Good Lord, Livia, you have me on the edge of my seat. You should do a podcast."

"I love podcasts, but it's not nearly as fun when it's happening to you," Livia muttered.

Marcel ignored her complaint. "Keep going."

Livia shivered as she grudgingly recalled the unnerving details of the morning.

"I got ready for work and drove away from the house like usual, but then I circled around the block and parked on the corner. I could see the house through my neighbor's hedges, but my car was out of sight."

"Sneaky. I like it." Marcel applauded her ingenuity. "Did you catch the thief?"

"About an hour later, I saw Jacob walking down the street. I couldn't believe it. He just strolled up the sidewalk and used the key I gave him to go inside like he owned the place."

"He *walked* to your house?" Marcel demanded. "I thought he was staying in a hotel near the airport."

"I don't know where he left his car. I assume he didn't want anyone to notice it in the driveway." A tight smile curved her lips. "Unfortunately for him, he'd underestimated Betty's obsession of keeping track of the neighborhood."

"Did you confront him?"

Livia cringed at the mere thought. She might be a feral, ruthless opponent in business deals, but in personal relationships? Hell, no.

"Don't be silly. I did what any other mature woman would do: I snuck into the backyard and peeked through the window."

"Good choice." Marcel looked riveted. As if Livia really was repeating what she'd heard on a podcast. Not revealing the painful events of her morning. "What was he doing?"

"He was in my bedroom, going through my dresser drawers. He looked like he was searching for something."

"Through your drawers? Seriously?" Marcel looked suitably scandalized. "What was he looking for? Money? A gun?" He grimaced. "Ew. Maybe he's one of those weirdos who smells women's panties."

Livia had stood on her back porch, peering into her bedroom with a numbed sense of disbelief. She'd already accepted that there was no legitimate reason for Jacob to be sneaking into her house at that hour. But the sight of him rifling through her drawers had still shocked her.

"I don't know what he was looking for. It's not like I hide anything with my undies."

"What happened next?"

"I was about to go in and confront him when I heard the front door of my house open and a stranger walked into my bedroom."

"Holy crap. A woman?"

"No, it was a man."

"Ah." Marcel waggled his brows. "Intrigue."

"There was intrigue," Livia agreed. "But not like you think. He wasn't there for a hookup with Jacob. The stranger walked into the bedroom and shoved Jacob against the wall like he was threatening him."

"Did Jacob know him?"

Livia took a second to sort through her memories. The last thing she'd expected was for some stranger to appear in her bedroom and attack Jacob. The whole encounter had taken on a strange, dreamlike quality.

"Jacob at least recognized him," she finally said. "They looked like they were arguing, but Jacob wasn't trying to fight back. I think he was trying to convince the man of something."

Marcel's amusement faded, as if he sensed Livia's smoldering sense of unease. She didn't know what was happening between the two men, but there'd been an ugly expression on Jacob's face that she'd never seen before.

"Did you call the cops?"

"No, the stranger left and, a few minutes later, Jacob took off."

Marcel clicked his tongue. "You should tell the police, Livia."

"And say what?" Livia spread her arms in a gesture of helplessness. "That the man who I willingly offered a key to my house showed up and searched through my underwear drawer? And that a stranger came in and pushed him and left? As far as I know, they didn't take anything, and didn't do any damage. I'm not sure there was any actual crime committed."

"Still . . . it's weird."

"It's beyond weird," Livia agreed, pulling her phone out of the leather satchel she'd slung over her shoulder. She searched through her most recent photos before turning the phone to show Marcel. "Which is why I took a picture of him through the window so he couldn't deny what I saw, and then sent him a text telling him to come by today and leave the key to my house. The creep."

Marcel narrowed his eyes, as if struggling to make out the blurry image. It wasn't entirely her fault. The thick screen over the window had cast a shadow and her hand had been shaking so badly she couldn't hold the phone still.

Obviously, it was enough to convince him she was telling the truth. Marcel shook his head, leaning back in his swivel chair.

"A shame. But I warned you when Jacob walked through the door that he was trouble."

"Bullshit." Livia dropped the phone back into her satchel. "You told me to—and I quote—'hit that fine thing.'"

Marcel tried and failed to look innocent. "Did I?"

Livia rolled her eyes. "It's my fault. I should never have listened to you. You have terrible taste in men."

"Brutal, but accurate," Marcel conceded.

"Love sucks," Livia muttered, stomping past the reception desk and into her office at the back of the building.

She might have terrible taste in men, but she was an amazing real estate agent.

Time to focus on what mattered. Making money.

Lots of money.

CHAPTER 2

New Orleans, LA
Monday, June 23rd

Livia arrived at her office bright and early to discover Marcel brewing himself a large cappuccino. He was the only one who knew how to work the complicated machine that had cost her a small fortune, and he took full advantage of his expertise. This morning he was stylishly attired in a tight, short-sleeved cashmere sweater and white slacks.

Livia had chosen a loose tunic dress that reached her ankles. Her brunette curls were knotted on top of her head, leaving a few tendrils to fall against her neck. It was too hot for her expensive skirts and tailored jackets. Plus, today she planned to inspect the new subdivision that a local developer had given her the opportunity to sell. The dozen homes were in various stages of construction and she kept a close eye on them. She wanted to make sure they were perfect before she put them on the market. Today was a day for comfort, not starch and high heels.

"Still nothing?" Marcel demanded the second she stepped through the front door.

Livia shook her head. There was no need to ask who he meant. They'd both been waiting on pins and needles for Jacob Pearson to come to the office and drop off her key.

"Nothing. I spent the weekend texting, calling, and leaving messages. He's ignored all of them."

Marcel sipped his cappuccino. "You have been well and truly ghosted, sweetie."

"Good riddance." Livia didn't have to pretend her indifference. She'd had five days to come to terms with the knowledge Jacob hadn't been the man of her dreams. He was just another loser who'd disappointed her. "I had the locks changed and upgraded the security system at my house. Time to move on."

Marcel sent her a horrified glance. "You're going to let him walk away without a proper goodbye?"

"Like I said. Good riddance."

"Girl, I don't think so." Crossing the room, Marcel settled behind his desk and logged into his computer. "You might not be a bitch, but thankfully I am petty enough for both of us."

Alarmed by the expression of determination on her friend's face, Livia hurried toward the desk.

"What are you going to do?"

"Leave a few messages on his social media." Marcel concentrated on his task. "The world should know that he's a creep who breaks into women's homes and sniffs their panties."

Livia flinched. "He didn't sniff my panties."

"You don't know that he wasn't going to. I mean, he had to be in your bedroom for a reason."

"Marcel, please," Livia protested.

She didn't mind humiliating Jacob. In fact, she hoped someday that he got exactly what he deserved. But she didn't want any public drama.

What if he tried to retaliate?

Marcel ignored her plea, leaning forward to study his monitor. "Wait. It's Pearson, right? P. E. A. R. S. O. N?"

"Yes, why?

"He doesn't have any social media accounts?"

"Of course he does. I checked after he asked me to join him for a drink. I've had too many jerks hit on me who have a wife and a pack of kids waiting for him at home."

Livia sighed at the memory of how eagerly she'd scoured his accounts, enlarging every picture of Jacob on the beach or in his expensive sports car. She'd made very sure there weren't any women standing next to him with a wedding ring on her finger.

"I can't find anything." Marcel glanced up with a frown. "At least none that look like your Jacob Pearson."

"He's not mine, thank God." Livia pulled out her phone. "I'll find it for you, but you're not leaving any messages."

"Party pooper."

"You mean mature adult?"

"No, I mean party pooper. Where's your sense of fun?"

"Childish revenge isn't my sense of . . ." The words dried on Livia's lips as she stared at her phone. She closed out the social app and opened another, then another. All of them showed the same thing. "What the hell is going on?" she muttered.

"Livia?"

"Someone deactivated his accounts." She glanced up to meet Marcel's curious gaze. "All of them."

"Bastard." Marcel shook his head in disgust. "He must be afraid you intend to out him as a weirdo."

"If that was the reason he could have easily blocked me," Livia pointed out, unable to dismiss a niggling anxiety. "Scrubbing his online accounts seems a little drastic."

"What about his business accounts?" Marcel suggested. "He's a financial advisor, isn't he?"

"He has a website." Livia used her phone to pull up his page. Or at least she tried. What she got was a warning that the website no longer existed. The anxiety turned up a dozen notches. "Shit. What's going on?"

She turned the phone for Marcel to see the blank page. His brows slowly lifted, as if struck by a sudden realization.

"Oh, Livia. You weren't ghosted. You were catfished."

Livia shoved the phone back into her satchel with a frown. She was still trying to accept the fact that Jacob had crashed into her life and then just as abruptly disappeared. Like a hit and run. Now she had to consider the fact that he wasn't Jacob at all? No. It was giving her whiplash.

"There has to be another explanation," she insisted. "Why would anyone catfish me?"

"I listened to a podcast about a dude who was dating over a dozen different women at the same time."

"Why?"

"When he was exposed, he said the women were giving him everything he wanted—sex and money and a place to stay. Plus, he liked the thrill of sneaking around. They didn't catch him for years."

"Gross." Livia made a sound of disgust. "Men."

Marcel held up a slender hand. "Again. Preaching to the choir."

Livia shook her head, stubbornly wanting to dismiss Marcel's warning. It didn't seem possible, but then again, she couldn't think of another reason for his social media and professional website to be wiped clean.

"If Jacob did catfish me, I still don't understand why," she grudgingly conceded. "It's not like I gave him any money."

"He did sneak into your house. Maybe he thought that you have something worth stealing. Cash. Jewelry. Antiques."

"I told him I put every penny I earn back into the business. I even admitted that I buy my clothes off-rack and that my car has over one hundred thousand miles. Hardly the sort of woman with expensive jewelry hidden in her drawers."

"Yes, but you're Livia Benoit."

"So?"

"So everyone in Louisiana recognizes the name Benoit."

Livia clenched her teeth. It was true that most people in the state would recognize the name Benoit. Her mother's ancestors had been powerful landowners for over two hundred years. Starting with the Willows, a large mansion surrounded by vast acres of farmland and bayous outside of New Orleans, they'd expanded their empire to own office buildings, shopping centers, and a chain of hotels from New Orleans to Baton Rouge. Over the years, their wealth and influence had diminished. Most dramatically since the death of her grandfather, Henri Benoit, who'd been a ruthless force of nature. But the name Benoit remained a formidable key to opening doors in Louisiana.

Both in society and politics.

"I've never been a part of the clan," she insisted. Her sole link to her extended family after being dumped into foster care was the mandatory summers at the Willows, where they attempted to mask their aversion to her presence. "I've earned everything I have." She paused, realizing that she wasn't being entirely honest. After the death of her grandfather ten years ago, she'd received a yearly lump of cash from his trust fund. It meant that she could buy her small home without draining funds from her business. "Mostly."

Marcel shrugged. "It doesn't change your name. Or the assumption that you must be loaded."

The knot of queasiness in the pit of her stomach doubled in size. Just when she thought her brief relationship with Jacob Pearson couldn't get worse, it did.

"Well, whatever his intention, he obviously realized I'm broke and decided to move on."

"Or he got what he wanted."

Livia shuddered. She was sick of Jacob Pearson and his lies. The sooner she got him out of her mind, the better.

"I'm telling you, there's nothing for him to get," she insisted. "My name might be Benoit, but it ends there. My supposed family pretend like I don't exist."

Marcel parted his lips, but whatever he was about to say was forgotten, as he abruptly recalled something.

"That's not entirely true," he said. "Unfortunately."

"Unfortunate for you or for me?"

"Both of us," Marcel warned. "Your aunt Delilah called this morning."

Livia groaned. Unfortunate was an understatement. Delilah Laurent-Benoit was married to Livia's uncle, Adrian Benoit—the older brother of her mother and the heir to the Willows, as well as her grandfather's businesses. She was also mother to Livia's only cousin, Celeste. She was three years younger than Livia, and the two couldn't have been more different.

Celeste had been adored by her parents, as well as spoiled rotten by Henri Benoit as a child. Livia had detested her. And since Celeste had grown up, she hadn't improved. She'd gone from a juvenile diva to a pampered, catty bitch.

"Did Delilah leave a message?"

"Not so much a message as a threat." Marcel paused for dramatic effect. "She said she was in New Orleans and intended to stop by and see you."

"Stop by here?" Livia demanded in horror. She could count on one hand how many times someone from the Benoit clan had visited her over the years.

"Yes."

"Did you tell her I was busy?"

"How? She just announced she was coming and hung up."

"Thanks."

Marcel looked offended. "What did you expect me to do?"

"What you always do with people who try to bully you. I've seen you make grown men cry."

"No way. She scares me."

"Me too," Livia muttered.

"We could close early and hit happy hour at the Tin Roof."

A pitcher of margaritas at the corner bar instead of being thrown to the lion? Or rather, the lioness? Yeah, that sounded perfect. The only problem was that she would later regret revealing her cowardice.

"Tempting, but I decided a long time ago I wasn't going to let my family intimidate me."

"What about me?" Marcel complained.

"Buckle up, buttercup." Livia headed around the desk, sending her friend a tight smile. "Word of warning, keep your head high and your spine straight, but don't look her directly in the eye. That's how she destroys your soul."

"That's not funny."

Continuing down the short hall into her office, Livia settled at her desk and tried to concentrate on the stack of bills awaiting her attention. She'd wasted far too much time dwelling on Jacob and his mysterious appearance and disappearance in her life, not to mention the effort and expense to upgrade her home security over the weekend.

She would not waste more time worrying about Delilah or what she might want.

Much to her surprise, Livia stayed busy enough to forget about the looming visit for most of the day. It helped that she had several potential clients call, plus a videoconference with a local developer who was converting a historic building into upscale apartments. Livia was eager to get her foot in the door before the units went on sale.

It was after four in the afternoon when she heard a woman's voice in the front lobby. The voice was too muffled to recognize, but it made the hair on the back of her neck stand on end. A sure sign that a Benoit was nearby.

A minute later, Delilah confirmed her fear by shoving open the door to her office without bothering to knock and stepping inside.

The tall, painfully thin woman was wearing a silk pantsuit in a pale green with an ivory camisole. The green brought out the expensive golden highlights in her red hair, which was cut into a short bob. Her dark brown eyes were hard and her lips pinched as she spared a glance around the office.

Delilah sniffed, as if annoyed she couldn't find any fault in the clean, timeless beauty of the elegant décor or the bank of windows that offered a view of the lake.

"I'll never understand why you hired a man to be your receptionist. He's so odd," she complained.

Livia narrowed her gaze, on instant defense as she slowly rose to her feet. She would not let the annoying woman peer down her long nose at her. Of course, she was still several inches shorter than her aunt, but it made her feel better.

"Marcel is my administrative assistant, not my receptionist, and this agency couldn't function without him."

Delilah sniffed. "I suppose you think having a man in the office makes you look trendy?"

Livia blinked. It was too simple to excuse the older woman's prejudices as being old-fashioned. She was deliberately obtuse, preferring to live in a bubble of privilege that ignored anything and everyone who didn't fit into her idea of what was proper.

"I think Marcel is the best choice for the position. No other motive." Livia's tone dripped with ice. "Why are you here, Delilah?"

"I'm in New Orleans to speak with the photographer who will be joining us at the Willows next week."

Livia winced at the mention of her upcoming visit to the remote estate. The Benoit family set aside the first two weeks of July for their reunion. A horrifying joke that was instituted in her grandfather's will. Each member of the family who wanted their yearly payout from the trust fund had to stay at the Willows. She assumed it was his way of controlling them from beyond the grave.

As far as Livia was concerned, it was sheer punishment. But she'd be damned if she let her share of the money go to one of her relatives. She'd walk through the pits of hell first.

Livia stared at her aunt in confusion. "You hired a photographer for our reunion? Why?"

"Don't be silly. Why would I hire him for our reunion? He will be there to take Celeste's engagement pictures."

"Celeste is engaged?" Livia didn't know why she was shocked by the announcement. Celeste was twenty-seven years old. Well past the usual age for Benoit women to get hitched. But then again, it was astonishing that any man would willingly tie himself to the shrew. "Congratulations," she choked out.

Delilah pulled her lips into a tight smile. "Yes, we're all very pleased. And Celeste is delighted. I've never seen her so happy."

"Anyone I know?"

"Winston."

"Who?"

"Winston Durand, the son of our neighbor, Gerald Durand." The smile widened with a smug satisfaction. "And his heir."

A distant memory clicked in Livia's brain. The Durands weren't as infamous as the Benoits, but they did have a large mansion not too far away from the Willows and a thriving car rental business.

"I've heard the name, but I don't think I've ever met him."

"Probably not. He attended a private school on the East Coast and spent his summers in Ireland with his mother's family. His grandfather is Sir Rowan Sullivan."

Livia shrugged. Was she supposed to be impressed? "Is that why you came by? To tell me about the engagement?"

"I also wanted to make sure that you packed a formal gown. We're hosting an engagement party next weekend."

"At the Willows?"

"Where else would we announce our daughter's engagement?"

Livia groaned. So much for thinking things couldn't get

worse. Now she was not only going to be stuck in the wilds of the bayous, surrounded by a family who'd tossed her away like trash, but she was going to be forced to endure Celeste's in-full princess form, prancing around and demanding constant attention.

Great. Just great.

"Then maybe we should reschedule the reunion," she suggested, prepared for Delilah to give a sharp shake of her head.

"That's impossible. Your grandfather's will is quite clear on the dates he expects us to be together. Besides, Celeste wanted to schedule the party when we are all together. We're family."

"If you say so."

Delilah's smile faded, her features tightening. At one time she'd no doubt been a beautiful woman, but her pinched expression had left behind lines that her expensive cosmetics could no longer disguise.

"This is an important time for Celeste. And for me," she chided. "I expect you to attend the various events we have planned for next week and smile for my very expensive photographer. That's not too much to ask, is it?"

"I suppose we'll find out." Livia abruptly sat down, grabbing a file off her desk. She'd had enough. More than enough. "Until then, I have to actually work to pay my bills. So if you don't mind . . ."

There was a tense pause, Delilah clearly surprised at the abrupt dismissal, then, with a click of her tongue, she was turning to head out of the office.

"I'll see you next week," she said as she stepped out the door.

"Can't wait."

Livia listened as Delilah marched down the hall, followed by the rattle of the glass front door being slammed shut. She squeezed her eyes shut as she braced herself for the shrill alarm that abruptly blasted through the air. For the past few weeks the security system had developed a glitch and the smallest thud or bang against a wall could set it off. She meant to have it fixed, but she never seemed to have the time.

There was the sound of footsteps hurrying toward the storage room where the control panel was located and a second later the ear-splitting noise was brought to a merciful end.

Livia heaved a weary sigh as Marcel appeared in the open doorway, his expression wry.

"I'm not sure, but it's possible there was actual steam coming out of that woman's ears. I think that's what set off the alarm. What did you do to her?"

"I exist. That seems to be enough to piss off my family."

"Same."

Livia leaned forward to close her laptop and scooped up her phone. There was no way she was going to concentrate after that ugly little scene. Reaching beneath her desk, she grabbed her purse.

"I'm going to take off early. I need some fresh air," she said, waving her hand in front of her face. Her aunt had left behind a cloud of expensive perfume. Like a fog of gloom.

"I'll lock up."

"Thanks, Marcel."

Walking toward the door, she stopped to give her friend a quick hug, shocking both of them. She wasn't a touchy-feely person, but today she needed to remember that there was someone in her world who actually liked her.

Pulling away, she awkwardly hurried out of the building and jumped into her car. She turned out of the lot, intending to head home. Delilah's arrival was a reminder that she hadn't even started to pack, and now she had to shop for new evening clothes. Celeste's unwelcomed engagement meant she couldn't hide in her rooms once she got to the Willows. The snobbish Benoits would insist on putting on a show for the guests who were bound to come and congratulate the happy couple. If she had to be there, she wasn't going to wear her one cocktail gown over and over.

She had some pride.

Lost in the dread of her upcoming trip to the Willows, Livia drove straight past the street to her house. But she didn't turn around. Instead, she continued through the thick city traffic, not really sure where she was going until she saw the exit for the airport.

Whipping the car in the turnoff lane, Livia ignored the blast of a horn from behind her and veered off the ramp. Then she veered off again, entering the parking lot of an extended-stay motel. The motel wasn't shabby, but it was far from new, and it'd been a shock to discover Jacob was staying there the first time she stopped by to pick him up. He'd explained that he was only there until he could buy a house, and he liked the fact that it was close to the airport. She'd accepted his explanation, in the same way she'd accepted everything else about him. Without question.

She slowly drove to the far end of the lot, her gaze scanning the vehicles parked in front of the one-story building with a line of metal doors. The dents suggested someone had kicked and potentially shot at them more than once.

Reaching the end of the building, Livia impulsively pressed on the brake as someone pulled open the last door. A large, middle-aged man stepped out and headed toward a nearby utility truck.

Not giving herself the chance to consider the danger, she rolled down her window a couple of inches and called out.

"Hi! Excuse me."

The man turned with a frown and strolled toward her. He was wearing a uniform with an insignia that matched the utility truck, but that didn't mean he couldn't be a serial killer. Still, her car door was locked and it was broad daylight. It wasn't that much of a risk, and she had to satisfy her gnawing curiosity.

The man reached the car and peered through the window. "Yes?"

"I'm looking for Jacob Pearson. Is he inside the room?" She nodded toward the door he'd just closed.

"Don't know him."

"Oh, I'm sorry." She silently cursed in frustration. She was too late. "He was staying in that room last week."

"Naw. Not in that room," the man said. "I've been here for over a month. You've made a mistake."

"You're sure?"

"I think I know where I've been staying."

"Right. Sorry."

Rolling up her window, Livia drove away with a numb sense of disbelief. She'd only been to the hotel a couple of times to pick up Jacob, and he'd been standing in front of the door when she'd pulled into the lot. She'd assumed that he didn't want her waiting around in such a sketchy location. Now she realized that she'd never actually seen him coming in or out of the room.

Because he'd never stayed there.

It'd been another lie.

Who the hell was Jacob Pearson? And why had he been in her life?

CHAPTER 3

Rushville, LA
Tuesday, July 1st

Bright and early, Livia packed her car and made the two-hour drive east of New Orleans. The Willows was built on a strip of land that was bordered by the Mississippi River on one side and protected wetlands on the other side. A graveled road led to the main estate that was hidden behind an elaborately scrolled wrought-iron gate. Her grandfather had been the one to add the fencing, as if living miles from the nearest town didn't keep them properly isolated.

Once off the main highway, Livia pulled into the small town that was the last stop before reaching the family estate. Rushville wasn't much more than a main street with a neat row of small businesses and a half dozen churches anchoring the clusters of neighborhoods. There was a park with a bandstand and playground that claimed a place of pride at the heart of town, serving as a gathering place for the locals. As Livia drove past, she smiled at the large red, white, and blue banners that were draped from the trees. They were preparing for the Fourth of

July picnic that would include a parade and the massive fireworks display that made her aunt Delilah crazy. She was of the firm opinion if she didn't organize and approve the event, it shouldn't happen.

About to turn onto the road that would lead out of town, Livia impulsively pulled up to the curb in front of the local bakery. If she was going to survive the next two weeks, she was going to need reinforcements. What better way than a hidden stash of cupcakes, peanut butter fudge, and pralines?

All the stuff she kept off-limits when she was home.

Leaving the bakery with a large pink box tied with a bow, Livia nearly ran down a woman who was striding past the store with a determined air of authority.

"Sorry," Livia muttered, stepping back as she clutched the box of pastries against her chest. That'd almost been a disaster.

The woman stopped, turning back to stare at Livia with wide eyes. "Livia?"

Livia frowned, her gaze sweeping over the tall, wiry frame that was covered by a brown uniform. A cop? Her gaze moved up to study the narrow face that was dominated by a pair of hazel eyes and framed by short, honey brown hair. There was a sprinkling of freckles on the pale skin and a smile that added an irresistible charm to her plain features.

"Bryce?" Livia felt a surge of happiness as she recognized her old friend, who'd made her summers at the Willows a little more bearable.

Bryce Swift had grown up in Rushville with her father, who'd allowed her to run wild. The near-feral girl had been the only one with the courage to defy Celeste Benoit's disdain for her cousin and make friends. In fact, Livia was fairly certain it was to spite Celeste that Bryce started sneaking onto the private grounds of the Willows to spend time with Livia in the first place.

Whatever the reason, the two had become fast friends.

Bryce moved forward to give Livia a hug, careful not to crush her box of pastries. "My God, it's been forever."

Livia tried to think of the last time she'd crossed paths with Bryce. "It was your wedding, right?" she at last determined. She had been a bridesmaid at the small but beautiful ceremony held in the park. "What was that? Six years ago?"

"Almost eight."

"Yikes. You're making me feel old."

"You want to feel old? I have a four-year-old daughter who reminds me every day that I'm creeping toward retirement."

"Seriously?" Livia felt a stab of surprise. Bryce had been such a rebel that it was hard to imagine her as a mother. Then she remembered the kind and fiercely loyal heart that her friend had hidden beneath her tough exterior. More than once, Bryce had protected Livia from the local kids who wanted to impress Celeste by being cruel to her unwelcomed cousin. Even when it meant getting in trouble herself. Bryce would be a perfect parent. Strong, but fully committed to loving her daughter. "Congratulations."

"Thanks. Josie is the light of my life."

"Are you living in Rushville?" Livia tried to recall what she'd heard about Bryce after her marriage. "I thought you moved to Baton Rouge when you and your new husband joined the FBI?"

"We did." There was a pain-filled pause. "Benjamin was killed in the line of duty three years ago."

"Oh, Bryce." Livia didn't know what to say. She'd never seen her friend so happy as she did on her wedding day. The very picture of a radiant bride. It was horrible to realize that their life together had been cut brutally short. "I'm so sorry. I didn't know."

Bryce shook her head, as if she was trying to deflect Livia's sympathy. No doubt she'd had more than enough pity over the past three years.

"It's okay," she murmured. "I mean, it's not okay, but we're managing. We moved back to Rushville so Josie could be close to her grandpa. I wouldn't be able to do this without him."

"Are you still with the FBI?"

"No, I left the agency. I'm a deputy at the local sheriff's office now. It gives me more time to spend with Josie."

That explained the brown uniform and the silver star on her shirt pocket. Livia resisted the urge to offer her sympathy again.

She sent her friend an understanding smile, well aware of the sacrifice Bryce had made for her daughter.

"Josie's lucky to have you."

"I try." Bryce flushed, as if Livia's soft words pleased her. "Why are you in town?" She held up a hand as Livia started to answer. "Never mind. It's the first of July. Time for the dreaded Benoit reunion."

"Even more dreaded this year."

"Why?"

"Celeste is having her engagement party this coming weekend."

Bryce didn't look surprised by the announcement. "I assume Winston Durand is the unlucky husband to be?"

"That's what I'm told."

"Good. Both are self-obsessed narcissists. They're perfect for each other."

Livia smiled. It was nice to know that her cousin wouldn't be ruining some decent man's life.

"Unfortunately, I'm stuck going to the stupid party, along with whatever mysterious events my aunt has planned during my obligatory imprisonment at the Willows."

Bryce nodded toward the pink box. "That explains the bakery pit stop."

"This is just to get through the next few days. I'll be back for more."

"Doesn't the Willows have a chef?"

"According to my aunt and uncle, he's the finest in Louisiana, but I'll be damned if I endure my relatives' patronizing stares if I so much as nibble on a dessert." The childhood trauma that had never healed cramped her stomach with dread. She would never forget the way her grandfather had scowled at her when she asked for a second slice of cake. Or his insistence that she complete one hundred morning laps in the pool to get rid of her chubby thighs. It'd been a deliberate attempt to humiliate her. "They are firm believers in women starving themselves for the sake of beauty."

"At this point, they've just become an outdated joke." Bryce rolled her eyes before thankfully changing the subject. "I hope you have some time to get together while you're here. Maybe grab lunch or a drink."

"I would love to," Livia eagerly agreed, reaching into her satchel to pull out her business card. "Here's my number."

"And here's mine." Bryce reached into her back pocket for a small notebook and pencil. She scribbled her number on it before handing it to Livia. "Not nearly as fancy."

"Fancy is overrated," Livia assured her, tucking the paper in her satchel. "And promise you'll call me whenever you have some free time. I'm going to need to get out of the Willows as much as possible. Otherwise, you'll probably find me locked in one of your cells. Or a padded room."

Bryce winked. "I promise to break you out."

"Thanks."

"That's what friends are for."

Livia turned away, pausing long enough to send her companion a wistful smile. "I've missed you, Bryce."

Bryce smiled back. "Same."

By late afternoon, Livia had unpacked her things and safely stored her pastries in the extensive suite at the back of the house.

She didn't mind being on the opposite side from the rest of the family. The more space, the better. And she preferred the view of the nearby wetlands. Beyond the line of weeping willows that marked the edge of the back lawn, the bayous loomed with a dark and sultry sense of forbidding danger, but they were at least honest. They *were* dangerous. Unlike the rest of the estate, which was lovely and graceful and perfectly manicured while hiding the fetid rot beneath the surface.

Plus, she couldn't see the swimming pool from her vantage point. She might not remember much about her mother, but she certainly didn't want to wake up every morning with a view of the spot where she jumped to her death.

Pacing from the massive bedroom into the attached sitting room, Livia abruptly headed out of her suite. The soft rose-and-ivory décor might be beautiful, but she felt like she was being smothered. Probably because she knew it had been picked out by her grandfather, who had never once asked her what she preferred when she visited. He assumed he knew best, and she should be overjoyed she was allowed to step foot on the hallowed grounds of the Willows.

She resisted the urge to creep down the back steps and instead boldly made her way down the double staircase that led to the large foyer with a black-and-white tiled floor and an enormous chandelier imported from Venice. There were several delicate tables with various urns and statues that were supposedly priceless antiques and a portrait of her grandfather over the main entrance to the formal salon.

Livia glanced up at the man who'd been such a dominant force in her life.

Henri Benoit had broad features with a prominent nose and heavy brows that were usually pulled together in a dark frown over his piercing blue eyes, and his silver-gray hair came to a widow's peak, emphasizing his wide forehead. There was an arrogance in his expression as he glared down at the lesser beings who dared to enter his home.

She wasn't sure if someone had intentionally put the picture in the foyer to keep out unwelcomed guests, or if her grandfather had actually liked the grim portrait. Probably both.

Shaking her head, Livia headed out of the double front doors and across the wide veranda. The white antebellum-style home had the mandatory fluted columns that held up the balconies that surrounded the second floor and large windows with heavy shutters that could be closed during the hottest part of the day. Or, God forbid, during a hurricane.

The main house stood proudly on the highest section of land, overshadowing the outbuildings that had either been converted into garages or a bathhouse for the outdoor pool or torn down completely to make room for the tennis courts.

She didn't have a destination in mind, but the sound of a muted conversation had her strolling along a flagstone pathway toward the sunken garden at the side of the house. There was only one entrance to get through the neatly trimmed hedges that framed the gardens. Like everything else at the Willows, the glorious beauty was hidden from view unless you were one of the few lucky souls to be blessed with Benoit blood running through your veins. It was as if her ancestors feared a random passerby would spoil the prized roses and marble fountains with a mere glance.

Reaching the edge of the terrace, Livia found herself distracted by a slender form standing near the outside hedge, as if hiding in the shadows. More curious than alarmed, she strolled forward, her brows lifting as she realized who was standing there.

"Hello, Delilah."

The older woman jerked, clearly caught off guard. Turning her head, she glared at Livia.

"What are you doing here? I thought you were resting in your rooms?"

"I was. Now I'm out getting some fresh air. What are you doing here?" Livia leaned forward. "Ah, a gap in the branches. Who are you spying on?"

Delilah reddened. "I'm not spying."

"You're hiding behind the bushes and peeking into the garden. It looks a lot like spying."

Gathering her composure, Delilah flicked a dismissive glance over Livia's casual shorts and sleeveless shirt. The older woman was wearing a tunic dress with heels despite the smothering heat, as if she expected some sort of badge of honor.

"I'm watching Celeste's interview with the *Rushville Gazette*," she at last admitted. "They asked to be the first to announce her engagement. I would have preferred to give the offer to one of the national magazines. Or even one of those online influencers. But the editor reminded me that it's the Benoit tradition to give his paper the scoop."

"So the prized fiancé has arrived." Livia shifted so she could see through the opening.

The garden was in full bloom with a profusion of roses that were planted in precise rows between the paved walkways and bubbling fountains. Her great-great-grandmother had chosen the layout to reflect the gardens of Versailles, albeit on a much smaller scale.

And at the center of the garden was her cousin Celeste, in all her glory.

Taller than Livia, Celeste had inherited her mother's slender frame and her father's brown hair, although Celeste kept her long tresses highlighted with streaks of honey and chestnut. Like her mother, she was wearing a tunic-style dress that emphasized her slender waist and long legs. Her exposed skin had been spraypainted to look as if she spent hours in the sun, and her nails were as long as daggers and painted a deep red.

There was no doubt who and what she was: a pampered daughter of a rich man who'd never had to work a day in her life.

Nepo baby.

"He was supposed to be home last night," Delilah answered Livia's question. "But his flight was delayed from Ireland." A smug smile touched her aunt's lips. "He's been over there for the past few weeks. He didn't arrive home until this morning. I'm sure he's exhausted, but he refused to reschedule. He's always determined to put Celeste first."

"Lucky gal," Livia drawled. "Was Winston visiting the royals?"

"You can mock if you want, but there is a distant connection to the royal family." Her smile never wavered. "And he wanted his grandparents' official blessing before the wedding."

"I assume that means they won't be attending the party?"

"None of Winston's family will be able to come. Such a shame."

"None of them?"

Livia studied the man who was standing next to her cousin. He had his back to her, but she could see that he was about the same height as Celeste, which would explain why she'd chosen flats instead of her usual designer heels. He was broad through the shoulders and chest. Not fat, but definitely thick beneath his crisp white shirt and black slacks. His hair was cut short, and shimmered a deep red in the late afternoon sunlight.

The two stood next to the central fountain while a middle-aged man asked them various questions and a young woman snapped pictures of the happy couple.

"Unfortunately not."

"Why won't they be here?" she asked, hoping there was some fun drama that might add a little spice to her boring week.

"His mother passed away a few years ago from a sudden heart attack, and his father's health is failing." Delilah clicked her tongue, as if annoyed by the Durand family's lack of endurance.

"No brothers or sisters?"

"He was an only child. Just like Celeste." The older woman's irritation faded. "They have a great deal in common: good looks, good breeding—"

"Stop," Livia interrupted.

"It matters," Delilah ruthlessly insisted. "Especially in this day and age."

"It matters if you're a racehorse, I guess. Otherwise . . ." Livia's disgust was forgotten as the interview ended and Winston stepped away from his fiancé, turning so Livia could see his profile. Her brows snapped together. There was something familiar about the line of his nose and the tilt of his head. As if she'd recently met him. But where? A second later, realization hit, smacking her in the face like a blow. "Oh my God."

"What's wrong?"

"That's Winston?" she breathed.

"Of course it's Winston. Who else would it be?"

"I've seen him." Livia instinctively reached into her pocket, only to come up empty. She'd left her phone in her suite.

"I'm sure you have. He lives in the neighborhood."

Livia struggled to think clearly. That profile was the same as the man who'd snuck into her house to attack Jacob Pearson. She was almost certain of it.

"Not here. In New Orleans."

"He's an important business executive. He travels to the city on a regular basis."

"He was . . ." Livia swallowed her words. She needed time to consider before she blurted out something she couldn't take back.

"He was what?" her aunt prodded.

"Never mind." Livia cleared her throat and stepped back. "I'll let you get back to your spying."

"I'm not spying," Delilah snapped before she could halt the words. Then, straightening her shoulders, she sent Livia a chiding glance. "Cocktails will be at six. I'm expecting guests, so please wear something appropriate."

"Whatever."

With a roll of her eyes, Livia turned to stroll back toward

the house. It wasn't until she was inside that she gave in to the sharp impulse to race to her rooms and grab her phone out of her satchel.

Then, with trembling fingers, she scrolled through the photos to pull up the grainy image of Jacob in her bedroom. It was even more blurry than she remembered and, zooming in, she realized that she'd only caught a portion of the stranger.

He looked like he had the same build as Winston Durand and was about the same height, although it was hard to tell since he was leaning forward as he pressed Jacob against the wall. And the profile looked similar, but if she was being honest, she couldn't deny that it might have been a thousand other men. Plus, there was the fact that he was supposedly in Ireland for the past few weeks.

She must have made a mistake, right?

No. Her gut instinct refused to accept the obvious. There was something about him that convinced her he'd been with Jacob that morning. She wouldn't rest until she knew one hundred percent it wasn't him.

CHAPTER 4

Not sure if she was imagining things to distract herself from being stuck at the Willows, not to mention enduring two weeks of Celeste's gloating at landing a rich husband with royal connections, Livia put on a black cocktail dress that hugged her curves and was cut low to emphasize her full breasts. It was her gown of choice when she was trying to aggravate her cousin, who hated when Livia attracted male attention.

Impervious to the knowledge she was being petty, Livia headed down to the private sitting room. She stepped inside, vaguely disappointed that Winston wasn't there. It was possible that he'd gone home to change for the festivities, but she was hoping he would arrive early to please his soon to be mother-in-law.

Glancing around the long room that was bigger than her entire house, Livia wasn't surprised to discover that Delilah had changed the furnishings since last year. The pale green and ivory sophistication had been replaced with bright turquoise couches that looked as uncomfortable as the yellow chairs strategically placed around the new white carpet. The original wallpaper remained along with the heavy crystal lights that spilled a dull glow over the room. Her grandfather had explicitly insisted that the bones of the house remained the same, but every year her aunt did her best to bury the past beneath layers of modern fixtures.

"Hello, Livia. Welcome home."

Her uncle stepped through the open French doors that led to the back terrace. The middle child and official heir of Henri and Olivia Benoit, Adrian was a slender man with dark brown hair that formed a widow's peak just like his father. His face wasn't as square, and it lacked the same defiant ruthlessness as Henri, but it was obvious he was a Benoit.

He was holding an empty crystal glass in his hand, as if he'd snuck down early to get his cocktail hour started. Livia arched a brow. She wasn't judging. There were more than a few nights she needed a glass of wine as soon as she walked into her house. But since her oldest aunt, Helene, was constantly criticized for her habit of overindulging, it was rare to see anyone drinking more than a sip of wine from the cellar that had cost her grandfather a small fortune.

"Hello, Adrian."

The older man moved to place his empty glass on the sideboard before turning back to study her with a practiced smile.

"I've been hearing good things about your agency, Livia. You landed the Hillcrest subdivision, didn't you?"

"I did," Livia admitted, surprised that word had already gotten around. She'd just signed the paperwork last week.

Was her uncle keeping track of her? She quickly dismissed the thought. When had anyone in this family ever given a damn about her?

"It's not easy to start a new business. You should be very proud."

"It's still a work in progress, but I'm hoping to expand by next year."

"You plan to expand?"

The hint of censure in her uncle's voice confused Livia. "Of course. Eventually I'll add in the territory outside of New Orleans. Many families are looking for property just beyond the city limits to build new homes or even choosing rural towns where the school districts are smaller. If I can get a foothold, then I'll hire a couple more agents to concentrate on those areas."

"But surely . . ."

She narrowed her gaze as he deliberately allowed his words to trail away. "But surely what?"

"Traditionally, a woman of your age would be thinking about settling down and starting a family."

His words didn't bother her. Adrian wasn't the first man to assume her priority in life was being a wife and mother. But even as her lips parted to inform him she didn't intend to become a brood mare for any man, she hastily swallowed the words.

This was the perfect opportunity to discover more about Winston Durand. And his connection to the mysterious Jacob Pearson.

"You mean traditionally like Celeste?" she asked, hiding her annoyance behind a bright smile.

"I hope she will carry on the Benoit legacy," he agreed.

"But they won't be Benoits, will they?"

"They will still have the blood of the Benoits running through their veins."

"Not really the same thing, though, is it?"

Adrian's jaw knotted as he clenched his teeth. "It will be the joining of two prestigious families," he managed to spit out. "We're all pleased."

Livia pursed her lips, as if searching her memories. "You know, I don't think I've ever met Winston. I hope he's a nice guy. It doesn't matter if he's from a prestigious family or not if Celeste ends up unhappy."

A portion of Adrian's irritation eased. "He's an intelligent young man with excellent manners and a good head on his shoulders. I'm sure Celeste will be very happy."

Livia noticed he said nothing about him being nice. Obviously, that wasn't a requirement to join the Benoit clan.

"What does he do? I assume he works?"

"Of course he does. He's the CEO of his father's car rental business that is spread through all fifty states, as well as the expansion he started when he was still in college to include yacht and jet rentals."

"Impressive. I suppose he has to travel a lot?"

"Unfortunately, he's gone more than he's home," Adrian agreed. "That's why they are planning to live at the Willows after the marriage. Celeste will be more comfortable at home. And, of course, we'll be here if she needs help with the children."

"Ah, yes, the future children that will have the Durand name after they're born," she couldn't resist pointing out in sweet tones even as she tucked away the knowledge that Winston could be gone for days or weeks with no one noticing.

"Did I hear my name?"

Livia jerked at the low voice that came from directly behind her. When had someone come into the room? And why had they deliberately crept up on her?

Whirling around, she found her cousin's fiancé regarding her with a curious gaze. Up close, she could make out the finer details of his face. The heavy brow and bluntly carved features that were more average than handsome. And the dark eyes that studied her with a chilly intensity. As if he didn't really like her. Or maybe it was just her imagination, she acknowledged.

Just as it might be her imagination that she was even more convinced that he'd been the stranger in her home with Jacob.

A shiver raced down her spine, but she forced herself to meet his steady gaze, relieved he didn't do the usual male inspection of her curvaceous body.

"Winston." Adrian moved to lay his hand on the younger man's shoulder. "Have you met my niece, Livia Benoit?"

A meaningless smile curved his lips. "No, I haven't had the pleasure." He nodded his head toward her. "Livia."

"Winston."

A silence stretched as the two stared at each other. At last, Adrian cleared his throat at the hint of tension in the air.

"Excuse me. I hear the guests arriving."

The older man scurried from the room and Livia turned until she was directly facing her companion.

"Are you sure we haven't met?" she boldly demanded. "You look very familiar."

Winston's bland expression never changed, but a wariness flickered in the depths of his eyes. The question had unnerved him.

"Please don't tell me that I have one of those faces that looks like everyone else?" he asked, his smile thawing. As if he was hoping to ease the stiffness between them. "Because I can assure you that I would remember if our paths had crossed."

"Maybe I saw you at an event. Do you spend much time in New Orleans?"

"Not anymore. My father's health is declining. These days I try to work from home as much as possible."

"I'm sorry."

"An unpleasant fact of life."

"True." Livia paused, as if trying to think of a way to change the depressing conversation. "Delilah mentioned you flew in from London this morning."

"Dublin," he corrected. "My grandparents own an estate in Ireland."

"An estate? I'm impressed. Lucky you."

"Very lucky," he agreed before pressing a hand against his mouth as if stifling a yawn. "I always enjoy my visits, but I'll admit the jet lag is killing me tonight. I must be getting old."

A sudden blast of expensive perfume wafted through the air before Celeste entered the room. She paused at the doorway, taking in the sight of her fiancé standing close to her cousin, her lips pursing in displeasure. Not that she would believe any man would prefer Livia to her, but she couldn't endure anyone receiving attention but herself. Typical narcissist. Tilting her chin, Celeste glided forward, once again wearing a pair of flat shoes instead of heels and a sparkly silver dress that started an inch above her breasts and ended an inch below her butt. Livia would be terrified that one wrong move and she'd be flashing the guests.

Reaching Winston's side, she wrapped her arm possessively through his, sending Livia a wintry smile.

"I see you have met my fiancé, Livia."

"I have."

"Your father introduced us, although Livia seems to think that we've met before," Winston said, his gaze never leaving Livia's face.

Celeste frowned. "Really? Where?"

Livia shrugged. It'd been a mistake to reveal she'd recognized Winston, she abruptly realized. If the man had a legitimate reason for being in her house, he would have admitted it when they first met. So either he really hadn't been there or he was trying to cover up what he'd been doing.

"I thought I saw him at the Black and Gold Charity Gala last week," she said in light tones. "But honestly, I meet dozens of people every week. Trying to keep them straight is why I hired an assistant."

Winston's expression remained impossible to read. "You work in real estate, right?"

"I do. I have an agency in New Orleans. If you ever decide to look for some property in the city, you should call me."

"Actually, I'm always looking for potential investment opportunities—"

"The photographer has arrived," Celeste interrupted Winston, pulling him toward the door. "I want to have a word with him before our session tomorrow." She glanced over her shoulder, sending Livia a smug glance. "You'll have to excuse us. Perhaps someday you'll discover that a bride-to-be can never rest."

Livia rolled her eyes as Celeste and the obedient Winston swept from the room. Then, ignoring the sounds of soft music that played in the background as the gathering guests mingled in the formal salon, she turned to stroll toward the sideboard that held a selection of brandy and whiskey and sweet ports.

Sometimes chocolate pastries weren't enough.

But before she reached the bar, she abruptly veered toward the open French doors. It was still an hour until dinner. Plenty of time to do some snooping.

She crossed the wide veranda and headed down the stairs to the pathway that led toward the circle driveway. If Winston was staying at his family estate, then he would have parked in front of the house.

Shrouded in the shadows of the hedges, Livia had a perfect view of the elegant guests through the arched windows of the salon. Mingling in small clusters, they grabbed fluted glasses of champagne from the trays of passing servants before moving to the next group. Like restless butterflies searching for nectar.

Celeste, of course, was posed in the center of the white-and-gold room, holding court with Delilah standing beside her. They flashed smiles and laughed on cue, like trained actors on a stage. Livia paused to admire the performance, her brows arching as she realized that the doting Winston was MIA. Had he already bailed on his new fiancée? She scanned the windows, finally spotting the man standing in the corner of the room. Next to him was her uncle Adrian, his hands motioning in sharp gestures. He was excited. Or pissed off. Suddenly, the two men glanced toward the door that led to the private sitting room. The room she just left.

Were they talking about her? Was it possible that Adrian knew Winston had been in her house? Maybe he'd sent the younger man . . .

A chill blasted through her, despite the thick night air. She'd hoped that her visit to the Willows would erase Jacob Pearson from her mind. It would be the one benefit to her mandatory stay. Now she was more obsessed than ever with Jacob and the reason he'd charmed his way into her life. And what his connection was to Winston. And perhaps her uncle.

Turning, she scurried down the pathway, taking time to grab a file from her car that she'd parked on the manicured lawn. She never used the garage space her uncle offered to her. She wanted to know she could make a quick getaway.

Once she had a legitimate reason for wandering around the front of the house, Livia casually strolled along the line of expensive vehicles. A Rolls-Royce. A Jag. Two Porsches. And a shiny black SUV with a vanity plate spelling the words WINSTUD. Gross. It had to be Winston.

She continued past the vehicle, covertly glancing around. It was still light outside, but thankfully, there was no one hanging around. The gathering wasn't large enough for her aunt to hire a valet. Assured she was alone, Livia circled back, peering through the windows of the SUV.

There wasn't much to see. Unlike her, Winston kept his vehicle annoyingly tidy. No empty coffee cups or takeout bags. No newspapers or stacks of files or unpaid parking tickets. The only thing visible was a rain jacket neatly folded in the back seat. A mandatory item for anyone living in Louisiana.

Or traveling to Ireland.

Not sure what she hoped to find, Livia cautiously grabbed the back door of the SUV and pulled it open. Afraid she might trigger an alarm, she breathed a sigh of relief when there was nothing but silence. It seemed doubtful that any of the guests were in a position to see the driveway, but her luck had been too crappy to take chances.

Grabbing the jacket, Livia searched the pockets, her heart leaping as she felt a narrow piece of paper. She pulled it out, tilting it toward the light. A receipt from a gas station. Hardly the smoking gun she'd been searching for, still she skimmed over the neatly printed numbers, before reading the name of the gas station. It was one of a large chain spread throughout New Orleans. Nothing unusual there. Then she reached the very bottom of the receipt where the date printed.

Her breath tangled in her throat. Last Thursday. Someone wearing the jacket in Winston Durand's SUV had gotten gas on Thursday. A date when he was supposedly in Ireland.

Carefully folding the jacket, Livia replaced it on the back seat and quietly closed the door. Then, licking her dry lips, she forced herself to stroll back toward the house.

The receipt wasn't absolute proof that Winston was lying about where he'd been last week. The jacket could belong to someone else. Or he could have lent the SUV to a friend while he was out of the country. But it did mean that Livia couldn't cross him off the list of suspects. He might very well have been the stranger meeting Jacob in her house.

Lost in her thoughts, Livia didn't notice the approaching shadow. Not until she was alerted by the crunch of footsteps on gravel.

Genuine fear clenched her heart as she came to a sharp halt. Had someone seen her snooping in Winston's vehicle? And if they had, what were they going to do about it?

"Who's there?" she called out.

"It's me, Livia." A tall form stepped around the front of the SUV, revealing Adrian Benoit. "What are you doing out here?"

Livia released a shaky breath. Not that she was entirely reassured. She hadn't forgotten her uncle's animated conversation with Winston as she strolled past the windows.

Livia managed a smile and lifted the folder she'd grabbed from her car. "I forgot a file I wanted to look over tonight," she murmured. "I'm going to run it up to my room before dinner."

Adrian looked suspicious, as if not entirely convinced by her handy-dandy cover story.

"Aren't you on vacation?"

"I own my own business. There's no such thing as a vacation."

His wariness visibly eased. "That's true enough."

"Speaking of businesses, how is yours doing?"

"Couldn't be better."

The words came too fast to be believable. "Lucky you. I currently have a dozen buildings I'm trying to sell. I don't suppose you're planning on purchasing new office spaces, are you?"

"Perhaps next year. After Celeste's marriage."

Livia arched a brow. Interesting. "Winston's joining the family business?"

"He has his own investments, but eventually we'll combine the two," he conceded.

Livia wondered how much her aunt and uncle were depending on the infusion of Durand money into the family coffers. She wasn't allowed to see the accounts for the Benoit fortune, but she'd heard rumors of her uncle selling off numerous properties in Baton Rouge and Lafayette.

"And Celeste?" Livia demanded.

"What about her?"

"She's not going to be a part of the empire?"

The older man looked confused. "Of course she'll be a part, but she's not interested in the day-to-day details of running the business."

Livia would bet every penny that Celeste hadn't been asked what she wanted. "I see."

Adrian clicked his tongue. "Not all women are committed to a career."

"Probably not." Livia shrugged. "I think we should all do what makes us happy, right?"

Adrian glanced toward the mansion that glowed with an artificial brightness, his expression bleak.

"Or what's necessary."

CHAPTER 5

For once, Livia was grateful that her aunt had invited a dozen guests to join them for dinner. Pasting a smile to her face, she nibbled the roasted pheasant as the elderly man seated next to her spent a solid two hours explaining his complicated family connection to the Benoits, and how they had assisted Livia's ancestors during their immigration from France to the new world. Nothing was required from her beyond an occasional nod of her head, as if she was listening to his rambling.

Barely waiting for the maid to whisk away the dessert plates, she jumped to her feet and disappeared to the blessed privacy of her rooms. She didn't want anyone watching as she paced the floor, trying to convince herself that she was overreacting.

Okay, it was possible that Winston had been the stranger in her house. He certainly looked familiar. And it was possible that he'd lied about being in Ireland. That receipt showing he was getting gas in New Orleans last Thursday hadn't appeared from nowhere. And it was possible that her uncle was involved in the mystery surrounding Winston Durand and Jacob Pearson. He'd been acting even stranger than usual since her arrival at the Willows.

But it was equally possible that none of those things were true.

Maybe Winston *had* been thousands of miles away, visiting his relatives in Ireland, when she'd seen Jacob sneaking around her house. And maybe someone else had used his vehicle.

And maybe her uncle was feeling overwhelmed by Celeste's upcoming wedding. There would be nonstop chaos at the Willows leading up to the lavish ceremony and reception. Not to mention the outrageous price tag.

By midnight, she'd accepted there was no dismissing her suspicions. And part of her didn't want to. Not when she had a legitimate means of answering the mystery that had gnawed at her since Jacob's disappearance.

Rummaging through her satchel, she at last pulled out Bryce's number and sent her a quick text, asking to meet her at the local dive the next day at noon. Only then did she crawl into bed and collapse in exhaustion.

The next morning, Livia ignored the bell for breakfast, preferring to hide in her rooms until it was time to head into Rushville. Then, slipping out the back door, she jogged to her car and jumped in, taking off before anyone could stop her. By noon, she'd settled into a dark booth at the back of the local restaurant, BB's Bar and Grill. It looked a breath from collapse, but served the best food in town.

The warped wooden boards matched the open-beamed ceiling and the heavy bar that ran the length of the room. There were a couple of round tables and a half dozen booths crammed into the narrow space. Close enough that any private conversations would have been easily overheard if it wasn't for the clamor of lunchtime guests and the jukebox that blared from the overhead speakers.

At five past noon, Bryce entered the bar and headed to the back booth. She was wearing her deputy uniform, but everyone in the place called out a greeting as she strolled past. Obviously, her position of authority didn't dim her popularity.

Livia smiled as her friend scooted into the booth, her short hair tousled from the wind.

"I know this is quick, but you did say you wanted to get together," Livia said in apologetic tones.

"No, no. I'm so happy you called. Although I have to be back at the office by one, so it will have to be quick. We'll plan a girl's night out for later in the week."

"Sounds perfect." Livia motioned toward the waitress. "What do you recommend?"

"I'm not a fan of fried food so I usually get the gumbo."

"That sounds delicious." Livia waited for the waitress to stop next to the booth. The middle-aged woman with dark hair pulled into a tight braid looked vaguely familiar, but Livia didn't know her name. "Two gumbos."

"And a skillet of cornbread with extra honey and butter," Bryce added.

Livia sighed with envy, her gaze skimming down her friend's body. Even in the bulky uniform, she looked leanly muscled, like a well-toned athlete. Livia, in contrast, was all soft curves in her khaki shorts and scooped tee.

"You always could eat like a linebacker and never put on a pound."

"My dad said it was the ornery in me." Bryce shrugged. "It burned away the calories."

"Well, he was right about the ornery."

Bryce tried to look innocent. "What? I was a perfect angel."

Livia snorted. "What about the time you threw a rock through your neighbor's window?"

"He called my mom a whore."

"Okay. He was a jerk." Livia wasn't fooled by her friend's light tone. Bryce had been deeply wounded when her mother had run off with the local dentist to start a new family in Dallas. Her father had tried his best to give her a stable home, but the number of hours he worked at the brickyard meant that Bryce spent most days without supervision. It was no wonder she'd run wild. "But what about the fake snake you left on the back terrace at the Willows?" Livia pressed. "My aunt nearly broke her hip."

"She wouldn't let you come to my birthday party."

"True. Such a bitch."

"Right?"

They shared a laugh at the memory of Delilah's shrill scream as she'd leaped off the stairs into a rosebush. Petty, but oh-so satisfying.

"Did you enjoy working for the FBI?" she asked.

"Loved it."

Livia tried to imagine her reckless, uninhibited friend enforcing the law. "I'll admit I never imagined you becoming a cop, but then again, you would have hated working in an office."

Bryce nodded. "Sitting at a desk isn't my favorite thing. Unfortunately, there's a lot more of that as a local deputy than when I was in Baton Rouge."

"I'm sorry you had to leave."

"It's all good." The words were stiff. "And what about you? How are things going?"

Livia mentally cursed herself. What was wrong with her? Of course Bryce didn't want to discuss being forced to leave the career of her dreams. With a determined effort, Livia launched into a series of funny stories about starting her business until the gumbo and cornbread arrived.

They had both cleaned their plates and had a second glass of iced tea when Bryce tossed aside her napkin and folded her arms on the table.

"Okay, Livia. Give."

"Excuse me?"

"I have a cop's instinct for trouble. Something's wrong. And it's not just because you're stuck with your family for the next couple of weeks."

Livia smiled wryly. Bryce had always been weirdly intuitive. With her police training, it would be even harder to fool her.

"I'm starting to feel guilty," she admitted.

"Guilty about what?"

Livia settled back against the wooden seat. "When I went to college my roommate was a nursing student. She was always complaining her friends and even strangers wanted her to diagnose a weird bump or rash. She hated it."

Bryce wrinkled her nose. "If you need me to diagnose a rash, you're out of luck."

"No. No rashes, I swear."

"But a police problem?"

"I'm not sure."

"Tell me." Bryce arched a brow as Livia hesitated. "I enjoy solving problems. It's my superpower."

"Okay. But stop me at any point. You're not going to hurt my feelings, I promise you."

As concisely as possible, Livia shared her relationship with Jacob Pearson from the day he'd walked into her agency looking to buy a house, to the day she'd caught him sneaking into her bedroom.

"Wait, wait." Bryce lifted a silencing hand, trying to absorb the wild tale. "This boyfriend was snooping through your drawers and then Winston Durand showed up at your house?"

Livia grabbed her phone she'd set on the table, pulling up the grainy image before shoving it toward her friend.

"Someone who resembles him," Livia backtracked her assertion. "I didn't get a good enough look at him to swear in court."

Bryce studied the picture. "I mean, it could be, but it's hard to tell."

"Yeah, I know. And he swears he was out of the country, although I happened to glance in his car last night—"

"'Happened to'?"

Livia shrugged. "I was passing by."

"Gotcha."

Livia hesitated. The next part was tricker to explain. "In the back seat I could see a receipt from a New Orleans gas station." She glossed over the fact that she'd broken into Winton's SUV and rifled through his jacket. "It was from last Thursday. When he was supposedly in Ireland."

Bryce's lips twitched, but she didn't press. What she didn't know couldn't hurt Livia.

"He could have let someone use his car while he was gone."

"It's possible, but it's also possible he lied about when he got back from Ireland. Or maybe he didn't go at all."

Bryce drummed her fingers on the table, her brow furrowed as she studied the blurry picture.

"Have you asked Jacob who it was?" She glanced up. "And what the hell he was doing in your bedroom?"

"I couldn't. He disappeared."

"Disappeared?"

"Yup."

"Literally? Figuratively?"

"Both." Livia spread her fingers. "Poof. He vanished into thin air. He doesn't answer his phone or texts. His social media is gone. Even his website is gone. It's like he never existed."

Bryce furrowed her brow. "Okay, Livia, this is creepy."

"Tell me about it."

"Send me that photo to this email address and I'll check him out." Bryce shoved the phone toward Livia before pulling a small notebook and pencil from her pocket and scribbling her private email on it.

Livia took the paper with a stab of unease. The best part of Bryce was her loyalty to the rare few she allowed into her life. It was also her worst trait. She would stand in front of a speeding truck to protect someone she loved.

"It won't get you in trouble, will it?"

"No. Finn is the current sheriff. He trusts my judgment."

"Finn." The name was familiar. Shuffling through her memories, Livia dredged up the image of a boy a couple of years older than her with long dark hair and stunning black eyes. He'd always been deeply tanned from the hours he spent as lifeguard at the public pool next to the park, with the sort of defined muscles that made the girls sigh. Livia didn't like to swim, but she made sure she spent time at the pool just to enjoy the view. "Griffin Maxwell?" She waited for Bryce's nod. "I remember him. He used to be smoking hot."

"He still is."

"I suppose he's married with a pack of kids?"

"Nope. Divorced. No kids."

It was Bryce's clipped tone that stirred Livia's suspicion. Her friend wasn't as indifferent to her boss as she wanted to pretend.

"Interesting."

Bryce abruptly slid out of the booth, shutting down the conversation. Yet another sign she had something to hide.

"I'll call you once I track down your mystery man."

"Thanks." Livia stood and hugged her friend. "I owe you."

"I haven't found anything yet."

"If anyone can, it's you."

CHAPTER 6

Rushville, LA
Wednesday, July 2nd

Bryce climbed the steps to the three-story brick building that served as the courthouse, sheriff's office, and a half dozen holding cells for the small parish. It wasn't fancy, but they thankfully didn't need an expensive CSI lab or SWAT team. The sheriff's office dealt with petty crimes and family dramas that needed a sympathetic, personal touch, not technology.

And occasionally, a stern warning.

Nothing at all like her job with the FBI.

Suppressing a sigh, Bryce stepped into the long, open space with a front reception desk that was manned by a silver-haired officer who should have retired years ago. Not that anyone had the guts to tell Chuck he should be home enjoying his days. And honestly, he did a good job of getting rid of bothersome visitors who were there to bitch about stuff the sheriff had no control over. Seriously, what did they expect Finn to do about the potholes in the road? Or locating their cat that wandered off a dozen times a week?

With a casual wave toward the older officer, who grunted in response—his version of *Welcome back*—Bryce took a seat at her desk. She'd chosen a spot near a window that overlooked the park. During the afternoon, her dad would take Josie to play on the swings. It gave Bryce a glimpse of her daughter enjoying her day. Plus, it meant she was facing away from Finn's office.

Not that she was worried about being distracted when she glanced through the glass wall that separated Finn from the rest of the room. Or at least that's what she told herself. Once upon a time, Griffin Maxwell had been her childhood crush. Like every other girl's in Rushville. But now she was a grown woman with a child and an aging father depending on her.

Finn was her boss. Nothing more.

As if testing her determination not to be distracted, Finn abruptly appeared next to the desk, leaning his hip against the corner. Bryce sucked in a slow breath, allowing her gaze to skim up the muscular body that filled out the brown uniform with mouth-watering perfection. Reaching the angular features, she studied the long, slender nose, the chiseled cheekbones, and the full lips that were curved into a half smile. He wasn't model-pretty, but he had a raw, compelling masculinity that was emphasized by his smoldering black eyes and the dark hair that was long enough to pull into a tail at his neck.

"How was lunch?" he asked.

"It was gumbo at BBs." Her tone was deliberately light.

"Ah." His smile widened. "So it was delicious."

She held up a finger. "I wasn't done. There was also a pan of cornbread with extra honey, and sweet tea."

"Nothing better."

"Exactly."

He folded his arms over his chest. "And how is Livia?"

"Troubled." The word had left Bryce's lips before she could consider the wisdom of sharing her friend's private business.

She trusted Finn. As a cop and as a person. He would never share anything she told him in secret. Plus, he was her boss. He had a right to know what she was working on when she was in the office. Even if it was on her own time.

His smile faded. "What's wrong?"

She shared the few details she knew about Jacob Pearson, well aware that there wasn't enough to warrant an official investigation, but fully committed to making sure her friend wasn't in danger.

It was clear that Finn remained on the fence. "Jacob Pearson sounds sketchy, but it's not really our jurisdiction," he pointed out.

"It might be."

"Why? You think he followed her to Rushville?"

"No, but Livia caught Jacob sneaking into her house a couple of weeks ago," she said. "And he wasn't alone. She thinks she saw Winston Durand come in and attack him."

Finn stiffened. "Winston Durand was in her house in New Orleans?"

"That's what she said." Bryce tapped on the keyboard of her computer, logging into her private email account. "Let's see if she sent the picture." She scanned through the junk until she found what she wanted. "Yep. Here it is."

"She's sure it was Winston?" Finn demanded, moving so he could peer over her shoulder.

Bryce breathed in the scent of a warm male soap, pretending the heat from his body wasn't sending tingles of pleasure down her spine. Since returning to Rushville she'd become the queen of denial.

"No, and this picture isn't exactly conclusive." She clicked on the email, opening the attachment to reveal the blurred picture from Livia's phone.

"That's an understatement," Finn murmured. "It could be anyone."

Finn straightened and stepped away, his expression hard to read. It was only then that Bryce remembered that the Maxwells were related to the Durands, like his grandfather had been a brother to Winston's grandfather or something.

"Sorry. I forgot he's a distant cousin, isn't he?"

He looked offended by the reminder. "*Very* distant. Just like I'm distantly related to half the people in this parish."

"True." In such a small town, it was hard not to have a family connection. She was different. Her family had originally lived in Chicago. They'd moved to Rushville when Bryce was a baby to get away from the big city. The one thing they hadn't considered was the possibility that Bryce's mom would grow bored with living in such a small town. Or that she'd take off with the first man who offered her a way out. "I promised to check out Jacob just to make sure he isn't a threat, but I'll do it in my personal time."

Finn waved a hand toward her computer. "No, go ahead and do it now. It's not like we have anything pressing to deal with."

"Really?"

"Livia will be in the area for the next couple of weeks," he said, revealing his awareness of Livia's compulsory visits to the Willows. Of course, most people in Rushville knew about Henri Benoit's crazy will. "It's our job to keep her safe."

"Thanks, Finn." She was genuinely grateful. "I hate to be late getting home to Josie."

"Speaking of Josie, did you find her stuffed hippo?"

Bryce's breath tangled in her throat. She didn't know why Finn's kindness toward Josie always caught her off guard. Maybe because most men didn't hide their boredom when she mentioned Josie. Even the ones who wanted to date her.

"My dad put it in the washer and forgot to tell me. A near tragedy averted."

"So peace has returned?"

"Don't be silly. Josie is four. This morning I fixed her the wrong cereal, socks are stupid, and the rain hurts her face."

Finn glanced toward the window where the early morning rain had given way to blue skies and smothering heat.

"Well, the rain can be unpleasant and socks *are* stupid. I can't comment on the cereal."

He glanced back at Bryce and they shared a smile. The sort that led to dangerous emotions and stupid decisions.

Bryce wiped the smile from her face. "You're sure you don't mind me investigating Jacob during office hours?"

"Go for it. I always liked Livia." Finn returned to his perch on the corner of her desk. "Thank God she wasn't like the rest of her family."

Bryce didn't miss the edge in his voice. "You don't like the Benoits very much, do you?"

"In my professional capacity, I consider them well-respected members of this community who pay their taxes and are generous with our local charities. An upstanding family that Rushville is honored to have as our neighbors."

"And in your unofficial capacity? It won't go past this office." She held up two fingers, pressing them together. "Scout's honor."

Finn shook his head, reaching to grab her hand and gently tug up a third finger.

"This is scout's honor."

He was bent forward, allowing her a glimpse into the velvet darkness of his eyes. Her mouth dried to the texture of the Sahara Desert.

"Of course you were a Boy Scout," she managed to mutter.

He released her hand with a shrug. "Law officers were either scouts or juvenile delinquents when they were young."

"We know which one I was." Leaning back in her wooden chair, she eyed him with genuine curiosity. "What do you have against the Benoits?"

"Old man Henri threatened to force my father out of office."

Finn's dad, Griffin Maxwell Sr., had served as sheriff in Rushville for thirty years. It wasn't until Finn agreed to run for the position that he'd been willing to retire. In all that time, Bryce couldn't recall ever hearing a bad word against him.

"Why?"

"It was back twenty-eight years or so ago. When Giselle Benoit supposedly jumped off the balcony of her bedroom into the empty swimming pool."

"That was Livia's mom, right?" Bryce asked. She had no memory of the woman, but she knew that she'd committed suicide when Livia was just a child.

"Yup."

"Wait. Did you say *supposedly*?"

He glanced over his shoulder, as if making sure Chuck couldn't overhear their conversation. "My dad didn't like to talk about it, but after Giselle's death he tried to get the details of exactly what happened, but Henri refused to let him on the property."

Bryce was confused. "Your dad was the sheriff. How could he stop him?"

"Easy. A few well-placed complaints to the mayor, a few more to his senator, and even one to the governor."

"You can't be serious."

"My dad was told in plain language to back off or he would be removed from office. The coroner ruled the death a suicide, and the case was closed."

Bryce wasn't surprised to discover that a bunch of politicians would bend the law for their rich friends. It happened all the time. Even in the FBI. But it baffled her they'd go to such an effort.

"Did your dad think there was something fishy about Giselle's death?"

"Not at first. It appeared to be exactly what Henri Benoit said it was: a tragic end to a beautiful young woman."

"Was there a note?"

"Yes. It said something like 'I can't go on.' Pretty generic and brief."

Bryce remained baffled. It certainly seemed like a suicide. "So why did your dad want to investigate?"

"Because a young, apparently healthy woman with a two-year-old baby and lavish lifestyle plunged to her death. It would have been malfeasance if he *hadn't* demanded an investigation."

"That's true."

"It probably would have been an open-and-shut case. There was nothing suspicious. Not until Henri went on a rampage, refusing to cooperate and dragging in his paid politicians." Finn's expression was hard, clearly showing his resentment for how his father had been treated. "Why go to that sort of effort if you don't have something to hide?"

His words echoed her own confusion. "Maybe because he was an arrogant ass," she offered.

"It could have been a way to flex his power," he reluctantly agreed, "but my dad never forgot."

"And you never forgave."

"It wasn't just what happened to my dad."

"Let me guess." She wrinkled her nose. "It's because Adrian Benoit is a condescending bore?"

"No. That was inevitable. It runs in the family."

"Okay." She considered the Benoit clan and their various methods of annoying the locals. "Is it because Delilah Benoit is constantly complaining about everything from the children in town daring to ride their bikes in the streets to the noise of the fireworks display on the Fourth of July?"

"She's a pain in the ass," Finn agreed. "But still not it."

"You can't mean poor Helene?" Bryce said, referring to the oldest Benoit. "She's just pathetic."

He firmly shook her head. "Not her."

"I give up. Tell me."

Bryce could see his jaw clench. "It's the fact that the family blocked the road to the bayous that crosses the edge of their property. Since the founding of Rushville, that pathway has been open so the citizens could have easy access to the federally protected wetlands. Now they're forced to drive an extra twenty miles, even assuming they have access to a vehicle. For some people in this area those lands are sacred. It's a crime the Benoits can trample over the rights of others just because they have money."

Bryce understood his frustration. His mother had family ties to the Native American tribes in the area. It was difficult enough to preserve their glorious heritage without the Benoits putting up unnecessary roadblocks.

"Did anyone ever make a formal protest?" she asked.

"None of the townsfolk were willing to risk antagonizing the Benoits, while the elders of the local tribe took a more long-term view of the situation."

"'Long-term'?"

"They were convinced that the land would purge itself of the taint when the time was right."

Bryce blinked. They considered the Benoits a taint on the land? Not that they were alone in their less than flattering opinion of the aloof, snobbish family, she silently acknowledged. There were plenty of townsfolk who held a grudge against their notorious neighbors and their attitude they were better than everyone else.

Before she could ask more about his father's interest in Giselle Benoit's death, the sound of a ringing phone had them turning toward Chuck, who picked up the landline on his desk. Times were changing, but Rushville was still remote enough to need old-fashioned technology. A minute later, he replaced the receiver and glanced toward Finn.

"That was old man Coulter. He said there's a stray dog in his garden and if we don't get out there, he's gonna shoot it."

Bryce started to rise to her feet only to be halted by Finn's hand on her shoulder. "I'll go. I promised to stop by the high school with some police tape so they can mark off the area in the parking lot for the Fourth of July floats to line up for the parade. I'll try to be back before five, but if not just lock the doors and go home."

"I don't mind staying until you get back."

"Go home."

She saluted with a teasing smile. "Aye, aye, Captain."

He studied her for a long, unnerving moment before strolling out of the office. Bryce released a shaky breath. Then, with a grim determination, she turned back to her computer. She didn't have time to waste on analyzing each word and glance that she shared with Sheriff Finn Maxwell, even if she wanted to. And she absolutely didn't.

Logging into her official software program, Bryce typed in Jacob Pearson's name and hit ENTER. She had access to information that wasn't available to the public, including crime records, whether they were currently incarcerated, and any aliases or nicknames.

A dozen files popped up, but a quick search was enough to reveal that none of them matched the man in Livia's picture. She expanded her search to the state of Louisiana. And then the rest of the country. There were a few Jacob Pearsons who matched the general description, but a deeper look eliminated them from her list.

After a solid two hours of searching, she had to accept the fact that Livia had been well and truly catfished. Whoever she'd been dating, it wasn't Jacob Pearson.

"Okay, mystery man." She rolled her head from side to side, loosening her neck muscles. "You wanna play? Let's go."

Livia took her time going back to the Willows. The gray clouds had drifted to the south, leaving a sun-drenched afternoon, and despite the heat and humidity, it was too nice to waste the day in her rooms. Taking a lazy stroll around Rushville, she'd wandered in and out of the small stores, and finally sat in the shade of the gazebo in the park. Around her, the citizens went about their business, none of them in a hurry to get stuff done. There was a different pace here. New Orleans was the intoxicating hustle and bustle of chicory coffee. Rushville was the slow decadence of molasses.

The heat finally forced her back to her car, but even as she parked in front of the sprawling mansion, she found her feet carrying her to the back of the house. She remained distracted by her conversation with Bryce and the suspicion that the fake Jacob Pearson was connected to Winston. Or worse, her uncle.

Which meant that Marcel had been right. Jacob's presence in her life had been because she was a Benoit.

A whisper of premonition brushed over her, leaving behind a heavy sense of dread. As if she was tainted by a darkness she couldn't see.

Bypassing the garden, Livia was climbing the steps to the back terrace when a movement out of the corner of her eye brought her to a sharp halt. Someone was roaming around. She frowned as her gaze skimmed over the vast lawn. There was no one there, but she was certain that she'd seen a shadow.

Without giving herself time to consider the wisdom of confronting a potential intruder, Livia angled past the tennis courts, intending to cut off whoever was back there. It wasn't until she reached the side of the pool house that she discovered the intruder was already escaping through the back gate set between a gap in the hedges.

Livia hesitated. She was willing to confront someone in the relative safety of the enclosed yard. She wasn't going into the swamps. End of story. But then the person stepped out of the shadows of the high hedges and into the sunshine and she realized it wasn't a stranger.

"Helene?" Livia stepped toward the tall woman, who was wearing a loose caftan that brushed the tops of her bare feet.

Her aunt continued to drift forward and with a muttered

curse, Livia hurried to catch up with her. The older woman had been a raging alcoholic for as long as Livia could remember. It wasn't safe for her to be out alone.

Darting through the open gate, Livia grabbed Helene's arm. "Are you okay?"

The last thing she expected was for the older woman to turn around and smack her across the face.

"Of course I'm okay," Helene snarled. "Get your hands off me."

"Fine." Livia released her hold on Helene's arm and stepped back. She wasn't injured, but her cheek was stinging from the blow. "Wander into the damned swamp if you want."

Helene paused, her blue eyes narrowing as she studied Livia. Her face was gaunt and deeply wrinkled and her long brown hair was heavily streaked with gray despite the fact that she couldn't be more than fifty-five or fifty-six years old.

"Who are you?" Her voice was rusty, as if she didn't use it much. She swayed forward, studying Livia with blatant suspicion. Then, without warning, she sucked in a sharp gasp. "Giselle."

Livia flinched. She'd seen a few pictures of her mother when she was young, but she'd never thought they resembled one another. Giselle's hair had been a lighter shade of brown and smooth as silk. Her face had been a delicate oval and her skin kissed by the sun, a perfect contrast with her bright blue eyes. She'd also been tall and slender and with a casual grace. Everything that Livia lacked.

"No. I'm Giselle's daughter." She had to force the words past her stiff lips.

"Giselle," Helene stubbornly repeated, her expression caught between joy and a strange, twisted horror. She reached out to grab Livia's hands. "Oh my God. I knew it. You're here."

"No. I'm Livia. Giselle is dead."

The bony fingers squeezed hard enough to make Livia hiss

in pain. It was only the fear that she might accidentally trip the older woman and break her hip that kept her from jerking free of her grasp.

"You're lying. She can't be dead. I've seen her."

"You've seen Giselle?" Livia demanded. "Where?"

Helene slowly turned her head to glance toward the nearby swamps. "She's out there."

It took a second to realize that Helene must be referring to the Benoit burial grounds that were tucked on a marshy spot of land that was protected by a circle of cypress trees.

"In the crypt?" she asked.

Helene shook her head. "She can't rest."

Livia forgot about her throbbing fingers as she studied her aunt with a sharp stab of curiosity. No one at the Willows was willing to discuss Giselle. It was like the family tried to erase her from their memories.

Only her ghost lingered.

"Why can't she rest?" Livia demanded.

"She's searching."

"Searching for what?"

Helene stared at her, a pained silence stretching between them. Then, with a strangled gasp, she spoke.

"Manny."

"Manny?" Livia furrowed her brows. "Is that a place? Or a person?"

"Manny, Manny, Manny," Helene chanted.

"Tell me—"

"Helene." A female voice cut through Livia's question as Janet Preston stepped through the back gate. The woman was a few years younger than Helene and had lived at the Willows as Helene's private nurse for the past twenty years. She was a small woman with sandy blond hair that she kept cut short and a square face. She rarely interacted with the rest of the family, but when she did she acted more like a drill sergeant than a nurse. “There you are.” She moved to stand next to Helene. “I’ve been looking for you everywhere.” With a stiff smile, she nodded toward Livia. “Hello, Livia. It’s good to see you.”

“Janet.”

“You’ll have to excuse us.” Janet firmly grabbed Helene’s arm, pulling her away. “It’s time for our afternoon tea.”

Helene tried to cling to Livia’s hands. “I’m sorry.”

“What?”

“Tell him I’m sorry.”

“Tell who?”

“Manny.”

“Manny? I don’t know who that is.”

“Manny, Manny, Manny.”

“That’s enough,” Janet said in stern tones, shoving Helene through the gate.

Livia glared at the nurse. “Wait. We were talking.”

“Not now,” Janet said, her expression grim. “She’s on new medication that’s affected her mind. Maybe after she’s had her tea and a nap, you can talk again.”

Livia stepped forward, intending to demand the right to speak to her aunt, but a glance at Helene’s anxious expression dried the words on her lips. Janet was right. The older woman was fading into a haze of confusion. She wasn’t in any condition to answer the questions that hammered through Livia with a ruthless hunger.

Fisting her hands, she watched the two women disappear, leaving her with a nagging desire to know the truth about Manny and why her aunt was sorry.

CHAPTER 7

The Willows
Wednesday, July 2nd

Livia slowly returned to her rooms, a trickle of sweat inching down her brow. The heat was oppressive in New Orleans, but this close to the swamps there was an extra layer of humidity that clung to her skin like a damp shroud. Intending to jump into the shower, Livia paused at her doorway. The heavy silence that filled the house assured her that most of the family were in their rooms, while the staff were no doubt scurrying around the kitchen as they prepared the lavish dinner.

It was a perfect opportunity to do more snooping.

With determined steps, she headed down the long corridor, passing through the main section of the house and into the family wing. She refused to tiptoe past her aunt and uncle's suite, reminding herself she wasn't doing anything wrong. Her encounter with Helene had stirred a vague memory.

She didn't know why it mattered. Who cared if her aunt was roaming the grounds, searching for her dead sister and sending her regrets to some unknown Manny? The older woman was clearly unstable. Livia would be better off concentrating on why Winston Durand had entered her house like he owned it. And his connection to Jacob.

Or better yet, she should be checking through her email to discover what disasters were piling up while she was out of her office. In a few days, she would collect her trust fund check and return to New Orleans. Once she was gone, her family and Winston Durand could rot in these swamps.

The defiant words were searing through her mind at the same time she was reaching out to shove open the door. Why fight her impulse? She was inevitably going to end up in her mother's rooms before leaving. It happened every time she stayed at the Willows. As if she hoped she would eventually feel a connection to the woman who'd given her birth and then a couple years later jumped to her death.

Stepping into a room that was decorated in elegant shades of cream and gold, she moved to the center of the carpet and turned in a slow circle. The ceiling was high, with a sparkling chandelier dangling in the center, and the wallpaper was an antique ivory shade to match the lush carpet. Thankfully, the French doors leading to the balcony were hidden behind heavy curtains, but the floor-to-ceiling windows were left uncovered, allowing the late afternoon sunlight to pour in.

This space, with its delicate furnishings and gold satin duvet, was designed for a pampered princess, not a new mother devoted to her child. In fact, the only indication that she had a baby was a framed picture of Livia on the nightstand next to the canopy bed.

Livia was told that she'd stayed in an attached suite with the nanny. She didn't have any memory of living at the Willows, but one peek into her old bedroom revealed it'd already been stripped down to a few stuffed toys and the clothes she'd outgrown. She'd been sent off to her foster family less than a month after her mother's death and her presence wiped away.

This room, though, had been preserved as if time stood still. The walk-in closet was still stuffed with Giselle's clothes, and her makeup was spread across the mirrored dresser. There was even a pair of fancy heels near the bed, as if she'd kicked them off before climbing onto the mattress. It looked like she might waltz through the door any minute.

The sound of a footstep behind her had Livia stifling a scream as she whirled toward the open door. Had Helene been right? Was Giselle's spirit roaming the grounds of the Willows?

"Livia." The voice shattered her moment of fear. It was male, and all too familiar. She stiffened as Adrian Benoit entered the room to regard her with a disapproving scowl. "What are you doing in here?"

Livia sucked in a deep breath, refusing to apologize. She had every right to be in the room.

"Just seeing if anything had changed," she smoothly lied.

His scowl deepened. He was wearing a gray tailored suit and a crisp white shirt, prepared for the evening despite the fact that it was only four o'clock. Did he get ready early so he could sneak down for a couple of drinks out of the critical gaze of his wife?

Probably, but who could blame him?

"Why would it change?" he asked, as if confused by the question.

"My mother has been dead for twenty-eight years. Haven't you ever thought about cleaning it out?" She didn't add that her own room had been emptied quick enough.

"Your grandfather requested it remain exactly as Giselle left it."

"Like a shrine?"

His jaw clenched. "I suppose that's what it is."

Livia turned to drift toward the dresser, picking up a crystal bottle of perfume and holding it close to her nose. She shivered at the light floral scent. She had no tangible memory of Giselle, but there were moments when she was certain she could recall her soft voice whispering in her ear and this unique fragrance.

"It's odd," she murmured.

"What is?"

Livia asked the question that had been troubling her for years. "Her clothes and stuff are here, but where is her purse or phone? Or even her computer? There's nothing personal except for a few trinkets. What happened to them?"

"I'm sure your grandfather had them locked away."

She turned back to study her uncle's grim expression. "Locked away where?"

He made a sound of impatience. "Livia, what is it you're looking for?"

"Answers."

"Answers to what?"

There were so many things she wanted to know, but suddenly nothing mattered but the oldest question of all.

"Everyone in this house refuses to talk about my mother."

Adrian flinched. "Don't, Livia. Not tonight."

This was the point where she was supposed to scurry away like a good girl. She'd been taught from an early age that it was rude to pry into the past.

"Not tonight, or not ever?" she challenged.

"It's a painful subject. You wouldn't understand, you were too young when she passed to share our grief."

Livia refused to back down. "You at least had the chance to know her as a real-life person and not just another tragic statistic."

His eyes widened. "Livia."

"It's true," she hissed. "You've reduced her memory to the way she died, not the way she lived." Livia spread her arms, glancing around the room that was filled with expensive items, but empty of personality. Her current bedroom in New Orleans was a messy collection of clothing and books and professional magazines she never got around to reading and Post-it notes with names or numbers stuck on the mirror. In one corner she had weights that were collecting dust along with a treadmill that was buried beneath a layer of blankets and clean sheets. One glance would be enough to reveal her age, her profession, and the fact that she knew how to be healthy but no desire to make the effort. This place was too sterile to hold any memories. "I want to know who she was growing up and becoming a woman," Livia confessed. "Did she like school? Did she get good grades? Was she on the softball team or in the school play? Did she go to the prom? What did she want to be when she grew up?" She hesitated before forcing out the most important question. "Did having me ruin her life?"

Adrian paled, as if genuinely pained by her probing. Then he astonished them both by answering.

"Giselle was a spoiled, defiant drama queen. She was constantly causing some sort of scene, as if she thrived in chaos." His lips twisted into a bittersweet smile. "But she was also vibrant and joyous and so charming no one could resist her. Not even my father. He worshipped the ground she walked on."

The words burst out of him as if they'd been bottled up for too long, and Livia felt a pang of gratitude. For once he was being completely honest, revealing his genuine emotion toward his young, impetuous sister.

"She was Henri's favorite?"

"Absolutely." His expression was oddly gentle. "But none of us minded. We all adored her."

Livia glanced toward the only indication that Giselle had been anything other than the pampered daughter of Henri Benoit. The framed photo of a smiling baby on the nightstand.

"Was she sad when she found out she was pregnant?"

"Not even for a second," Adrian said without hesitation. "She was delighted. And once you were born, she loved you more than anyone or anything in this world."

"Then why did she . . ." The words dried on her lips.

"I don't have the answers you want, Livia," he murmured, his moment of vulnerability hardening into stark rejection. "Drinks will be served at six. Delilah would appreciate if everyone could be on time."

With his warning delivered, Adrian turned on his heel and left the room. Livia waited until his footsteps faded before she crossed toward the bed. Her uncle hadn't given her answers, but he'd eased a fear that had haunted her since the days she'd discovered her mother had committed suicide.

Giselle hadn't jumped from her balcony because Livia had destroyed her future. She'd wanted a baby, and whatever else was going wrong in her life, she loved Livia.

The words meant more to her than Adrian would ever realize.

Marveling at the warmth that spread through her, Livia absently bent down to flip aside the gold duvet and reach beneath the mattress. She shoved her hand deeper, at last finding the thin scrapbook and pulling it out.

It was the only personal item she'd ever found over the years of searching the room, and she assumed that was only because her mother had kept it hidden. Otherwise, it would have disappeared with her phone and computer.

Livia didn't really understand why it was under the mattress. There were a few fading pictures stuck between the pages, mostly of the family around the estate. There were several of Giselle's mother, Olivia Benoit, who had died just months before Livia had been born. She'd been a short, curvaceous woman with a gentle smile and a love for gardening. In each picture she was trimming rosebushes or sitting in the glass greenhouse that had since then fallen into disrepair. They were just pictures, but Livia had always thought she could feel the love between Giselle and her mother. There was something different in the careful angles and lighting of the photos when compared to the casual poses that focused on Henri, or Giselle's siblings.

But none of them seemed out of the ordinary. Just the usual family events that happened on a routine basis. Which made it weird for Giselle to hide them under her mattress.

Flipping through the pages that were yellowed and brittle from age, Livia found the picture that she was looking for. In the center of the photo was a gleaming black limo that her grandfather had used when he traveled to visit the various properties spread around the state. Standing next to the vehicle was a stranger who was running a wet sponge over the hood, obviously cleaning the limo. A chauffeur? Probably.

He was tall and dark and gorgeous as he glanced toward the camera with a wicked smile. He had his shirt off to reveal a toned chest and rock-hard abdomen. Exactly the sort of eye candy who would turn the head of an impressionable teenager.

Livia had occasionally wondered if Giselle had been infatuated with the man. And if their relationship had gone beyond casual. After all, Livia had no clue who her father was, or even if he'd been informed he had a child. Maybe he'd seduced Giselle before moving on to a new job.

Then again, she couldn't imagine Henri Benoit tolerating any hired help who didn't understand their place in the rigid hierarchy of the Willows. Even if her mother had been impetuous and spoiled, any staff member would understand Giselle was off-limits.

In the distant background, Livia could see the blurred image of Helene, who was facing toward a tall, gray-haired man. Livia recognized him as Helene's husband. From the gossip Livia had pieced together, Helene had just turned eighteen when Henri married her off to the wealthy Lance Prescott, who was looking for a mother for his two young boys. Lance had lost his first wife less than six months before his wedding to Helene and, from all reports, it hadn't been a happy union. They divorced less than ten years later, and Lance moved away with his boys, never to return to the Willows.

Absently wondering if her aunt had started drinking after the marriage, and if that was the reason Lance had left, Livia pulled out the photo and flipped it over. It was one of the few pictures that had her mother's handwriting on the back.

The ink was fading, but she could clearly make out the words *Car wash day with Manny. Dreamy.*

Livia felt a stab of satisfaction. Manny. She knew the name struck a chord of memory.

Did it answer any questions?

No, not really. But then again, she proved her aunt hadn't been babbling incoherently. There really had been a Manny at the estate. And if Helene was confusing the past with the present, then she might genuinely think that Giselle was still alive and Manny was still the chauffer.

At least one mystery partially cleared.

Tucking the photo back into the plastic sleeve, Livia flipped the scrapbook closed with more force than she intended. There was the sound of crackling as the inner lining of the book came loose and a sheet of paper flew onto the mattress. Livia cursed at her carelessness, grabbing the folded piece of paper and gently smoothing it flat.

It didn't look like someone had ripped it from a notebook. It was too small and made from a thick ivory paper with the date stamped at the top. Maybe a sheet from a personal diary? She shrugged, her attention focused on her mother's handwriting in the center of the page.

Rice. Lake Oaks Park at 2 p.m.

Livia frowned. It looked like her mother had scribbled down an appointment. Was she going on a picnic and bringing some rice? Weird. There was a Lake Oaks Park close to her office in New Orleans, but it was nothing more than a small strip of land next to Lake Pontchartrain with some trees and a couple picnic tables. Not a tourist destination. Or even a romantic spot to meet a potential lover.

She opened the scrapbook to see where the paper had come from, her confusion deepening as she realized that the lining had been pulled off and then glued back together, hiding the note. That's why she'd never seen it before. It wasn't until the glue had dried up and she'd slammed the book shut that it'd parted to allow it to fly out.

But why would her mother hide it? A secret meeting? With who? And what was with the rice?

Baffled, Livia returned her attention to the wrinkled paper, her gaze lingering on the date stamped at the top.

Monday, September 29, 1997.

Her heart came to a painful stop. Her mother had committed suicide on September 28th. One day before her appointment in Lake Oaks Park. Well, assuming that she hadn't torn out a random page from her diary to jot down the note. It seemed weird. Did people contemplating suicide make plans? And why hide the note?

None of it made sense.

The distant sound of the grandfather clock striking five at last shattered Livia's dark musings. She still needed to shower and change before she was expected downstairs. And as much as she wanted to stay and figure out the meaning of the strange message, it was more important to concentrate on the present. And whether Winston and her uncle were involved with Jacob Pearson.

Tucking the scrapbook under the mattress, Livia smoothed the duvet into place before scurrying back to her rooms. An hour later, she was scrubbed clean with her hair pulled into a messy knot on top her head and wearing a silver lamé jumpsuit. The outfit was elegant but comfortable, plus she could wear a pair of flats. She wasn't sure why she wanted the feeling she could flee at a moment's notice, but it was unshakable.

At a few minutes after six, she was downstairs in the formal salon, staring out the arched windows as Winston Durand walked up the steps to enter the front door. He wore a casual tan suit and white shirt. Had he spent the day at his family estate? It was impossible to know. He could have been anywhere.

She was silently debating on the best means of following him around without being noticed when her aunt swept into the room. Livia groaned, prepping herself for the inevitable attack as Delilah marched to stand directly in front of her. On cue, Delilah's gaze narrowed as she took in Livia's sparkly jumpsuit.

"An interesting outfit," she at last said.

Livia smiled, pretending the words were a compliment. "Thank you. Marcel helped me choose it."

"Your receptionist?"

"Assistant," Livia corrected. "And he has excellent taste."

Delilah parted her lips, but before she could really piss Livia off by insulting her friend, Celeste entered the room, clinging to the arm of Winston as he moved to greet her.

"Oh, there's Celeste. She's wearing Chanel tonight," Delilah cooed. "Always classy."

Livia studied the short black dress with spaghetti straps and scooped neckline.

"You must be right. I saw several women wearing that exact gown at the Black and Gold Gala in New Orleans." Livia smiled sweetly. "It's obviously a very popular design."

Her aunt's expression hardened, as if trying to decide if she was more annoyed by Livia's dismissal of Celeste's expensive gown or the revelation that Livia had attended the most exclusive gala in New Orleans.

Livia bit her tongue, reminding herself that she was downstairs early in order to find out more about Winston and any potential connection to Jacob Pearson, not to insult her aunt and cousin. As much fun as that might be.

"They make a lovely couple," she choked out.

Delilah sniffed, no doubt sensing Livia's lack of sincerity.

"Yes. Yes, they do," she said, finally forcing herself to accept the compliment. "Celeste, of course, had her choice of men. I don't know how many of them proposed. To be honest, I lost count over the years. But I'm glad she waited for the right man before saying yes."

Livia managed a smile. "Have they been dating for long?"

"They dated off and on since Winston returned from college, but it wasn't serious until a few months ago. Neither of them were in a hurry to settle down and I think Celeste wanted to be sure that Winston was ready to be a devoted husband and father. She's like me—unwilling to compromise when it comes to putting family first."

Livia smiled wryly. "Family first" had never included her. She'd been handed off like a stray dog.

"Adrian mentioned they intended to live at the Willows after the wedding?"

"Yes." Delilah looked smug. Had she manipulated her daughter into staying home? She'd always been overprotective. Livia wouldn't doubt that the older woman had done everything in her power to keep Celeste from escaping her lavish prison. "It's the perfect solution since Winston has to travel so much."

"Celeste doesn't enjoy traveling with him?"

"He's busy with his business. She would be bored. At least here she can spend time with her friends. And eventually her children."

The words echoed what Adrian had told her, and Livia wondered how often Delilah had repeated them before she got everyone on board with her desire to keep Celeste secluded at the Willows.

"It's a shame that Celeste couldn't at least have gone with him to Ireland to announce their engagement to the royals. I would think that they would want to do that together."

Delilah shrugged. "It was a last-minute decision for Winston to fly over and speak with them in person. And I needed Celeste here to help with the preparations for this week."

"How last minute?"

Delilah's brows snapped together. "What does it matter?"

Livia deliberately turned away from the happy couple, who were quietly discussing some subject that made Celeste frown. She'd pressed far enough for one night. She didn't want to make her aunt suspicion.

And at least she'd discovered that Winston's supposed trip to Ireland hadn't been planned weeks in advance. Which made it more likely it'd been a cover story so he could be in New Orleans without anyone knowing.

"Just making conversation," Livia murmured. "Will there be any guests joining us tonight?"

"Just the photographer. He wants a few pictures of the family in a casual setting."

Casual? Livia resisted the urge to roll her eyes. Instead, she grasped the opportunity to satisfy yet another puzzle gnawing at her.

"Then Helene will be joining us?"

Delilah looked surprised by the question. "No. She prefers to have a tray in her room."

"That's a shame. I ran into her today. She was in the back garden."

"Was she?" Delilah shrugged. "I suppose that's a good thing. She needs to get some fresh air every now and then."

"I'm not sure if it was good or not. I had to stop her from wandering into the swamp."

Delilah sent her a startled glance. "She was out there alone? Janet is supposed to be with her when she leaves her rooms."

"I can understand why she needs someone with her. At first she thought I was my mother."

"She must have been drinking."

Livia didn't miss the edge of disgust in Delilah's tone. She'd always treated her sister-in-law like she was a nasty secret. Kind of like she treated Livia.

"It's possible she was drinking," Livia conceded. "When I caught up to her she was babbling about someone named Danny . . . no, that's not right." Livia pretended to search her memory for the name. "Manny. Yes, that's it. Manny."

Delilah froze. Just like that. Her body went rigid and her face was wiped of all expression. Then, with remarkable composure, she relaxed her muscles and managed a stiff smile.

"Probably a character off one of those reality shows she watches," she smoothly suggested. "She constantly has the television blaring. Night and day."

"No." Livia shook her head, deciding on a direct approach. This wasn't like her investigation into the mysterious Jacob Pearson. She had every right to know about her mother and why she'd been driven to suicide. "I think he was the chauffeur here at the Willows. Helene claimed she'd seen my mom looking for him. And that she was sorry about something."

Delilah clicked her tongue. "I've warned Adrian that his sister needs to be put in a home where she can be properly looked after. Maybe now he'll listen to me." The appearance of a tall, slender man with an expensive camera hung around his neck gave Delilah the perfect opportunity to escape the uncomfortable conversation. "Excuse me."

Livia watched her aunt hurry to greet her guest, tucking away the knowledge that Manny was obviously a sensitive subject. And that Delilah was afraid that Helene might accidentally reveal something they were trying to keep secret.

Apparently she needed to find Manny and ask him.

Just as soon as she figured out why Jacob Pearson had catfished her, why Winston had attacked him, and what the hell they were looking for in her underwear drawer.

CHAPTER 8

Livia escaped the tedious dinner before the dessert was served. It wasn't like she was going to eat it anyway. But once she was in her suite, she couldn't relax. Instead she spent the next three hours pacing the floor. How was she supposed to stop the questions that were spinning through her mind, like a hamster stuck on a wheel?

Only when she reached the point of utter exhaustion did she finally tumble into a deep sleep. Perhaps that explained why she didn't hear her phone buzz at three a.m. In fact, it wasn't until she climbed out of bed the next morning that she realized she'd received an alert from her home security system that there was movement on her front porch.

There was no way it'd been a deliveryman. Or even a curious neighbor. Not at that hour. It was possible that there'd been a stray dog that had set off the alarm, but she hadn't bothered to connect the system to her phone before leaving town. Honestly, after Jacob disappeared, she didn't think it was necessary.

Which meant she would have to go to the city and check the video from her house.

Pulling on a pair of khaki shorts and a loose smock top,

Livia brushed her teeth and knotted her hair on top of her head before grabbing her purse and hurrying out of the house.

It wasn't until she was starting the engine of her car that she grimly paused to consider what she was doing.

It didn't seem dangerous to drive back to New Orleans to check out her house. It was broad daylight. And whoever—or whatever—had been sneaking around was long gone. But then again, what if they weren't long gone? What if they deliberately set off the alarm in the hope she would come back to New Orleans? It could be a trap.

Ignoring her dislike of asking for help, Livia grabbed her phone to send a text to Bryce, telling her friend about the trespasser and that she was headed to her house in New Orleans. At least someone would know where she was and hopefully come looking for her if she didn't return. She didn't trust her family to care one way or another.

A second later, she got a text back from Bryce, telling Livia that she was coming by to pick her up and for Livia to wait by the front gate.

Reluctantly shutting off the engine, Livia walked down the long driveway and through the narrow door next to the formal gates. She was anxious to be on her way to New Orleans, but she was equally anxious to discover if her friend had information on Jacob Pearson.

She was left waiting for less than ten minutes when a brown SUV with a sheriff's decal painted on the side stopped directly in front of her. The passenger window slid down and Bryce's voice floated through the air.

"Get in."

With a lift of her brows, Livia climbed into the vehicle and pulled on her seat belt. A second later, they were rattling down the gravel.

"Where are we going?"

"New Orleans."

"Wait. I just wanted to let you know where I was heading. I didn't mean you had to drive me there," Livia protested.

The SUV picked up speed as they hit the paved road that skirted the edge of Rushville.

"I know, but I need to go to New Orleans, so we might as well combine our trips."

Bryce was wearing a pair of jeans and a casual T-shirt, which Livia assumed meant that she was off duty. Then again, she was driving her official vehicle.

"Why are you going to the city?"

"I'm hoping to interview Jacob Pearson."

Livia sucked in a shocked breath. "You found him?"

"Not exactly."

"What does that mean?"

"There's no Jacob Pearson that matches the photo you sent me. At least not in our system."

Livia released her breath with a harsh sigh. "Damn."

"That was my first reaction. So last night I sent the picture to a friend in the FBI." Bryce held up a hand as Livia stiffened at the thought of involving the FBI in her petty problems. "Strictly off the record, I promise."

"Did they recognize him?"

"Morgan ran a facial recognition and got a hit on an ex–New Orleans cop named Larry Sutton."

"A cop?" Livia struggled to accept what her friend was saying. "Are you sure?"

"Ex-cop," Bryce emphasized. "He was fired for taking bribes. And no, it's not certain it's him. The image was fuzzy and Morgan warned me that there was only a fifty-fifty shot that it's the right guy."

Livia dismissed the warning. "Did you get any information on Larry Sutton?"

Bryce veered onto the exit road that would lead to the highway. "He has an office in New Orleans and he's a licensed private investigator."

"Private investigator?" Livia grunted, feeling as if she'd taken a physical blow. Then, with a shudder of reluctance, she forced herself to dredge up her unwelcomed memories of Jacob Pearson. When they'd first met she hadn't questioned his claim that he was in finance. Despite his easy charm, he'd possessed a natural air of authority along with a hint of arrogance. Something she expected from a successful businessman. But those were also the personality traits of a cop. And the fact that he'd been caught taking bribes wasn't at all shocking. The creep had lied about everything. "I should have sensed that there was something sleazy about him," she muttered, angry that she'd been so easily conned.

"Let's not jump to conclusions until we know for certain," Bryce warned. "Larry Sutton is an ex-cop and current private investigator. We don't know he's Jacob Pearson the catfish. If it is the same guy, I promise you we'll find out what game he was playing and if someone was paying him to play it."

With a shake of her head, Livia turned her thoughts from *who* had been lying to her to *why* they'd been lying.

A private investigator didn't randomly catfish women. They were paid to hunt down missing people or expose secrets, right? She wasn't missing. And as far as she knew she didn't have any secrets. So why?

"It's surreal. I'm so ordinary." She glanced out the passenger window as they hit the highway and zoomed toward New Orleans. Her stomach was twisted into a tight knot. "Actually, I'm probably the most boring person I know. It doesn't make any sense to have a private investigator going to such extremes."

"Hopefully we'll soon have the answers to your questions."

"Yes, Lord. Please," Livia rasped, her mind struggling to accept that there was yet another massive twist in her brief, regrettable relationship with Jacob Pearson. It felt like a prank that'd spiraled out of control. Or a case of mistaken identity. Maybe he realized it was a different woman he was supposed to be investigating and that's why he'd disappeared.

"Are you okay, Livia?"

Livia glanced toward her companion, abruptly realizing she was being completely self-absorbed. She hadn't bothered to question how much time Bryce had spent digging up information on Jacob Pearson or even how she was able to do this road trip on a weekday. Some friend she was.

"What about your job?" she demanded. "I don't want you having to use your personal time off to do this. I can check out Larry Sutton on my own."

"I'm on official duty. Finn insisted."

"That's remarkably generous of him."

Bryce kept her gaze locked on the thickening traffic. "Not really. You're currently staying in our official district. It's our job to protect you along with the other citizens of Rushville. It's always possible that Jacob Pearson might follow you to the Willows."

Her voice was oddly stiff, as if there was something she wasn't willing to share, but Livia didn't press. It was enough to know that Bryce had convinced the sheriff to allow her to include the investigation into her duties. Gratitude raced through Livia.

"Thank you. But what about—"

"Josie is spending the next week with Benjamin's parents," Bryce interrupted before Livia could ask if she was taking Bryce away from her daughter. "They always rent a cabin in the Ozarks during the Fourth of July for a family reunion. Josie loves it. There's a huge lake and playground, plus she gets to spend time with her cousins who she rarely gets to see. It's good for her."

"What about you?"

Bryce looked confused. "What about me?"

"Are you okay with her being gone?"

"Absolutely," Bryce admitted with a refreshing honesty. "I adore my daughter, but I feel no shame in fantasizing about a few peaceful nights soaking in a hot bubble bath and sipping a cold glass of wine."

Livia smiled, suddenly wondering if Bryce's stiff tone when she was referring to Finn Maxwell was personal.

"Are you alone in that bubble bath fantasy?"

"Livia."

Livia chuckled at the unmistakable chastisement. "Fine, you can keep your fantasies to yourself. I promise we'll be back to Rushville in time for a full soak. Both with bubbles and wine."

"No worries. If we're late we'll stop for dinner and a drink on the way home."

Livia settled back in her seat. "Sounds great."

Reaching the outskirts of New Orleans, Bryce exited off the highway and slowed to a crawl as she zigzagged through the streets. It was an older section of town where cars parked next to the curb, leaving a narrow path that was barely wide enough for the large SUV.

"Tell me about the intruder at your house," Bryce demanded.

The knot returned to Livia's stomach. Or maybe it hadn't really disappeared, she just hadn't noticed it.

"I'm not really sure if there was an intruder or not," she confessed. "I had an alert that there was movement on my porch at three a.m. I suppose it could have been a stray dog, but I want to check it out."

"Can you pull up the video on your phone?"

"No. Unfortunately, I set up the app so I get an alert if the camera is activated, but I didn't bother to sync the video before I left town. I had the locks and security system changed after I caught Jacob in the house."

"Good call."

Livia agreed. The changes had felt excessive when she assumed she'd just been ghosted by Jacob. Now she wished she'd gone bigger and better with the security.

"I want to make sure no one got into the house last night and that there wasn't any damage."

"And it gives you a perfect excuse to spend a few hours away from the Willows."

"There's that," Livia agreed. It hadn't been a conscious decision, but there was no doubt she was always eager to escape from the shadows of the family mansion. "You know, it's been strange being back at the Willows."

"Isn't it always?"

"Stranger than usual."

"Why do you say that?"

Livia took a second to pinpoint to source of her unease since arriving at the family mansion.

"I think it started with my suspicion that Winston might be the second guy in my house," she at last concluded. "And then wondering if Adrian might be involved."

"Wait." Bryce sent her a startled glance. "Adrian? Your uncle Adrian?"

"I saw him whispering with Winston."

"That's it?"

"No. It wasn't just the whispering." Livia struggled to pinpoint her suspicions. "I can't explain it. It was more a vibe than anything. They were acting . . . weird. And then I found Helene roaming toward the swamps, and she was muttering about seeing my mother and the old chauffeur, Manny somebody-or-other."

"She's not exactly stable," Bryce pointed out.

Livia heaved a harsh sigh. "That's true."

There was a brief silence as Livia recalled her awkward encounter with her aunt. It was more than just her fear that Winston was somehow connected to Jacob Pearson. The unease that kept her stomach in a knot was nothing new. It'd been there for as long as she could remember. But until the past couple of days, she'd refused to examine the unpleasant sensation. It was enough to know she would travel to the Willows, collect her portion of the trust fund, and leave without delving into the darkness that haunted the family estate.

Why bother? It wasn't like they considered her as more than an interloper.

This time, it wasn't as easy to ignore the bubbling tensions just beneath the surface.

"What is it, Livia?" Bryce demanded.

"I think deep down I've always sensed that my family was hiding something from me. But in the past, I assumed it had to do with my father. They've always refused to tell me anything about him."

"Yeah, I always thought that was odd they kept that a secret," Bryce agreed. "Did you check your birth certificate?"

"Yup, no father listed." The first thing Livia had done when she turned eighteen was get a copy of her birth certificate. She'd been deeply disappointed when she realized it wasn't going to give her the answer that had haunted her for years. "It used to bother me. Now, I'm pretty sure I'm better off not knowing."

"You're probably right. You have enough family drama in your life."

Livia rolled her eyes. "Beyond enough."

"So what do you think they're hiding from you?"

"Something to do with my mother's death."

It was the first time that Livia had spoken the words out loud and she was shocked by how right they felt. As if the truth had been lurking just out of sight.

Bryce sucked in a loud breath, as if Livia's confession had struck a nerve. "Seriously?"

"What is it?" Livia demanded. "Do you know something about her suicide?"

"No. Of course not." With a visible effort, Bryce managed to relax her stiff muscles. "Like everyone else in Rushville, I always assumed it was a suicide."

Livia frowned at her friend's strange reaction. "Do you think I'm crazy?"

"I think you're stressed. But I also think you should trust your gut."

"My gut hasn't been very dependable lately, but since I'm

stuck at the Willows for the next couple of weeks, I might as well indulge my curiosity."

"What do you intend to do?"

"I'm not really sure. No one in my family will discuss my mother or what happened that night. They act as if mentioning her name is some sort of sacrilege to her memory. Even her room has been stripped of anything that might give me a clue to who she was or why she might have been driven to such an extreme need to end her life. No. Wait." Livia had nearly forgotten the scrapbook she'd discovered. "I do have an idea. If we have some time we might swing by Lake Oaks Park."

"Why?"

"I found a note my mother hid beneath her mattress, it said 'Rice. Lake Oaks Park at 2 p.m.'"

Bryce sent her a confused glance. "That's it?"

"That's it." Livia shivered, the sensation of a ghostly hand sweeping over her face. "Except for it was written on a page that was dated for the day after she died."

CHAPTER 9

New Orleans, LA
Thursday, July 3rd

Bryce slowed the SUV, turning the corner onto a one-way street. New Orleans was like most older cities with clusters of areas that had fallen into grim neglect that were weirdly bordered by lavish mansions.

This neighborhood was worn and slightly shabby, but it maintained the elegant atmosphere of days gone by. Most of the houses were built in the Craftsman style with covered porches and dormer windows. They were perched on wide plots of land with driveways that circled behind the homes to hidden garages. A few of them had neatly trimmed hedges to block off their property, while others were cleared to welcome passing pedestrians. It was clearly a mishmash of aging locals who refused to give up their homes, and small businesses looking for affordable office space.

"That's the address," Bryce said, pulling into the driveway to study the house.

It was one story, although there was a window beneath the

sharply pitched roof to suggest a partial attic. The siding was a faded gray with white shutters and a covered porch. The tall windows were wood-framed and obviously original, as was the ornate railing that framed the porch. It had recently been painted white to match the wooden sign that swayed in the wind: SUTTON PRIVATE INVESTIGATIONS.

"This must be the place," Livia said, the words sharp as if she was forcing them between her clenched teeth.

Bryce shot her friend a quick glance, noting the tense lines of her profile. Livia was practically vibrating with the need to confront the man who'd lied and manipulated her into a relationship before mysteriously disappearing.

"Do you want to wait out here?" Bryce asked.

Livia made a choked sound of disbelief. "Absolutely not."

"Okay, but remember priorities." Bryce pointed a warning finger at her companion. "We're here for information first. Once we get the answer to why he lied to you, *then* you can punch him in the face."

"I prefer a kick to his nuts."

"Always a good choice." Bryce shoved open her door. "But first we talk."

Livia didn't answer as she exited the SUV and headed up the sidewalk. Bryce could only hope her friend didn't go feral once she was face-to-face with Larry Sutton.

Hurrying forward, Bryce moved past Livia to take the lead as they crossed the porch and opened the glass door. A welcomed wave of air-conditioning greeted them as they entered the front lobby that had once been the living room, with built-in bookcases and a wood-plank floor. There was a small desk near the front door and another, larger desk at the back of the space with two leather chairs in front of it. As if waiting for clients.

Unfortunately, there was no Jacob Pearson or Larry Sutton, just a large, middle-aged woman with hair chopped short and dyed a bright red. She had dark eyes coated in layers of makeup and she was wearing a yellow pantsuit that went out of fashion in the eighties. Currently she was standing next to the desk, tossing various items into a cardboard box.

"We're closed," the woman announced, barely glancing at them as she continued to fill the box.

"We need to talk to Larry Sutton," Bryce announced, her gaze moving from the woman to the small plaque on the front of the desk that was embossed with the name CHERRY RYAN, SECRETARY. "Cherry."

"A lot of people need to talk to Larry Sutton." The woman grabbed the plaque and threw it into the box. At the same time, the old-fashioned landline on her desk released a shrill ring. "Me included."

"He's not here?" Bryce demanded.

"Does it look like he's here?"

Bryce narrowed her eyes at the flippant answer, pulling out her badge. "We have some questions."

For the first time since they'd entered the office, Cherry turned toward them, belatedly realizing they weren't potential clients.

"Shit," she muttered, her eyes skimming over Bryce's official badge. "I knew it."

Bryce tucked the badge into her back pocket. "Knew what?"

"That he was in trouble. I mean, worse trouble than usual." Cherry shook her head in disgust. "Did he piss off the cops? Is that why he's laying low?"

Bryce arched a brow. "Does he spend a lot of time in trouble?"

Cherry shrugged. "Most of the time he stays on the right side of the law, but he's a private investigator. It's his job to lie, cheat, and spy on people. He has a real talent for it."

"No crap," Livia muttered in a soft voice.

"What's he done now?" Cherry asked.

Bryce managed a meaningless smile. "Like I said, I have a few questions for him."

Cherry waved a hand around the empty office. "I'm not covering for him if that's what you're thinking. He isn't here."

"Do you have a number where I can contact him?"

The woman leaned forward to grab a business card off the desk and handed it to Bryce. It was too generic to have more than Larry Sutton's name, address, and two phone numbers.

"Try the bottom number," Cherry said. "That's his cell phone. He's not answering the phone for me, but you might have more luck."

Bryce tucked the card into her pocket with her phone, her gaze sweeping over the office. She didn't expect to find Larry hiding under the desk, but she was searching for any hint that he'd bolted out the back door when he caught sight of Livia.

There was nothing.

No half-filled coffee cups, no open files on the desk, even the computer was powered down. It didn't look like he'd been around for a while. She felt a burst of frustration. She wouldn't have asked Livia to join her if she hadn't been confident she was about to expose Jacob Pearson as Larry Sutton, Private Investigator.

She should have remembered the age-old adage of all law enforcement officers: when you were on the hunt for a suspect, whatever could go wrong would go wrong.

"When was the last time you spoke to him?"

"Two weeks ago."

"He hasn't been into the office?"

"Nope."

The answer caught Bryce off guard. It wasn't surprising he'd been avoiding Livia if he suspected his cover had been blown. But why not come to his office? He surely had other clients?

"Is that unusual?" she asked.

"Not when he's working on a case," Cherry said. "He's disappeared for months before. But he always answers his phone.

Or at least he gets back to me if I leave a message. This time"—she snapped her fingers—"nada."

"You didn't report him missing?"

Cherry looked baffled. "Why would I? He's not my kid. Although he acts like it. Besides, I didn't think he would want me involving the cops."

"Why not?"

The older woman shrugged, returning to her task of placing the items from her desk into the box.

"Larry isn't a bad guy, but he has some pretty sketchy clients. I warned him more than once he was going to get involved in a situation that was going to get him thrown in jail."

"Can you be more specific? 'Sketchy' in the fact that they're criminals?"

"A few. Not drug dealers or local thugs, but a few have been arrested for money laundering or counterfeiting."

Out of the corner of her eye, Bryce caught Livia shuddering in disgust. Poor thing. She'd had no idea she'd been dating a man who would be involved with crooks.

"What did he do for them?"

"Usually it was following around a wife or girlfriend to see if they were cheating. Or doing background checks on the people who work for them."

Bryce arched a brow. "Criminals have background checks done on their employees?"

Cherry shrugged. "Usually they wanted to know if the person was a gambler or into drugs. Those sorts of employees can be desperate enough to do anything, including stealing from someone they know will put a bullet in their head."

Larry Sutton was even sleazier than Bryce expected, which might explain why he'd decided to disappear. There were some bad guys in New Orleans you didn't want to make mad. And if you did, it was wise to slink into the shadows until it was safe to come out.

On the other hand, his sketchy client list made his connection to Livia all the more confusing. She didn't hang out with criminals, and even though the Benoits were arrogant jerks, she'd never heard rumors that they were anything but upstanding citizens.

So if he had been pretending to be Jacob Pearson and then felt the need to disappear, who the hell hired him?

"Do you know the name of his current client?" she asked, already prepared for Cherry's sharp shake of her head.

Was there some unseen force trying to keep Jacob Pearson from being found?

"Most of our clients are run through the regular billing system," Cherry said. "But there are a few that he takes off the books. They usually pay in cash."

"What about his current client?"

"One of those who prefer to be off the books. He never came into the office or called the main number for the business. Everything went privately through Larry."

Bryce ignored Livia's muttered curses, concentrating on Cherry's words. "But it's a he?"

The secretary hesitated. "I'm not sure. I just assumed," she at last admitted.

It could have been a simple assumption, then again, it could have been that Larry used the male pronoun when talking about the client.

With a shrug, Cherry gathered up the last of the items on the desk and tossed them in the box.

"Why are you packing?" Bryce demanded.

Cherry sniffed. "I've put up with a lot over the past ten years—Larry's sexist jokes, his habit of having friends over after hours and leaving this place a mess. The angry ex-girlfriends and unhappy clients. But I'm not going to spend another second here without getting paid."

"When were you supposed to get your pay?"

"Last Friday. I have the check for me and the guy who cuts the grass made out and left on his desk." She nodded toward the back of the room. "All he had to do was sign them."

"Has he ever missed payroll before?"

"Maybe a day or two, but not this long," Cherry conceded. "I left a dozen messages warning him I was out of here if he didn't come in and sign the damned check." Cherry picked up the box, her expression grim. "His loss."

Bryce considered the various options. It was possible that Larry Sutton had moved on to a new case and was too preoccupied to deal with his office. It was more likely that something had happened during his previous job that had driven him into hiding. He might even be out of town.

The question was whether it was the same client who had hired him to spy on Livia. And if her friend was in equal danger.

"Before you leave, I need Larry's home address."

Cherry glanced around the office. "This is it."

"Here?"

"He crashes in the attic when he's between girlfriends."

Bryce glanced toward the door at the back of the office. She assumed that led to the staircase.

"Have you checked up there?"

Cherry looked offended by the question. "Of course I did. He hasn't been around. I cleaned out his fridge last week."

Bryce swallowed a sigh. It was sounding more and more like Larry had skipped town. "Do you have an emergency contact?"

"You're looking at her."

"No family?"

"None he ever talked about."

Bryce felt another surge of frustration. She'd tracked down trained assassins with less effort.

"What about girlfriends?"

Cherry shrugged. "What about them?"

"Do you have any names or numbers?"

"I'm his secretary, not his wife." The woman grimaced. "Thank God. I would have beat him to death with a skillet if I'd been married to the bastard. Now I need to go find a new job."

"Do you mind if we look around?"

"Knock yourself out. Have a nice day."

Without a backward glance, Cherry headed out of the office. Bryce followed behind, latching the door as the woman disappeared down the sidewalk. She didn't want to be caught by surprise while they were searching the place. Whoever Larry was hiding from might decide to pay a visit. Especially if they knew Livia was here.

"Do think something happened to Jacob?" Livia asked, her tone indicating she was more frustrated than sad at the thought her ex-boyfriend might have been hurt. "I mean, he not only ghosted me, but he's disappeared from his job."

"I suppose it's possible considering the implication that he worked with the sort of people who might be willing to get rid of someone who crossed them," Bryce said, although she wasn't ready to leap to any conclusions. "But Cherry seemed more convinced that Larry was just laying low. Until we know for certain one way or another, I think we should assume that he's alive and well."

"True. He's obviously a sleazeball. I doubt he'd care that he left his staff without a paycheck."

"Let's check out the attic."

Bryce took the lead, touching the handgun that she'd holstered beneath her shirt. She didn't intend to use it unless they were under extreme circumstances, but it was reassuring to know she had easy access to a weapon.

Her agreement to help Livia had been an impulsive decision that she assumed would take a couple hours of her time. She'd track down the idiot who'd tried to catfish her friend and send him a stern warning. That would be that. It'd never occurred to her that it would turn into a full-fledged manhunt that now included the New Orleans underworld.

Pushing open the door behind the second desk, Bryce discovered a short hallway that led to a bathroom and a storage space stuffed with filing cabinets and plastic tubs piled to the ceiling. At the end was a set of stairs that led to the narrow attic with a sloped ceiling and bare, wood-plank floor. It was an open space with a bed shoved under the lone window and a narrow counter that held a hot plate and a small microwave.

It was unpleasantly claustrophobic. Probably because there were stacks of dirty dishes, empty bottles of booze, and takeout boxes near the microwave, while wrinkled clothes were tossed in every corner. It looked like a frat boy's apartment, not a trained policeman's.

"What a mess." Livia turned in a slow circle. "Gross."

"Yeah, don't touch anything." Bryce moved toward the chair where a dozen magazines were stacked. She rolled her eyes. Porn, of course. "We were given permission to be here but I don't have jurisdiction if we find a clue. Look around and see if there's anything that might reveal if Larry Sutton is also Jacob Pearson."

A second later she heard Livia's sharp gasp. "It's him."

Bryce turned to discover her friend standing next to the nightstand near the bed. She hurried to join her, bending down to study the framed picture of a man standing near a lake, holding a fish in one hand and a rod in the other. Behind the man she could see a cabin with a sign carved over the door.

"That's the man who called himself Jacob Pearson?" she asked, trying to match the fuzzy image that Livia had sent her with this photo. "You're sure?"

"Absolutely."

Livia reached out, almost as if she intended to smash the picture, but Bryce caught her arm and pulled her back.

"No, don't touch," she warned. "This is confirmation that

Jacob Pearson and Larry Sutton are the same man, but we still don't know what's happened to him. I don't want to disturb anything."

Digging her phone out of her pocket, Bryce took a picture of the photo before turning and taking pictures of the rest of the attic. It was easy to overlook things when you were doing a quick walk-through. She would study the images later to see if she missed an obvious clue.

Once she was done, Bryce tucked her phone away and walked toward the sheet that was hung from a rod tacked onto the wall. She pulled it aside to reveal the closet that was stuffed with a vast assortment of clothes.

No. Not clothes, she silently corrected herself. Costumes.

At one end there were expensive, tailored suits, including a tux, followed by cashmere sweaters and slacks. There were more casual jeans and shirts in the center and at the other end were a dozen uniforms—utility worker, security guard, cop, military officer, chef—and scrubs with badges that had Larry Sutton's picture with a variety of names printed beneath them. There were even a couple of dresses, as if he'd been in drag for one of his jobs.

"The man might be a sleaze, but he was thorough," Bryce said. "He could blend into any background with this stuff. Unfortunately, there's no way to tell if anything is missing. If he packed a bag and left town, we'd never know."

"He probably got paid and is enjoying a vacation on the beach," Livia snapped.

"It's possible. At least we know that Jacob Pearson never existed and that we're searching for Larry Sutton, ex-cop and current private investigator. He can't hide forever." Bryce dropped the curtain. "Let's get out of here."

CHAPTER 10

They returned to Bryce's SUV and, giving her friend the address to her house, Livia settled back in the leather seat and considered what they'd learned.

She knew that Jacob was Larry Sutton. And that he was a private investigator. And that he'd disappeared. All significant discoveries, but they didn't really answer any of the questions that haunted her.

Why had Larry manipulated his way into her life? Who had hired him? What was he looking for in her house? And why had he suddenly taken off?

Bryce allowed her to stew in silence for several minutes, but at last she gave in to the concern that had been shimmering in her eyes since they'd left the office.

"Are you okay?" She shook her head as the words burst out. "Sorry, I keep asking that, don't I?"

"I don't mind," Livia assured her friend, watching the neighborhoods blend from residential to touristy to business to residential again. "Honestly, I'm not sure if I'm okay or not."

"What's bothering you?"

"My relationship with Jacob Pearson keeps getting more

bizarre. It was bad enough when I thought he was another run-of-the-mill creep who was sniffing through my underwear drawer. But then he disappeared along with all his social media and I thought I'd been catfished. Which was strange, but it happens. And now I find out he's a private investigator." She hesitated, waiting for the knot in her stomach to tighten. Instead, she felt nothing. Was she finally numb? "I don't even know what to do with that," she admitted. "It just doesn't make sense."

"You're right. It doesn't make sense. We need to figure out who hired him."

Livia flinched. She was still trying to process the fact that Jacob had been a private investigator. She hadn't reached the part where she worried about who had hired him.

"It had to have been Winston." Livia pointed out the obvious choice.

"If Winston was the man you saw in your house it would make sense," Bryce agreed.

"But why? I never met Winston until a couple days ago. He had no reason to spy on me." Livia frowned as she remembered the scene in her bedroom. "And why did he shove Larry against the wall? He was clearly angry, but does that mean he's the reason that Larry disappeared?"

Bryce shook her head. "I don't have any answers. And we're still not sure that it was Winston you saw through the window."

Livia sighed. She'd dredged up the memory a hundred times, but she couldn't be sure who'd been in her bedroom with Larry Sutton. She suspected it was Winston, but if she was put on the witness stand she'd have to admit it was no more than a gut instinct.

"Who else could it be?" she finally demanded.

"I'm not sure, but until we do have a way to verify the intruder, it would be dangerous to leap to conclusions. We might overlook something important."

"You're right," Livia agreed. "And even if it was Winston he might be the middleman. Maybe he hired Larry for someone else." As soon as the words left her mouth, Livia realized how silly she sounded. "I'm starting to talk like a character in a cheesy detective show."

"We'll get the answers. It's just a matter of finding Larry Sutton and forcing him to tell us who hired him and what they wanted."

Livia wished she shared her friend's confidence. "Easier said than done."

Bryce clicked her tongue. "You haven't forgotten how stubborn I am, have you? I once went two full days without eating because my dad said I couldn't have anything until I finished the broccoli on my plate. I was ten years old. That's not to mention the nights I spent on our roof trying to catch our neighbor sneaking out to meet his receptionist in the orchard behind our house. It took over a month but I finally got a picture of him. That was the last time he tried to claim that our garden shed was on his property."

A small smile tugged at Livia's lips, her tension easing at Bryce's mischievous boast. Her friend was right. Livia had never met anyone who was more tenacious than Bryce when she was on a mission.

"No, I haven't forgotten. If anyone can track him down it's you."

They turned onto the street that ran in front of Livia's house. "Let's briefly assume that Sutton wasn't hired by Winston or your uncle," Bryce suggested. "Is there anyone that might have a grudge against you? A rival real estate agent? An ex-lover? A client?"

Livia silently considered the people who might hold a grudge. There were a few fellow agents who'd been infuriated by her rapid rise to the top. More than one had accused her of using her connection to the Benoit clan to open doors. And others had hinted she must be sleeping with the developers to get such lucrative contracts selling their new homes. But it was competitive bull crap that happened all the time.

"I'm sure there are a few people in my life who wouldn't mind getting revenge. You can't build your own business without stepping on a few toes. Especially if you're a woman," she admitted. "But they wouldn't have any reason to sneak around my house. If they wanted to hurt me they would spread nasty rumors about my agency. Or vandalize one of the properties I'm trying to sell."

"What about ex-lovers?"

"Few and far between." Livia didn't bother to scroll through her previous relationships. They'd been too shallow to stir up a desire for revenge. "None of them were serious enough for either of us to care when we stopped seeing each other."

"You'd be surprised," Bryce said. "There are some men who can't handle rejection, even if they pretend they're indifferent."

Livia gave a firm shake of her head. "It would be a stretch for them to remember my name, let alone be bitter enough to cough up money for a private detective."

"Okay," Bryce conceded. "I just don't want to get locked in one direction with no real proof."

Livia knew Bryce was referring to her belief that this was somehow connected to her family. She also knew her friend was right. It would be all too easy to allow her feelings for the Benoits to blind her to other potential suspects.

Belatedly realizing they were nearly at her house, Livia pointed toward the approaching driveway.

"Pull in here."

Bryce turned into the driveway and shut off the engine. She leaned forward to study the house that was small but sturdy, with the unique details that came with homes that had been built by hand, not constructed by developers who concentrated on volume, not quality.

"Nice," Bryce said.

Livia felt a stab of pride. "Nothing fancy, but it's mine."

"That's everything."

"Yes."

She shared a smile with her friend. Independence meant everything to girls who'd grown up with the knowledge they had no one to depend on but themselves. Still, looking back, Livia couldn't regret her struggles. It'd given her a strength that she might never have had if she'd been handed everything on a silver platter.

Like her cousin.

Livia was mildly amazed by the realization. For the first time ever, she felt sorry for Celeste. The beautiful woman might have a life of luxury, but she would always be at the mercy of her mother. And eventually Winston.

What a terrible fate.

Bryce held out her hand. "Can I have your house key?"

Livia dug into her purse. "Why?"

"I'm going to check out the house before you come in."

"Bryce."

Bryce snatched the key from Livia's fingers, pushing open the door of the SUV. "I'm trained to see stuff you aren't. And if this is a crime scene we don't want any evidence disturbed before I call the local police to investigate."

Livia scowled. "You're using the same old excuse to try and keep me out of the way."

"Look, if I decide to buy a house I'll let you be the expert without trying to tell you how to do your job." Bryce held her gaze. "Deal?"

Livia released a noisy sigh. "Deal."

With a nod, Bryce slid out of the vehicle and walked toward the front porch. Her head swiveled from side to side as if she were looking for anyone hidden in the bushes. Or perhaps she hoped the intruder had left behind a clue that would reveal who'd been sneaking around. Then, reaching the door, she shoved it open and stepped inside.

Ten minutes later, she was jogging back to the SUV. "It doesn't look like anything has been disturbed. Let's check out the security tape."

Bryce eagerly joined her friend, hurrying up the driveway and onto the porch before stepping through the open door. Without warning, she found her steps faltering as she was wrapped in the familiar scent of lavender and polished wood. It smelled like home and she winced at the pang of longing that clenched her heart.

The Willows would never be more than a place she was duty bound to visit. The sprawling mansion was as formal and rigid as a museum, with shadows that pressed against her with the threat of a storm brewing just out of sight. The entire estate was shrouded in an ominous atmosphere that Livia had assumed was a product of her overactive imagination.

Now she wasn't so sure.

With a shake of her head, Livia led her companion into the spare bedroom that she used as a home office. She slid into a seat at the small desk and fired up her spare laptop. The screen flickered to life and she searched for the security program. It took a couple of minutes to get the stupid thing open and the video downloaded, but at last she had what she wanted. Waiting for Bryce to lean over her shoulder, she slowly searched through the footage.

There was nothing to see beyond a few kids cutting through the edge of her lawn and the postman delivering her mail, until the video reached 3:13 in the morning.

"There," Bryce breathed, pointing toward the figure that stepped out of the darkness to cross her porch. "Can you pause it?"

"I think so. Hold on." Livia tapped on the keyboard. She didn't know what she was doing, so she used the old "try everything" approach to stop the footage. At last she hit the right button, freezing the video so they could study the intruder. Livia tapped again, eventually finding a way to zoom in. "There."

They leaned forward, squinting at the dark image. It was clear enough to make out the shape of a person. It looked too broad through the shoulders to be a woman, but that was about all she could make out. The intruder was wearing a ski mask to hide his face, along with the hood pulled up on his heavy sweatshirt.

"Whoever it is knew they were on camera and were afraid of being identified. I don't know if it's because they're a pro or if they're afraid you might recognize them." There was an edge of frustration in Bryce's voice. "Is there anything you've seen before? The hoodie? The shoes?"

"No, I can't even tell how tall they are or their body weight. It's all kind of a blur." Livia was equally frustrated. "So much for my upgraded system."

"They're never great. Not even the ones we have at the office. Can you zoom out again?" Bryce leaned even closer to the screen as Livia widened the view to take in the intruder and a portion of the porch. "What's that?"

The image was frozen at the spot where the man was reaching for the doorknob. It wasn't until Bryce pointed at the glint of moonlight off a small piece of metal that Livia noticed he was holding something in his fingers.

"A key," she breathed. "Jacob. It has to be."

"Let's watch the rest of the video," Bryce suggested.

Livia tapped a key and the intruder was once again in motion, bending forward as he tried to unlock the door. There was a hesitation, as if he was confused why he couldn't get inside, then with an angry gesture, he slammed his hand against the door and turned to stalk off the porch, disappearing into the darkness.

"Why didn't the key work?" Bryce asked in confusion.

"I had the locks changed at the same time I changed the security system," Livia reminded her friend. "The key I gave him doesn't work, but Jacob wouldn't have known that."

"Right. I forgot." Bryce straightened. "Did Jacob know you were going to be out of town?"

"Yes. I even mentioned the exact dates I'd be gone." Livia clenched her hands into tight fists, feeling like an idiot. "I asked him to come down and join me for lunch if he had the chance. I might as well have invited him to break into my home and steal me blind while I was gone."

Bryce frowned. "But when he was in your house before, he didn't try to steal anything, did he?"

"I don't think so," Livia conceded. "And he'd been here often enough to know that I didn't have anything of value except for my computer and a television that's at least five years old."

"You said you saw him searching through the dresser in your bedroom."

"I'll show you."

Livia shut down the computer and headed out of the office and into the bedroom across the hallway. She ignored the unmade bed and stacks of laundry that needed to be put away as she headed for the low dresser shoved against the far wall. Bryce wasn't here to inspect her housekeeping skills.

Opening the top drawers, she stepped back so Bryce could see inside. "Look for yourself. It wouldn't take long to realize there's nothing in there."

Bryce pushed aside the nightgowns and lingerie, before shaking her head in confusion. "Do you ever have cash laying around from your agency?"

"Never. It's all electronic transfers. And I never personally have any money here. It's easier to use my credit card." Livia glanced around the bedroom. She loved the sense of coziness in the small space, but anyone hoping for a quick score would be disappointed. There were no hidden safes, no locked drawers, no jewelry boxes. Nothing but clothes, shoes, and files from the office. "Besides, he's supposed to be a private investigator, not a thief."

"He could be both," Bryce said, holding up her hand as Livia's lips parted to protest. "I know, I'm reaching." Her hand abruptly dropped and her eyes widened. "Wait."

"What is it?"

"I just thought of something." Bryce planted her hands on her hips, her brow furrowed. "If I'd been hired to spy on you, I wouldn't depend on the limited amount of time I could spend in your company. The best way to find out whatever information I was hired to get would be to plant a camera or a listening device in the house. Maybe both."

"You're right." Livia thought back to Jacob's ready agreement to stay in during the evenings rather than go to a fancy restaurant. And his insistence that he wanted to make her dinner and have it ready for her when she came home. God, she'd been such a sap. He could have told her any lie and she would have swallowed it without question. "That could be the reason he wanted the key. So he could come in and set up his spy stuff."

Bryce's lips twitched at Livia's less than technical terms. "And maybe whoever hired him wasn't happy with his intrusive methods," she added. "That's why he was annoyed when he came into your house and discovered Jacob in your bedroom hiding his camera."

It made sense. It would explain why Jacob had manufactured their relationship and why he'd been in such a hurry to get the key to her house. And even why he'd disappeared. Maybe whoever had hired him had decided he didn't like Larry Sutton's method of investigation and run him out of town.

"But why come back last night?"

"He could have left something behind," Bryce suggested. "Spy stuff is expensive."

"Okay. Let's look around."

Livia headed for her closet, trying not to dwell on the possibility that she'd been on camera during her most private moments. Was anything more intrusive than spying on her walking around naked or dancing to her favorite music? Or even while she was sleeping. God, it gave her the creeps. Shoving aside her clothes, Livia ran her hands inside the closet before doing the same around the trim. Then she moved to the windows before tossing aside the stacks of laundry she needed to put away, and even shoving aside her neglected treadmill to do a full inspection of the wall. Behind her, Bryce was doing the same.

At last she conceded defeat. "If there's a camera here, he hid it too good for me to find," she told her friend.

"Agreed." Bryce closed the dresser drawers and straightened. "Do you need anything while we're here?"

"Everything." The word burst from Livia's mouth, a sense of dread crawling down her spine. "I don't want to go back to the Willows." She shook her head, pressing her hand against her stomach. The knot was back in full force. "I should be grateful to be away from this house where two men have been sneaking around spying on me, but I'd rather be here than at the family mansion. How sad is that?"

Bryce moved to lay a comforting hand on her shoulder. "It's just for a few more days, and then you'll be done with your obligatory visit. By then we'll have tracked down Larry Sutton and warned him what will happen to him if he steps foot on your property again."

Livia struggled to cling to her friend's assurances. "Okay."

Together they left the house, pausing to lock the door before climbing into Bryce's SUV and backing out of the driveway.

"One good thing is that if it really was Sutton trying to sneak into your house last night, we know he's still in New

Orleans," Bryce pointed out. "That will make it a lot easier to track him down."

Bryce shivered." It can't be soon enough for me."

"I know."

They had reached the corner of the block when Livia remembered she had another reason for wanting to return to New Orleans.

"Do you mind driving past Lake Oaks Park on our way out of town?"

Bryce sent her a smile. "I have a better idea. Let's pick up a couple of sandwiches and have lunch there. It's a perfect day for a picnic and neither of us is in a hurry to get back to Rushville, are we?"

"Absolutely not."

Bryce turned onto the main road leading to the lake, detouring into the drive-thru of a small restaurant that was famous for their shrimp po' boy sandwiches, before they were zooming down Lakeshore Drive and, at last, pulling into the small park.

Slowing to a crawl, Bryce drove along the edge of the picnic areas before rounding the patches of trees and finally along the lane that offered a view of the lake. At last she parked near a wooden table and carried their lunches to take a seat.

"There's not much to see," Bryce murmured.

"No," Livia agreed. It was called a park but it was closer to a rest stop. Which was probably why they were the only visitors despite the beautiful day and the fact that it was noon. The perfect time to take a break from work and get out for some fresh air. "Why would my mother make an appointment to meet someone here? And why bring rice?"

"It had to be some sort of picnic or carry-in dinner."

Livia reached to open the bag of takeout food, her gaze skimming over the grooves carved into the wooden table. Abruptly she froze.

"Or a name," she breathed.

"Nice," Bryce retorted. "You're absolutely right. Rice is a common name. It could have been the person she was meeting."

The explanation felt right. The message made much more sense if Rice was a person, not a tasty side dish. But it still left a dozen questions.

"Again, why here?" Livia demanded.

"It's not very private." Bryce swiveled her head from side to side. "I can see from one end to the other and anyone driving past would have a clear view. It doesn't feel like the place to meet up with a secret lover."

"Or a drug dealer."

Livia winced. She'd never said the words out loud, but it wasn't the first time she'd wondered if Giselle had chosen a lifestyle that might have driven her to suicide. It was an obvious explanation. A young mother who'd become addicted might feel the best way to protect her daughter and family from her illness would be by jumping from the balcony. It was one of the reasons she'd never probed too hard for an explanation for her mother's shocking death.

Bryce glanced around. "You know, this place is strangely familiar."

"You've been here?"

"No, but I drove by it more than once," Bryce said, her brow furrowed. "I just can't remember where I was going."

Livia nodded toward the thick traffic that was zooming past them. "That's a main road so it wouldn't be surprising."

Bryce clicked her tongue. "It's going to nag at me until I remember."

Livia sucked in a slow breath, clearing her mind of Jacob Pearson and her mother's mysterious note. For a couple hours she wanted to enjoy lunch with her friend.

She dug into the bag to pull out a small box that had been packed separately from the sandwiches.

"Until you remember, let's devour these beignets while they're still warm," she announced, flipping open the box to reveal the warm doughy goodness rolled in layers of powdered sugar.

"Dessert first?" Bryce grabbed a beignet and shoved it into her mouth, powdered sugar coating her chin. "I knew there was a reason I loved you."

CHAPTER 11

The Willows
Thursday, July 3rd

Livia was back at the Willows by midafternoon. The heat was oppressive, smothering the estate in a humid layer of haze, but she forced herself to stroll slowly around the edge of the mansion to the back terrace. It was the time of day most of the family were in their rooms, relaxing before the busy evening ahead. If one of them happened to glance out the window, she wanted them to assume she was taking a leisurely walk.

Ignoring the entrance to the private family salon, Livia continued down the terrace to enter through the servants' doorway. It was left unlocked during the day, allowing her to slip into the empty kitchen. Then, walking through the doorway directly to her right, she tiptoed her way through the back hallway that ran the length of the house.

On the way back from New Orleans, she'd brooded on who had hired Larry Sutton to spy on her, and why. Two questions she didn't know how to answer. Not until she realized there might be some proof.

Larry Sutton was an immoral creep who was clearly willing to do anything for a quick buck. Which meant that he wasn't working for free. There had to be some sort of money trail, right? She didn't have any way to discover if Winston was the one to hire him, but she could check out her uncle Adrian.

Thankfully, she'd spent enough time as a child exploring the secret entrances that were hidden throughout the house. It meant she could enter the library through a concealed doorway that had been forgotten by the rest of the family.

Stepping through the narrow opening, she paused to appreciate the impressive room with towering shelves stuffed with leather-bound books and glass cases that protected the ancient maps her ancestors collected over the years. It was stunningly beautiful, but she'd rarely spent any time there.

The library directly connected to her grandfather's private office and was strictly off-limits to everyone unless they'd been explicitly invited by the old man.

Not that she cared. For as long as she could remember, she'd made it her life's purpose to avoid Henri Benoit. Even after he died, she didn't feel comfortable this close to his private domain. As if his disapproving scowl was glaring down at her from the heavens. Or, more likely, glaring up from the pits of hell.

Besides, there was nothing of interest in this elegant room. She'd always been an avid reader, but she came from a bunch of egomaniacs who were obsessed with their legacy. They had books detailing their family tree in excruciating detail, following the life of each and every ancestor who led back to French royalty. They also had the original blueprints and sketches created during the building of the Willows. Plus the hundreds of articles written about the place over the years. But that's where the library collection ended.

The only time she'd come in here was to prove she could use the secret door to enter and leave without anyone noticing.

Now she boldly stepped into the room and glanced around. Nothing had changed in the past thirty years. She doubted anything had changed in the past century, unless you counted the electricity, internet, and fancy computer system she could glimpse on the walnut desk in the attached office. This was the very heart of Benoit power. The spot where misogyny and a stubborn tradition combined to keep the family line churning toward oblivion.

With a shrug, Livia inched her way along the shelves, her gaze locked on the main door of the library. Like her grandfather, Adrian kept the door locked so no one could enter without his permission, but that didn't mean he might not decide to put in a few hours of work.

At last slipping into the office, Livia crossed directly to the desk. As she'd hoped, there were stacks of papers and ledgers in various piles along with a dozen bills marked with LAST NOTICE. Her uncle was just like his father. They distrusted computers and insisted on having hard copies of every contract and business transaction.

Taking a quick glance through the bills that indicated serious problems with Benoit Enterprises, she turned her attention to the ledgers. Adrian was meticulous in keeping a running account for his various properties, including a tally of the money coming in compared to the expenses. There was also a listing of expenses that were taken out of a central business account. Office supplies and other daily incidentals that were lumped together. If Adrian had been paying Larry Sutton out of that slush fund it would be impossible to know without a copy of the bank statements.

She was glancing toward the computer, wondering if she could figure out her uncle's password, when the click of a lock echoed through the silence.

With a muttered curse, she hurried to inch open one of the windows, hoping Adrian wouldn't notice with the shade pulled down. Then stepping through the French doors and onto the back terrace, she pressed herself against the wall near the window.

Seconds later, she heard Adrian's voice drifting out of the office.

"Connect me to Mr. Edwards. Tell him it's Adrian Benoit." There was a short pause. "Quincy, I have a question concerning the Slidell account. . . . Yes, I'm well aware it's been closed and the funds deposited back to my private account. My question is how we can make any evidence of it disappear. . . . No. I mean, erase any trace of the account and the transfers from your system so that no one can ever prove it existed. . . . Yes, this is a personal request. Of course I will be happy to return the favor in the future. We've been friends long enough for you to know my word is good."

Livia press a hand to her mouth to stifle her gasp. He had to be talking about money he sent to Larry Sutton, right? Why else would he suddenly be so desperate to keep the account he used a secret?

Obviously her uncle somehow realized that she'd discovered that Jacob Pearson was actually Larry Sutton. Maybe he even knew she'd gone to the New Orleans office today. The secretary, Cherry, had pretended not to recognize Livia, but that didn't mean she wasn't a liar like her boss. If she'd made a call to Adrian warning him that Livia was on Sutton's trail, he'd be desperate to cover up his connection to the private investigator.

And what about Winston Durand? Was he involved? She was still convinced he'd been the one with Larry in her house.

"Adrian? Adrian, are you in here?" Delilah's impatient voice cut through the thick air like a knife. "The photographer is looking for you."

"I have to go," Adrian muttered, cutting the call short as he rushed to obey his wife. "I'm coming."

Livia hesitated, debating whether to go back into the office. It was probably a waste of time, she at last concluded. Her uncle was obviously erasing every connection to Larry Sutton. Which meant he'd no doubt disposed of any paper trail that would lead to the private investigator. She would have to find some other way to prove he'd hired the sleazebag.

Heading off the terrace, Livia angled across the lawn toward the back gate. She had no desire to return to her rooms and pace the floor. Not when she was still processing the conversation she'd overheard between her uncle and his banker. As tempting as it was to leap to the conclusion her family was involved in spying on her, she knew it was a mistake to act as if she had solid proof.

Yeah, she had circumstantial evidence and gut instincts, but until she and Bryce tracked down Larry Sutton, it was impossible to know for certain. Not that she was going to quit digging, she acknowledged, stepping through the gate and heading toward the small cemetery near the family chapel. She had to do something to keep herself occupied over the next few days.

Skirting past the chapel that was nothing more than an empty shell with a couple of rotting pews inside, Livia stepped into the marble mausoleum. She passed by the plaques embossed with the names of her ancestors until she reached the one belonging to her mother.

GISELLE OLIVIA BENOIT – BELOVED DAUGHTER WHO WAS TAKEN TOO SOON

Rubbing her fingers over the angel carved into the marble, Livia tried to conjure up the image of her mother. As usual, it was a wasted effort. She couldn't recall a face or a tangible moment they shared together. The memories were too fragmented. A scent. A feeling. A soft whisper in her ear.

With a grimace, Livia dropped her hand. She kept hoping each time she came into this place it would be different. There had to be some connection with the woman who'd given her birth. A soul-deep love that should transcend death. But it was always the same: an emptiness that couldn't be filled by a crypt on the edge of the swamp.

Stepping out of the mausoleum, Livia froze as a shadow darted into the thick trees that framed the edge of the bayou. What was that? She hadn't gotten a real look at it, just a flicker of movement out of the corner of her eye. There was no way to know if it'd been a person or an animal, or even the swaying of a tree branch.

Livia waited, straining to hear footsteps. When there was nothing, not even the rustle of leaves, she scurried back to the estate. She wasn't afraid, she assured herself, but that close to the swamps there were all sorts of dangers.

Alligators, wild dogs, and even a few cougars. Better safe than sorry.

She didn't slow until she was through the gate and passing by the tennis courts. Then, coming to a halt, she gathered her shaken composure. Now that she was back within the manicured grounds of the Willows, she felt silly at being spooked by what was probably nothing.

Refusing to give in to the urge to lock herself in her rooms, Livia glanced around, her gaze catching sight of the wind vane on top of the old stables. The center was shaped like a rooster with metal arrows showing the four directions: north, south, east, and west. The air was soggy, but there was enough of a breeze to send it spinning.

The stables had been converted to garages long before she was born, but she'd never bothered to do more than peek inside them. When she was a young girl she thought they smelled like gas fumes and old oil, and as she got older she just wasn't interested.

Now she crossed the lawn with firm steps, careful to keep her eyes averted from the nearby pool. It was a habit she'd developed as a young child. Reaching the long building that had been recently painted a bright white with black trim, she punched in the code to open the door. Thankfully, it was the same code used to open the front gates. Probably not the best security system, but a stroke of luck for Livia.

Stepping into the gloomy darkness, she fumbled for the overhead light. It took some searching, but at last her fingers brushed over the switch on the wall and a bright glow drove away the shadows. Entering the garage, she closed the door and walked past the neat row of expensive cars—a BMW, two Mercedes sports cars, and a Land Rover. At the end of the line was an old Ford Taurus that no doubt belonged to Janet, and a vehicle covered by a heavy tarp that had belonged to her grandfather.

Now that she knew there'd been a chauffeur at the Willows, she assumed there must be some sort of luxury sedan under the tarp. By the time she was old enough to remember her grandfather, he'd rarely left the estate, demanding any business dealings be conducted in his private office. But it was easy to imagine Henri Benoit lounging in the back seat while a uniformed servant drove him to his various businesses.

She also suspected that the staircase she'd noticed at the back of the garage led to a private apartment for the chauffeur. She hadn't thought about the purpose of the upper floor until now, but it was the only thing that made sense.

Threading her way through the cars, Livia hesitated at the bottom step, glancing out the window to make sure there was no one approaching the garage. When she was sure there was no one in sight, she headed up the stairs.

The wood creaked beneath her feet, disturbing the thick silence that filled the garage. The noise made her wonder if anyone had bothered to climb the stairs since her grandfather's death. Maybe not since the last chauffeur left the estate.

Her suspicions were confirmed when she pushed open the wooden door at the top of the stairs and entered a large loft.

It had a narrow bed pushed against the wall and a matching dresser next to it. There was a kitchenette built into the far corner, if you could call it that. There was a sink, a microwave on a narrow counter along with a tiny fridge, and a TV tray with one wooden chair. Beyond the kitchen doorway she could see a cramped bathroom with a toilet and shower, but no sink.

It was barren, but private. If she had to work for the Benoits she'd take this cramped space over a room in the Willows any day of the week. Heading toward the bed, she lifted the mattress, then lowered herself to her knees to look underneath. There was nothing to see but dust bunnies and a used condom.

"Ew."

Livia shoved herself upright and moved to check out the kitchenette. It was equally empty, and thankfully devoid of condoms. A peek in the bathroom assured her there nothing to see here.

Livia placed her hands on her hips, not sure what she'd hoped to find. Maybe a few personal items that would give her a clue to Manny's life. Or a hint of why he'd left. Perhaps most importantly, she'd wanted to see if he had a connection to her mother. A futile wish, she acknowledged, turning to cross back toward the door.

Her breath caught in her throat. Had she shut it? Or did it close on its own?

Reaching out, she grabbed the knob and gave the door a shove. It opened a fraction. Just far enough to prove it wasn't locked, but it hit something that prevented it from moving any farther. Almost like someone had wedged it shut.

"Hello?" She slammed her hand against the wooden panels. "I'm in here. Let me out." She pounded it again. "Hey! Let me out."

She pressed her ear against the crack between the door and frame, straining to hear sounds of movement in the garage. Silence. Whoever had jammed the door was gone.

Or worse.

Livia abruptly stepped away from the door, her hand pressed against her racing heart. What if they were down there waiting? She'd tried to dismiss the possibility that she'd been followed to the mausoleum, but obviously her sense of unease had been right. Someone had been creeping behind her and now they'd trailed her into the garage.

Horror swept over her like a black cloud.

Why? Why would they lock her in here? If they wanted to hurt her it made more sense to attack her when she was in the cemetery. If someone threw her body into the swamps it could take weeks to find her. Assuming anyone would bother to look. And she wasn't going to die up here. Not when she could call for help.

Still, there had been a reason someone had locked her in this room. Either a tasteless joke or a warning. She was betting on the warning.

She reached into her purse for her phone, only to hesitate. It wasn't the instinctive aversion of making a spectacle of herself in front of her family that made her pause. After all, one of them was quite likely the culprit. And she could easily call Bryce to come and get her out. But whoever had jammed the door thought she was stuck.

This would be the perfect opportunity to sneak out and expose the jerk.

Spinning around, Livia darted toward the window and flipped the flimsy locks. She shoved on the frame, grunting in frustration when it refused to budge. The wood had warped over the years. Livia braced her legs and leaned forward, putting her weight behind her next shove. There was a cracking sound, as if a part of the wood had splintered, then the window jerked upward far enough for her to crawl through.

Livia hurriedly grabbed the chair and shoved it against the wall. Then, refusing to consider the danger of dropping from a second-story window or confronting her stalker, she looped one leg over the sill and then the other, balancing for a second as she glanced down, trying to choose a landing spot.

This was stupid, she silently told herself. She should call Bryce and wait for her to come and clear the door. That was the sensible thing to do. Only she wasn't going to be sensible, she acknowledged, spotting a pile of clippings from the recently mowed yard.

Sending up a prayer that she didn't break her leg, Livia shoved herself off the ledge. She squeezed her eyes shut as the wind whipped past her, tugging at her clothing. It lasted a mere second, but her stomach had completed a full flop by the time she hit the ground.

She missed the pile of clippings, of course. Her crappy luck sent her flying too far. Thankfully, the spongy ground kept her from any permanent damage. Taking a second to regain her balance, Livia limped toward the back of the garage, her heart pounding so loudly she couldn't hear anything else.

Once she reached the shadows, she inched her way toward the end of the building, hoping she could catch the stalker as they came out of the garage. Reaching the corner, she leaned forward to study the graveled driveway.

There was no one in sight. Livia rounded the building, pausing to peek in the window. The light had been switched off, plunging the garage into shadows. She assumed whoever had been inside had already fled. Why risk stumbling through the dark?

Muttering a curse, Livia picked up her pace, ignoring the twinge in her ankle as she reached the stone pathway that led toward the back terrace. It hadn't been her imagination that she'd been locked in the abandoned apartment. Someone had to be lurking just out of sight.

She'd reached the pool house before she heard footsteps heading her way. Coming to a halt, she watched as Celeste suddenly appeared. Her cousin was already dressed for dinner in a sleek silver gown and matching ballet flats. She had her hair braided into a complicated knot on top of her head that was held in place with diamond-studded clips, and a layer of perfect makeup disguised any potential flaws.

Livia halted. It seemed doubtful Celeste could be the stalker. Not only was she immaculate from head to toe, but also her shoes were too delicate to survive the muck. You couldn't sneak around the swamps without getting filthy.

As if to prove her point, Celeste pinched her lips as she ran her gaze over Livia's grass-stained shorts and the sweat dripping from her face.

"Good Lord, Livia. What happened to you?"

Livia impatiently glanced over her cousin's shoulder. There was no one in sight.

"Nothing," she muttered, conceding defeat. Whoever had locked her in had disappeared.

"You look a mess." Celeste reached out to flick her fingers over Livia's hair. "You have cobwebs stuck on you."

Livia stepped back. She wasn't going to reveal what had happened. Not until she'd talked to Bryce.

"I went to the family crypt to pay my respects."

Celeste wrinkled her nose. It was doubtful the woman had stepped foot in the mausoleum since their grandfather had passed.

"Respect? You've never had any respect for the family."

Livia shrugged. "Probably because I've never been a real member of this family. You and your mother have gone out of your way to make sure of that. Whenever I visit you make me feel like an intruder."

"You are. The Willows is our home. Never yours." Celeste smiled with a smug cruelty, as if she thought Livia would be wounded.

"More like a prison." Livia didn't have to fake her shiver

of revulsion as she glanced toward the house that spread over the land like a cancer. "You're all stuffed in there like rats in a maze, and you don't even know you're trapped."

Celeste jerked, as if Livia had slapped her. "Don't pretend that you're not jealous of me and the fact that I'll inherit this estate," she hissed. "Not to mention the fact that I'm about to marry a rich, handsome man with his own inheritance. When we combine the Willows with the Durand property we'll have one of the largest estates in all of Louisiana."

"I notice there was no mention of marrying the man you love," Livia pointed out in dry tones.

"Of course I love Winston."

"If you say so."

"He's a wonderful man who treats me like a princess." Celeste flushed with irritation as Livia abruptly laughed at her conceited boast. "What's so funny?"

"Who wants to be a princess?"

"Every woman."

"Not me."

Celeste sent her a sour glare. "Shocker."

Livia allowed her gaze to once again roam over the looming mansion. When she was young, she'd shared a small ranch-style house with her foster parents. It'd been built on a narrow lot and looked like every other house on the block. It was plain and boring and she hadn't been particularly close with the couple paid to raise her, but she hadn't been unhappy.

She'd had plenty of friends in the neighborhood and enough freedom to make mistakes and discover what she enjoyed doing. Most importantly, her life hadn't been mapped out for her. She'd been allowed to dream of any future she wanted. It wouldn't have mattered if she decided she wanted to become the next president or settle down on a farm in Indiana and raise alpacas.

She'd been free of the Benoit legacy. Thank God.

"I would be bored out of my mind stuck out here in the

swamps with nothing to do but roam around this oversized house and paint my nails," she finally murmured, returning her attention to her cousin. "Now you're going to be handed off to a man so you can continue to live in the swamps and paint your nails while he flies around the world enjoying his life. Wait." She snapped her fingers. "I forgot, you'll also get to pop out a baby or two to continue the less than worthy line of the Benoits. Boring."

Celeste's flush deepened to an ugly red, her eyes smoldering with fury. Livia had hit a raw nerve, even if her cousin would rather die than admit it.

"I suppose slaving away in an office and going home to an empty house is better?" she snapped.

"At least I'm in charge of my life. I don't have to depend on Mommy and Daddy or a rich husband to support me."

"At least my mommy didn't jump off the balcony to get away from me."

Livia glared at her cousin as a shocked silence stretched between them. She knew that the venomous attack had been retaliation for mocking Celeste's shallow life, but that didn't make the words hurt any less.

At a loss for words, Livia told herself to walk away. Why give the bitch the satisfaction of knowing she'd hit where Livia was most vulnerable? But before she could move, a harsh voice came from behind her.

"Giselle didn't jump, you stupid girl."

With a small gasp, Livia whirled around to discover Helene standing directly behind her. Where had she come from? And why hadn't she heard the older woman approaching?

"What are you doing out here?" Celeste demanded.

Helene strolled past Livia to study her niece with an arrogant sneer. The older woman was wearing one of her loose caftans with her hair hanging down her back, but she still managed to look regal. A true Benoit.

"This is my home," Helene drawled.

"Not for long. My mother said she intends to find a nice room for you in the local looney bin."

Livia studied her cousin. She'd seen that stubbornly defiant expression before. Usually when Celeste had done something wrong but was refusing to admit her guilt.

"Delilah is as stupid as you if she thinks she can force me out of here." Helene smiled. "My father knew exactly what kind of woman she is. He arranged his will to ensure that I would be welcomed to stay at the Willows until the day I die."

"You shouldn't say stuff like that," Celeste hissed. "Not in this house."

With a last jaundiced glare at Livia, Celeste turned and flounced back to the house.

"Such a shame." Helene clicked her tongue. "Celeste was an unpleasant child, but I hoped she would soften as she matured. Instead, she went from unpleasant to nasty."

Livia stepped toward her aunt. She didn't care about Celeste. Her cousin was a rancid bitch and always had been. Her only interest was in Helene's fervent denial when she'd first approached them.

"Why did you say my mother didn't jump?"

Helene blinked, then with a suspicious speed, she was no longer the arrogant daughter of Henri Benoit, but instead the confused woman who drifted around the estate like a ghost.

"Did I? Are you sure?"

"Yes," Livia insisted. "You don't believe she committed suicide?"

Helene waved a hand in a vague gesture. "I told you. I see her. Her spirit will never leave this place. She was loved."

Livia curled her hands into tight fists. As much as she wanted to give her aunt a sharp shake, she knew it was a waste of energy.

"If she was so loved, then why did she jump?"

Helene flinched. "She wasn't thinking clearly."

"Was she unhappy before . . ." The words stuck in Livia's throat. "Before that night?"

"Not unhappy. She was angry. I'd never seen her so furious."

Livia barely dared to breathe. That was the most information she'd gotten since she discovered her mother hadn't fallen from her balcony as she'd been told as a child, but that she'd jumped.

"Angry with who?"

"It doesn't matter."

"It matters to me," Livia insisted. "I need to know what happened."

"Love. Betrayal. It festers. Festers and festers and festers." Helene turned to stare at the pool that was covered, as if trying to protect the past. Or keep it hidden. "Until you slice out the evil or die from the poison."

"Who betrayed her?"

"Everyone."

"You mean, everyone in the family? Or—"

"She's here," Helene interrupted, leaning toward Livia. For once, there was no smell of alcohol clinging to her breath, but the clouds had returned to her eyes. As if she was losing touch with reality. "Do you feel her? She watches us. She's afraid." Helene sent her a worried frown. "She whispers you're in danger."

The sensation of invisible fingers brushing over her cheek sent a chill inching down Livia's spine. No. Sucking in a sharp breath, she dismissed the fear that it was Giselle sending a warning from the grave.

Hadn't she decided when she was standing in the mausoleum that she had no connection to her mother?

Still, she turned the conversation from Giselle Benoit. Helene's insistence that the dead woman was watching over them was starting to freak her out.

"What about Manny?" she demanded. The missing chauffeur might have some insights into the Benoit family dynamics and what was happening before Giselle ended her life. "Where is he?"

Helene glanced toward the garage. "He's gone."

"Where did he go?"

"My father got rid of him."

"He was fired?"

"Yes."

"Why?"

Helene's expression hardened, her tone bitter. "Henri Benoit didn't need a reason. This was his house and we were all his puppets."

"Even my mother?"

"No. Giselle refused to bend to his will." Helene visibly shivered despite the smothering heat. "Now she's free. Just like you're free." Without warning, the older woman grabbed Livia's hand and gave it a painful squeeze. "Don't let this place pull you in. It's toxic. Stay free."

With her warning delivered, Helene released Livia's hand and turned to drift back to the house.

Livia watched her go, her mind churning over the events of the day. So far she'd watched a security tape with a hooded figure that might or might not be Larry Sutton trying to break into her house in New Orleans, enjoyed a lunch in the park where her mother was supposed to have a meeting the day after she died, been locked in an empty apartment above the garage, and exchanged a vicious battle of words with her cousin.

All in all, an eventful day. But amazingly, the fear that was humming through her body when she'd realized the door to the apartment was jammed had transformed to anger.

She didn't know who was stalking her. Or why. Or if they had any connection to Larry Sutton. But she did know that she wasn't going to become a willing victim.

She was Livia Benoit. Granddaughter to Henri Benoit.

One way or another, she was going to figure out what was going on. And if it was someone in her family, she would make them pay.

CHAPTER 12

Rushville, LA
Friday, July 4th

The next morning, Bryce positioned her SUV at the front of the Fourth of July parade, leading them through the streets of Rushville. At last reaching the downtown park where the crowd had gathered to enjoy the local barbeque and vendor booths, she shut off the flashing lights and shrill sirens of her SUV and drove back to the courthouse. She was always happy to be included in the festivities, and she hadn't minded when Finn asked her to take point on the parade this year, but now she was eager to return to the office for a quick lunch before heading out on patrol.

Parking in front of the courthouse, Bryce jogged up the steps, listening to the distant sound of the high school band playing "God Bless America." Her lips twitched at the uneven drumbeats and shrill squeaks of the clarinets. Small-town celebrations weren't as polished or elaborate as the big cities', but everyone was welcomed to join in, regardless of talent.

Pushing open the front door, she breathed a sigh of relief as the air-conditioning swept around her. The day was another scorcher with enough humidity to make her consider moving back to Chicago. She had a few distant cousins there, and while the winters might be a pain, the summers didn't make her feel like she was living in the pits of hell.

With a shake of her head, she entered the sheriff's office. As much as she hated the grinding heat, she wasn't going to uproot Josie again.

"Do you have a sec?"

Bryce was jerked out of her musings as Finn appeared from the back room and waved for her to join him.

"Sure." Her stomach growled in protest at the delay in lunch, but Bryce obediently hurried into Finn's office. "What is it?"

Finn returned to his seat behind his desk, pointing at the screen of his computer.

"I did a little digging on Larry Sutton."

Bryce blinked in surprise. She'd shared the limited amount of information they'd gathered during their trip to New Orleans, but she hadn't expected him to join the investigation.

"You didn't have to do that."

He shrugged. "I know. I had some time on my hands and I reached out to a friend who is a cop in New Orleans."

Bryce stepped closer to the desk, savoring the warm scent of his cologne. "Did you find out anything?"

"Not a lot. Unfortunately, my friend didn't join the force until after Sutton had been fired, but he'd heard stories about him."

"What sort of stories?"

"The usual—taking bribes, pocketing evidence, changing eyewitness accounts."

Bryce made a sound of disgust. She had run into corrupt cops before, but it never made it easier to accept when one was exposed. They were supposed to be the good guys.

"Anything violent?" she asked.

Finn shook his head. The sunlight streamed through the window behind him, reflecting off the glossy darkness of his hair and emphasizing the velvet softness of his dark eyes.

"There were no complaints of brutality against him, although he was in more than a few fights. He also had a habit of sleeping with the wives of his fellow cops."

"Yeah, that sounds right," she said, recalling his secretary's confession that he bounced from woman to woman. "A true sleazebag, as Livia would say. Did your friend say whether the cops had any dealings with Sutton since he became a private investigator?"

"He was given several warnings for trespassing, as well as two for stalking," Finn said. "Sutton claimed he was working a job and they let him off with a warning."

"Of course they did," Bryce said dryly.

"There was also a call from a neighbor about a public disturbance."

"What happened?"

"Supposedly a woman showed up at Sutton's office with a gun."

"That doesn't surprise me," Bryce drawled. "An unhappy client or ex-girlfriend?"

"Both. He'd been working for her husband to locate the prized Porsche she'd hidden in a storage shed. It sounded like he used the same tactics that he used on Livia." Finn's jaw tightened. The sheriff was a patient, empathetic lawman who tried to understand both sides of an issue, but he had a fierce sense of justice. The thought that Sutton had taken advantage of Livia to earn a few bucks had obviously infuriated him. "First he seduced her to try to get information, and when that didn't work, he broke into her house to search for the address of the storage unit."

"A shame she didn't get off a shot." Bryce held up her hand as Finn arched a brow. "I don't mean I wish she'd hit him with a bullet. But if she could have got off a warning shot, he might have thought twice about his life choices."

"Doubtful."

"You're right." Her stomach grumbled in protest. She was an hour past lunchtime. "Anything else?"

Finn grabbed a sheet of paper off his desk. "As I said, there were never any formal charges brought against Sutton after he left the force, but whenever the cops were called to investigate a complaint against him, they made a running list of his aliases. It's possible that he's using one to avoid Livia." He handed her the paper. "At least it's a starting place."

"Nice. Thank you, Finn." She glanced down at the list of names. There were at least a half dozen. "This is really helpful."

"I'm not just another handsome face."

Bryce briefly forgot how to breathe. Finn was right. He was much more than a handsome face. He was smart and sexy and loyal. The sort of man that made a woman forget to be sensible.

She took a step back. Both physically and mentally. "I'll do some searching on these names when I'm done with patrol."

Finn narrowed his gaze, but his expression never changed. "Are you going to watch the fireworks at the park tonight?"

Bryce was caught off guard by the question. "I haven't decided."

"You should," he urged. "You won't be on duty. Take some time to enjoy the holiday."

"Is that an order?" she teased, her mouth oddly dry.

He held her gaze. "A personal request."

Laying in her bed until well past ten a.m., Livia at last hopped in the shower and prepared for the day. Her aunt had announced during dinner last night that they would be lunching at the Rushville Country Club with their fancy friends, pointedly not including Livia in the invitation.

Fine with her. She'd rather starve than be forced to eat lunch with a bunch of stuck-up prigs who slammed gin and tonics for breakfast.

Besides, it gave her the perfect opportunity to do some sleuthing.

Waiting until she heard the Land Rover crunch down the driveway, Livia pulled her hair into a high ponytail and slipped on a casual pair of jean shorts, a red T-shirt, and sneakers. She hoped to blend in with the locals who would be flooding the area for the Fourth of July festivities.

Tucking her phone in her back pocket, Livia left the house through the back and crossed toward the gate that opened into the swamps. She wasn't deliberately putting herself in danger, but she was determined to get answers. And that meant discovering who'd hired Larry Sutton. And why.

She'd already searched her uncle's office. Now she hoped to find a way to slip into Winston's house while he was busy at the country club.

Reaching the narrow path that led from the swamps into Rushville, Livia strolled at a leisurely pace. There was nothing to see or hear beyond the rustle of leaves from the thick vegetation that lined the path and the occasional scuttle of a small rodent, but there was always the possibility there were unseen eyes watching her. She didn't want to attract attention, and more importantly, she wanted to hear if anything or anyone was following her.

Once she neared the Durand estate, she slowed her pace even more, her gaze sweeping over the backyard protected by a low brick wall that framed the large estate. There was no formal garden, but there was a large pond with a fountain in the center, surrounded by flowering plants.

The house itself was more Acadian in style than plantation. It had a wide, wraparound porch with white wicker furniture and large ceiling fans to keep the family cool during the summer heat. The windows were tall with huge wooden shutters and a steep roof that was covered with clay tiles and decorative gutters.

Not as imposing as the Willows, but it made a statement of wealth. She assumed that was the purpose.

Livia stopped near the massive azalea bush that spilled over the top of the wall, pretending to smell one of the blooms. There was no sound coming from the house, and no lights in the windows, but she didn't have a good view of the garage or driveway. She couldn't be sure that Winston had left.

Trying to decide whether to risk climbing over the wall, Livia muttered a curse as the French doors opened and a slender figure headed in her direction. Was someone monitoring the security cameras? Or had she tripped some sort of hidden alarm?

Keeping her head lowered, as if fascinated by the flower, Livia watched the stranger approaching. She looked younger than Livia with shimmering red hair that flowed down her back and pale, perfect skin. Her eyes were surprisingly dark and thickly lashed, her full lips painted a bright pink. She was . . . what was the word? Sultry. Yep, that fit her to perfection, Livia decided.

She was wearing tight jeans and a sleeveless white sweater that clung to her large bust with remarkable tenacity.

"Are you lost?" she demanded in sharp, suspicious tones.

Livia pretended to jerk in shock, as if she hadn't noticed the woman approaching.

"Goodness. You startled me."

The woman took a slow inventory of Livia, as if silently calculating the worth of each piece of clothing. Obviously, Livia's off-the-rack style wasn't impressive enough to earn her more than a dismissive sniff.

"This is private property."

"I wasn't going past the wall," Livia assured her. "I just wanted to smell the flowers."

The woman pointed toward the road. "That's private as well."

"Really? I thought the pathway was open to the public?"

"The Benoits had the road closed to vehicles years ago and Winston recently requested the closure be extended to pedestrians after his father became ill. Mr. Durand gets agitated if he sees strangers near the house."

So who agreed to the outrageous request? Livia silently wondered. Probably the mayor, who had always been in the pockets of his rich citizens.

"I heard Mr. Durand was unwell. I'm so sorry." With an effort she kept her disgust leashed. Trust a rich man to block off an entire road because he didn't like having the public near his house. "Do you work for Winston?"

"I'm Mr. Durand's nurse, Tara Warner. Who are you?"

Livia tried not to judge. After all, there were plenty of beautiful women that worked hard in their chosen professions.

"Livia Benoit."

The woman's eyes widened. "Livia? You're the . . ."

Livia's lips twisted. Her reputation had obviously preceded her. "Black sheep of the family? Yes. That's me."

Tara cleared her throat, swiftly regaining her composure. "I was going to say you're the cousin who lives in New Orleans. Winston mentioned you were staying at the Willows for the next couple of weeks."

"The return of the prodigal granddaughter. Or something like that," Livia admitted. "I didn't realize my cousin was freshly engaged and that we'd be hosting endless events."

"Everyone is very happy," Tara said.

Not everyone, Livia silently acknowledged, easily detecting the edge in the woman's voice. It would have been wrong to jump to the conclusion that Winston had hired this particular nurse because she was gorgeous, but she sensed that Tara looked at him as more than an employer.

Was that because she'd hoped to land a rich husband when she took the job? Or because the two of them were lovers?

Livia shook her head. Did she care? Not really.

Right now she was there to get information on Winston. If she couldn't get inside the house, then maybe the nurse could share some insight.

"And Mr. Durand? Is he happy about the engagement?"

"Of course, although he can't be involved in any of the celebrations." Tara glanced back at the house, her attention focused on an upstairs window that overlooked the pond. "He's bedridden."

"How awful. I didn't know it was so bad," Livia lied. "It must be hard on him to be missing all the fun."

"I suppose."

"And then Celeste mentioned that Winston does a lot of traveling. It must be very lonely for him. No wonder he hired a nurse to keep him company."

Tara shrugged. "Mr. Durand understands. He depends on his son to keep his business running smoothly."

"But it's not always business, is it?" Livia pressed. "Doesn't he travel overseas to visit his mother's family?"

"Only when necessary. He tries his best to be here for his father." Tara allowed a smug smile to curve her lips. "Lately he prefers to spend his evenings close to home."

Livia ignored the less than subtle hint that Tara was the reason that Winston preferred to be close.

"Really?" Livia stared at Tara as if confused. "I could have sworn that Winston told me that he spent the last couple of weeks in Ireland visiting his grandparents. Was I mistaken?"

Confusion flickered over the nurse's beautiful features. Then, with a sharp intake of breath, she pasted on a smile.

"Yes. That's right."

"Did you know he'd left the country?"

"Of course. He always keeps me informed of where he will be in case I need to get ahold of him."

She was a good liar, but Livia could hear the nervous edge in her voice. She would bet money this woman was working with Winston to hide his true whereabouts last week. And she was worried that she'd nearly given away the game.

"He implied it was a last-minute decision," Livia said.

"I really wouldn't know."

"Does he often take off with no warning?"

Tara squared her shoulders. Did she remember that the best defense was a good offense? "What are you asking?"

"Nothing." Livia shrugged. "When we were chatting I was trying to imagine taking off to Ireland on a whim. It must be nice. It would take me months of planning and a second mortgage to pay for the trip."

"It wasn't on a whim. He travels there regularly to visit his grandparents," she said, the words sounding practiced. "He's very devoted to his family."

"So you said." Livia paused. "And what about Celeste? Is he devoted to her as well?"

A dark emotion flared through Tara's eyes before she was taking a step backward.

"I should get back to my patient."

Livia silently chided her rash questions. It was a mistake to have reminded this woman that Winston was engaged.

"Wait," she called out.

Tara glanced over her shoulder with an impatient expression. "What now?"

"How long have you worked here?"

"A few months."

Livia pulled her phone out of her back pocket. "Do you live at the estate?"

The impatience shifted to wariness. "I do. Why?"

"I was supposed to meet a friend of mine at the fireworks display. I was sure he said he took this path all the time." Livia pulled up the photo of Larry Sutton she'd found on the internet. It was a few years old, but it was better than the fuzzy image she'd taken through the window. A shame she hadn't bothered to take any photos when they were dating. Maybe she'd already known he wasn't sticking around long enough for her to waste her storage. She turned the phone so Tara could see the screen. "You haven't seen him, have you?"

Tara leaned forward, her expression never changing as she studied the picture. "No. I don't think so. There's not many people who walk back here." She straightened. "I really should go."

The nurse strolled away, glancing over her shoulder as she reached the pond.

"Nice to meet you, Tara."

Livia lifted a hand to wave at the glaring woman before forcing herself to continue down the path. She didn't doubt Tara intended to watch until she was sure that Livia wasn't going to sneak back.

CHAPTER 13

Livia continued down the pathway and into town. She'd never really spent time enjoying the Fourth of July activities with the locals. Her aunt had refused to let her come when she was younger and she wasn't interested when she got older.

Now as she wandered through the busy park, she belatedly realized what she was missing.

The stalls were overflowing with home-crafted goodies and fatty foods that made her mouth water. Corn dogs, funnel cakes, BBQ ribs, and platters of jambalaya. Collecting enough food to feed a family of four, Livia found a seat in the shade of a weeping willow and watched the various entertainments enjoy their big moment on the bandstand.

The talent was questionable, but the enthusiasm made up for the out-of-tune songs and awkward dance routines. She even enjoyed the hog-calling contest that had the audience on their feet yelling for their favorite. It was the sort of small-town fun that made Rushville a special place to live.

Feeling relaxed for the first time in weeks, Livia lost track of time. It wasn't until the trucks arrived with piles of fireworks that she realized that the afternoon had passed and dusk was spreading across the horizon.

With a click of her tongue, Livia rose to her feet and dumped her empty plates in the nearest trash can. She wasn't in a hurry to return to the Willows, but she didn't want to be walking home after dark. She might be willing to continue digging into who hired Larry Sutton, but she wasn't stupid. She'd already been locked in the garage. Who knew what might happen if she was caught wandering around at night.

She crossed toward the back of the park, avoiding the crush of people who headed to watch the fireworks being unloaded. There'd been a few curious glances throughout the afternoon, but no one had approached her. Which was fine. She was there to relax, not to answer questions about her family. Or worse, about herself. She just wanted to blend into the background and disappear without attracting attention.

Moving behind the bandstand, Livia picked up her pace, not hearing the footsteps behind her. It wasn't until a hand reached out to grasp her shoulder, forcing her to stop, that she realized she'd been followed.

Glaring over her shoulder, Livia froze as she discovered Winston Durand standing directly behind her.

"Hello, Livia," he drawled, his handsome features looking oddly sinister in the fading light.

"Winston." Stiffening her spine, Livia shrugged off his hand and turned to face him. There were a hundred people in the park. He couldn't risk hurting her in such a public setting. Could he? "I didn't expect to see you in town. My aunt hates these local events."

"They're at the Willows."

"And Celeste?"

"She's with them. They're meeting with the photographer to select which picture to use on the wedding invitations."

Livia arched a brow. "Shouldn't you be there?"

A hard, humorless smile curved his lips. "My opinion on the invitations isn't needed or welcomed."

"Why not? It's your wedding too."

"This is Celeste's big day. I'm just there to support her."

Did he think he sounded like a loyal fiancé? If so, he was completely mistaken. He came off as a man who didn't give a crap about his upcoming wedding. Not that she cared one way or another.

"So instead you came to watch the fireworks?"

"No. I was looking for you."

Unease crawled down her spine. He was staring at her with an unnerving intensity.

"Why?" she demanded.

"Tara texted me to say that you'd been to my estate."

Livia blinked. The nurse had gone to the effort to text Winston about a random pedestrian when he was lunching with his soon to be in-laws? Interesting.

"I wasn't at your estate," she corrected him. "I was walking down the public pathway and she scurried out of your house to accuse me of trespassing."

"I apologize." There was no hint of regret in his hard tone. "I've asked the staff to keep an eye open for any paparazzi lurking around the house. I don't want my father disturbed."

Livia snorted. "Paparazzi? In Rushville?"

"It sounds ridiculous, but both Celeste and I have social connections. That unfortunately means we're the targets of the worst sort of troll looking for a scandal."

The explanation sounded practiced. As if he'd prepared for the day someone accused him of abusing his power.

"That's a lot of effort to avoid someone taking a picture." Livia lifted her brows. "Unless there actually is a scandal for them to expose?"

His jaw clenched. "I'm just a boring businessman who's trying to do the best for his father and his new fiancée."

"Okay." She stared at him with blatant disbelief. "Did you hunt me down just because I was walking by your house?"

"Tara also said you were asking a lot of questions."

"There weren't a lot of questions. We had a brief, meaningless conversation, nothing worth sending texts about. Unless the two of you share every intimate detail of your day?"

"We communicate whenever she is concerned about my father's welfare," he snapped, a hint of frustration in his voice. He came there expecting to bully her into backing off. He hadn't expected her to fight back.

"Me strolling past your house is hardly a threat to anyone."

He hesitated, as if trying to decide whether to let it drop to prove he had nothing to hide or to press his warning to try and intimidate her.

At last he went with the intimidation route. No surprise. He possessed the arrogance of a privileged rich man who demanded obedience from the lesser folks.

"Tara felt uncomfortable with your interest into my father's health and my own travel schedules," he said in accusing tones. "She thought you were trying to pry information out of her."

"Why would I do that? Unless you're hiding something."

"You've already tried to convince Celeste that I'm lying about having met you before."

"That was an honest mistake."

"And now you are digging for something else to cause trouble for me. Are you trying to jeopardize my engagement to your cousin?"

Livia paused. Was that what had him worried? That she was going to do something to hurt his relationship with the Benoits? Or was he afraid she might discover he'd hired a private detective?

Maybe both.

"I have no interest in your relationship with Celeste," she assured him. "In fact, I hope you both have a long and happy life together."

Perhaps sensing the sincerity in her words, Winston stepped

back. "I trust you're being honest, Livia. We're going to be family and I'd prefer that we be friends. But I won't hesitate to be your enemy if you threaten me or my future with the Benoits. Enjoy the fireworks."

With a stiff nod of his head, Winston stepped past her and headed toward his vehicle parked near the line of portable potties. Livia glared at his back, hoping his expensive SUV smelled like a sewer. The jerk.

It was obvious that her snooping around was bothering him. Unfortunately, there was more than one possible reason he should be concerned.

"Livia?" A new form appeared beside Livia, but this time she felt nothing but relief as she turned to discover Bryce regarding her with a worried expression. "What happened?"

Livia shuddered, wrapping her arms around her waist. How could she be cold when it was a hundred smothering degrees in the park?

"I'm not entirely sure, but I'm convinced that Winston Durand is hiding something," she muttered.

Bryce shot a glance toward the SUV that peeled away with the soft purr only an expensive engine could produce.

"Why? What has he done?"

"Nothing yet," Livia conceded. "But I was walking behind his house today—"

"Livia," Bryce interrupted with a frown.

"I was on the public pathway." Livia rolled her eyes. "Or at least what used to be the public pathway."

"Yeah, the Benoits and Durands have a nasty habit of claiming land that doesn't belong to them."

"How do you think they got so rich?" Livia asked in dry tones.

"Was Winston mad you were trespassing?"

"No, it was the pretty young nurse who got her panties in a twist."

"Tara?"

"Yup. She tried to run me off and we had a short conversation before I left."

Bryce studied Livia with a suspicious expression. "That's it?"

"I might have mentioned Winston's trip to Ireland last week. I swear Tara looked completely baffled. As if she didn't know what I was talking about." Livia shrugged. "Then suddenly she was falling over herself to reassure me that of course Winston had been visiting his grandparents and she knew all about the overseas trip."

"Maybe she legitimately forgot," Bryce suggested. "I've only met the woman a couple of times, but she seemed like the sort of person who was more interested in herself and not so much in other people. Not very nurse-like."

"I agree, but while Winston might be able to lie to everyone else about his whereabouts, he would want his father's nurse to know his exact location in case she needed to get ahold of him in a hurry. And he probably warned her not to say anything if she was asked."

Bryce didn't look convinced by her convoluted logic. "That's a lot of assumptions, Livia."

"True, but I have another one. I think Tara and Winston are sleeping together."

Bryce took a second to process Livia's accusations. At last she shook her head.

"I don't really know Winston. He went to private school when he was younger and he spent his summers in Ireland, but I don't doubt that he's like most rich men who are convinced that they have the God-given right to do whatever they want to do to whoever they want. He could be dangerous, Livia."

Livia agreed with her friend. Winston Durand had the polished sophistication of most rich people, but there was something hard and ruthless just beneath the surface.

"I'm more and more convinced he had something to do with

hiring Larry Sutton. Along with my uncle." Abruptly recalling what she'd overheard the day before, Livia shared Adrian's conversation with the mysterious banker. "He has to be covering his payments to Sutton, right?"

"It's possible," Bryce slowly agreed. "But I can't do anything about it until I have probable cause to get a warrant and look at the accounts."

"But what if the bank gets rid of the evidence?"

"You agreed to let me do the investigating," Bryce reminded Livia in stern tones. "You've already alerted Winston that you suspect him. He'll be on his guard now."

"I only asked a few questions."

"Let me handle this. It's what I do, remember?"

Livia released a shaky sigh as a restless urge to march back to the Willows and scream at the top of her lungs surged through her.

"I have to do something. I feel like I'm drowning in secrets," she rasped, glad she hadn't mentioned the fact that she'd been locked in the empty chauffeur apartment. Bryce was worried enough. "I need answers."

Sensing her frustration, Bryce reached to lay a hand on her shoulder. "We'll get them, I promise. I have a few new leads on tracking down Sutton. I'll tell you about it tomorrow."

Livia parted her lips to demand her friend tell her immediately when she caught sight of a man crossing toward them with a determined stride.

He was taller than most of the crowd who were drifting back to the park as they lost interest in the tedious job of setting up the firework display. But it wasn't his height that made women stop in their tracks to watch him pass by.

"Dear Lord, is that Finn?" she breathed. She was firmly off men, but that didn't mean she couldn't appreciate his fiercely carved features that were framed by his dark, glossy hair and the muscled perfection of his body.

Bryce stiffened as she glanced over her shoulder. "Yes."

"Damn. He's more gorgeous than I remember." Glancing back at Bryce, she realized her friend was wearing casual shorts and a cotton shirt that was tied at the waist to reveal her firm stomach. It was the outfit of a woman intending to enjoy her evening. Livia waved her hands to send her friend toward the delicious sheriff. "You're right. We'll talk tomorrow. Go get him, girl."

Bryce sent her a stern frown. "I want your promise not to do anything foolish."

"You have it, as long as *you* promise to be outrageously foolish with that delicious snack."

Bryce flushed, but she didn't hesitate to turn and scurry toward Finn. Livia watched her friend with a wry smile.

Her own life was a mess, but she was happy that Bryce had a second chance at happiness. Everyone deserved that.

And maybe someday, she would have her own second chance.

Until then . . . she trusted no one.

CHAPTER 14

The Willows
Saturday, July 5th

Livia was showered and dressed in casual shorts and a white cotton shirt shortly after dawn. It'd been another restless night, but she wasn't going to stay in bed. Why toss and turn when she could be out trying to answer the questions that nagged at her?

Pulling her hair into a ponytail, Livia headed down the backstairs. She'd assumed that she would be the only one up and about at such an early hour, but as she reached the bottom step, she could hear the clatter of pans from the kitchen and the sound of vacuuming from the front salon.

With a click of her tongue, Livia hurried toward the door that opened onto the back terrace. She'd forgotten the big shindig was tonight. The house would be buzzing all day with cleaners, florists, caterers, and the extra serving staff that had been hired for the event. Pure chaos. And a perfect excuse to get away from the Willows for the day.

First, however, she had something she wanted to do.

Moving along the edge of the terrace, Livia jogged down the steps and past the covered pool. She hissed at the sensation of an icy shadow reaching out, as if it intended to suck her beneath the canvas cover.

A part of her wished the family didn't treat the pool as some sort of morgue. At least if it was filled with water and surrounded by chairs it wouldn't feel like there was a perpetual gloom hanging over the place. People might even stop dwelling on how Giselle Benoit died and instead on how she'd lived. Another part couldn't bear the thought of her mother's memory being tarnished by plastic patio furnishings and beach balls.

With a shake of her head, Livia followed the path until she reached the garage. Then, tapping in the code, she pushed open the door and switched on the lights. She was careful to take a thorough survey of the interior before she fully stepped into the long building, and even then, she left the door open. She didn't care if anyone inside the house noticed what she was doing. She was more worried about getting locked in.

Once convinced she was alone, Livia crossed the cement floor and climbed the steps to the apartment. A grim satisfaction settled in the center of her being. The door was closed and at the bottom a rubber wedge had been shoved beneath it.

Grabbing her phone, she leaned forward to take a picture. It hadn't been a figment of her imagination. Someone had deliberately tried to lock her in the apartment.

She left the wedge where it was as she headed back down the stairs. She had proof that the door had been deliberately jammed, but that didn't tell her who was responsible.

Still holding her phone in her hand, Livia felt the vibration of an incoming text. Glancing down, she read the message from Bryce, inviting her to come to the sheriff's office whenever she had time.

Perfect. She stopped at the bottom of the staircase to let

Bryce know she'd be there in a few minutes. Anything to get her away from the frenzied preparation for the lavish party.

She was taking a step forward when something near the workbench built against the back wall captured her attention. With a frown, she moved forward, bending down to grab the small pile of fabric. It was silky, with a bright gold-and-blue pattern. Not the sort of thing you would use as a rag in the garage.

Holding it up, she watched as it unfolded to reveal a long, narrow scarf. It was definitely for a woman. Maybe something to cover your hair if you were driving a convertible. Or maybe wrapped around your neck at a fancy nightclub? Lifting it to her face, she pressed the silky fabric against her nose. There was a scent clinging to the fabric. It was faint, as if it had faded over weeks. Perhaps years. And it was familiar.

Was it someone who lived in the Willows? Probably.

Absently folding the scarf into a small square, she stuffed it in her back pocket. There was every possibility that it could have fallen out of a car when someone was getting out. Certainly it looked like something her aunt would wear. Or even Helene.

But why would it be at the back of the garage? There was no dust on it, so it couldn't have been there for more than a few days.

Battling the urge to connect it to the jerk who'd shoved the wedge under the apartment door, Livia headed out of the garage and around the side of the house. She had a spare set of keys in the glove compartment of her car. Not the safest choice, but she had a habit of forgetting her keys when she was hurrying out of the house in the morning or locking them in the office in the evening. Besides, it wasn't like anyone was going to steal the crappy thing.

Skirting the edge of the garden, Livia angled around the corner of the house, intending to slip away unnoticed. It wasn't until she caught sight of the front yard that she realized she'd miscalculated her escape route. Not only was the driveway already filled with delivery vans, but her aunt was standing on the bottom step of the porch, directing the florists where to place the large pots of flowers in front of the house.

Despite her elegant sundress and glittery sandals, Delilah looked like a general as she bullied the uniformed men to haul the heavy pots from one location to another, determined to have the perfect profusion of color as the guests arrived.

Livia slowed her pace, hoping to avoid detection, but with an uncanny ability to sense a deserter to the cause, the older woman swiveled her head to stab Livia with a warning frown.

"Livia. Where are you going?"

Livia shrugged. "Into town."

Delilah marched toward her in full battle mode. "Why?"

"I'm meeting Bryce in town."

"Who?"

"My friend. Bryce Swift."

"Does it have to be this morning?" she demanded. "Have you considered the idea we might need you here?"

"Why would you need me? It's not my party."

Delilah clicked her tongue in disapproval. "And you don't care if your cousin's engagement announcement is a success?"

"Not really."

Delilah looked shocked, as if unable to believe anyone would be indifferent to Celeste's stunning triumph in landing a rich husband.

"That's very selfish," she accused.

"It's honest," Livia corrected her aunt. "And I don't remember you arranging a party and inviting the press when I started my agency. In fact, you didn't bother showing up for my grand opening."

Delilah flinched. Not out of guilt, Livia was sure. The older woman simply hadn't expected the direct attack.

"Because I assumed you invited us to show off your connection to the Benoit family, not out of a desire to share your special night with us," she finally shot back.

Livia stared at the older woman. Her aunt couldn't be serious? When in her life had she tried to trade in on her family connections?

"I have the name Benoit, I don't have to drag you out of the bayous to prove our relationship."

"Fine." Delilah pressed her lips in a tight line. "Did you really want us there?" It was Livia's turn to flinch. They both knew that the invitation had been one of obligation, not from any real desire for them to show up. "You see?" her aunt pressed. "The rift between us isn't all our fault. You've made it clear you consider us the enemy."

Livia tilted her chin, refusing to be branded the bad guy. "Do you blame me? How would Celeste feel if she'd been handed off to strangers instead of being raised here with her family?"

Delilah glanced toward the workers who continued to carry massive flower arrangements out of the vans. Was she worried they weren't following her orders? Or that one of the staff might overhear their conversation?

"That was your grandfather's decision," she at last snapped in a low voice.

Livia shrugged. "And no one bothered to fight for me to come home."

"The Willows belonged to Henri. His word was law."

Livia didn't miss the edge of bitterness in her aunt's voice. It was a reminder that life with Henri Benoit couldn't have been pleasant. Still, the older man had at least tolerated Adrian and his family. That was better than her.

"And he didn't want me," she said in flat tones.

"He said that you were a painful reminder of what he lost."

Livia snorted. It was the same tired excuse they always used.

If Henri had loved her mother so much, then why wouldn't he do everything in his power to keep her daughter with him?

Squashing the ancient sense of injustice, Livia instead concentrated on the unexpected encounter with her aunt. During the long hours of the night, she'd promised herself she would use every minute she was stuck at the Willows to uncover the truth. Not just the truth of her family's potential connection to Larry Sutton, but her increasing certainty that there was a secret surrounding her mother's death.

"And what was the excuse for keeping Helene's sons from visiting?" she abruptly demanded.

Delilah looked confused. "Who?"

Livia arched a brow. She'd never really questioned why Helene's former family never bothered to spend time at the Willows. Who cared? It wasn't until she started poking into the past that she recognized that the stepkids had been erased from Benoit history even more thoroughly than she had.

"You know, Helene's stepchildren," she reminded her aunt. "I don't remember their names? Pat or Bob or something."

"You mean Patrick and Bradley?" Delilah continued to look confused, as if she couldn't imagine why Livia would be interested.

"That sounds right. Why haven't I ever seen them here?"

"I suppose they didn't want to come back after the divorce."

"Even though Helene helped raised them?"

Delilah made a choked sound. "She hardly raised them. She was married to Lance, but she had a full-time nanny for his sons, along with a tutor who came every day after school to help with their homework."

Livia studied her aunt's grim expression. She acted as if Helene had committed some terrible sin by handing off her kids to the hired help.

"Same thing most women would do if they had the money." Livia held Delilah's gaze. "The same thing you and my mom did."

Delilah sniffed. "Actually, it wasn't the same. Not at all." An ancient grievance hardened the woman's expression. "Helene's husband paid for extra staff to take care of his boys, and Giselle was encouraged by Henri to have a live-in nanny so she didn't have to deal with the more tedious tasks of childrearing. I, on the other hand, was expected to make do with an occasional babysitter who might come for an hour or two to help me." She clicked her tongue. "Not that I minded, of course. I adored Celeste."

Livia ignored the petulant complaint. The woman obviously bore a grudge against her sisters-in-law. Then again, there was no doubt she loved her daughter. Sometimes too much.

"Where did the boys go after they left here?" she asked, genuinely curious.

"They went with their father back to Baton Rouge. A few months later, Lance was remarried."

"Are they still there?"

"No, I heard they moved to New Orleans after college." Delilah pursed her lips. "Over the years they've opened a restaurant and a couple of bars, but they never lasted more than a few months. I can't imagine how much of their father's inheritance they've wasted. A shame."

"And they never returned to see Helene?"

"I told you they didn't." Delilah narrowed her gaze. "What's your interest in them?"

Livia shrugged. "Nothing really. I just find it strange that they could have lived in this house for years, but never felt the urge to come back and visit their stepmother and family. I didn't know if it was their decision or if my grandfather told them not to return."

Delilah abruptly glanced away, as if trying to hide a sudden emotion. "There was an unpleasant end to the marriage. It was better for everyone to have a clean break," she said stiffly.

"Even for Helene?"

"Especially for Helene." As if unnerved by the trend of the conversation, Delilah lifted a diamond-ladened hand to wave it toward Livia's car. "Go meet your friend. I have a thousand details that need my attention."

Livia's mild curiosity ramped up a notch. Delilah was obviously reluctant to discuss what had happened between Helene and her ex. Had Henri been the driving force behind the divorce? Was it possible he'd discovered something about his son-in-law that he feared might tarnish the Benoit name? Or maybe Helene's husband wasn't willing to share his enormous wealth with the fading Benoits.

Something to consider. Especially since Helene's husband had moved out of the Willows a few months before her mother's suicide. Was it connected? Who knew. Clearly the family was having issues.

Livia tucked away the question to ponder later as her aunt turned toward the house.

"Wait," she called out, reaching into her back pocket to pull out the scarf.

Glancing back, Delilah sent her a glare that would make most people tremble in fear. Livia was thankfully impervious.

"Now what?" the older woman snapped.

Livia held out the scarf. "I think you dropped this in the garage yesterday."

"I doubt that." Delilah flicked a disinterested glance toward the folded length of satin. "Where did you get it?"

"Near the stairs that lead to the apartment."

"What were you doing back there?"

"Passing through," Livia hedged, giving the scarf a shake so it spilled out to its full length. "Is this yours?"

Delilah parted her lips to deny ownership, but the words seemed to stick in her throat as her eyes widened. She recognized the scarf, Livia silently acknowledged. But that wasn't the reason the color was suddenly draining from her face and her hands clenched into tight fists. The older woman was bothered by the sight of the scarf.

"What's wrong?" Livia demanded.

"Nothing." With obvious reluctance, Delilah reached out to snatch the scarf from Livia's hand. "You're right, this is mine. Thank you."

She was lying, but why?

Did she know who owned the scarf? And more importantly, did she know if the owner had tried to lock Livia in the upstairs apartment?

The questions hovered on Livia's lips, but with a swirl of her sundress Delilah was heading toward the florist vans with a rigid spine that warned she was done with the conversation.

Livia watched her stiff retreat, feeling like she'd discovered something important. She just couldn't pinpoint exactly what it was.

Knowing that it would be a waste of time to dwell on the strange itch in the back of her mind, Livia headed toward her car. Eventually her brain would spit out what was troubling her. Until then she had other worries waiting for her attention.

Weaving her way through the thickening line of vehicles, Livia squeezed through the open gates and drove into Rushville. Unlike the Willows, the town was smothered in a layer of quiet lethargy as the citizens slept off their late-night festivities. Zigzagging through the empty streets, Livia parked in front of the courthouse and headed inside.

Most of the offices were closed, making it easy to follow the sound of a ringing phone to the door with a painted glass window assuring her she was in the right spot. She pushed it open and stepped inside, only marginally surprised that there wasn't more security. In a town like Rushville they didn't expect trouble. Not until it happened.

Livia's lips twitched as she caught sight of the elderly man seated behind the reception desk, his voice gruff as he answered the old-fashioned landline. He looked like he came direct from some casting office. The perfect small-town grumpy deputy with a heart of gold.

Hovering near the desk, Livia was relieved when her friend appeared from the back of the long room. She felt weirdly uncomfortable. Just like she felt when a cop was driving behind her. There was a tingling sense of fear that she might be in trouble even if she hadn't done anything wrong.

Bryce reached her side and waved her hand toward a desk set against the far wall.

"I'm over here."

Together they crossed the room, an old air conditioner vibrating against the planked floor and rattling the nearby window. It sounded as if it was losing its battle to combat the humid heat. It felt like it too. Livia could already feel her top sticking to her lower back.

Bryce didn't seem to notice despite the fact that she was wearing her brown uniform with a wide belt loaded with handcuffs, a walkie-talkie, and her service weapon. She looked as cool as the proverbial cucumber.

Pulling a ladder-backed chair next to the desk, Bryce arranged it so Livia could see the computer screen. Then, waiting until Livia was sitting, she took her own chair, her brows lowering as she studied Livia.

"Are you okay? You look tired."

"I haven't been sleeping very well."

"Hopefully today will help with that."

"Did you find something?"

Bryce grabbed a piece of paper off the desk. "Finn uncovered a few of Larry Sutton's aliases. I thought we could skim through social media and see if you recognize anything."

"Nice." Livia settled back in her chair. It wasn't a direct lead, but it was at least somewhere to start. "And speaking of Finn . . ."

"Absolutely not." Bryce sent a quick glance toward the back office. It looked empty, but her friend was clearly horrified at the direction of the conversation.

"At least tell me if the two of you—"

"No."

"Fine." Livia reluctantly conceded defeat. It was unfair, of course. How was she supposed to live vicariously through her friend if Bryce refused to share the intimate details of her time with the delicious sheriff? "Can I ask how Finn got these names?" she instead asked.

"He has a friend who works for the New Orleans Police Department. Sutton has had more than one brush with the law since becoming a private investigator."

"No surprise there. How many names did he get?"

"Five. Not including Jacob Pearson."

"At least six aliases?" Livia's breath hissed between her teeth. "The jerk."

"Weapons-grade jerk." Bryce placed the paper on the desk and tapped on the keyboard in front of her. "We might as well start with the top name."

A dozen or so links popped up, but none of them resembled Larry Sutton. "Nothing," Livia muttered.

"Number two."

Bryce typed in the name. There weren't any social media pages attached to it, but a dozen pictures with a bleached blonde popped up, along with a familiar man standing next to her.

"That's him," Livia said.

"Do you recognize the woman?"

Livia studied the images. The woman was in her mid- to late thirties with a round face and long hair. She looked like she'd been pretty in the past, but the years of tanning and smoking had taken a toll.

"No."

Bryce scanned through the pictures. They looked like a regular couple, posing on a boat in the middle of a lake, and one of them standing in front of a bar with an alligator drinking a beer painted on the window behind them.

"Not much else to see," Bryce had at last conceded. "Name number three." Again they came up empty. "Hmm. Number four."

This time, a couple social media pages popped up, both with Larry Sutton's photo at the top.

"He didn't bother to pull down this profile." Livia leaned forward, a small flare of hope racing through her.

"No, but it hasn't been updated for over three years," Bryce pointed out. "I'm not sure how helpful it will be."

They swiped through the entries that claimed he was a pharmaceutical salesman who traveled the country, a race car driver on the weekends, and able to speak four languages. Livia snorted. It was a wonder he hadn't announced he was busy curing cancer in the evenings.

"Wait." She grabbed Bryce's hand as they scrolled past a cluster of pictures that had obviously been taken during a New Year's Eve party.

Bryce sent her a hopeful glance. "You recognize something?"

"That sign in the background." She pointed toward one of the pictures. It had a cluster of customers in a shadowed bar. They were all wearing hats with flutes of champagne they were lifting in a boozy toast. Her fingertip touched the alligator drinking beer painted on the window behind the men. "It has to be the same place we saw him with in the pictures with the blonde. I mean, there can't be more than one bar with that cheesy logo."

"You're right."

Bryce enlarged the photo until they could read the name of the establishment painted over the top of the alligator. It was backward, but it was easy enough to make out the words.

Gator Brew.

Bryce pulled up a new page and typed the name into a search engine. A second later, she had the website pulled up.

"Here we go. Gator Bob's Pub. Home of the famous Gator Brew. Whatever the heck that is. The address is in La Harpe."

"Where?"

"It's a small town not far from New Orleans." Bryce tapped her fingers on the desk, as if lost in thought. "I wonder if the bartender is still working there."

"There's only one way to find out." Livia abruptly rose to her feet. Her nerves felt as if they'd been scraped raw. She needed to be out doing something. Anything.

"True," Bryce agreed, shoving herself out of her chair to send Livia a stern glance. "I'll let you know what I find out."

"I want to go."

"No, Livia." Bryce used her cop voice, shutting down any argument. "If this man is a friend of Larry Sutton he might decide we're a threat. In these small towns people are willing to take matters into their own hands."

Livia shivered. She was so accustomed to the looming sense of danger since she'd caught sight of Jacob sneaking into her house that she occasionally forgot that someone might actually get hurt. The last thing she wanted was for her friend to put herself at risk.

"All the more reason for me to go with you," she insisted.

"I'm trained to deal with trouble," Bryce retorted. "And it will be much easier if I don't have to worry about protecting you."

"I can take care of myself."

"Livia. You agreed to let me do the investigating."

"Did I?"

Bryce narrowed her gaze, unwilling to budge. "You can't go. You have an engagement party tonight, don't you?"

It was a low blow, but effective. As much as Livia wanted to go in search of the missing Larry Sutton, she couldn't miss the party. Whatever her feelings toward her family and the Benoit legacy, she tried to avoid publicly insulting them. People would be looking to see if she was there or if she'd decided to snub her cousin. She wasn't going to give them a reason to gossip.

"Fine," she muttered, pointing a finger toward her friend. "But call me the second you find out something."

"I promise."

CHAPTER 15

La Harpe, LA
Saturday, July 5th

It didn't take GPS to locate Gator Bob's Pub. La Harpe was a town of five hundred citizens who crowded together along the edge of the bayou. A handful of businesses lined the downtown square, but only one had a gator holding a beer painted on the front window.

Pulling into an empty spot directly in front of the narrow brick building with a tin roof, Bryce strapped her gun beneath her shirt before she locked the SUV and headed inside. She didn't expect any trouble, but she hadn't been exaggerating when she'd warned Livia that these small towns could be dangerous. They didn't like outsiders poking into their business. Especially if the outsider also happened to be a law official.

Glancing up and down the empty sidewalk, Bryce pushed open the glass door, wincing at the bell that jingled her arrival. In the thick silence of the shadowed space it sounded unnaturally loud. She stepped inside, immediately smacked in the face with the pungent stench of sour beer and stale popcorn.

She paused to skim her gaze over the heavy wooden bar along one side of the room with a smoky glass behind it and shelves lined with bottles of liquor. The bar itself was carved from a dark wood that was polished until it glowed and edged with brass trim. There were a handful of round wooden tables in the center of the space and at the very back were a couple booths. One booth was currently occupied with four middle-aged men who were slumped in the leather seats as if they'd started drinking last night and hadn't stopped.

Unfortunately, none of them resembled Larry Sutton. And none of them bothered to glance her way as she strolled toward the bar. She assumed that meant they didn't work there.

"Pull up a seat," a gruff voice called out on cue. "I'll be right there."

A minute later, a swinging door next to the booths was shoved open and a big man carrying a tray of glass mugs appeared. He looked to be over six feet and at least three hundred pounds. He was wearing worn jeans and a T-shirt with the Gator Brew logo on the front that was stretched so tight she feared it might split up the side when he lowered the tray onto one of the tables.

At last turning toward her, he reached up to smooth back his few remaining strands of gray hair, looking mildly surprised to discover a stranger.

"If you're looking for lunch, you'll have to go to the café on the corner. I don't serve food," he warned.

"Officer Swift." Bryce pulled out her badge and held it toward him.

"A cop?" He allowed his dark gaze to skim down her body, admiring her white shorts and long, bare legs. "Shame."

Bryce snapped the badge shut. "Trust me, that's not how you want to start this conversation."

The man flinched at the icy warning in her voice. "Right." He cleared his throat. "If this is about my liquor license I just had it renewed. I have the paperwork in the back."

"I'm not here about your liquor license. I'm looking for information. Are you the owner?"

"I am. Bob Payson."

She glanced around the nearly empty bar. It was just after noon. Too early for anyone but hardened drinkers to be in a pub.

"I'm trying to track down a customer of yours."

Bob scowled, his beefy face flushing as if she'd insulted him. "I'm no snitch."

"He's not in trouble."

"Then why are you looking for him?"

"There's a possibility he's missing."

"A possibility?" Bob's suspicion deepened. He obviously had trust issues when it came to cops. "What's that mean?"

"Can we sit down?"

His jaw bunched. Was he considering the pleasure of telling her no? If he was, he wisely squashed the urge and nodded toward the nearby table. He moved to take a seat, waiting for her to join him before he folded his arms over his chest and eyed her warily. "So who's missing?"

"Larry Sutton."

"Sutton?" Bob stared at her as if he thought she was joking. "Naw. You got your wires crossed," he at last assured her. "Larry is always disappearing, but that doesn't mean he's missing. I promise he'll pop back up when he's done with whatever job he's working."

Bryce leaned back in her seat, adding his name to the list of people who believed Larry Sutton had simply gone off the grid.

"When was the last time you saw him?"

"I don't remember." Bob looked unconcerned. "At least not an exact date."

"Try," Bryce insisted.

Bob glanced toward the bar, as if seeking inspiration. "It's been a few months for sure . . ." He abruptly snapped his fingers, glancing back at Livia. "Wait. I do remember. He was here for our big Gator Bash. I know that for sure."

"What's a Gator Bash?"

"I opened this place in 2005. It was March twenty-fifth, to be exact. And ever since then I host an appreciation night on that date for some of my most loyal customers." He shrugged. "I tap a keg, we play darts and cards, eventually there's a fight. Good times."

"And Larry Sutton is a loyal customer?"

"More than that. He's been with me from the beginning. In fact, he loaned me some money to help tide me over the first couple of months."

"Larry is from La Harpe?"

"Not exactly. He owned a cabin with his wife a few miles away from here. But he would stop in for a beer after working his shift in New Orleans."

Bryce felt a stab of shock. "He's married?"

"He was. Poor dude. His wife was gunned down not long after I opened this place."

"What happened?"

"She worked at a convenience store near the highway. One night a meth head came in and shot everyone in the store. He got away with less than fifty bucks." Bob shook his head. "Tragic."

"Gunned down." That was a very specific term. "You're right, it is tragic," Bryce breathed.

"Larry was never the same after that."

A remembered pain sliced through Bryce's heart. She understood the shocking pain of losing a spouse to gun violence, although she'd probably been more prepared than Larry Sutton. Benjamin's position in the FBI meant he walked into danger on a daily basis. Just as she had.

Still, the shock had left her tumbling into a dark depression that had only been eased when her father had insisted that she and Josie come stay with him.

"No one is ever prepared to lose a loved one." There was a raw sincerity in her voice. "Especially when they're young."

"It was more than that." Bob's expression was grim. "The bastard who killed her was never charged with her murder. Larry was convinced the cops didn't bother to investigate because the prime suspect was related to the local sheriff at the time. No one knows for sure."

Bryce considered what she'd discovered about Larry Sutton. It fit that he'd developed a disdain for the justice system that had failed him. And perhaps explained why he'd chosen to use his authority to abuse the system.

"That could make a man bitter."

"Exactly. He left the area and moved to New Orleans. He even bought a fancy car and a watch that cost more than this bar." Bob shook his head. "His wife would have been horrified. She believed in a simple life."

"Sounds like he came into some money." Bryce studied the man across the table, curious at how much he knew about his friend. "Life insurance on his wife?"

Bob glanced away. "Maybe. I mean . . . I guess it was. He stopped coming out here so much and I kind of lost touch with him."

Bryce smiled in satisfaction. He knew he was a dirty cop. "Then he got fired?"

"He claimed he was framed, but I don't think he really cared. He was a cop because that's what he'd been before his life was destroyed." The large man cleared his throat, as if regretting he'd revealed so much about his friend. "Sorry, I kind of veered off track."

"No. I need this information," she insisted. "I assume you knew he became a private investigator."

Bob nodded. "That's when he started coming out here again. He seemed happier, although I don't think he ever fully got over his grief."

Bryce studied the large man. It was time to find out how far he would go to help his friend.

"Did he bring his clients to this place?"

"He might have."

"And you knew that he was using aliases to trick people?"

Bob stiffened. He hadn't been expecting the question. The urge to deny any knowledge of Larry's deceptions warred with the unease of lying to a cop. At last he tried to hedge.

"Larry helped me out more than once over the years," he muttered.

"That wasn't my question."

Another painful pause. "Yeah, okay," he finally burst out. "When he asked me to use a different name for him every now and then, I didn't care. Why would I? He was just doing his job."

Bryce narrowed her eyes, thinking of Livia's raw sense of betrayal. "I'm not sure the women he lied to and manipulated would agree."

"Is that what this is about? Did some woman call the cops because he lied to her?"

Bryce arched a brow, her expression hard at his dismissive tone. "I'm here because I'm trying to get a feel for who Sutton is and where he might go if he wanted to disappear."

He hunched his shoulders, no doubt sensing her annoyance at his lack of sympathy for Larry's victims.

"It could be anywhere, really. He once spent a month living on the streets in an effort to find the missing daughter of one of those mega-church preachers. He was filthy and covered in bug bites by the time he tracked her down, but the father paid him a damned fortune."

"According to his secretary, she hasn't seen or heard from him in days despite her efforts to contact him. She was packing up her things when I went to the office. She said that he might disappear for a few days or even weeks, but he always returned her calls. And this was the first time he'd ever missed signing the payroll."

Bob paused, as if suddenly taking her concern for Larry Sutton seriously. "That's strange, even for Larry," he conceded. "He can be a selfish bastard, but the one thing he cares about is his business. And that includes Cherry."

"Where would he go if he needed to lay low for a while?"

"I really don't know."

With a grunt of annoyance, Bryce leaned forward, folding her arms on the table as she glared at her companion.

"Look, Bob, I get that you feel some sort of loyalty to the guy, but I'm not looking to arrest him. I just want to know that he's okay."

Bob licked his lips. "Like a wellness check?"

"Something like that," she said, dodging a direct answer. "Does he have any family in this area?"

"He never spoke about any family. I got the feeling that he'd taken off from home when he was young and never looked back."

Bryce ground her teeth. Of course he couldn't have a large extended family that she could use to track him down.

"What about close friends who would let him camp on their couch?"

"Not that I know about. At least not in this town. He's burned a lot of bridges over the years."

"There has to be someplace he crashes," she insisted, refusing to concede defeat. "He has too many enemies not to have a hiding spot."

Bob heaved a deep sigh. "If he isn't with one of his current girlfriends, I suppose he could be at one of the cheap hotels he uses when he's avoiding an angry husband or unhappy client," he reluctantly revealed.

Bryce felt her first prick of hope since driving to La Harpe. Reaching into her purse, she pulled out a small notebook and a pen, shoving them across the table.

"Write them down for me." She watched in silence as Bob

jotted down the name of three hotels before shoving the notebook back. She read through the list, not surprised when she didn't recognize any of them. "These are all in New Orleans?"

"Yep."

"Thanks." Bryce rose to her feet, once again reaching into her purse. She pulled out a business card and handed it to Bob. "If you hear from Larry, give me a call. I think he might be in danger."

Bob frowned as he studied the information on the card. "Rushville? Where's that?"

"A little dot in the bayou."

The man's suspicions returned. "Why would you be looking for Larry?"

"Like I said, I just need to make sure nothing's happened to him."

With a nod, Bryce headed toward the door. She didn't have much confidence that Gator Bob would call if he heard from Larry, but she at least knew that there was every possibility that Larry would reappear when he got tired of hiding.

Like sludge bubbling to the top of a landfill.

The trick was to be prepared to corner him before he could disappear again.

CHAPTER 16

The Willows
Saturday, July 5th

The engagement party was in full swing, allowing Livia the opportunity to slip into the shadows. From there she could watch the spectacle of designer-dressed guests mingling through the formal salon and spilling onto the front terrace. Livia didn't recognize most of the crowd, although her cousin had assured her that there were a dozen influencers among the guests and at least two mainstream journalists.

Honestly, Livia had been mildly surprised by the mediocre feel of the party. And not just the guests who were on the lower rung of the social ladder. The food had been locally catered, not flown in from some chichi restaurant in New Orleans. And recorded music drifted from hidden speakers. She'd expected a stringed quartet at the very least.

It reinforced Livia's suspicion that the Benoits were struggling financially.

Thank goodness her yearly inheritance came from a trust fund set up through her grandfather's lawyer, and not left in

Adrian's hands. She had no doubt the account would have been emptied long ago.

Sipping from the glass of champagne she'd grabbed before the precious vintage was gone, Livia concentrated on Celeste as she stood in the center of the room, surrounded by her bridesmaids as the photographer weaved around them snapping pictures.

Was her smile just a little too wide? Her back a little too stiff? She looked like a woman pretending to be deliriously happy. And the gaggle around her didn't even pretend. They were blatantly bored by their role as background props for the bride-to-be.

She supposed if you lived a fake existence built on image it was hard to be relegated to second place.

"Hello, Livia. You look like you're enjoying the circus as much as I am."

With a tiny jerk, Livia glanced toward the man who'd silently appeared next to her. He was about her height but twice as wide, with thick muscles that didn't come from the gym. He looked to be a couple years older than her, although his face was deeply tanned and weathered, as if he spent a lot of time in the sun, and his dark hair had a few strands of silver. His eyes were a rich brown and they held a warmth that she didn't often see from guests in this house.

He looked vaguely familiar, but the tux and black bow tie were throwing her off. It wasn't until she noticed the crescent-shaped scar on the edge of his jaw that recognition hit.

"Robbie Broussard?" She instinctively leaned forward to give him a hug, relieved to have one friendly face in the dismal crowd. "Oh my God, I haven't seen you forever. What are you doing here?"

"Your uncle invited me."

"Seriously?"

Livia winced the second the impulsive question left her lips. She didn't mean to be rude, but Robbie Broussard was the son of the gardener who'd kept the grounds at the Willows immaculately trimmed and the gardens in full, glorious bloom. During her summers Robbie would tag along with his father, and Livia would lure him away from his chores to play tag in the bayous or steal cookies from the kitchen. It'd been during one of their adventures that Livia had dared Robbie to climb on top of the family mausoleum. He'd slipped and fallen, busting his jaw on the way down.

He'd bled so much that Livia had been terrified that he was dying, but Robbie's dad had assured her that she wasn't going to be punished. He'd also added that Robbie needed his brain rattled for doing something so foolish.

Livia's grandfather, however, hadn't been nearly so forgiving.

It was the last time she'd been allowed to play with Robbie.

"A shock, right?" Robbie said in dry tones.

"No, I mean . . ."

"It's okay." His smile assured her that he wasn't offended. "I've done some work for him." Reaching into his pocket, he pulled out a business card and handed it to her.

"'Broussard Landscaping and Ornamental Gardens,'" Livia read out loud, impressed by the intricate logo and gold trim on the card. "Very fancy."

"Not really." Robbie shrugged. "My dad was a gardener and barely made enough to provide for his family. I do basically the same thing, but I can charge an obscene fee because I call myself a landscaper."

She waved her glass toward the nearby crowd. "It's a rich person thing. They don't care about value, they care about image. If you convince them you're worth a fortune, that's what they'll pay."

"Exactly," he agreed.

A slow smile curved her lips. "Good for you, Robbie. It couldn't happen to a better guy."

He shrugged. "I'm not going to lie, there was a petty satisfaction in getting the invitation. Once upon a time, I would have been stuck using the back door to enter the Willows. Now I'm a guest. Go figure."

Livia chuckled. "Same."

They shared a rueful glance as Robbie leaned against one of the fluted marble columns that ran the length of the room.

"I heard you opened your own business, is that right?"

"I did." It was Livia's turn to pull a business card out of the red satin clutch that matched her halter-style gown. She handed it to Robbie.

"'Benoit Real Estate Agency. New Orleans.'" He sent her a smile. "Congrats."

Livia lifted her glass in a toast. "Here's to walking through the front door."

"Cheers." He tapped the edge with his own glass. "Since you're still using the Benoit name I assume you're not married?"

"Nope. You?"

"Yeah, I married Kim Walden. We went to school together."

Livia glanced toward the crowd. She didn't remember anyone named Kim, but she assumed that his wife would be nearby.

"Is she here?"

"She's home with our son, Caleb." Robbie lifted a defensive hand as she instinctively turned back to stab him with a glare. "Hey, it's her choice. I begged her to come, but she hates these events. Staying with Caleb is just an excuse to avoid them."

Livia relaxed. She should have known Robbie wouldn't be the kind of guy to be out partying while his wife was home with a baby.

"I don't blame her."

"Me either. If I didn't need references from these people to expand my business I would be home with the family." He stiffened, abruptly recalling who he was talking to. "Sorry, I probably shouldn't admit that to a member of the Benoit clan."

Livia clicked her tongue. "We both know I've never been a part of the clan."

He slowly nodded. "Does it bother you?"

"It used to, but over the years I decided I would never have fit in with the Benoits, even if hell had frozen over and they decided to welcome me with open arms." She nodded toward the tall, handsome man who was standing in a corner with Adrian. They had their heads close together as if they were discussing something they didn't want overheard. It was an increasingly common sight. As if the two men had something that was demanding their mutual attention. "Winston is more comfortable at the Willows than I'll ever be."

Robbie made a sound of uncertainty. "Do you think he's comfortable?"

"You don't?"

"I'm not sure." He shrugged, his gaze locked on Winston, who continued his intense conversation with Adrian. "I suppose he seems happy enough."

Livia stepped closer, her mild pleasure in reconnecting with Robbie replaced with a tingle of curiosity.

"You know something," she breathed.

Robbie froze, as if realizing he'd said more than he should have. "Nah. What could I know? I'm just the gardener."

She clicked her tongue. "You don't fool me, Robbie Broussard. Share."

He pretended to consider her demand before he chuckled. "Okay, okay." He motioned for her to step closer. "I've done quite a bit of work at the Durand estate since Winston took over from his father. He had the back patio refurbished and tore out the old pool to replace it with a pond. And during the three or four months I was working there he had at least a dozen different women staying with him. Sometimes more than one."

Livia wasn't surprised. Winston had the vibe of a man who enjoyed women. The more the better.

"Sowing his wild oats?" she asked.

"And then some." Robbie nodded toward Celeste, who was

still posing for the photographer. "In fact he was still sowing those oats right up to the night he was seen holding hands with your cousin at the country club gala." He lowered his voice another notch. "I know for a fact he'd just flown back from Monte Carlo that morning with a swimsuit model who was still at his house. I was trimming the hedges in the backyard when I saw her sunbathing by the newly finished pond."

"He does enjoy collecting pretty women," she agreed, recalling her stroll behind the Durand estate. "Have you seen his nurse?"

"Tara Warner? Yeah, the town was buzzing after Winston hired her."

"I'm surprised that Celeste tolerates having her under his roof." Livia glanced toward her cousin. "She's never been one to allow competition. When we were young my grandfather bought me a fancy dress to wear when I spent the summer. We had dinner one night at the country club and a creepy old man said I looked like a princess. The next morning I woke up to find the dress cut into a dozen ribbons and tossed on my bed."

"Sounds like Celeste," Robbie agreed. "But when it comes to Winston she might not have any choice."

"Why do you say that?"

"I shouldn't gossip about my clients. Kim tells me it's a bad habit," Robbie muttered.

"Trust me, no one here has any intention of noticing that I exist. You can tell me anything and it's not going be repeated."

Robbie's brief wariness melted away. They'd shared a childhood where they'd both been outsiders at the Willows. He knew she was the one Benoit who could be trusted.

"You know Winston casually dated Celeste over the years." He waited for her nod. "I overheard him telling his dad that your aunt and uncle were dangling Celeste like a baited hook in an attempt to land a rich husband. He also said that he didn't mind having her in his bed, but that he would rather be castrated than have the Benoit clan permanently clinging to him like a bunch of leeches."

"Castrated?" Livia made a face. "Strong words from someone who struts around like an alpha male. I wonder what made him change his mind."

"I suppose people change. But it does seem weird."

"Very weird."

Livia mulled over what Robbie had told her. She didn't doubt for a second that her aunt and uncle would angle to get the biggest bang for their buck when it came to Celeste. After all, she was beautiful, well connected, and willing to play the role of happy homemaker. The perfect partner for a man in search of a trophy wife.

She also understood Winston's reluctance to spend the rest of his life supporting the Benoits in the style they were accustomed to enjoying.

What baffled her was why Winston would have gone from calling Celeste a leech to putting a ring on her finger. It had to be a powerful incentive.

Or threat . . .

Did Adrian have something on the younger man? Had he blackmailed Winston into proposing?

It would explain so many things.

"Speaking of castration . . ." Robbie cleared his throat, looking uncomfortable. "That's what is gonna happen to me if Kim finds out I'm revealing secrets about my clients."

Livia managed a smile as Robbie straightened from the column, as if he was preparing to move on.

"No worries," she assured him, resisting the urge to ask if they could get together later. She sensed he already regretted sharing what he'd overheard. Then she was struck with a sudden inspiration. "Is your dad still in the area?"

"He is. Still living in the same old house behind the bakery. I've tried a dozen times to get him to move to a new home. I even offered to build onto our place after my mom passed a few years ago. He refuses to budge." Robbie rolled his eyes. "He says he likes the smell of baking bread early in the morning."

"Can't beat the smell of baking bread," she pointed out.

"He's a stubborn pain in the ass, but one who's earned the right to live where he wants."

"Do you think he would mind if I visited him?"

"He would love it," Robbie assured her. "He hates being retired, but his arthritis keeps him from leaving the house much these days. I know he gets bored." Robbie nodded toward someone across the room. "I'm being summoned," he murmured, sending her a warm smile. "It's good to see you, Livia. I really mean that."

"You too."

Livia watched Robbie melt into the kaleidoscope of guests before she set aside her half-empty glass and edged her way toward the side door. She'd made her mandatory appearance, now she wanted to be anywhere but there.

Unfortunately, she couldn't get to her rooms without using the main door, which meant risking the notice of her eagle-eyed aunt. She would have to sneak through the gardens to the back of the house.

Not that she minded a short stroll in the night air, she decided as she stepped outside. The soft breeze cleared away the expensive perfume that was clogging her sinuses and muted the music until it was nothing more than a distant hum.

Sucking in a deep breath, she strolled along the pathway, savoring the sense of peace. For now the Willows was too busy pandering to the spoiled Celeste to notice her, which meant she could simply enjoy the elegant sense of ageless beauty as it bathed in the silver moonlight.

The rare sense of contentment didn't last as she turned the corner and climbed the stairs to the terrace. It was much darker back here and the faint sounds of the party were drowned out by the incessant drone of frogs and the buzz of insects from the nearby swamp.

Suddenly she was acutely aware of how alone she was.

It seemed doubtful that anyone would be brazen enough to attack her when there were a hundred guests, staff, and family members stuffed into the Willows, but still . . .

Would anyone be able to hear her scream?

A whisper of fear fluttered over her, leaving behind a layer of goose bumps. She didn't want to be out here alone, but even as she turned to scurry through the back door of the house, she was brought to a sharp halt as she caught sight of a light burning in the loft of the garage.

She froze. Her aunt had no doubt hired a few locals to act as valets, and of course there were a dozen employees that were serving drinks, and handing out hors d'oeuvres, but none of them would have any reason to be in the apartment over the garage. So why was a light on?

Livia stood still, caught between the urge to discover who was in the apartment and the knowledge she should be in her rooms with the door locked and bolted.

At last she compromised.

She wouldn't go to the garage. Not when it felt like a blatant trap. But if she could find a spot where she could see past the pool house that was blocking her view, she might get a glimpse into one of the lower windows. If someone was in there, they wouldn't be expecting her to be going to her rooms yet, right? She might be able to recognize the person wandering around as they waited for her to check out the light.

It was a long shot, but she wasn't going to risk leaving the terrace.

Concentrating on the darkness ahead of her, Livia didn't notice the door to her uncle's office slide open. In fact, it wasn't until she heard the click of leather soles against the stone terrace that she realized she was no longer alone.

It didn't occur to her to run. Or even scream. Instead, her first instinct was to turn and fight whoever was sneaking up behind her. A brave and utterly stupid decision.

And completely useless.

She was still trying to spin around when the hands smacked into her back, sending her stumbling forward. With a cry of shock, Livia toppled off-balance, her stupid heels making everything worse.

Windmilling her arms as she staggered down the shallow steps, she desperately struggled to avoid breaking a bone or smacking her head against the hard stone. And for a second she hoped she might avoid disaster. Then the toe of her shoe caught the edge of the tarp pulled tight over the empty pool and she plunged face-first into the canvas tarp.

Tumbling through the darkness, her heart froze in place, a sense of horror blasting through her.

Someone was trying to kill her in the exact spot her mother had died.

CHAPTER 17

The Willows
Sunday, July 6th

Livia didn't remember much about her wild scramble over the tarp to reach the far side of the pool. Or her frantic flight into the house and up the stairs to lock herself in her rooms.

She only knew that she spent the rest of the night pacing the floor, her phone clutched in her hand. She was calling Bryce the second she heard anyone outside her door. No matter how late it was.

Thankfully, the hours passed without further incidents, and by the time dawn was cresting over the bayous, she was showered and dressed and out of the house.

For a brief moment last night she'd tried to pretend that the Willows was just a beautiful estate and that her imagination had turned it into a menacing nightmare. Now she knew she'd been right. Either the place was haunted by ghosts or it had been infected with the evil of some demon that had crept from the depths of the swamp.

Once in her car, Livia locked her doors and stomped on

the gas as she zoomed down the driveway at a speed that sent gravel spraying into the air. She only slowed long enough to allow the gates to open before zipping through and heading toward town.

A part of her wanted to keep driving. To head back to New Orleans and forget all about her family and their creepy estate. Unfortunately, she had bills to pay. Which meant she had to stay the full two weeks to get her check from the trust fund.

Plus, there was no guarantee that returning to her house would end her danger.

She had no idea who'd pushed her last night.

Or why.

It would be easy to assume it was connected to her mother. It couldn't be a coincidence she'd been pushed into the pool where Giselle had plummeted to her death. But then again, if someone was determined to frighten her, what better way than making her believe she was being terrorized by a ghost?

Reaching the edge of Rushville, Livia shoved away the questions spinning through her weary mind and concentrated on her surroundings. The town wasn't big enough to have a lot of traffic, but the locals tended to stop in the middle of the road to chat with a passing neighbor. Or just to gawk at someone's new car. She didn't want to backend someone because she was distracted.

A few minutes later she was parked in front of a shotgun house that was painted a bright yellow with green shutters. Like most homes in the neighborhood, it was built in a long, narrow design with a gabled roof and a small porch outlined with a white railing and dominated by a wooden swing.

She breathed a sigh of relief when she caught sight of the large, middle-aged man with thinning black hair and a square, weathered face sitting on the swing. It'd been years since she'd last seen Remy Broussard, but he hadn't changed much. A few more pounds on his broad frame and a few more wrinkles on his tanned face, but the same welcoming smile on his lips as she climbed out of her car and walked up the pathway.

The scent of warm bread and freshly brewed coffee wafted on the morning breeze, reminding Livia of Robbie's complaint that his father refused to move. In this moment she understood why.

She climbed the steps, relieved she didn't have to knock on the door. It made it seem like this was a casual encounter, not that she had tracked him down to grill him about the past.

"Good morning, Remy," she said, moving to stand next to the swing. "I'm not sure if you remember me—"

"'Course I do," Remy interrupted, his smile widening. "Little Livvy. All grown up now."

Livia glanced down at the cut-off shorts and sleeveless T-shirt she'd pulled on after her shower.

"And then some, unfortunately."

"Looks good on you. Better than skin and bones," Remy insisted, pushing himself to his feet with some effort. Obviously his arthritis was bothering him this morning. "Come in. I have a pot of coffee on the stove."

Livia followed him into the small living room that opened to the even smaller dining room and then directly to the kitchen at the back of the house. Everything was well worn, as if it'd been around as long as Remy had owned the house, but it was scrubbed ruthlessly clean and freshly painted.

This was a man who took pride in his property.

Moving to the stove, Remy poured her a mug of the thick chiccory brew out of an old-fashioned coffeepot.

"Sugar? Cream?"

"Both," she requested, hiding her shudder. She could already smell the coffee. It was going to be strong enough to wake the dead.

"Good girl."

He doused the black liquid with a dollop of cream and a

healthy portion of sugar before handing her the mug and motioning toward the small, Formica-topped table.

They settled on the folding chairs and Livia reluctantly took a sip of the steaming hot liquid, promptly burning her tongue.

"I spoke with Robbie last night," she said, placing the mug on the table. The stuff was way too bitter to tolerate, even with the sugar and cream.

"Did you?" Remy looked surprised. "Is he doing work at the Willows?"

"No, he was there for Celeste and Winston's engagement party."

"Ah, right. Forgot about that." He smiled wryly. "Robbie told me he'd been invited, but I didn't pay much attention to when it was happening."

"You must be very proud of your son."

"I am," he agreed without hesitation. "But because he's a hard worker who built a business with his own hands, not because he's invited to fancy parties. No offense intended."

Livia nodded. This man had always been polite when he was working at the Willows, but never subservient. He wanted to do a good job and go home. He wasn't there to make friends with his rich employees.

"None taken, I'm not of a fan of fancy parties either, but I didn't have much choice." She sighed. "I'm stuck at the Willows for another week."

"Never understood that."

"Understood what?"

"Why Henri insisted you all gather together every summer like swallows returning to their nest."

"More like vipers." Livia snorted. "I assume it was my grandfather's way of controlling us from the grave. If he'd had my portion of the trust fund automatically deposited into my bank account I would never have come back once I was of age to decline his invitations."

"That sounds like the old man. He always wanted to be in charge."

A massive understatement, Livia silently acknowledged. Her grandfather turned manipulation into an Olympic sport. A master puppeteer pulling the strings. But while he could force the people who depended on his wealth to bend to his will, he couldn't force them to love him.

A strange chill crawled over her skin. As if her grandfather was punishing her for her petty pleasure in imagining him dying alone and despised in his big, four-poster bed.

"When did you start working for the Benoits?" she abruptly demanded, banishing the terrible image.

"Let me think." Remy tapped the blunt tip of his finger on the table, as if searching his mind for the date. "I first started gardening with the March sisters. That was before your time. They owned a big house next to the interstate. It was torn down when they built the new access road. A shame. The house was falling apart, but they had the most beautiful gardens. Then I started working part-time for the Durands and eventually added in the Willows. I think it must have been in the mid-eighties when I started there. Later I included a couple businesses like the bank and Baptist church."

She'd known that he wasn't full-time at the Willows, but she hadn't realized he'd been spread so thin.

"That's a lot."

"It was, but there's something special about spending your day surrounded by nature. Never seems like work."

Livia wasn't an outdoor sort of gal, but she could understand why someone would find peace in a garden.

"It sounds nice."

"Those were the days." Remy held up his hand to reveal the swollen joints of his fingers. "They pass too quickly."

Livia folded her arms on the table and leaned forward. "Tell me about them."

He hesitated. "You sure? Did Robbie ask you to stop by and keep me company? I know he worries I spend too much time alone."

"No, I'm genuinely interested."

Remy studied her with a curious expression. "What do you want to know?"

"Tell me about the Benoits back in the day."

He shrugged, sipping his coffee before answering. "I suppose they were pretty much like they are today."

"Arrogant, entitled, and insufferable?"

His lips twitched. "Your words, not mine."

"What about my mom?"

"Ah, now. Giselle was different."

"How?"

Remy set aside his empty mug. "Don't get me wrong. She could be arrogant, no doubt about that. You can't be that pretty and rich and spoiled and not be full of yourself. But she wasn't stuffy and she was never mean-spirited." He smiled at some memory. "And she never treated people like they were beneath her, including me. She used to bring me lemonade on hot days and insist I take a break. She even gave me a box of my favorite pralines every Christmas. She knew how much I loved them, but I hated to spend the money for the treats."

Warmth spread through Livia at his words. As she'd told Adrian, it was so hard to think of her mother without her memory being tainted by the mystery and agony of her death. She needed to know more about the woman who had created her.

"You liked her?"

"I did. Everyone did," Remy said. "She had a way about her that put you at ease. As if you'd been friends for a long time." He paused, pursing his lips. "I don't think the old man liked that."

"Why not?"

"He was old-school. There were people his sort talked to and those who were beneath his notice."

"Like the hired staff?"

"Exactly."

Livia had no trouble imagining her grandfather's snobbish disapproval. The question was how far her mother might have gone to aggravate her overbearing father.

"Do you remember the chauffeur?" she asked, still bothered by Helene's vague reference to her mother's ghost searching for the mysterious Manny. Was her aunt unstable? Absolutely. But that didn't mean she wasn't fully aware of the family secrets. And her grandfather would certainly have disapproved of her mother being friendly with a good-looking member of his staff. "I think his name was Manny something or other."

"I remember a driver. What was his name?" Remy struggled to dredge through his memories. "Baxter. Yeah, that was it. Charles Baxter," he finally said. "He worked for your family for at least fifty years before he retired."

"But no Manny?"

Remy started to shake his head only to hesitate. "You know, now that I think about it, there was a young guy there for a couple years. It was after Charles retired. Can't remember his name. I'm not sure I ever talked to him. Kept to himself in his apartment over the garage most of the time."

"Do you know if he was friendly with my mom?" Livia asked. "Maybe friendlier than he should be?"

"Nope." Remy firmly shook his head. "Never heard anything like that. Why do you ask?"

Livia waved her hand in a dismissive gesture. "I was curious, that's all. I wondered why he seemed to have disappeared so quickly. I thought maybe he was caught being too familiar with my mom and had been run off."

"I doubt that." Remy snorted at the mere thought. "If your mom was dating the hired help she wouldn't have bothered to keep it a secret. Just the opposite. I think she would have flaunted it just to piss off the old man."

That was exactly what she'd been thinking, Livia reluctantly conceded. "It's curious he vanished without a trace."

"I don't know that he vanished," Remy protested. "Your grandfather wasn't an easy man to work for and Charles had been with him for years. I'm not sure anyone could replace him. And after your mother died, Henri didn't really need a driver. He rarely left the house."

Livia swallowed a sigh. Manny felt like a dead end. Literally. Time to move on.

"Yeah, being Henri Benoit's granddaughter was challenging enough," she agreed. "I can't imagine working for him."

"He was tough, but he was never stingy." Remy, surprisingly, was defending his one-time employer. "Especially when it came to the Willows. Not like . . ." He coughed, realizing he'd been about to insult one of her relatives.

"Uncle Adrian?"

"I'll just say that he'd not famous for his generosity around this neighborhood," he hedged.

"You're not telling me anything I haven't heard before," she assured her companion. "I'm not involved in the family business, thank God, but I suspect it's gone downhill since my grandfather's death."

"I don't know anything about the business either, but the Willows isn't like it used to be, that's for sure." Remy rose to his feet, crossing to the stove to refill his mug. He waved the coffeepot in her direction, but Livia hastily shook her head. Remy returned to his seat, sipping his hot coffee as he reminisced about the good old days. "Once their parties weren't a bunch of locals and a few gossip rags. They hosted the governor and senators and a few big wigs from Hollywood who did some filming in the area. And the entertainment came out of New Orleans. Jazz players and singers from the nightclub would perform in the back garden. I could sit on my porch and listen to them."

"I'm sure Delilah would be thrilled to have those sorts of parties, but I doubt they could afford it now."

"True," Remy agreed. "It's not just the cost of food and stuff. You need a full staff. Back then they had a housekeeper and cook and a couple of maids, plus they always hired me to set up the stage and chairs in the gardens and Charles to act as the valet. Everything was first class."

Livia felt a pang of regret. She didn't have any memories of those days. The Willows had always seemed like a mausoleum to her, not a place where people were eager to gather. But she'd heard enough stories to know that there'd been a time when Louisiana's social elite had flocked to this tiny corner of the bayous. It was a shame that she'd never been able to see the house before the ghosts had shrouded it in darkness.

"Do you remember when it changed?"

"'Course I do. It was the day your mother died. Henri was never the same. He closed the shutters on the house when he went into mourning. No more lavish parties or weekend guests. The whole family practically disappeared for the next couple of years. I think it was your aunt Delilah that at last insisted they start doing some entertaining, but it wasn't like back in the day."

Livia resisted the urge to roll her eyes. She didn't doubt that Delilah had been foaming at the mouth during the long bout of mourning. She hadn't married Adrian Benoit to be trapped in the middle of nowhere with no ability to show off her supposed wealth.

"What about Aunt Helene?" Livia had never really considered the idea that her oldest aunt had been a person with hopes and dreams before she started lobotomizing herself with alcohol. "Did she ever do any entertaining?"

"Not really. She never had your mother's beauty or Adrian's

ambition. And, I hate to say it, but she didn't really mix well with others. I don't know if it was because she was shy or just thought she was better than people in this town, but she was never a favorite." Remy took a deep gulp of his coffee, and Livia marveled at the amount of caffeine that had to be running through his veins. She'd be jittery all day if she drank more than a few sips. "But eventually your grandfather decided it was time for her to get married and he started inviting men with the sort of money and pedigree he wanted for his daughter."

Livia sucked in a sharp breath. "My *grandfather* decided it was time for her to get married? Not Helene?"

Remy shrugged. "Back in his day I think it was a normal thing. And as far as I know, Helene didn't argue about it. A few months later she was married." He tsked. "Unfortunately."

Livia squashed her burst of anger at the thought that Helene had been bartered off like a prized cow. Maybe her aunt had been happy to land a rich husband. She was more interested in the hint of disgust in Remy's tone.

"You didn't like Lance Prescott?"

The older man struggled and failed to contain his disdain. "I didn't really know him, but he managed to stir up a lot of ill will around here, I can tell you that."

"What did he do?"

"He hadn't moved into the Willows for more than a few weeks when one of his boys was swimming at the old rock quarry. The boy got a bump on the head. Or maybe a cut on his lip, I can't remember, except I know it wasn't much. But Prescott was furious and he stormed down to the city hall threatening the town with a lawsuit unless they put up a fence up so no one could get into the quarry. It was the best swimming hole in town before they finally built the pool and everyone was locked out." He shook his head. "I broke my arm out there one summer when I was little. My mom whupped me and told me to be more careful."

"Yeah, I can't imagine that made him popular in Rushville."

"That wasn't all, he threatened another lawsuit to close down the flea market they used to have in the city park on Saturday mornings."

"Why did he care about a flea market?"

Remy's features hardened. "He claimed they were selling stolen merchandise, which was a load of hogwash. My auntie had a booth there selling her homemade fudge and my cousin would sharpen knives for a few cents. Just a way to make some extra cash for the locals."

"I'm confused." Livia studied Remy's clenched jaw. "Why would he claim that they were selling stolen stuff?"

"He was pissy because one of the flea market vendors backed into his fancy car one morning and drove away before he could make them pay for the damages."

"That was it? He closed down the whole flea market because of a dent?"

"Yup."

Livia shook her head. Lance Prescott was clearly one of those petty, self-entitled jerks that thought they ruled the world.

"No wonder Helene divorced him."

"I don't think she did," Remy said. "Prescott left her. Or at least that's what I heard happened."

"Did you also hear why?"

"The rumor was that she refused to give him a child."

Livia blinked. It wasn't what she'd expected to hear. She'd assumed that Henri was responsible for running off his son-in-law. He controlled everything that happened in the Willows. If Henri had forced Helene to get married, then he would be equally comfortable in forcing her to divorce him.

"Helene refused to have a baby? Or she couldn't get pregnant?" Livia asked, inwardly confused why a man with two sons would care about more kids. Unless he was one of those gross rich dudes who was convinced it was his duty to spread his seed far and wide. She frowned when the older man lowered his head, as if hoping to avoid the question. "Remy?"

Reluctantly he met her searching gaze. "Actually there were whispers she got rid of one."

"An abortion?"

He held up a hand at her shocked tone. "It was just rumors. Anyway, he packed up his brats and moved away. No one blamed Helene. If she'd had a kid then she would never have been free of him."

Livia didn't judge her aunt for her decision. It didn't matter whether she had an abortion, or if something else had destroyed her marriage. She just knew that the result was a broken woman who drifted through life in a haze.

"I'm not sure she is free," Livia muttered.

"Are any of us?" Remy lifted his hand to stare ruefully at his swollen joints. "At least she isn't stuck living with that miserable ass." He lowered his hand. "And neither are we."

"But at what cost?" Livia shivered, once again feeling the heavy presence of her grandfather. "A shame she didn't escape the Willows."

"It's not an easy place to leave." Remy nodded toward the back door that had been left open to allow the breeze to tunnel through the long, narrow house. "Feel lucky you got out so young."

Livia glanced toward the pool of sunshine that spread across the worn tiled floor, the shadows that threatened to wrap around her banished by the knowledge she could stand up and walk away. In fact, she could get in her car and never return to this part of Louisiana.

It was a freedom the rest of the Benoits would never have.

"You know, Remy, I think you're right," she said. "I used to be annoyed that I'd been given away like an unwanted puppy after my mother died, but it forced me to become independent." She slowly rose to her feet, smiling at the older man. "A gift from Grandpa Henri. Thanks for chatting with me."

"Happy to see you." Remy struggled to stand, a warm smile curving his lips. "And don't be a stranger. I'm out on the porch most mornings."

"I'll be back," she promised, stepping toward the back door.

"Livia."

"Yeah?" She glanced back to discover Remy staring at her with a sudden frown.

"Be careful. The Willows isn't a place to go digging. Let the past rest in peace."

Let the past rest in peace . . .

The words whirled through Livia's mind as she drove back to the Willows. She didn't know if Remy had any actual knowledge of the secrets that had been buried by the Benoit clan, or if he'd simply sensed that there was a darkness haunting the estate. Either way, the warning should have sent her scurrying back to her rooms, where she could remain behind locked doors until she could get her trust fund money and leave. That was the smart thing to do.

So of course she did just the opposite

Once back at the Willows she parked in her usual spot and strolled around the side of the house. She silently warned herself to act casual, but she knew that if anyone was watching her they would instantly sense something was up. Her movements were jerky and she was glancing from side to side, searching for potential enemies preparing to leap at her from the shadows.

Her hope was that the family was sleeping in late after a night of festivities while the staff was busy cleaning up the mess left behind by the guests.

Rounding the back of the house, she continued at a measured pace, her gaze sweeping over the terrace, searching for any clue left behind by the jerk who'd attacked her the night before. Predictably, there was nothing out of place. No outline of a footprint. No stray cigarette butt. Not even a silk scarf carefully arranged for her to discover.

Her steps slowed and her stomach twisted as she reached the pool. There was no indication that she'd scrambled across the tarp in an effort to flee her assailant. It was still pulled tight over the empty pool. Maybe the layer of dust was disturbed, but that was it.

If she didn't have bruises on the palms of her hands where she'd tried to break her fall, she might be able to convince herself that the shove and her tumble toward the pool had been nothing more than a nightmare.

A shiver raced through her and she paused, glancing up at the balcony directly over her head.

That's where her mother had stood. Had she'd lingered for a long time, contemplating the voice whispering for her to end it all? More importantly, had she given any thought at all to the daughter she was leaving behind? It seemed doubtful since she hadn't bothered to write a note for Livia. Not even a scribbled "I love you" on a scrap of paper.

Then again, maybe she hadn't lingered on the balcony. Maybe the pain had been too overwhelming and she'd been driven to leap over the railing of the balcony to find peace from her demons.

Livia shook her head. She would never know what was in Giselle's mind when she took her life, but there were other answers she could uncover.

Or at least, that was the hope.

Forcing her oddly heavy feet to carry her forward, Livia used the servants' entrance to step into the kitchen. The room was thankfully empty for the moment, although she assumed the cook would soon be starting lunch. For now Livia was able to scurry across the tiled floor and through the open doorway into the narrow hallway without being noticed.

During the long hours she'd spent pacing the floor last night she'd dredged up an ancient memory of spying on her grandfather when she was very young. It hadn't really been intentional. She'd been playing with her dolls on the back terrace when her attention had been captured by her grandfather shutting the blinds to his office.

The suspicion that he was doing something secret had naturally stirred her curiosity and, creeping to the doors, she'd peeked through the narrow crack in the blinds to watch the older man standing in front of the massive globe that was perched on a wooden stand. As she watched, he grabbed the sides of the globe and twisted it until he could lift off the top half and set it aside. Then he reached into the bottom half that was obviously hollow to pull out a black velvet bag. Livia had easily recognized it as one of the bags that held the Benoit family jewels. Her grandfather had occasionally had them delivered by a servant during formal dinners to pull out the sparkling necklaces and earrings so he could spew boring stories about which relative had bought the expensive bauble and how many times a Benoit woman had worn the jewelry during a visit to Buckingham Palace, or attending an inauguration, or dinner at the governor's mansion.

Livia had quickly lost interest and returned to her dolls. Even as a child she'd known those shiny gems would never belong to her. She was very much Cinderella, according to the Benoit clan. Celeste was the princess.

It wasn't until late last night that she'd suddenly recalled that neither Delilah nor Celeste had been wearing one of her grandmother's lavish designs. Delilah's only jewelry had been the gaudy diamond rings that she'd collected since being married to Adrian, and Celeste had been wearing a simple strand of pearls along with her engagement ring.

It might have been an attempt at understated elegance, but Livia doubted they were capable of resisting the urge to show off their wealth.

So why not haul out the pretty baubles?

Livia's first guess was that they no longer owned them. After all, if the Benoit fortune was gone then the fastest way to raise money would be to sell off the family's prized possessions. Starting with the stuff that wouldn't be noticed by anyone outside the Willows.

It wouldn't directly answer any questions, but it might give a motivation to why Adrian and Winston were acting so weird.

Maybe they hired a private investigator to see if she had been smart enough to invest her trust fund into the stock market or real estate and now had a nest egg worth stealing.

Or more likely, they were trying to discover if she'd gone to a lawyer to set up a last will and testament. If something happened to her without a legal beneficiary then her share of the trust fund would go back to the Benoits. And as far as she knew they'd also get her house and business since they were her closest family. It wouldn't make them rich, but it would keep the creditors at bay until they could get Celeste married and pregnant.

A wild theory, but one that would explain more than a few things that had happened to her over the past month.

Using the hidden door, Livia crept through the library and into her uncle's office, silently shutting and locking the door behind her before moving to the globe in the corner of the room. Her hands were shaking as she reached out to place them on the sides of the globe, just like she'd seen her grandfather do. Then she gave it a twist, satisfaction stabbing through her as a loud click reverberated through the silence.

It sounded like the tripping of a lock.

Pulling on the top of the globe, she was prepared for it to separate from the bottom half, but she hadn't expected it to be so heavy. Obviously it was from a time when craftsmen used solid materials that were built to last.

Grunting as she stumbled backward, Livia hastily set the globe on her uncle's desk before turning back to peer inside the empty shell that remained on the wooden stand.

"I knew it," she muttered, easily able to see that there were no black velvet bags or long leather boxes.

So what had happened to her grandmother's emerald necklace? Or the ruby one? Or the diamond pendant with its matching brooch? She'd seen pictures of Delilah in the papers wearing the emeralds at one charity event or another. And that had been after her grandfather's death.

That meant they'd been handed down.

She tapped her fingers on the edge of the bottom globe. It was possible her uncle had moved them to a different room in the house. Or even took them to a safety deposit box at the bank. But Livia didn't think that was the answer. Not when last night's party would have been the perfect opportunity to show them off.

With her suspicions confirmed, Livia started to step back only to hesitate. There weren't any jewels in the hidden safe, but there were several sheets of paper in the bottom along with a thick document, folded and wrapped in a faux leather cover.

With a quick glance toward the closed door, Livia reached in to grab the papers. She wrinkled her nose as she realized they were more unpaid bills, including two mortgage payments on an office building in Baton Rouge. Strange. The commercial properties had been paid off during her grandfather's time as head of the family. It was something he bragged about with monotonous regularity. Which meant that Adrian had borrowed money against the property and was clearly struggling to repay the loan.

Dropping the bills back into the globe, Livia pulled out the leather-covered document. She'd already guessed what it was. She'd been in real estate long enough to recognize a deed of property.

She unfolded the stiff papers, her brows drawing together as she scanned through the legal mumbo jumbo. This wasn't a deed for an office building or shopping center. It wasn't even a rental property. It was a detached, single-family home in Slidell, Louisiana, that had been purchased almost thirty years ago.

Confused, Livia pulled out her phone to take a picture of the address.

Why would the Benoits own a house in Slidell? And why would the deed be hidden in the globe and not filed with the other legal paperwork?

It had to be because Adrian didn't want anyone to know he owned the house.

She narrowed her eyes. Was it possible Adrian had purchased the place for his secret lover? It was hard to imagine her uncle having enough passion to go to the effort of driving to Slidell to meet with a mistress, let alone spending the cash to keep her in relatively decent comfort. But who knew what was hidden beneath his pretense of stiff propriety?

He could be a full-fledged freak as far as she knew.

Still she couldn't make herself accept the easy explanation. There was something niggling in the back of her mind.

Something about the deed.

Livia sucked in a sharp breath. No, it wasn't the deed that set off her alarms. It was the address.

Slidell. Just like the bank account he wanted closed and erased from records.

Were the two connected?

Livia dropped the deed back into the globe, trying to sift through the various possibilities. The property had been purchased decades ago, but Adrian was only now trying to close the bank account. Did that mean the two weren't connected? Or had something recently happened to worry him that his secret might be exposed?

Something like her catching his private investigator sneaking into her house and pawing through her underwear drawer.

Maybe he'd closed down the account because he'd been using it to pay Larry Sutton and he didn't want the creep connected to him. Or maybe . . .

The breath was squeezed from her lungs.

Maybe he didn't want the Slidell bank account to lead to the house because that's where he'd stashed the private investigator until Livia lost interest in looking for him.

It was yet another wild theory, but that was all she had at this point.

Certainly it was worth a quick drive to Slidell to check it out.

CHAPTER 18

Slidell, LA
Sunday, July 6th

Taking the longer route to the northeast shore of Lake Pontchartrain, Livia easily blended in with the church traffic as they returned home after a meal in one of the numerous local diners.

She didn't really have a plan as she zigzagged through the narrow streets of Slidell. She wasn't foolish enough to show up and knock on the front door. No, that wasn't true. She *was* that foolish, but the knowledge Bryce would be furious with her squashed the urge to take such a bold approach. Instead, she intended to cruise past the house and see if she could spot any vehicle in the driveway. Or maybe a last name printed on a mailbox or carved into a log and arranged in the front yard. Those chunky decorations were popular right now.

At last turning onto the street she'd been searching for, Livia slowed to a mere crawl, her heart jumping as she saw something even better than a last name on a mailbox.

There was a FOR SALE sign stuck in the middle of the lawn.

Circling the block, Livia parked on the opposite side of the street and shut off the engine. Then leaning back, she studied the house with the eye of a real estate agent.

It wasn't the small bungalow she'd been expecting. The sort of modest, inconspicuous place you expected a man to buy for his mistress.

This two-story brick house was twice the size of its neighbors, with a massive yard and ancient weeping willows perfectly framing the wide patio with fluted columns. The tall windows were mullioned with heavy wooden shutters and an upper balcony ran the length of the front of the house. The white trim had been recently painted and the shingled roof was in good condition. There was a detached four-car garage to one side, and a glass sunroom addition on the other side. The backyard was fenced in, blocking her view, but she could see the top of a gazebo from where she was sitting.

It was designed to demand attention and, unless the inside was completely trashed, it was easily worth half a million dollars.

The thought had barely formed when Livia abruptly pulled out her phone to send a text to the real estate agent, requesting a tour. She now had the perfect excuse to get inside the house. The woman responded within seconds, saying she would be there ASAP.

Livia grabbed her purse and dropped her phone inside before shoving open her door and climbing out of the car. She wasn't willing to risk confronting whoever was in the house before she came to Slidell, but now she strolled forward with a casual confidence.

If you put your house on the market, you had to expect people to come poking around, right?

Avoiding the front door, Livia crossed the brick-paved driveway to peek into the garage. It was dark inside, but she could tell it was empty. Next she strolled to glance into the backyard. Besides the gazebo there was a koi pond and a garden shed decorated with hanging flower baskets that overflowed with fuchsia and petunia blooms. It was all well tended, but it felt professionally staged. There weren't any personal items—no furniture on the covered patio, no equipment to care for the lawn, not even a stray garden gnome.

At last, Livia turned toward the nearby house, her heart suddenly racing and a layer of goose bumps coating her bare arms despite the smothering heat. Until this moment she'd managed to pretend she was doing a routine inspection on a property she was interested in selling. Just another day in the life of a real estate agent. Now her stomach cramped with unease as she forced her heavy feet to carry her toward the nearest window.

This had seemed like a great idea when she'd been sitting in her car. Just stroll up like any other potential buyer and do a little poking around. All perfectly normal when there was a house for sale, right?

But the closer she got to the window, the more she felt like there was a target right between her eyes.

Telling herself she was being an idiot, Livia finally reached the house and leaned forward to peer through the clear glass. It was obvious at first glance that she was looking into an informal living room that was connected to the open kitchen. It was equally obvious that the furniture and wall decorations had been removed, leaving behind a barren space to be filled by the next owner. And what she could see of the white French-style kitchen warned that it was equally empty. Not even a stray glass next to the sink.

Livia clicked her tongue, caught between relief and a surge of disappointment. Not only was it growing doubtful that Larry Sutton was hiding at this location, but the fact that it was on the market explained why her uncle was keeping the deed in an easy-to-reach location.

Not that she was fully satisfied.

She wanted to know why her uncle would own a fancy

home in Slidell. Especially if they were having money issues. And why no one had ever mentioned this place.

It was at last the sound of a lid snapping closed that jerked Livia out of her thoughts.

Leaning to the side, Livia glanced across the street to where an elderly lady wearing her going-to-church pantsuit was closing her trash can with more force than necessary. Livia arched her brows. Was the neighbor warning her that she'd been spotted? It certainly seemed like it.

Livia watched as the woman turned to head back into her house, her spine stiff as if she felt like she'd done her neighborly duty to scare off a trespasser. She was clearly the sort of person who kept a close eye on what was happening around her, and willing to take action when she thought it was necessary.

With a renewed sense of purpose, Livia squared her shoulders and sauntered across the street. She'd just spotted the local nosy neighbor. Every block had one. She was the perfect person to give Livia the info on who had been living in her uncle's house and why they'd left.

Careful to stay on guard, Livia swept a professional gaze over the house as she stepped onto the porch. It was a bland, ranch-style place with a mixture of brick and green siding. The windows were small and most were covered by old-fashioned blinds that blocked the sunlight. A decent enough property that matched most of the other homes in town, Livia silently concluded, but it couldn't compare to her uncle's house.

Livia knocked on the door at the same time she reached into her purse to pull out a business card. Then, pasting a smile on her lips, she watched as the woman cautiously cracked open the door.

Up close the neighbor looked to be in her early seventies with iron-gray hair cut short and styled like a helmet. Her square face was deeply lined and her current expression was hard with suspicion.

"Yes?" she demanded, her voice gruff.

"Hi, I'm Livia, a real estate agent from New Orleans." She held up her business card. "Do you have a minute?"

"No need to go on." The woman glanced toward the card with a sniff. "I told the other real estate agent I'm not interested in selling. They'll have to haul me out of this house feetfirst. Probably sooner rather than later, considering my heart condition and the incompetency of the doctors these days, but until then, I intend to stay."

Livia's smile never wavered. The woman might not be interested in selling her house, but she clearly enjoyed talking.

"I don't blame you. It's a charming house and it's obvious that you take excellent care of the property," Livia said in admiring tones. "And the neighborhood seems to be equally charming."

"For the most part." The woman's tension eased and she opened the door another couple inches, allowing Livia a glimpse of her living room, which was crammed with heavy furniture and a collection of porcelain figurines. "There are a few bad seeds, of course. These days you can't keep them out, can you?" She glared toward the yard next door where a couple of kids bikes were lying in the driveway along with an inflatable pool. "A shame."

"Actually that's why I knocked on your door." Livia lowered her hand, still holding the business card. "Ms. . . ?"

"Just Flora. Flora Gibbs."

"Nice to meet you Flora. Such a beautiful name. The goddess of flowers, right?"

The woman looked surprised by Livia's awareness of the origin of her name. "Yes. It was my mother's idea. She was an avid gardener, unlike me. I don't have her green thumb, unfortunately. My late husband used to say I could kill a plant just by walking past it."

"I'm sorry for your loss," Livia murmured.

Flora shrugged. "It was years ago. A sudden heart attack. It was a shock, but I'm glad he didn't suffer."

"You live here alone now?"

The suspicion returned as Flora narrowed her dark eyes. "I do, but that doesn't mean you can railroad me into selling."

"I would never dream of pressuring anyone to sell," Livia assured her. "I'm here to represent an investment firm who is interested in purchasing private property in this area, but I'm only looking at homes that are currently on the market."

The suspicion remained. "You mean they want to put some sort of business across the street?"

"Just the opposite. They want to buy residential homes to rent out, but only in safe, quiet neighborhoods with good schools, and only to tenants who have been through a thorough background search and who are willing to sign long-term contracts. That's why I want to talk to a few of the locals. I need to be sure this is the sort of location they would want to invest in."

Flora considered the advantages and disadvantages of Livia's impulsive lie before giving a grudging nod. Clearly having a vetted renter across the street was better than risking an unsuitable owner who might move in and spoil her view.

"Well, as I said, there are a few less than desirable residents, but for the most part we're good, God-fearing people who live in peace."

"That's exactly what I want to hear." Livia turned so she was standing sideways on the porch. "Can I ask about the house across the street that's for sale?"

"What about it?"

"Has it been empty for long?"

"About three months now. Ever since Estelle died."

"Was Estelle the owner?"

"Yes, we were friends for years. We sat right there on her front patio and had coffee every morning come rain or shine." Flora nodded toward the empty house. "And we drove to church every Sunday before going to get us some lunch. It won't be the same without her."

"I'm sorry. Was she about your age?" Livia kept her tone casual.

"Yes, and before you ask she lived very quietly and she kept an immaculate house. You should have seen her tulips in the springtime. She kept huge baskets of them on her front patio. All different colors." Flora heaved a sigh. "I'll admit that I've been dreading whoever moves in next. They couldn't possibly be as good a neighbor." Livia battled to keep her expression smooth as Flora rambled on. Unless Adrian had a thing for older woman, then Estelle hadn't been his secret lover. So who was she and what was her connection to the Benoits? Livia's attention returned to Flora as the older woman gave a loud click of her tongue. "Then again, as much as I hate the thought of anyone moving into Estelle's home, an empty house is an invitation to criminals. I had to call the police after Estelle died when I saw a man wandering around the house, peeking in the windows and trying to force open the front door. In broad daylight. These thieves have no fear anymore. Just do what they want to poor folks."

Livia felt a surge of genuine sympathy. "You're right, that is brazen, but it is an unfortunate side effect of a For Sale sign going up. Criminals assume the house is empty and try to take advantage."

"This was before the sign went up," Flora corrected her. "Estelle wasn't even cold in her grave. And you know, at first I thought it must be a distant relative or someone from the bank."

"Why do you say that?"

"They were wearing a nice suit and tie. What sort of thief wears a suit?" Flora sounded outraged that the criminal had tried to deceive her with respectable clothing. "But then, if you're going around during the day I suppose you don't want to look like a thug." She shook her head. "To tell the truth, I wouldn't have called the police until I saw him ramming his shoulder into the front door, trying to break in."

Livia's first impulse was to dismiss the mysterious thief. There was nothing unusual about someone trying to break into an empty house. But the fact that he was wearing a suit was strange. And so was the boldness of trying to get in during the day. That sounded more like someone searching for something in particular, not a random crime.

"Did he get in?"

"No. When he heard the sirens coming he took off. That's when I knew for sure he was up to no good. I mean, why wouldn't he stay around if he had a legitimate reason to be there?"

A good question. On impulse, Livia pulled out her phone. She'd taken a handful of photos during Celeste's engagement party. She would never have bothered to capture the moment, but Marcel had bullied her into promising that she'd take some pictures so he could see the various gowns of the guests when she returned to New Orleans.

"Can you describe him?" she demanded as she scrolled through the images.

"Like I said, he was dressed in a suit and clean shaven. I think his hair was light. Maybe it was gray. I couldn't really tell. I do remember thinking he was a nice-looking man, and that it was a shame he'd chosen a life of crime." Flora made a sharp sound of annoyance. "I said as much to the policeman. A mistake, I'll tell you. The obnoxious man acted as if I was a silly old lady who made up the intruder just to get some attention. My husband never trusted law officials. Or politicians. I can't say I blame him."

Locating a picture that included Adrian, Livia expanded it until his image was in the middle of the screen. It wasn't great. He had been standing across the room from her and the lighting was bad, but it was clear enough to determine his height and size beneath his elegant tux. Plus, he was staring straight at her, giving a clear view of his features.

She turned the phone to show Flora. "This wouldn't happen to be the man you saw, would it?" she asked.

The older woman leaned forward, her brow furrowed as she studied the photo. "No, the thief was younger, I'm sure of that," she at last said, straightening to glance back at Livia. "About your age I would say. And he was wider. Not fat, but nicely toned. All over. He looked like he was one of those guys who liked to spend their days in the gym. At least when he wasn't breaking into homes."

Livia felt a flare of amusement at the older woman's dedication to her "neighborhood watch." It was remarkably thorough.

Then her amusement abruptly vanished. It wasn't that long ago that Livia had been similarly captivated by a stranger's bulging muscles and hard ass shown to advantage by his expensive suit.

Barely daring to breathe, Livia turned her phone back so she could once again scroll through the pictures until she found the image she wanted. She expanded it before she held the screen toward Flora.

"What about this man?"

Flora pursed her lips, taking her time as she studied the picture of Larry Sutton. Was she trying to sort through her memories of the thief? Livia didn't try to rush her. She needed the truth, not a vague guess that might lead her down the wrong path.

"That could be him. I can't say for sure, but yes. He looks very similar." Flora sent Livia a curious glance. "Is he a well-known thief?"

Livia dropped the phone into her purse. That wasn't a firm identification, but it was enough to consider the possibility that it had been Larry snooping around the house.

Now the question was why.

"Actually, he's not a thief at all. He's been trying to lure away my client by offering him homes before they go on the market."

"He's a real estate agent?" Flora was clearly skeptical. "Why would he try to break in?"

"To get pictures and dimensions of the property to send to my clients before me," Livia glibly lied. She didn't blame the woman for being confused. It'd been a terrible explanation. In her defense, she'd never been good under pressure. She'd frozen the one and only time she'd tried to sneak out of school and gotten got by the principal. Time for a distraction. "Do you remember the exact day you saw him?"

"You better believe I remember the exact day. It was just a couple hours after Estelle's funeral. I was pulling my car into the garage when I spotted him. No respect at all."

"And he hasn't been back?"

Flora shook her head. She looked disappointed that the trespasser hadn't been caught in the act. Livia was equally disappointed. If there was a formal police report she would know exactly who'd tried to break in.

"Not that I've noticed," Flora admitted. "But there's been the real estate lady coming and going with people to look at the house."

"No one else that might seem out of place?"

"Not that I recall."

Livia swallowed a sigh of frustration. For now the intruder was a dead end. Time to move on to a new line of questioning.

"It's a large place for a woman on her own. Estelle didn't have any family who lived there with her?" she asked.

"No. She never married and she didn't have any kids. After her parents died she was all alone in the world."

"How sad."

Livia expected the usual condescending agreement that an unwed woman deserved to be pitied. She got it all the time from her married friends. Poor Livia, all alone. Instead, Flora sniffed, shooting an envious glance toward her friend's elegant home.

"I don't know. She seemed happy enough. And why wouldn't

she be? She inherited enough money to buy a nice house and live in comfort with no need to get married. And as for kids . . ." Flora shrugged. "She told me that she'd had enough of children when she worked as a nanny. Never wanted any of her own."

Livia's mind went blank. Just like that. One minute she'd been wondering how to find a connection between Adrian and the churchgoing, tulip-loving older lady and the next she had a horrid fear she knew exactly how they were connected.

"She worked as a nanny?"

"Yes, she told me she started with a family when she turned seventeen. She'd always wanted to travel and they were heading to France for three years. After that, she moved from place to place. She preferred to be with babies and toddlers so she usually left after a couple years."

Livia's mouth was so dry it was hard to form the words. "What was Estelle's last name?"

"Gates."

"Stella Gates?"

Flora pursed her lips in disapproval. "She didn't like the name Stella. She said she'd used it because her mother's name was Estelle, but after her mom died she went back to using her full name."

Livia pressed a hand to the center of her chest. Her heart was racing so fast it was painful.

"Oh my God."

"What's wrong? Are you sick?" Flora studied her with a concerned frown.

"I . . . no, I'm fine." Livia sucked in a ragged breath, struggling to regain her composure. Now more than ever she needed a clear mind. "I just realized I've heard her name before."

"Really?"

"I'm related to the Benoits," she said, aware that Flora had barely glanced at her business card. She didn't know her name or the name of her agency.

Flora blinked, as if wondering if Livia was simply bragging about her relationship to the powerful Benoit clan. Then, she appeared to recall something her friend had told her.

"That's right. Estelle worked for the Benoits. It was at that place . . ." Her words trailed away as she searched her memory. "What was it called?"

"The Willows."

"Yes, that's it." There was a hint of disapproval in Flora's tone. Had Stella shared some stories about living with the Benoits? Or did Flora just resent rich people? She'd already indicated she had a chip on her shoulder when it came to the police. "She was there a couple of years, I think," the older woman continued. "Did you know her?"

"Not personally, but I'm currently staying at the Willows. I had no idea their old nanny was the one selling this house when I drove to Slidell."

"What a small world."

"Amazingly small." Livia didn't have to fake her fierce agreement. "Did she ever talk about her life at the Willows?"

Flora's features tightened. "Not really."

"That's surprising," she murmured, sending the older woman a smile. As if they shared secret. "I've heard all the rumors. Henri Benoit was generous with his fancy friends, but notoriously cheap when it came to paying his employees and still expecting them to work like slaves."

"Well, I don't think she minded the work. In fact, I think she was very fond of the baby she was looking after, but she said there was some sort of nasty situation and the child moved away. I never got the details."

Was she referring to Giselle's suicide? Or was there some other nasty situation?

"She didn't tell you anything about what happened?"

"Nothing. In fact, she only mentioned her time with the family on a couple of occasions." Flora squashed any hope that she had information that could help Livia discover why Stella was living in a fancy house owned by Adrian Benoit. "She didn't like to talk about her previous work. In a lot of ways she was a very private person."

Livia arched her brows. She must have been very private if Flora hadn't managed to wring out any information over the course of several years. That didn't necessarily mean she'd been hiding anything. The woman might simply believe in discretion when it came to her past employers.

"And none of the Benoits ever visited her after she moved into the house?" she asked.

Flora looked shocked by the question. "I sincerely doubt it. Folks like that don't remember their old servants, let alone come visit them." She glanced back at her own modest home, her lips thinning to a bitter frown. "But it's the same everywhere, isn't it? My husband worked in a bank for almost thirty years, but when he died do you think one of them ever came to see if I was okay or if I needed anything? All I got was a box of his belongings and a sympathy card. No loyalty these days, if you ask me."

Hard to argue with that, Livia silently acknowledged. The business world was a cutthroat place. If you got sick, or died, they moved on to someone new without missing a beat.

"Do you happen to know why Estelle chose this location to settle?"

"Her parents were from the area. They passed several years ago, but that's one reason she became a nanny for the Benoits. She wanted to be closer to home after her mother was diagnosed with cancer. Then, of course, she got her inheritance and was able to retire and take care of them full-time."

"So her inheritance didn't come from her parents?"

"No, I don't think so. She mentioned her father had worked on a shrimp boat and her mother had worked at a nursing home. I doubt they would be able to save up such a nice fortune."

Flora sounded genuinely sad her friend was gone, but the envious expression returned as she stared at the house across the street. "I don't know where the money came from, but something she said made me think it was a previous employer who'd left it to her. Enough to buy her own home and live a life of comfort. Lucky for her."

Was it luck? Or something else? That was a lot of money to get from a former employer. Especially if she didn't stay in one place more than a couple of years. Enough money that there had to be some way to find out if the "inheritance" had come from the Benoits, even if her uncle was scrambling to cover his tracks.

A problem to worry about later. For now . . .

Her lips parted to ask if Stella had any other friends she could chat with, but the sound of a car pulling into the driveway across the street interrupted her. The real estate agent had arrived.

Resisting the urge to ignore the interruption, Livia once again held out a business card.

"Thanks so much for answering my questions, Flora. And if you think of anything that I should know about the house be sure and give me a call."

The woman reluctantly took the card, but Livia didn't have any hope that she would call. She might enjoy a chat on the porch, but she wasn't thrilled at the thought of some mysterious investor buying up property in her neighborhood.

Retracing her steps to Stella's house, Livia slid into her role of real estate agent with a sense of relief. She'd been a professional long enough to appear calm and composed, even when her thoughts were a tangled mess of confusion.

Introducing herself to the middle-aged woman with dark hair styled in a bob and wearing a suit jacket and white slacks, Livia quizzed her on the expected topics.

Taxes, zoning, crime rate, HOA fees and school district.

As they spoke, they wandered around the outside of the property, before the agent used the pad key to open the door and lead Livia inside. As she'd suspected, it was empty of furniture and personal belongings that might give her insight into Stella Gates. It did, however, confirm Livia's initial listing price. The high ceilings in the front room and the stone fireplace actually amped up the worth of the property. If her old nanny had somehow compelled Adrian to buy this place and give her a yearly allowance, she had to have an amazing amount of leverage over him.

Pretending to study the window frames and turning the faucets off and on, Livia strolled from room to room.

"Can you tell me about the previous tenant?" she at last asked in a casual tone.

"She was an older lady. No children or pets. And no smoking," the agent was quick to point out. "And as you can tell she was very tidy. She kept the property in pristine condition."

Too pristine. Livia headed into the kitchen, opening drawers in a vain hope of stumbling across a scrap of paper or old photograph that had been overlooked.

"I was speaking with the neighbor and she said that the tenant had recently passed," Livia murmured, turning back to the agent as she conceded defeat.

"That's right, but not in the house," the agent insisted. "She was in the hospital."

Livia sent the older woman a reassuring smile. "My only interest is making sure that the property deed has gone through probate and there's no messy inheritance battle. I just had a deal in New Orleans that ended up in the courts when the kids couldn't agree how to split up the profits. I'd prefer to avoid that if possible."

"Ah, I see. No worries here. The deed to the property is owned by an investment company. There are no liens or potential lawsuits. It's all very straightforward."

Livia glanced toward the windows that offered a distant view of the lake. How did she get the information that would reveal why Stella was living in a half-million-dollar house that was owned by her family? It seemed unlikely the agent would have any details. Maybe Stella had a lawyer? Or a financial advisor?

She was still floundering when she was distracted by the buzz of her phone.

Reaching into her purse she pulled it out and glanced at the screen. Her brows snapped together as she recognized the number.

"I'm sorry. It's my office," she said. "I have to take this."

"Of course."

With a nod, the agent turned to leave the kitchen, giving Livia privacy as she connected the call.

"Marcel? What are you doing in the office on a Sunday?" she demanded, knowing it had to be an emergency. She was right. "Oh my God. I'll be right there."

CHAPTER 19

New Orleans, LA
Sunday, July 6th

Livia was furious by the time she'd pulled to a halt behind the police car blocking the street in front of her office. It hadn't been a long drive, but there'd been plenty of time for her to mull over Marcel's revelation that some idiot had destroyed her window in a drive-by shooting.

She should have been terrified. There was no way it had been a random act of violence. Whoever had shot out her window had done so on purpose. But despite her frayed nerves, the more she thought about the attack the more her blood boiled.

She'd already been locked in an empty apartment and shoved onto the tarp covering the pool where her mother had died. Now her office had been vandalized.

The more she thought about the escalating harassment, the more she wanted to punch someone.

Forcing herself to take a deep breath, Livia climbed out of her car and approached the uniformed patrolman who was waiting for her in front of her office.

He had a youthful face set in sullen lines, as if he'd rather be on a high-speed chase or maybe working undercover with drug traffickers. Anything but waiting to take a statement about a busted window.

From his expression, Livia was already prepared for his uninspired questioning. Did she have surveillance? Yes, but only inside the office. Did she have any disgruntled former clients or employees? None that would shoot at her office. Any vengeful exes? She gave him Larry Sutton's name. He wasn't really an ex, but she was already convinced he was guilty.

The man jotted the name down and, with a promise to return tomorrow to speak with the other business owners in the area, he then climbed in his patrol car and zoomed away.

Livia headed into the office, not surprised to discover Marcel on his phone as he stood at the far side of the lobby. Livia took a second to study the damage.

It wasn't as bad as she'd expected. There was glass scattered over the carpet and two bullet holes were visible in the far wall, but it was all surface stuff. Nothing that couldn't be fixed.

Still, the sight of the damage struck sparks off her already smoldering temper.

"What a mess," she growled, planting her hands on her hips.

Marcel ended his call and strolled to stand next to her. He was wearing a pair of khaki shorts and loose cotton shirt. The casual style only emphasized his natural elegance.

Livia, on the other hand, was hot and sweaty from standing in the heat while she chatted with Flora. And honestly, she was pretty sure she hadn't brushed her hair since she'd stepped out of the shower hours ago.

"Yeah, on the bright side, there was no one here when the lunatic shot up the place," Marcel murmured.

Livia sent him a jaundiced glare. "There is no bright side."

"Oh, thank God," Marcel breathed, glancing toward the

broken glass that glittered like tiny daggers in the late afternoon sunlight. "It's a total mess."

"We'll have to call the lumberyard and get some plywood for the window."

"No worries. I'll call my cousin Darius. He can swing by and get the plywood and put it up for us today. Plus, for the right price I can get him to order and replace the window so we don't have to worry about it. He's always looking for a way to make a quick buck."

The heavy sense of dread that had been pressing on her shoulders abruptly lifted. Not because Marcel was dealing with the situation—that was why she'd hired him to be her assistant, after all. It was the reassurance that he hadn't been injured or traumatized by the shooting.

Even when he'd assured her on the phone that the office had been empty and that he had everything under control, she'd needed to see him in person to be one hundred percent certain.

That was also the reason she'd been so damned mad.

It was one thing for her to be in danger. But she couldn't bear the thought that her friend, or even one of her clients, might have been injured.

"Thanks, Marcel." She sent him a weary smile. "I knew I could depend on you."

"I'll also contacted a professional cleaning company. We don't want any stray shards of glass stabbing into one of our clients. More importantly, we don't want one stabbing into me." Marcel held out his bare arm. "Look at this delicate skin. It would be a crime against nature to have it scarred. And I suppose we'll have to have the holes in the wall patched and painted."

"Agreed." She knew her companion was trying to lighten her dark mood. "And I'll call the insurance agent and get the tedious process rolling."

Marcel shuddered. "Better you than me."

Livia glanced toward her office before giving a sharp shake of her head. She didn't have the energy for the inevitable fight. Not today.

"That can wait until morning."

"Yes. And I can handle things here. At least now that you've gotten rid of that annoyingly stubborn cop. I think he suspected I was the one responsible for the shooting." Marcel rolled his eyes. "As if I'd stay around to make a police report." He waved a hand toward the door. "You should get back to the homestead before they use your absence as an excuse to vote you off the island. Or whatever it is rich people do to steal other people's money."

"Exist. That's all they have to do," Livia said dryly. "They're like black holes sucking up the wealth around them."

Marcel chuckled. "Truth."

Livia heaved a sigh. She didn't want to think about the Willows or her family. Or their connection to what had happened to her office. They were another problem she was putting off until tomorrow.

"I'm going to spend the night in New Orleans." She held up her hand as Marcel started to protest. "The family has an agreement that an emergency can override the clause. A few years ago, Delilah had to spend the entire two weeks with her mother, who was in the hospital after she'd fallen and broken her hip. I can't imagine that she was any help to the poor old woman, but I'm sure she didn't want to waste the money on hiring a nurse."

"Wait." Marcel arched a teasing brow. "You didn't shoot out the window so you could escape the family for a night, did you?"

"I'm not that desperate." Livia paused, abruptly realizing just how badly she wanted to stay in New Orleans. "Not yet," she added.

Marcel's amusement faded. "What's happened?"

"Nothing. Everything." She shrugged. "The usual."

"No, there's something." Marcel leaned forward, studying her face with an unnerving intensity. "You look like you haven't slept in a week."

"Probably because I haven't," she admitted, running her fingers through her tangled curls. She wasn't overly vain, but she hated feeling grubby.

"Does it have to do with Jacob Pearson?" Marcel narrowed his eyes. "The bastard."

"It's a lot more complicated than that," she admitted. I'll tell you everything I know later. Right now I just want something to eat and a hot shower."

Marcel reluctantly squashed his curiosity. "What can I do to help?"

"Just having you deal with this mess is more than enough."

He grabbed her hand, giving it a gentle squeeze. "Go home and get some rest."

"Thanks, Marcel. I don't know what I'd do without you."

"It would be a struggle."

"That's for sure," she breathed, leaning forward to kiss his cheek.

He waved her away, scowling to hide his pleasure at her fierce sincerity. "Go. I got this."

Returning to her car, Livia sent a quick text to Bryce. She didn't want her friend worried when she didn't return to Rushville. Then, feeling like she was running on autopilot, she drove to her house.

Pulling into the driveway, she parked her car and headed to the front porch. Once she opened the door, however, she shook off the numb detachment. Despite her anxious need to be safely tucked in her own home and surrounded by her personal belongings, she hadn't forgotten that there'd been more than one intruder lurking around.

It was possible that someone had shot out her window to

lure her back to New Orleans. If they'd followed her here, then they might be waiting for the opportunity to . . .

Actually, she didn't know what they might want from her. But she was going to be on guard.

Leaning forward, Livia switched on the lights, cautiously glancing around the living room before stepping inside. She closed and locked the door behind her before moving from window to window to make sure they were locked, and then closed the curtains. She wasn't going to risk exposing herself to a shooter who might be standing outside. Next, she went from room to room, opening closet doors and peeking under the bed.

Only when she was certain that she was alone did she grab some clean clothes from her bedroom and lock herself in the bathroom to take a shower. Eventually she ran out of hot water and, drying off, she pulled on her fresh clothes before doing another sweep of the house.

Confident she was alone, Livia headed into the spare bedroom. Her laptop was at the Willows, but she could use her old computer to do a search of Stella Gates.

There wasn't much to find. Just a few articles about her donating cakes and pies to her local church charity events and one mention of her winning a five-hundred-dollar scratch-off ticket. Flora had been right. Stella really was lucky. But nothing about her life before she moved to Slidell or her time working as a nanny.

Accepting that it was yet another dead end, at least until she had a chance to confront her uncle with what she'd discovered, Livia returned to the living room and ordered a pizza from her favorite restaurant. For the next few hours she was going to veg on the couch and mindlessly stare at the TV. Tomorrow she would start again.

She turned on her favorite reality show and was headed into the kitchen to grab a soda when the knock on the door shattered the illusion of peace. It was too quick for the pizza delivery, but there was the possibility that it was one of her neighbors checking on her.

Grabbing a butcher knife from the wooden block on her counter, Livia commanded her heavy feet to carry her forward. It seemed unlikely that a criminal would knock before carrying out some heinous act, but she wasn't taking any chances.

Once in the living room, she parted the heavy curtains a sliver, peeking at the slender form standing on her front porch. A blast of surprise raced through her as she dropped the knife on the coffee table and pulled open the front door.

"Bryce." She swept a gaze over the tall woman's casual jeans and New Orleans Saints T-shirt. "What are you doing here?"

"You don't think I'm going to let you stay here on your own, do you?" Bryce held up her hand, her irresistible smile curving her lips. "Plus, this bottle of wine isn't going to drink itself."

Livia stepped back to let her friend into the house, feeling a shocking jolt of relief at having someone staying with her. This was her home, but as long as there was some crazed madman—or madwoman—out there tormenting and stalking her, she would never feel completely safe.

Still, it was too much to ask poor Bryce to give up her rare free time to babysit her.

"There's no need for this, Bryce," she insisted as the woman shrugged off a backpack and tossed it on the floor. "I appreciate your concern, but you have better things to do with your Sunday evening."

"Sadly, I don't," she informed Livia. "My dad is at church playing bingo, and Josie won't be home for a few days."

"And the yummy Sheriff Finn?" Livia couldn't resist asking.

The hazel eyes narrowed. "Stop."

"Okay. I won't deny that I appreciate your company. And I definitely need your detective skills. But first, you get comfortable while I pour us a glass of this." Livia leaned forward to pluck the bottle from her friend's firm grasp. "I have a pizza ordered with the works. Is that okay with you?"

"Perfect." Bryce pulled her phone out of her back pocket before strolling with the grace of an athlete to drop onto the couch.

Livia returned to the kitchen, opening the wine and pouring two glasses. She also grabbed a bag of chips and the candy bars she kept in her emergency stash.

Bryce smiled as Livia returned, placing everything on the low coffee table. "Girls' dinner. My favorite." Leaning forward, Bryce grabbed one of the wineglasses, briefly stiffening as she caught sight of the butcher knife that Livia had dropped there earlier. Opening the bag of chips, she took a handful before settling back and studying Livia with a grim expression. "First, tell me what brought you back to New Orleans."

"Marcel called to tell me the office alarms had gone off, and when he went to check out what was wrong, he found that someone had driven by and shot out the front window."

Bryce was in instant cop mode. "Shot? You're sure?"

"There were bullet holes in my wall. More damage I have to have fixed."

"No other buildings were hit?"

"Not on that block. The patrolman who answered Marcel's nine-one-one call is supposed to be investigating if there were any other victims."

"Then the assumption is that you were deliberately targeted by the shooter?"

Livia grimaced. It sounded worse when her friend said it like that. "I guess so."

"No eyewitnesses or video surveillance?"

"The cop who I talked to promised he would check around tomorrow, but it sounded like he was already dismissing it as a group of teenagers taking random potshots." Livia grabbed her wine and took a deep drink. "I'm pretty sure that any search for the perp or perps is going to be pretty low on their to-do list."

Bryce nibbled on her chips, her gaze never wavering from Livia's face. "You think you know who did it?" she abruptly asked.

"My guess would be that Larry Sutton pulled the trigger at the request of either Adrian or Winston." Livia shrugged. "Maybe both."

"Why?"

"Because I'm getting too close."

"Too close to what?"

"That's the question, isn't it?" Livia muttered. "I thought it all started a couple of months ago. The day a man calling himself Jacob Pearson strolled into my office and started flirting. But that's wrong. Something happened in the past that started all this and now it's snowballing."

Bryce settled back in her cushion. "I'm listening."

Pouring them both a fresh glass of wine, Livia told her friend about her conversation with Remy earlier in the day and his implication that the Benoits were looking for a wealthy son-in-law to bail them out of financial ruin. And then her determination to discover if things had gotten bad enough to sell off the family jewels. She hadn't bothered to mention that she'd been locked in the apartment or shoved into the pool. She could share that information later. For now she didn't want her friend to get bogged down in worry for her.

A wasted effort, of course.

Bryce listened in silence, one of the traits that made her such a great cop. She had the ability to absorb all the information before making any judgments. But once Livia reached the part of the story where she'd gone in search of who was living in the house listed on the deed, she couldn't hold back her outrage.

"Wait." She carefully set her wineglass on the table before leaning toward Livia with a frown of disbelief. "You went to Slidell to investigate a mysterious house on your own?"

"I wasn't investigating," Livia protested. "Not really. I just thought I would drive past and check out the place."

Bryce made a sound of frustration. "You snuck into your uncle's private office and broke into his safe to discover a deed that just happened to be conveniently hidden inside it. Did it ever occur to you that it could be a trap?"

Livia was instantly on the defensive. Her friend had a point. It could very well have been a way to lure her to that particular location. But she truly didn't think so.

"My uncle's not that clever," she muttered.

"Livia."

"Okay, I should have been more careful," she conceded, anxious to move on. "Do you want to know what I found out?"

Bryce continued to glare at Livia before at last heaving a resigned sigh. "You know I do."

Repeating her conversation with Flora, Livia shared everything she'd learned, along with a precise description of the house.

"And your old nanny was living there?" Bryce demanded in surprise.

"Yes."

"The Benoits must have a hell of a retirement plan."

Livia snorted. "I can guarantee you that my family has never paid a penny more than absolutely necessary. At least to anyone unfortunate enough to work for them."

"It's weird." Bryce furrowed her brow. "I could understand giving her a house to stay in if she was still caring for you."

"I couldn't." Livia recalled the cramped ranch home she'd lived in until she turned eighteen. "They certainly weren't so generous to my foster family."

"Interesting. So what did she do that was so special?" Bryce leaned back, as if silently sorting through the various possibilities.

"I've been racking my brain trying to figure it out. My best guess is that Stella Gates knew something that one or more of the Benoits didn't want shared with the world." Livia drained the last of her wine. "Or with another Benoit," she added. "I don't doubt for one second they all have sins they're willing to pay to keep hidden."

"Blackmail?"

"Why else would they let her stay in a fancy home and pay her enough to live without having to work? Especially when the family is struggling to pay their bills."

Bryce held up a warning hand. "Wait. We don't know that she wasn't paying rent. Or that she hadn't actually inherited enough money to live on."

"If that was true, then why was my uncle desperately trying to convince his banker to erase all trace of his Slidell account?" Livia demanded. "You don't do that for a legitimate rental property. He's hiding something—either for himself or for someone else."

"Okay, I agree. It does sound sketchy," Bryce conceded.

"There's more. The neighbor mentioned that she'd seen a man trying to break into Stella's house on the day of her funeral."

"Not that unusual, unfortunately. Even in Rushville an empty house is an invitation for criminals."

"Maybe not unusual, but the thief was wearing a suit during the break-in. And when I showed her a picture of Larry Sutton, Flora said the intruder looked like him."

Bryce blinked, as if struggling to follow Livia's rambling accusations. "Why would Larry Sutton try to break into your old nanny's house? And why would he be wearing a suit?"

Livia set aside her empty glass. She could feel a warm glow spreading through her body, assuring her that she'd had enough. At least until she could get something more substantial in her belly.

"What if he wanted people to believe that he was at the house because he'd just come from Stella's funeral and was a relative who had every right to be there?" Livia suggested. "I'm sure that most people wouldn't have given him a second glance. Even Flora said that she wasn't going to call the cops until she saw him trying to break open the front door."

Bryce arched her brows. "So once again the nosy neighbor is Larry Sutton's nemesis?"

"Exactly." A grim smile twisted Livia's lips. "It's fitting, really. No amount of technology can compete with a bored old lady staring out the window."

"True, but that doesn't explain what Larry was doing there."

A knock on the door interrupted the conversation.

"Hold on." Livia jumped to her feet and crossed the living room to grab the purse that she'd tossed on a chair. Five minutes later, she had the pizza box open on the coffee table and they were wolfing down the greasy, doughy goodness as if they hadn't eaten in days. It wasn't until they'd satisfied their immediate hunger that Livia went to the kitchen to get a handful of napkins and another bottle of wine from her cupboard.

Bryce leaned back with a sigh, sipping her fresh glass of wine. "Let's go back to the beginning and walk through your theory."

Livia settled in the corner of the couch, her legs curled beneath her. "Okay."

"Stella Gates is hired by your mother after you were born."

Livia slowly shook her head, suddenly realizing that it'd been a mistake to assume it was her mother who'd hired a nanny to take care of her.

"Actually, it wouldn't have been my mother's decision. Henri Benoit controlled everything that happened at the Willows—including the staff," she said.

"All right, so Henri hired her to come and help your mother after you were born."

"Yes, but why?"

Bryce looked confused. "That's what rich people do. They have babies and then pay someone else to take care of them."

"Just yesterday, Delilah was complaining that she'd had to make do with a part-time babysitter to help her with Celeste, although Henri had been happy to pay for a live-in nanny for his precious Giselle. At the time I thought she was just jealous because my grandfather obviously loved my mother more than Adrian. Now I wonder why Henri had been so generous."

Bryce shrugged. "Your mother was young. Maybe he was worried she wasn't ready for the responsibility."

It was a logical explanation, but Livia had a feeling her grandfather would be the petty sort of man to punish his daughter by refusing to help with her unwanted child.

"Or maybe he didn't trust her," Livia suggested. "What if he was paying Stella extra to spy on my mother?"

"Why would he do that?"

"He couldn't have been happy that his princess had a baby without a husband. Preferably a rich one. He would want to make sure that he kept her under firm control so she didn't make any other embarrassing mistakes."

Bryce didn't look convinced. "Your mother lived in his house in the middle of the swamp. That's about as controlling as you can get."

"My mother had obviously managed to sneak around and get pregnant. It was possible she was continuing to sneak around to stay in contact with my father. Whoever the hell he was."

Bryce's eyes softened, but she was smart enough to know that Livia didn't want her pity. You couldn't miss what you never had, so Livia rarely thought about the fact that she had no clue who'd gotten her mother pregnant.

Now, however, it was possible that his identity had put the recent chaos into motion, even if he'd been a minor player. Like the butterfly effect.

"You think he was someone local?"

She wrinkled her nose. When she'd been very young she'd occasionally wondered if her father might be nearby, but sheer survival had forced her to squash the urge to look for resemblances in the men she passed on the streets of Rushville.

"I'm not sure, but there must be a reason why no one is willing to talk about him. Either he dumped her and disappeared after discovering she was pregnant, or, more likely, he was somehow unwelcomed at the Willows."

"Maybe he was already married."

"Yeah. I've considered that, but I'm pretty sure my grandfather would have bullied whoever it was to leave their family and marry my mother," Livia said. "He wouldn't have cared who was hurt in the process as long as the Benoit honor was restored."

Bryce nodded, sipping her wine as she mulled over what Livia had told her. Her expression was pensive, as if she wasn't entirely satisfied with the direction of her thoughts. At last she gave a sharp shake of her head.

"You know, I'm willing to speculate that Stella had some sort of information that one or more of your relatives were willing to pay to keep secret. Why else would she be living in a home owned by the Benoits? And why else would your uncle try to hide an account that might be connected to the nanny?" Bryce conceded. "But why would they be worried about your father, or anything else to do with your mother, once she was gone? Any potential scandal no longer mattered, did it?"

Livia considered the question. Bryce was right. Not because her mother was dead, but because her grandfather was. He was the one who would have been wounded by his beloved daughter's memory being tarnished. The rest of the Benoits couldn't care less if Giselle's name was dragged through the mud.

"Agreed," she murmured. "It must be some other secret."

"Stella did live at the Willows for at least a couple years." Bryce tapped her finger against the edge of her glass. "It's possible that she saw something. Or overheard a private conversation. And after your mother's death, she decided to cash in."

"It's more than possible," Livia muttered. "They are hiding something. I've sensed it all along."

"But what?"

"I don't know. I truly don't."

Silence settled between the two women as they pondered the fragmented clues that refused to fit into a cohesive picture. They knew that Larry Sutton was a private investigator who'd pretended to be Jacob Pearson to worm his way into her life. But they had no idea who'd hired him, or why he'd been sneaking into her house and searching through her drawers. They knew that Stella Gates had once been her nanny, but they had no idea why the Benoit family had given her a fancy house to live in, and potentially a monthly salary.

What was the connection?

"Okay." Bryce at last broke the silence. "Someone in the Benoit clan obviously knew that your nanny was in the house for the past . . . what? Twenty-eight or twenty-nine years?

"Yes, the property didn't go up for sale until after her funeral."

"And your uncle just closed the bank account?"

"Yes."

Bryce pursed her lips. "If they knew where she lived, and that she was now dead, why hire Larry Sutton to break into her house?"

"It could be that Stella took something from the Willows and they were trying to get it back before the house was sold," Livia suggested. "Maybe some sort of document. Or picture."

"But if they owned the house, they wouldn't have to break in, would they?"

"If Stella was smart she would have changed the locks the day she moved in," Livia said dryly. "She had to know you can never trust a Benoit."

Bryce shook her head. "Even if there was a lease agreement between the Benoits and Stella and she'd locked them out, the contract would have ended the day she died. Whoever owns the property would have every right to go inside."

Livia clicked her tongue, annoyed with herself. "You're right, I should have thought about that."

"You have a lot on your mind."

"Yeah, but it's my job." With an effort she squashed her irritation. There were probably lots of things she was missing. All she could do was try to concentrate on what was important. "So does that mean Larry Sutton was hired by someone else to break into the house?"

"The first person who comes to mind is Winston Durand," Bryce said. "He's one of our top suspects and he's the one who wouldn't have the legal authority to search Stella's house."

"I'm still sure it was Winston who came looking for Larry the day I caught him in my house. Which means he knows the private investigator," Livia agreed, her tone uncertain. "But I thought Winston and Adrian were working together. And what interest would Winston have in my old nanny?"

"I'm more interested in what interest he has in *you*," Bryce retorted. "You never had any contact with Stella, have you?"

"None." It was the one thing that Livia could say with confidence. "I don't even remember her."

"Could she have called your office to try and sell her house before it reverted back to your family? Or could she have questions about her rights as a renter?"

It was a reasonable hypothesis. The older woman might have been pressured by Adrian to get out of her home when the business went downhill. There was a lot of potential income wrapped up in the property. Stella might have heard that Livia worked in real estate and hoped that she could convince her uncle to let her stay.

"If she did, I never got the message. Which is highly unlikely. Marcel is an amazing assistant. He's meticulous in keeping track of potential clients."

Bryce heaved a loud sigh. "It's so confusing. Why would your uncle allow your former nanny to be living in a house belonging to the Benoits, and potentially be giving her some sort of allowance? And why was he keeping it a secret? And why had Larry Sutton tried to break in after the funeral?"

"All great questions with no answers."

"And why was Larry Sutton . . . wait." Bryce cut off her words. "When was the funeral?"

For once, Livia had an answer. "I looked it up on the computer. April twenty-seventh. It was a graveside service at ten in the morning."

"And when did Larry show up at your office pretending to be Jacob Pearson?"

"May fourteenth." Livia made a sound of disgust. "How sad is it that I remember the exact date?"

"Two weeks after Stella died. Why did he go from her house in Slidell to New Orleans to create Jacob Pearson and lure you into a relationship? There has to be a link between the two events."

Livia shivered. As happy as she was to be in her own home, there were still unpleasant memories of Jacob lingering in the back of her mind. They wouldn't be completely banished until she discovered exactly why he'd abused her trust. And more importantly, if he was still a threat.

"A thousand whys with zero answers," she muttered. "And I have another one. Why shoot out the window of my office?"

"That one is easy," Bryce surprised her by insisting.

"Is it?"

"Either it's a warning for you to stop poking into the past. Or, for some reason, they wanted to lure you away from the Willows."

Livia's head was starting to spin, but she reached for the bottle on the table and poured herself another glass of wine.

"I think you're right. This was a warning. And not the first one," she said. "Someone is worried about me digging up old skeletons."

Bryce frowned. "What else happened?"

Accepting that she couldn't keep her friend in the dark any longer, Livia shared her encounters with the mysterious stalker. Not surprisingly, Bryce was instantly furious.

"Dammit, Livia, why didn't you tell me before now? You can't go back there. You're not safe."

"You think I'm any safer here?" Livia reached out to grab her friend's hand, giving her fingers a small squeeze. "The only way to end this is to expose whoever is behind the attacks."

Bryce looked grim, but she understood that Livia couldn't lock herself in this house forever.

"We will." She clutched Livia's hand, her words sounding like a solemn pledge. "We're going to expose them and throw their asses in jail."

"Amen."

CHAPTER 20

New Orleans, LA
Monday July 7th

Bryce woke the next morning with a dry mouth and a stiff neck. The dry mouth was a result of too much wine and the stiff neck was from a night spent on the narrow couch.

It was the sort of morning that begged her to squeeze her eyes shut and fall back asleep. Maybe when she woke the next time the pounding behind her eyes would be gone.

Instead, she struggled to her feet and stumbled into the shower, turning on the cold water until she was shivering and wide awake. Then, brewing a pot of coffee, she pulled on fresh clothes and made a quick phone call.

Once she was sure she had everything in place, she poured a mug of coffee and entered Livia's bedroom.

"Hey, sleepyhead, wake up," she said loud enough to jerk the snoring woman out of her deep sleep.

With a groan, Livia rolled over, shoving her tangled hair out of her face.

"You're up early," she groaned. "And annoyingly chipper considering we didn't go to bed until after two."

"Get dressed," Bryce commanded. "We have an appointment."

"What?" Livia struggled to sit up. "An appointment with who?"

Bryce leaned forward to hand her friend the fresh mug of coffee. "We'll talk on the way. Chop-chop."

Livia blinked. "'Chop-chop'?"

"Get a move on it," Bryce clarified.

Livia pouted, then, realizing that Bryce wasn't going to go away until she had agreed to get out of bed, she heaved a deep sigh.

"Fine." She sipped the coffee as she tossed aside the covers. "I'm moving."

Convinced that her friend was awake, Bryce went back to the living room to tidy up the mess they'd left behind. Then, gathering up what she'd brought with her, she headed out to her SUV.

While she waited for Livia she called Josie to say hi, not surprised by her daughter's joyous laughter as she relayed the various adventures that she'd been enjoying with her cousins. Although Bryce missed her little girl with a fierce urgency, she was deeply grateful to Benjamin's parents for ensuring that Josie remained an important member of their family. They kept his memory alive in her bruised heart in a way she couldn't.

Once she disconnected, she sent Finn a text, telling him she would be into the office later than usual. He sent back a quick reply assuring her that he had everything covered and to enjoy her day. A wry smile curved her lips, her thumb touching the words on the screen. Finn Maxwell was making it tough to convince herself she wasn't ready to be romantically involved.

Her dangerous thoughts were thankfully shattered as the front door opened and Livia appeared, wearing a pair of white shorts and a stretchy yellow top, with her damp hair pulled into a high ponytail. Even at a distance, her face was pale with shadows from their late night under her eyes; still, she looked beautiful.

If Bryce was a vain woman she might hate Livia Benoit. Pretty, smart, and related to the most powerful family in Louisiana—everything a woman could want.

Thankfully, Bryce *wasn't* vain, and she'd never once wished she could change places with her friend.

"Ready?" she asked as Livia climbed into the SUV.

"I'm not sure. Ready for what?" Livia demanded as she pulled on her seatbelt.

"When I woke up this morning I had a weird feeling of déjà vu," Bryce said, backing out of the driveway.

"Because you were sleeping on the couch?"

"Because I was sleeping on the couch in New Orleans." Bryce gunned the engine and headed south.

"Why would that give you déjà vu?"

"Not long after I graduated from the FBI academy, I came to New Orleans for a six-week training program. I had a stipend to pay for my lodgings, but a friend let me crash at her apartment so I could pocket the money. I was newly married and we needed the cash."

Livia watched the passing homes as they continued to weave their way through the quiet neighborhood.

"Are we going to your friend's apartment?"

Shaking her head, Bryce turned onto a main road that was still packed with rush-hour traffic.

"When I remembered staying in New Orleans, I also remembered driving to the FBI offices. The route took me right past Lake Oaks Park."

Livia looked confused, as if her brain was still sluggish from the wine. Then her eyes abruptly widened.

"The park where my mother was supposed to have her mysterious meeting."

"Exactly. I knew there was a reason it was so familiar when we went there."

Livia took a moment, as if considering what Bryce had just told her. "Maybe I need more coffee, but I'm still confused. Are we going to the park?"

"Yes, but I'm not done telling you what else I remembered."

"Okay. What else?"

"During my training, the special agent in charge of the local office would stop by to chat with us. His name was Jonathon Rice."

"I still don't . . . wait." Livia sucked in an audible gasp, her hand pressing against her heart, as if it was racing. "Rice? Oh my God. That was the name on my mom's note. You think she was meeting at the park with the FBI?"

On cue, the Lake Oaks Park came into view and Bryce veered onto the exit to pull into the empty parking lot.

"The field office is just down the road." She pointed along the lakeshore. "It's not fancy, but it's close enough to the main road to be easily visible when you go there. This would be a perfect meeting place if your mom didn't want to be seen going into a building owned by the feds."

Livia slowly nodded. "That makes sense, but why would she need the FBI?"

"I don't know, but I took a chance and called Special Agent Rice before I woke you up. He agreed to meet us this morning at his house."

Livia bit her bottom lip, looking torn between hope and resignation that they were falling down another rabbit hole.

"It's kind of a stretch."

"Only one way to find out."

Punching in the address she'd gotten from Jonathon Rice, Bryce followed the GPS directions to the outskirts of New Orleans.

It was a quiet neighborhood with small, farm-style homes arranged in neat rows. They were unique enough to give them character, but each was painted white with green shutters and black doors. Was there some sort of homeowners association that required the color combination? She was guessing yes when she noticed the recently mowed lawns and precisely trimmed hedges.

She smiled as she pulled into the driveway of the corner house. It made sense that a lawman would choose a neighborhood with rigid rules and regulations. They were trained to appreciate people who lived by proper procedure.

Double-checking to be sure she was at the right address, Bryce exited the SUV, waiting for Livia to join her before climbing onto the small porch that was covered by a green-and-white awning.

Lifting her hand, she started to rap on the door only to have it pulled open by a tall, lean man with dark skin and gray hair buzzed close to his scalp. Jonathon Rice hadn't changed much over the past few years. He still stood with his back straight and his shoulders squared as if about to march into battle, and his features were still remarkably smooth despite the fact that he must be in his sixties.

"Special Agent Swift," he murmured, his dark gaze sweeping toward Livia as if surprised she wasn't alone.

"It's Deputy Swift now, but please call me Bryce," she said.

He nodded. "And I'm Jonathon." Stepping back, he waved them into the long, narrow living room that was sparsely furnished with a nondescript couch and two matching armchairs. It would have been depressingly boring if it wasn't for the bookshelf that stretched to the ceiling with leather-bound books and the large window overlooking the front yard. "I'm surprised you left the agency, Bryce," Jonathon said with a blunt honesty. "I watched your training and marked you as someone who was going to make her way to the top of the FBI."

Bryce felt the familiar pang of loss flare through her. Her future with the FBI had ended the day Benjamin had been shot.

"It's a long story." She nodded toward her companion, eager to change the subject. "This is my friend. Livia Benoit."

The older man arched a brow. "Benoit?"

Bryce nodded. "Henri Benoit's granddaughter."

"I see." His expression revealed he didn't understand at all, but he was willing to be polite. "Please, have a seat."

Bryce and Livia moved to perch on the couch. "Thank you for seeing me on such short notice," Bryce said.

Jonathon shrugged. "I retired a couple of years ago. Shortly after my wife passed. I have nothing but time on my hands now. Can I get you something to drink? Coffee? Tea?"

"Nothing for me, thank you," Bryce declined as Livia shook her head.

Jonathon moved to settle in the nearest armchair, leaning forward as he studied Bryce with an intense curiosity.

"I assume this has something to do with a case you're working on?"

"It does, but it's not official so if you don't feel comfortable answering my questions I'll completely understand," she told him.

His brows inched higher. "Ask them and I'll decide if I'm comfortable."

Bryce didn't try to beat around the bush. Ever since Livia had revealed she'd been attacked by some unknown stalker, there'd been a new urgency in discovering the truth of who had hired Larry Sutton to spy on her friend and why.

"Did you ever meet with or investigate anyone from the Benoit family during your time at the FBI?" she demanded.

A sudden comprehension spread across Jonathon's face. As if the reason for her presence was suddenly explained.

Hope bloomed in the center of Bryce's heart. Maybe this wasn't a wild-goose chase after all.

A second later, her hopes were dashed as Jonathon gave an emphatic shake of his head. "No."

Bryce exchanged a disappointed glance with Livia before turning back to the retired FBI agent.

"Then I apologize. I'm afraid I wasted your time."

"Wait," Jonathon insisted as Bryce started to rise to her feet. "I said I didn't *meet* with anyone from the Benoit family. But I did speak with one."

Bryce instantly forgot her disappointment. This was what she was hoping to hear. "Who?"

"Giselle Benoit." He confirmed her suspicion. "She contacted me . . . hmm, it must be twenty-seven or maybe twenty-eight years ago."

"What did she want?" Bryce asked.

"She requested a meeting. We set the time, but she never showed up. A couple days later, I heard that she'd committed suicide." His gaze shifted toward the silent Livia. "I assume she was a relative of yours?"

"My mother."

"I'm sorry."

Bryce didn't give her friend time to respond. She'd easily fallen back into her interrogator mode, questioning a potential witness.

"Were you supposed to meet at Lake Oaks Park?"

He took a minute to consider the question. "Like I said, it was a long time ago, but that sounds right. It was a convenient location for people who wanted to meet in an informal setting. Or the people who didn't want anyone to know they were talking to an FBI agent."

"She called the office?"

"Yes, she said that she had vital information to pass along."

"Did she say what that information was?"

Without warning, Jonathon rose to his feet. "Wait here a minute. I'll get the file."

Bryce studied him in surprise. "You have the file here?"

"It was never an official report."

"So why keep it?"

"I kept it because I thought it might be important after I

heard Ms. Benoit had died." He shrugged. "But when there was no investigation I packed it away and forgot all about it."

"You kept it here, not at your office?" Bryce pressed.

A slow smile curled his lips. As if he approved of her question. "Very good, Bryce. At that time, the Benoits had the sort of power to make investigations disappear." He shot Livia a quick glance before heading toward the arched opening that led into a narrow hallway. "Excuse me."

There was a tense silence as Bryce and Livia waited for the man's return. Neither wanted to be the one to suggest their luck might finally have turned. Everyone knew that was a jinx.

Within minutes, Jonathon was back holding a thin manilla folder. He waved it in the air as he resumed his seat.

"This is it. As you can see, it's not much."

Bryce resisted the urge to reach out and snatch the folder from his hand. She sensed that Jonathon was pleased to have the opportunity to be included in the investigation. She wasn't going to take that away from him.

"Any information would be greatly appreciated," she assured him.

Flipping open the folder, Jonathon pulled out a sheet of paper. Bryce blinked. He hadn't lied when he said he didn't have much intel.

"I jotted down a few notes during our phone conversation," he explained. "Back then I was a young field agent so it didn't occur to me to pass the call up to someone with more authority once she said the name Giselle Benoit."

"I'm relieved you didn't." Bryce didn't doubt that any file mentioning the Benoits would have been conveniently lost over the years. It was unfortunate, but justice would always be for sale when it came with enough money and power. "What did she say?"

"She told me that she'd witnessed a crime at the Willows."

Bryce stiffened. "Wait. She used that word—'crime'?—not something illegal?"

"Crime." He turned the page so she could see the neatly written note. "I underlined the word."

"Interesting." Bryce tried not to read too much into Giselle's claim. A crime could be anything from littering to murder. Still, it did make it sound as if it was a particular act that had prompted her to call the FBI, not an ongoing series of events.

Jonathon turned the paper back to read the rest of his notes. "I suggested that she call her local law enforcement and speak with them, but she insisted that they were too afraid of her father to investigate." The older man paused, sending Livia a tight smile. "If I'm being honest, I thought she was being overly dramatic. She sounded upset on the phone and I assumed she was a rich, spoiled girl who was mad at her parents and wanted to punish them. I regret that now."

Livia's face was pale, her hands clenched in her lap. It was obvious she was struggling to control her emotions.

"But you agreed to a meeting?" Bryce asked, diverting the attention back to herself.

"Yes. She said she would keep calling until she found someone who would believe her, so I finally suggested we meet at the park. That way I didn't look foolish if it turned out to be nothing more than a childish tantrum, and she didn't have to worry about anyone in her family finding out she'd called us."

"But she never showed up?"

"Correct."

There was a pause, as if Jonathon was done with the conversation. With a low hiss of frustration, Livia abruptly surged to her feet, glaring at the older man.

"That's it?" she rasped. "That's all she said?"

Jonathon lifted his head, his dark gaze taking in the tension vibrating through Livia's body before returning to study her flushed face. At last he gave a slow nod, as if coming to some sort of decision of whether or not to reveal what was on the paper.

"There was one more thing," he admitted. "I have quotes around it, so I must have thought it was odd."

"Tell me," Livia demanded.

"Your mother said that the Benoits couldn't hide their sins in the swamps. Not anymore. This time they were going to pay."

CHAPTER 21

New Orleans, LA
Monday, July 7th

Livia was distantly aware of Bryce taking charge of the pleasantries as she thanked Special Agent Jonathon Rice for sharing his information and requesting that he contact her if he remembered anything else. She even realized that her friend had grabbed her upper arm to steer her out of the house and into the SUV parked in the driveway.

But she was lost in the fog that had wrapped around her brain the moment the FBI agent revealed that her mother had called him to report a crime. What had happened that prompted Giselle Benoit to go to such an extreme measure? And how far had someone gone to keep her from revealing what she knew?

"It can't be a coincidence," she abruptly blurted out, shaken out of her daze as they drove past the park where her mother was supposed to meet Agent Rice.

How different would her life have been if Giselle had managed to live long enough to keep her appointment? Would her mother still be here? Would she have exposed the Benoit family and raised Livia with all the love that had been denied her?

"What can't be a coincidence?" Bryce broke into Livia's bout of self-pity.

Livia turned her head to study her friend's grim profile. "The fact that my mom contacted the FBI to report a crime and two days later she's found dead."

Bryce hesitated. "I don't want to leap to conclusions, but I agree the timing is suspect," she at last admitted.

"Why couldn't she have just told Agent Rice what happened when she called him?"

"It would have solved a lot of problems." Bryce shrugged. "But she was probably at the Willows. It's possible that she was afraid someone might be eavesdropping on her calls. Back then, not everyone had cell phones. And even if they did, the service in such a remote area would have been sketchy at best."

Livia nodded. Even now the cell service at the Willows was unpredictable. "True."

"And maybe she wanted to meet with the FBI agent before she revealed her information to decide whether or not she could trust him."

A chill crawled over Livia, as if her mother were reaching out from the grave. Livia shivered. It felt like a warning.

"It must have been so awful for her," Livia breathed. "She not only had to choose between loyalty to her family and her conscience, but she couldn't know who would help her and who might betray her."

"Yeah, it must have been tough," Bryce agreed.

With an effort, Livia battled back the looming sense of dread. They had a few clues. She intended to follow them regardless of the danger.

"You asked if she specifically said the word 'crime.' Why?"

They turned onto the road that would lead them back to Livia's house. "In my experience, people say 'crime' when they've just experienced or witnessed a violent event. Like a mugging, or a hit and run or a robbery," Bryce explained, slowing the SUV as they turned onto a narrow street. "But if they're reporting a teller skimming money out of the till, or a fake charity taking advantage of the elderly, they're more likely to say that someone is doing something illegal."

Livia slowly nodded. It did make sense. "So my mom witnessed a crime and decided to contact the FBI," she said, speaking her thoughts out loud. "It had to have been serious."

"Agreed. That's not something you do on a whim."

"Unfortunately, it doesn't help us figure out what happened or who was responsible for the crime."

"It does take Winston and Celeste off the list."

Livia frowned. "I suppose you're right. Celeste wasn't even born yet. Does that mean I made a mistake about seeing Winston in my house?"

"It's possible."

Frustration seared through Livia. She'd been so certain she'd seen Winston arguing with Larry Sutton in her bedroom. So what other clues had she gotten wrong or just flat out missed? The thought was enough to make her scream.

"One step forward and two steps backward," she muttered. "How are we supposed to uncover a crime that happened almost thirty years ago?"

"I'm not sure," Bryce bluntly admitted, pulling into Livia's driveway. "We don't know which member of your family committed the crime. Or where it happened."

"Wait."

Bryce turned in her seat to study Livia with a curious gaze. "What is it?"

"We do know where it happened."

"We do?"

"My mother told Agent Rice that the Benoits couldn't hide their sins in the swamps. Not anymore."

"Yes." Bryce furrowed her brow. "That has to mean something. But what do you hide in the swamps? Some sort of evidence?"

"A body?" Livia suggested. "Toxic waste?"

"They did close off the road leading into the bayous behind the house," Bryce said. "The townsfolk were furious, but according to Finn's dad the mayor allowed the Benoits to do whatever they wanted."

"There's something back there," Livia said with a sudden surge of certainty. It didn't matter that a second ago she'd been regretting leaping to the conclusion that it had been Winston in her house. This time she was sure her instincts were right. "Something they don't want found." She sucked in a sharp breath, hit by a sudden suspicion. "And Stella Gates knew about it."

Bryce tapped her fingers on the steering wheel as she considered the pros and cons of Livia's words.

"A good theory, but how is Larry Sutton involved?" Bryce demanded. "And why did he go to so much trouble to worm his way into your life?"

Livia heaved a harsh sigh. She didn't have an answer to the perfectly logical questions. She'd been a baby when her mother died.

"It's annoying that we can't track Sutton down."

"Beyond frustrating." Bryce smacked her palm against the steering wheel. Then her jaw tightened and she was abruptly backing out of the driveway and heading south. "We need to talk to his friend again."

Livia settled back in her seat, not complaining at being back on the road. The last thing she wanted was to sit around her house stewing on what had happened to her mother. As long as she was moving she felt as if she was doing something.

"What friend?" she asked.

"Gator Bob."

It took a second for Livia to recall who Bryce meant. "Oh, the guy who owns the bar in La Harpe?"

"Yup."

Livia was confused. "You think he knows where Larry might be hiding?"

"It's a long shot, but I'm hoping that he has a few more suggestions. Or if we're lucky, he might have heard from Larry in the last day or so."

"Why not?" Livia agreed. "It's not like we have a dozen other clues to follow."

"First we'll swing past Sutton's office to make sure he isn't back at work."

The zigzagged their way through the suburbs to park in front of the house that had been converted into a private investigator office. Leaving the SUV, they climbed onto the porch and knocked on the door. There was no answer and Livia moved to the front window to peer inside. It was dark enough to reveal the flashing red light on the landline. No one had bothered to listen to the messages.

"I don't think he's here," she said.

"On to Gator Bob's," Bryce announced, turning to head back to the SUV.

Livia hurried to join her, barely getting her seat belt buckled before they were zooming down the street.

Waiting until Bryce had navigated through the thick traffic to reach the edge of town, Livia at last broke the silence.

"Do you think the bar will be open this early? It's not even eleven yet."

Bryce shrugged. "If not we'll have something to eat at the local diner and wait for him to show up."

"Sounds like a plan." On cue, Livia's stomach rumbled in anticipation. When Bryce had woken her up, she'd still been recovering from a night of too much wine and junk food. Coffee had been more than enough to satisfy her. Now her body was demanding genuine substance. "I'm starving."

"Yeah, that pizza is long gone."

Bryce pressed her foot on the accelerator to send them racing down the highway. The traffic had thinned to a mere trickle as they headed deeper into bayou country, giving them an open lane to race past the empty wetlands. It wasn't until they neared the turnoff to La Harpe that Bryce abruptly swung her SUV onto the shoulder and slammed on the brakes.

"What's wrong?" Livia glanced toward the barren landscape. "Did you see something?"

"That sign." Bryce pointed through the front windshield toward the faded billboard directly ahead of them.

Livia leaned forward, reading out loud. "'Cypress Cove Landing. RV and Tent Campground. Hunting and fishing available in season. Next exit.'" She glanced back at her friend. "I don't understand. What about it?"

"I've seen it before."

"The campground?"

"No, the sign." Bryce reached into her purse to pull out her phone, impatiently scrolling through her pictures. "This was in Larry Sutton's apartment."

Livia leaned to the side as Bryce turned her phone to show the image on the screen. It was Larry Sutton standing in front of a cabin holding a fish. Just over his shoulder was a sign that matched the billboard, although on a much smaller scale. She had a vague memory of seeing the framed photograph when they'd searched the loft above Sutton's office.

"Okay. He visited the campground and caught—"

"No," Bryce interrupted, using her fingers to zoom in on the sign. "See? The sign behind him shows that the campground is another ten miles down the road. Sutton is standing in front of his own cabin."

Livia wasn't ready to make the leap. The official campground might be ten miles away, but that didn't mean they didn't have cabins spread around the area.

"Why do you think he owns it?"

Bryce settled back in her seat, leaving her phone in Livia's hand. "When I was asking Bob about Larry Sutton, he mentioned that Sutton and his wife lived in this area. That's why he was so familiar with his bar. It wasn't until his wife was shot and killed that he decided to move to New Orleans. He never said that Larry sold his first house. I just assumed he had." Bryce clicked her tongue, as if annoyed with herself. "A rookie mistake. You know the old saying about assuming."

"But what about the hotels he said that Larry used as hideaways? Why would he use them if he had a cabin?"

"Red herrings. Sutton probably pretended to stay at them to fool his target. Just like he did when he was dating you. Didn't you tell me that he had you pick him up, but when you went back there was someone else in the room?"

"Yes." Livia hissed out the word between clenched teeth, the same anger she'd felt when she'd realized she'd been catfished racing through her. "The jerk."

"I doubt he ever stayed in any of the hotels he mentioned to his friend," Bryce continued. "Instead, he bounced from girlfriend to girlfriend, occasionally sleeping at his office and keeping his cabin a complete secret. That way he would always have a safe place to disappear when things got too messy."

"That makes sense."

"It's worth checking out."

Livia sent her companion a confused glance. "We don't have the address."

"We know it's ten miles from that campground." Bryce nodded toward the billboard and then toward the exit. "If the cabin is on this road we should be able to spot it. Keep an eye open as I drive."

"Okay." Holding the phone so she could use the picture of Sutton to match against any cabins they passed, Livia turned in her seat to stare out the passenger window.

Bryce put the SUV in gear and they slowly pulled off the

highway and rolled down a narrow road that wound its way through the thick, mossy ground and stunted trees. Over the past hour, low clouds had rolled in from the gulf, obscuring the sun and giving the impression they were wrapped in a dull gray.

Like a shroud . . .

The thought sent a chill down Livia's spine, and once again she was certain there was a soft voice of warning whispering in the back of her mind. Could it be her mother? Or just a figment of her imagination?

Determined not to give in to a creeping sense of anxiety, Livia gritted her teeth and kept her gaze locked on the passing scenery. The wetlands were a flat expanse that seemed to go on forever. It should have made it easy to spot any buildings from miles away. Unfortunately, there were large tangles of overgrown vegetation along with dozens of road signs that blocked the view.

They crawled along at a snail's pace, the road angling upward as they reached solid ground that swelled between narrow channels of water. The cypress trees thickened along the edge of the road, making it even more difficult to see the occasional cabin that dotted the patches of dry land.

"Wait," Livia breathed, holding up the phone as she caught sight of a roof through the branches. "That looks like the frame of the cabin."

Bryce swerved onto the shoulder and put the SUV into park. Then, unsnapping her seat belt, she bent down to pull her service gun from the locked container under her seat. Making sure the safety was on, she pushed open her door.

"Stay here."

"No, Bryce." Ignoring her friend's glare, Livia climbed out of the vehicle and folded her arms over chest. "I'll stay behind you, but we're in this together."

Bryce looked like she wanted to toss her back into the SUV, but with a glance around their isolated surroundings, she gave a sharp nod. No doubt she was weighing whether Livia would be in as much danger alone on the deserted road as trailing along with her.

"Fine." Bryce pointed a warning finger at Livia. "But if he's here, let me do the talking."

Keeping her weapon in her hand, Bryce ignored the narrow path that circled past the vegetation, instead battling her way through the overgrown bushes to approach the cabin from the side.

They halted in the lacy canopy of a weeping willow, studying the weathered structure that looked like it'd been abandoned for years. The sideboards had long ago lost any paint and the windows were covered by layers of dirt. Even the tin roof had rusted until it looked on the verge of collapse.

Still, there were signs that the place wasn't as deserted as someone wanted a casual passerby to believe. The windows were dirty, but more than one had been replaced and there was a pile of firewood that had been recently chopped. Plus there were tire tracks pressed into the grass, as if someone had driven up in a heavy vehicle and parked in front of the narrow porch.

Clearly noticing the tire tracks at the same time as Livia, Bryce stepped to the side to peer toward the back of the cabin.

"I don't see a car here, but there's a shed behind the house. It could be hidden in there." She sent Livia a stern frown. "I'm going to knock on the door. You stay behind me."

Livia nodded, following on Bryce's heel as she crossed the spongy ground and climbed the one step onto the porch. The wooden planks sagged beneath their combined weight, but thankfully they didn't splinter. Bryce rapped on the screen door.

Livia's mouth was weirdly dry as they waited for any sound of approaching footsteps. There was nothing. Not unless you counted the sound of buzzing insects. The eternal song of the bayous.

With a frown, Bryce pulled open the screen door and rapped

on the wooden one behind it. Surprisingly, it slid open, as if someone hadn't managed to get it firmly latched. A bad feeling washed over Livia. Had a malignant spirit had been released from the cabin to slither past them?

She sensed Bryce's shiver, as if she'd experienced the same sensation of evil, but with a grim expression she stepped through the opening.

"Hello?" Bryce called out. "I'm looking for Larry Sutton. I'm Deputy Swift." She paused, her words echoing through the empty space. "If anyone is here, show yourself."

Livia entered the cabin behind Bryce, careful to give the woman plenty of space in case she needed to back out of there in a hurry. A quick glance was enough to warn her that they weren't the first person to come looking for Larry Sutton. The small living room was littered with papers and books that had been pulled out of the desk in a corner and off the narrow bookcase. Even the cushions had been jerked off the couch and slashed, as if someone was searching for something hidden inside.

"The place has been trashed," she muttered, her gaze moving to the door leading to the kitchen. That room appeared to have received the same treatment. There were broken plates and pans scattered across a linoleum floor and cabinet doors left hanging open. "Do you think Larry still owns it?"

"Looks like it." Bryce pointed toward the framed photo that was hanging cattywampus on the paneled wall. Even at a distance Livia could see a young Larry Sutton standing next to a pretty blond-haired woman in a simple wedding gown. "That must be his wife, who was killed."

Livia grimaced. A lingering violence hung in the air. As if the fury sizzling from the intruder had stayed long after they'd disappeared.

"I guess someone came looking for Larry and they weren't happy when they couldn't find him."

"Or they were looking for something," Bryce suggested,

crossing to peek into the kitchen before moving to the second opening that proved to be a bedroom and attached bathroom.

"Maybe Larry found an incriminating piece of evidence against the Benoits and someone wanted it back," Livia suggested.

"That's a logical guess," Bryce agreed, wandering toward the desk as her gaze kept watch on the open door to make sure no one was trying to sneak up on them. "He seems the sort of guy who would get hired to find something, then once he had his hands on the prize, he would turn around and blackmail his client to get it."

Livia watched her friend tiptoe over the papers that were tossed on the floor, trying to imagine what the private investigator might have been told to find, and why whoever trashed this cabin would be so anxious to get their hands on it.

Was it the information her mother had been intending to hand over to the FBI? And if so, why wait almost thirty years to go looking for it? It's not like anything had changed . . .

Wait. Livia sucked in a sharp breath. Something *had* changed. Stella Gates had died.

"What if he got it from Stella Gates?" Livia's heart skipped a beat, a surge of excitement racing through her. For the first time since she'd discovered that Jacob Pearson was a fraud, she was convinced she'd just grasped a sliver of the truth. "She shared rooms with me and my mother at the Willows. Who else would have been so close to Giselle just before she died?"

Bryce sent her a puzzled glance. "You think your nanny was responsible for her dying?"

Livia shook her head, struggling to arrange her chaotic thoughts. "No, I think Stella would have known why my mother was going to the FBI. And after she died, Stella might have taken the evidence and hidden it somewhere the Benoits couldn't find so she could get money from them. Then once they realized Stella had died, they panicked and hired Larry Sutton to find it."

Bryce slowly nodded. "I see where you're going with this, but I thought Larry Sutton was run off by the nosy neighbor?"

"He was, but that doesn't mean he couldn't have come back later that night."

"And then he decided to blackmail your family?"

"It's possible. It could explain why he went into hiding." Livia glanced toward the shredded cushions. "Obviously someone is willing to go to a lot of effort to get their hands on whatever he has."

"But why pull you into his dangerous game?"

Livia's certainty faltered at the blunt question. It was the missing factor. The one thing that didn't fit her theory.

She heaved a harsh sigh. "I don't have a clue."

"We should get out of here," Bryce abruptly announced, heading for the door. "If Sutton happens to show up, he'll be in his rights to shoot us."

Livia didn't protest. She wanted out of the cabin, with its messy clutter and air of desperation. As they stepped off the porch, however, she reached out to touch Bryce's shoulder.

"Wait. Shouldn't we check out the shed? Just to see if there's anything inside it?"

Bryce hesitated, visibly torn between the urge to get Livia away from potential danger and the knowledge that they needed to search for any clue that might reveal why someone had torn the cabin upside down.

"A quick peek and then we're out of here." Bryce glanced toward the leaden sky that threatened rain at any moment. "This place is giving me the heebie-jeebies."

"Me too. It's creepy as hell."

With steps that were close to a jog, they circled the cabin and moved toward the shed that was in even worse condition. The entire structure tilted to the side, as if stubborn perseverance was the only thing keeping it from collapsing.

Bryce headed toward the sliding barn doors at the front of

the shed, shaking her head to indicate they were locked. Livia walked to the side to peer through the tiny window. The panes were dirty and the inside was shadowed, but she was able to make out a vague shape.

"It's too dark to see much, but I think there's a car inside," she announced, pulling out her phone and turning on the flashlight. Then, shining the light through the window, she pressed her nose against the filthy pane. "Wait. That looks like the car Larry was driving when he was pretending to be Jacob," she breathed, swiveling the light to sweep over the familiar vehicle, stiffening as she caught sight of the shadowed lump on the ground. "And there's something on the floor next to the door."

"Shit." Bryce was leaping into action even as Livia tried to make out what she was seeing. It wasn't until she heard the splintering of rotting wood that she realized her friend had kicked open the doors. Light spilled into the space, revealing the form was a man lying on his side.

With a gasp, Livia rushed to the front of the shed, her heart thundering so loud she could barely hear Bryce's sharp command.

"Stay back, Livia. That's an order."

Skidding to a halt, Livia watched in horror as Bryce carefully rolled Larry Sutton onto his back, his face covered in dried blood as he stared sightlessly at Bryce, who leaned over him, her hand pressed against his neck.

"Is he. . . ?" The question lodged in her throat. The smell alone told her that there was no need to ask if he was dead.

Bryce straightened, her face grim. "Call nine-one-one."

CHAPTER 22

New Orleans, LA
Tuesday, July 8th

It was after midnight before Bryce and Livia were released by the police. They'd been grilled for hours, but each of them had stubbornly stuck to their story that they'd rehearsed, waiting for the cops to arrive at the cabin.

They had claimed that Livia requested that Bryce locate her boyfriend, Jacob Pearson, who'd gone missing. Livia insisted that she didn't want to cause any trouble and that she'd just wanted to make sure he was okay. Bryce explained that she'd managed to discover that Jacob was, in fact, Larry Sutton and they'd gone to the cabin to ask why he'd lied. The last thing they'd expected was to find him dead.

None of it was a lie, it just wasn't the full truth.

Thankfully, the fact that Larry Sutton had obviously been dead for days, combined with Bryce's position as a law officer, not to mention the fact that the private investigator was a notorious liar and cheat, had meant that they'd eventually been released with the promise they would return if there were any more questions.

Now they sat in the SUV, staring at the dark, nearly empty parking lot as they recovered from the grueling day.

Bryce knew that Livia must be in a lingering state of shock. Not only had her friend spent the past week being tormented by a mysterious stalker, now she'd stumbled across the dead body of the man who'd seduced and then catfished her.

It had to be messing with her mind.

And if Bryce was being honest, she had to admit she was equally rattled by the gruesome find. It wasn't the first dead body that she'd been around, but it was the first one that had been so far into decomposition. Far enough that she hadn't been able to determine how he'd died, although she suspected a gunshot wound to the back of his head.

Giving her friend the time and space to process her complicated emotions, Bryce was caught off guard when Livia abruptly reached out to grasp her hand.

"I'm sorry."

Bryce blinked in confusion. "Sorry for what?"

"That I dragged you into this mess." Livia made a sound of disgust. "Look at us: hungry, covered in dust, and sitting in the parking lot of the New Orleans Police Department after being interrogated for hours about finding my ex's dead body. You should be out enjoying your evening."

Bryce shrugged. "This sort of mess is my daily job," she assured her friend. "And I'm glad you did get me involved."

"But—"

"I was thinking while we were stuck waiting between interviews," Bryce interrupted, not wanting her friend to wallow in guilt. The danger she was in had increased dramatically. After all, being worried that the Benoits were hiding a secret was one thing, finding dead bodies was another level. "What if Larry Sutton was in your house to hide whatever he found?"

As she'd hoped, Livia was instantly distracted. "Why would he hide it at my house?"

"It's the last place your family would look," she pointed out. "And maybe he wanted you to have it if something happened to him."

"If he did, he hid it too well for me to find," Livia said, making clear the obvious. "I searched my place from top to bottom after you suggested he might be spying on me. There's nothing there."

Bryce sighed. It'd been nothing more than a fleeting thought. "I suppose it wouldn't explain why he went to the effort of dating you. He could have broken into your house and left the item without anyone knowing he'd been there." She shook her head in frustration. "Okay, we leave out why Larry Sutton involved you. It still seems likely that he went to Stella's house to find something."

Livia turned in her seat, her face bathed in the glow of the nearby streetlight. She looked pale and weary, but her expression was one of grim determination as she shoved aside her guilt and returned her attention to sorting through what they knew.

"We just can't be sure if he got it or not," she pointed out.

"His death indicates that he did. Why else kill him?" Bryce paused as she considered what they'd seen at the cabin. There was every appearance that the place had been ransacked. As if someone was searching for something. Or angry that Sutton failed to have what they wanted. But they didn't have any actual evidence. And she couldn't allow herself to simply assume they knew what had happened. It might have been done deliberately to throw them off the track.

"You thought of something?" Livia demanded as the silence stretched.

"It's possible that one of your family found what they were searching for without his help."

Livia furrowed her brow. "Then why kill him?"

"To keep his mouth shut. He was the one person who knew why Stella was blackmailing them. With Stella buried and

Larry rotting in his shed, they no longer had to worry about their secret being revealed."

"True."

Bryce heaved a sigh. She was tired and it was an effort to think clearly. She was starting to grasp at straws.

"But once again, that doesn't explain why Sutton contacted you. Or why you've been threatened since your arrival at the Willows."

"Wait." Livia abruptly tensed, her eyes widening. "I think I know."

"Really? Tell me."

"When I went to Stella's house, it was empty."

"Okay."

"Who took her stuff? Flora told me that Stella didn't have any family. And since the house technically belongs to the Benoits, it had to be one of them who packed up Stella's things and moved them out before the house went on the market."

Bryce nodded. Unless the house reverted to the bank, the owner would be responsible for emptying out the contents.

"Moved them where? To a storage locker?"

"If I was trying to get rid of her stuff, I would contact the local charities to donate the larger household stuff. I'm sure most of them would come and pick up the furniture and dishes. But the personal items would have to be packed up by Adrian or someone in the family and taken to the Willows. Especially if they wanted to ensure there was nothing incriminating in her stuff that might end up in the hands of some stranger."

"Why the Willows? Why not the dump?"

"Where else could they know for certain it would stay hidden?" Livia insisted, leaning forward as if a sudden surge of adrenaline had seared away her weariness. "And why else has at least one of them been trying to frighten me away from the estate?"

"That's what you think they were doing?"

"It makes more sense than someone trying to kill me and choosing such ridiculous ways to do it," Livia said. "I mean, come on. Locking me in an apartment above the garage with a window, not to mention being close enough to the main house to yell for help. And then pushing me on top of a tarp? It was creepy, but not lethal."

"Okay." Bryce nodded in agreement. If someone wanted Livia dead, they wouldn't have given her so many warnings. Not unless they were playing with her before the kill, a warning voice whispered in the back of her mind. "The theory still leaves questions, but I agree it needs to be checked out. Where would they hide her personal belongings?"

Livia considered the question. "Not in the main house," she finally decided. "At least not while they're inviting members of the press into the house on a daily basis for Celeste's engagement. There's too great a risk that some inquisitive reporter might poke their nose where it doesn't belong."

"The garage?"

Livia shook her head. "I would have seen boxes or totes when I was out there. The stuff has to be in the swamp." Livia sent Bryce a smile edged with bitterness. "After all, my mother warned the FBI agent that it's a family tradition to hide our sins out there, right?"

It was another wild guess, but Bryce couldn't deny that Livia made a good point. Not only were the bayous vast enough to hide thousands of sins, but the Benoits had gone to a lot of effort to keep people away. Everyone assumed it was because they snobbishly wanted to keep out the riffraff. What if they blocked the road because they had something to hide?

"That would be unfortunate," Bryce said. "Things—along with people—have a habit of disappearing in the bayous."

"Not if we get there quick enough." Livia abruptly swiveled in her seat, reaching to pull on her seat belt. "Whatever they might have hidden in the past is probably gone, but Stella's house has only been on the market a few weeks. It wouldn't have time to disappear."

Bryce switched on the engine. It was late, but she felt the same urgency as Livia. Once word got out that Larry Sutton's body had been found, whoever killed him might not wait for the swamp to do its thing. They would want to destroy any evidence ASAP. "I'll drop you off at your house and go look for it."

"No." Livia reached out to grab Bryce's arm. "*We'll* go look for it."

"Dammit, Livia—"

"I'm safer with you than on my own," Livia interrupted. "Especially now that word will be spreading that I found Larry Sutton's body. If they were willing to kill him, they would certainly be willing to kill me. Especially if they were afraid I could expose them." She held up her hand as Bryce's lips parted to continue her argument. "Besides, you'll need my help to find the stuff."

Bryce scowled, but she put the SUV in gear and drove out of the parking lot. Livia's words echoed her own worries. Could she really leave her friend alone in New Orleans? No. Absolutely not. Not when there was a crazed killer on the loose. And she couldn't take her to the Willows. At least not to the house where her family was waiting.

The only alternative was to go together to search the bayou.

"Fine," Bryce conceded defeat, turning onto the road leading out of town. "But this is still just a theory. I don't want you to get your hopes up when we don't know if anything is there."

Livia settled back in her seat, her expression grim. "Something is out there. I should have suspected it a long time ago."

"Suspected what?"

"When I was a child, the bayous were off-limits."

"That's not really a surprise. They were off-limits to most kids in the area." Bryce's father had spent hours going over the various dangers to be found in the wetlands surrounding Rushville when they'd first moved there. "All of us were warned to stay away from them."

"Yeah, and that's why I didn't really think about it at the time. But beyond the general warnings of snakes and alligators, my uncle had a specific location that was marked off with old oil barrels that he told me never to go near. He said that there was a quagmire in the center of that spot. And that if I got caught in it I would die before anyone could find me."

Bryce tried to remember if she'd ever noticed any oil barrels when she'd been poking around the bayous. Just because her father had warned her to stay away, didn't mean that she'd listened. Her rabid curiosity was always getting her in trouble. It was also one of the reasons she'd gone into law enforcement.

She had to dig out every secret and get to the bottom of every mystery.

"I assume you never went there?" she asked her friend.

"No way. The mere thought of being sucked into a muddy grave gave me nightmares." Livia sent her a small frown as if sensing that Bryce was going to suggest that she wait in the vehicle while Bryce went in search of any hidden evidence. "But I know the exact spot. Which is why you need me along. I can lead you straight to it."

Bryce clicked her tongue as she veered onto the highway. "It's no wonder you've been so successful selling real estate. You can talk people into doing anything. No matter how crazy."

"I wish that was true. I'd be a rich woman."

Bryce pressed the cruise control as they sped down the empty road. She'd known Livia for years, but she never really thought about her as one of the Benoits. Not like Adrian or the snooty Celeste.

"Do you ever regret not being the one to inherit the family business?" she asked, genuinely curious. "I mean, everyone in my family is dirt poor. I can't imagine having rich relatives constantly shoving their wealth in my face."

"Not until recently," Livia said, a hint of frustration in her tone. "I have zero doubt that my uncle has managed to destroy what my ancestors created. I don't care what happens to the Benoits, but there are a lot of employees who depend on us to give them a paycheck." She shook her head. "I certainly couldn't have done any worse in protecting their futures."

"Have you considered the fact that you might have a shot at running the company once the truth is revealed?" Bryce demanded. "Whatever that truth might be?"

Livia snorted. "My uncle would never give up control."

"He might not have a choice."

Livia sent her a shocked glance, as if she hadn't even considered what would happen if Adrian was connected to Larry Sutton's death. Then she shook away the suggestion with palpable revulsion.

"Even if you're right, everything would go to Celeste, thank God."

"You wouldn't fight her?"

"No."

Bryce arched her brows. She'd never liked spending time at the Willows, but there was no denying it was a beautiful estate that had to be worth a couple million dollars. Maybe more. Would Livia really give up such a lavish property so easily?

"It's a lot to walk away from," she pointed out.

Livia shuddered. "I would rather watch it burn to the ground than own it. I think it's cursed."

Bryce returned her attention to the dark highway, suddenly reminded of Finn's words when he spoke about the mansion.

"You're not the only one," she murmured. "There are people in Rushville who believe the land belongs to the original tribes who lived in the bayou and that it was stolen by the Benoits."

Bryce could feel Livia studying her with an unwavering intensity. "Do those people include the gorgeous Sheriff Finn?"

Bryce felt her cheeks redden and she silently cursed her reaction. She had to stop acting like a teenager with a crush whenever Finn's name was mentioned.

"He did mention that some of the elders spoke of the land eventually purging itself of its taint," she admitted.

"Taint?" Livia sucked in a sharp breath. "That's the word he used?"

"Sorry, I probably shouldn't have repeated that." Bryce regretted her loose tongue. "You know how people talk in a small town."

"No, it's fine. I think they're right. There's some sort of taint or curse hanging over the Willows. And it's only getting worse." Bryce felt her friend shiver. "The ghosts refuse to rest. At some point the darkness has to be exorcised."

Her words whispered through the air, hanging between them like a harbinger of doom. Bryce tightened her fingers on the steering wheel, pressing her foot on the gas pedal. Neither spoke as they reached Rushville and Bryce circled the edge of town to take the road that had once led to the swamps. A few miles down the narrow lane, Bryce reached down to shut off her headlights before she gunned the engine and drove straight through the single chain that was stretched from one fence post to another. There'd never been a proper gate put up since everyone in the area understood that the Benoits would have you thrown in jail if they caught you anywhere near their land.

Bryce made a face as she heard the chain scrape against her bumper, but it quickly snapped, allowing her to hope that it hadn't done more than cosmetic damage. The vehicle technically belonged to the parish. She didn't want the headache of filling out endless forms to get it repaired.

They slowly bumped and rattled their way past the Durand estate before pulling off the road to park behind a large elderberry bush. Off to the left, the soft glow of outdoor lights from the Willows spilled across the road.

"This is as close as I can get without being seen from the

house," Bryce announced, crawling out of the SUV and opening the door to the back seat so she could grab a flashlight and her phone.

Livia quickly joined her, pointing to a narrow gap in the thick vegetation directly in front of them. "The spot we're looking for is toward the center of the bayou. Not far from the old trading post."

"I'm going to send Finn a text, to tell him where we're going," Bryce said, quickly typing in a short message before shoving the phone into her back pocket. "I'm not expecting any trouble, but better safe than sorry."

"Good idea," Livia agreed.

Together they entered the bushes and tangled vines that formed a physical barrier along the edge of the swamp. Bryce cursed as a thorn scratched her cheek, pausing to switch on the heavy-duty flashlight. They were far enough away from the road not to attract attention and she wasn't going to risk falling into one of the canals that spread like spiderwebs through the mossy ground. Not only was the brackish water disgusting, but there were alligators and snakes and a dozen other nasty critters waiting in the shallows.

Livia forged ahead, shoving aside the low tree branches and battling through the undergrowth. She was clearly a woman on a mission and while Bryce sympathized with her impatience, she didn't want her friend stumbling into trouble.

"Careful, Livia," she called out in soft tones. "Your uncle might not have been lying about the quagmire."

Livia didn't look back, but she did slow her pace as the ground grew spongy beneath their feet and the bushes were replaced with tufts of cattails. Even the trees transformed from towering barriers that blocked their path into hollow gray stumps that stuck out from pools of water.

They were reaching the center of the swamp.

"There." Livia abruptly broke the silence, pointing toward

a large lump of darkness just ahead of them. "Do you see that?"

Bryce aimed her flashlight toward the mound. The glow reflected off a smooth surface, revealing it wasn't natural.

"It looks like a tarp," Bryce said, cautiously walking forward. She cursed as she nearly stumbled over a hard object that had sunk into the boggy ground. Presumably it was one of the barrels that Adrian had placed around the supposed quagmire. Over the years it had disintegrated into a pile of rusty metal. Thank God she'd recently had her tetanus booster. Cautiously stepping over the death trap, she swept a beam of light over the black plastic-coated tarp, making sure there were no nasty snakes curled on the top. Then she motioned for Livia to walk to the other side of the mound. "You take that end and we'll pull it off without disrupting what's underneath." She waited for Livia to move into place. "Ready?"

Livia nodded and they both bent down to grab the edge of the plastic cover, gently peeling it back to reveal the contents hidden underneath.

"Yes. We were right," Livia breathed.

Bryce studied the cardboard boxes that were piled in a haphazard heap. As if someone had tossed them out of the back of a vehicle. Leaning forward, she grabbed the top box.

"Clothes in this one." She pushed it aside to open the next box. "Towels. And sheets."

"I've got two boxes of cookbooks over here," Livia muttered. "Who needs so many cookbooks? And what is this?" She pulled something out of the third box, holding it up to reveal a small ceramic statue. "Chicken figurines? There must be a hundred of them."

Bryce pushed aside box after box that were filled with silverware and cooking utensils until she found a smaller box that was stuffed with manilla file folders.

"Here we go."

Squatting down, Bryce pulled out the files and flipped them open, one by one.

There was the sound of squelching footsteps wading through the mud before Livia was crouching beside her.

"What did you find?"

"I'm assuming it came out of Stella's filing cabinet." Bryce skimmed through the stacks of papers. "Taxes. Bills. Bank statements. All of them have Stella Gates's name on them." Bryce reached the end of the files, setting aside the taxes and bank statements. She'd go through those later. It was impossible to know if there was anything sketchy or illegal in them until she could get them to the office. She leaned forward, peering into the bottom of the container. "What's this?"

Reaching in, she grabbed the shoebox and pulled it out. Livia scooted closer as Bryce pushed off the lid.

"What's inside?" she asked.

"Trinkets." Bryce flicked through the keychains and postcards that Stella had collected from her trips to Dollywood and the Grand Ole Opry. Below them was a stack of old pictures. "And these." She handed the photos to Livia, shining the flashlight on them. "Do you recognize anyone?"

Livia shuffled through the first few, shaking her head. Then suddenly she sucked in a sharp breath.

"This is my mom." She tilted the picture so Bryce could see a beautiful young woman with long honey brown hair and piercing blue eyes. She was standing in front of the Willows with a baby cradled in her arms. "That's me she's holding."

Bryce studied the picture. There was nothing to indicate there was anything out of the ordinary. Just the opposite. Giselle was smiling widely, her happiness unmistakable.

She placed the photo on top of the files to keep it dry. She didn't doubt Livia would want to keep it.

"What are the other pictures?"

"More of me," Livia said with a tremor in her voice. As if she was touched by the knowledge that her old nanny had kept so many photos of her. She flicked through the pictures of her as a baby lying on a blanket and crawling through the garden and splashing in the bathtub until she reached the last photo. "This one is different."

Bryce leaned toward Livia, her brows tugging together as she studied the strange man with dark hair who was wearing a uniform and leaning against a gleaming limo.

"A chauffeur?" Bryce shook her head. "Is he a relative of Stella's?"

"No, it's Manny." With an unmistakable surge of excitement, Livia flipped the photo over. As if she was expecting to find something. "Look. Stella wrote on the back."

Bryce read the scribbled words out loud. "'I know what happened.'" She glanced toward Livia. "Do you know what this means?"

"No, but Manny has to be involved with the mystery. There was a picture of him hidden in my mother's private scrapbook."

"He worked for the Benoits?"

"For a couple of years, then he just disappeared. No one seems to know what happened to him."

"We need to track him down." Bryce plucked the picture from Livia's fingers and placed it with the other picture and the files. Then she put the shoebox back into the container and straightened. "For now, I think we've hit a dead end."

"Again," Livia muttered as she pushed herself upright. "I really thought that this time . . ." Livia's words died away as she pointed to a spot a few feet away. "Wait. Is that another tarp?"

Bryce skimmed the light over the low mound. It was covered with a thick moss, but it did stick out of the ground as if there was something buried there.

"Let's look." Bryce cautiously inched her way across the ground that was becoming increasingly saturated. Her feet were soaking wet, the smell of rotting plants and stagnant water thick in the air. She grimaced, refusing to imagine how many bloodsucking insects and slimy reptiles were hidden in the muck. "This one's been here a long time," she said.

"Whatever is under there is big," Livia said, boldly reaching out to grab a handful of the decaying tarp.

She gave it a sharp tug, but the moss and vines kept it firmly lodged in place. Thankfully the material had rotted enough that it split beneath the pressure, ripping in half to reveal a rusty object beneath.

"What is that?" Bryce grabbed another section of the tarp, giving it a sharp tug until it shredded away. Once she had one side exposed, she aimed the flashlight to reveal the dull gleam of black paint. "A car?"

"Oh my God," Livia abruptly muttered. "Not just a car. It's my grandfather's limo. This was his prized possession."

It was hard to visualize the rusty, filthy shell as a fancy limo, but there was no mistaking the sleek lines and once gleaming chrome detailing. "Why would such an expensive vehicle be left to rust in the swamp?"

"I have no idea."

Bryce rounded the vehicle that was half submerged in the mud, continuing to pull away the decaying tarp. As she reached the front, she exposed the hood that was deeply dented, as if someone had smashed it into . . . something. It was hard to say exactly what.

"Maybe this is why," she said, waiting for Livia to join her. "It was obviously in an accident."

"This is the same car that was in the photo hidden in Stella's shoebox," Livia reminded Bryce. "Did Manny damage the car? Is that how he's involved?"

"That's too much of a coincidence for it not to be connected," Bryce agreed, abruptly shoving the files and pictures she'd kept from Stella's belongings and handing them to Livia. Then, pulling out her phone, she took several photos of the abandoned limo.

"This is something the sheriff needs to investigate," she decided, shoving her phone back into her pocket. "If we're on public land, then at the very least the Benoits are polluting the waterways." On the point of turning around to lead Livia out of the swamps, Bryce froze at the rustle of leaves. Something was moving behind them. She swung her flashlight from side to side. "Did you hear that?"

"Hear what?"

Bryce continued to search the darkness, her instincts screaming they were no longer alone. It wasn't just the rustle of leaves. It was the prickling awareness of a predator who was creeping closer.

But even on full alert, Bryce nearly missed the shadowed form weaving through the stunted trees. It was only because the flashlight glinted off the metal weapon the shadowed intruder was holding that she had time to leap to the side, shoving her companion to the ground as the crack of a gunshot echoed through the bayou.

Her ears were still ringing when a white-hot pain seared along the side of her neck. It felt like someone was pressing a branding iron against her skin. She hissed, tasting her blood as it splattered over her face, and she belatedly realized that a bullet had sliced past her throat, deep enough to gouge through the flesh, but hopefully missing her jugular vein.

Pressing her hand against the wound that continued to bleed, Bryce had enough sense to fall at an angle as she heard another shot ringing through the air. She needed to get away from the shooter long enough for her to call Finn for backup. Or maybe she would sneak back to her SUV where she'd left her gun.

The frantic plans were still swirling through her mind when her head smacked against something hard. She'd hit the bumper of the limo that was sticking out of the mud.

Pain ricocheted through her, joining the burning agony still throbbing in her throat. Then, to her horror, she realized that her vision was starting to narrow. She was going to pass out and there wasn't a damned thing she could do to stop it.

Strangely, her last thought wasn't one of fear. Being a law officer meant she'd already prepared herself to face death. It was an aching sadness that poor Josie was going to grow up without knowing how desperately her parents loved her.

CHAPTER 23

The Willows
Tuesday, July 8th

Livia crawled through the thick undergrowth, her muscles trembling and her heart lodged in her throat. She'd lost the files and pictures she'd been holding, but she didn't dare look back as she angled away from the shooter and in the general direction of the Willows.

Every instinct screamed for her to stay and fight. What if she left and something worse happened to Bryce? But while she might be able to draw the attention of the shooter away from her injured friend, she couldn't stop him. Or her. Not without a weapon. If she stayed they would both die.

Her only hope was getting to a phone and calling for help.

Ignoring the layer of slime coating her from head to toe, Livia pushed her way through the thickening vegetation, barely daring to breathe.

Who was out there shooting? Someone from her family? That seemed the most obvious conclusion. Who else had such easy access to the swamp? No. She would be a fool to leap to conclusions, she silently warned herself. It was most likely a family member who tossed Stella's belongings into the swamp, but she'd just come from New Orleans. They could have been followed by whoever had killed Larry Sutton.

Trembling with exhaustion and on the edge of panic, Livia at last reached the road behind the Willows.

Crouching in the weeds, she debated her options.

She could run back to the SUV, but she was fairly certain that Bryce had locked it before they'd headed into the swamp. Which meant she'd have to smash the window to get to her phone. Something that was bound to attract the attention of the shooter. Plus, it would add extra time to calling for help.

Or she could sneak into the Willows and contact the sheriff.

She didn't trust her family. Not a single one of them. And if they caught her, she didn't know what would happen. But it was a risk she was willing to take.

Keeping the vivid memory of hearing Bryce hit the ground with a pained gasp in the forefront of her mind, Livia squashed the terror thundering through her and grimly straightened. Her friend was hurt. Maybe even dying. The quicker she got help, the better.

Her knees felt weak, but she managed to jog across the narrow path, picking up speed as she pushed open the back gate and headed toward the pool house. She paused long enough to check for movement, her gaze scanning the back terrace before she was once again moving forward.

The house was bathed in darkness, but Livia remained cautious as she closed the gap to climb the shallow steps. Once on the terrace, she pressed herself close to the house and slid her way to the French doors that opened to her uncle's office. It was one of the few rooms that had a landline she could use to call the sheriff.

Her heart was beating so loud she wouldn't be able to hear

an elephant stomping around the room, but she still pressed her ear against the glass panes.

When she was convinced that there was no one inside, she reached for the handle and shoved against the door. It swung open with surprising ease, something that should have worried her. Unfortunately, she was too focused on getting to the desk to think clearly.

A mistake she instantly regretted as she stepped into the room and the overhead light was abruptly switched on. Livia froze like a deer in the headlights. Narrowing her eyes against the unexpected brightness, she could see the vague outline of a form as it stepped into the office from the library.

Locked in place, Livia released a primal cry of sheer terror.

"Livia?" A familiar female voice cut through her screams. "What are you doing?"

Livia blinked, her eyes at last adjusting enough to make out the older woman's mussed brown hair and gaunt form covered by a silk robe that fell to her feet.

"Helene?" Livia released a shaky breath, the surge of adrenaline draining to leave her feeling even more weak than before. "Oh, thank God it's you."

The older woman moved to the center of the office, her gaze sweeping over Livia, who was caked in mud and visibly trembling.

"What on earth happened?"

Livia turned to shut the French doors behind her, struggling to speak. "In the swamp."

"What about the swamp?"

"Someone was shooting at us."

"Shooting? Are you injured?"

Livia turned back, surprised to find Helene standing directly in front of her. "Not me. Bryce."

Helene looked confused. "Who?"

"Bryce Swift. She's a local deputy."

"She was with you in the swamp?" The older woman looked more annoyed than concerned.

"Yes."

Helene heaved a sigh. "Unfortunate."

"It's more than unfortunate," Livia snapped, stepping around the older woman. "I have to call the sheriff."

Helene moved to the side, blocking her path. "I don't think so."

"What?" For the first time since Helene had made her dramatic entrance, Livia truly studied her aunt. The older woman was dressed as if she'd just crawled out of bed, and her hair hung over her shoulders in tangles, but there was a hectic glitter in the blue eyes and a flush on her cheeks. Anger surged through Livia and she had to battle against the urge to shove the woman out of her way. Helene was fragile enough she might break a bone if she pushed too hard. "Damn, of course you have to be drunk when I need your help," Livia muttered, moving around her aggravating relative.

"No, I'm not drunk." Helene once again moved to block Livia's path. Only this time, she reached into the pocket of her robe to pull out a small handgun. "I'm disappointed."

Stunned by the unexpected turn events, Livia's gaze lowered to the weapon that was pointed directly at her heart.

"Helene?"

"Why didn't you leave?" the older woman snapped.

Livia licked her dry lips. She didn't understand. Was Helene behind the madness? Hiring Larry Sutton to spy on her and then killing him? Terrifying her with stupid pranks? Loading up Stella's belongings and dumping them in the swamp?

It seemed impossible.

And it was, she abruptly realized. Helene couldn't have been in the swamp shooting at her. She would be covered in mud and out of breath if she'd just come from there.

So what the hell was going on?

"What are you talking about?" Livia demanded, taking a cautious step forward.

If she could get close enough to Helene, she could try to overpower her. Helene might be holding the gun with the sort of confidence that warned she was a woman who knew how to use it, but there was no mistaking the tremors that occasionally shook her hand. It wouldn't take much to knock the gun from her fingers.

As long as she didn't shoot Livia before she could get in striking distance.

"I gave you warnings that even an idiot could understand," Helene hissed. "You aren't wanted here."

Livia narrowed her eyes. Maybe Helene hadn't been in the swamps, but she'd been responsible for tormenting her.

"You locked me in the garage," Livia accused.

"Yes."

"And left behind the scarf for me to find."

The older woman nodded. "It belonged to your mother."

Livia clenched her teeth. No wonder she recognized the perfume clinging to the silk. And why Delilah had looked so shocked when Livia had showed it to her.

"And pushed me into the pool."

Helene clicked her tongue, clearly feeling zero guilt. "I had to do something."

"Why?"

"Why? Because you were stirring up the angry spirits." Livia could see the violent tremor that raced through the woman. "Why can't you let them rest in peace?"

With an effort, Livia leashed the panic thundering through her. She had to get past the older woman so she could reach the phone and save Bryce.

Which meant she had to keep her distracted long enough to grab the gun.

"What spirits? My mother's?"

The blue eyes dimmed, as if Helene's brief grip on reality was fading. "She keeps whispering. Over and over." The older woman glanced toward the French doors, as if afraid that her mother was about to walk through them. No. Livia abruptly stiffened. Her gaze was on the covered pool outside the doors. "I can't get away from her."

Livia stared at her aunt, all the vague suspicions and questions surrounding her mother's death coalescing into a grim certainty. She could see it in her aunt's haunted expression.

"Because she didn't jump, did she? She was thrown off that balcony."

Helene winced, as if she'd taken a physical blow. "She was like you. She wouldn't stop pushing and pushing. I warned her too, but she wouldn't listen."

"So you killed her."

"Me?" Helene audibly gasped at the accusation. "No, of course not. I would never hurt my sister. I loved Giselle."

Livia hesitated. There was a throbbing sincerity in Helene's voice that was unmistakable.

"But she did something to anger the family?" she pressed, taking another step forward.

As desperately as she wanted to know what happened to her mother, it was far more urgent she get to a phone.

"She was always doing something to anger the family." Helene's mood snapped from grieving sister to jealous shrew in the blink of an eye. "Not that it mattered. She was the princess. She never had to face the consequences. Not like me."

"What consequences?"

"Loss." Helene's gaze strayed back to the pool. "So much loss. It's suffocating."

Another surge of anger raced through Livia. How dare this woman act as if she'd been the one to suffer? Giselle was dead, and Livia had been forced to grow up without her mother. With an effort, she squashed her resentment. It didn't seem smart to piss off the woman holding the gun.

"Are you talking about the loss of your sister?" she instead asked in a voice that was almost steady.

"She was one, but not the greatest."

Livia frowned, not sure what the older woman meant. "Do you mean your husband leaving?"

Helene blinked, as if caught off guard by the question. Then she released a sharp laugh. "God, no. The happiest day of my life was when Lance walked out of the door." She pressed a hand against her stomach. "That coldhearted bastard cost me everything."

Livia abruptly recalled Remy telling her that there'd been rumors of an abortion.

"Your baby?" she guessed.

"Lance and my father insisted I get rid of my child." Helene's face twisted with a sorrow that came from her very soul. "I refused, but in the end I lost her anyway. Along with Manu."

Livia shook her head, trying to keep up with the words Helene was spitting out as if they were poison. And maybe they were. They'd obviously been festering inside the older woman for years.

She caught the main storyline. Helene was married to a man she hated, and he'd wanted her to have an abortion. And for some reason, Henri wanted her to have an abortion as well. Which didn't make sense. Why wouldn't they want . . .

Her dulled brain at last realized that "Manu" wasn't a strange way to say she'd lost everything. It was a name.

"Manu?" Livia furrowed her brow, realizing that there was something familiar about it. "Of course," she breathed, the pieces falling together. Well, at least a couple of pieces. "You mean Manny? The chauffeur?"

Helene's features softened, as if just the mention of the man was enough to make her melt.

"Manu was his real name. He was the only person to truly love me."

"So . . . you had an affair with the chauffeur and got pregnant. Then your husband and father insisted that you get an abortion?"

Helene tilted her chin in a gesture of defiance. "I'm not ashamed. I wanted my baby."

"And that's when your husband left," Livia finished her thought.

"Good riddance. I thought that I could at last be happy." Helene's soft glow hardened to a bitterness that made her look years older. "But Lance left behind his malignant hatred for the child. I lost the babe a few days later."

Livia swallowed a sigh. It was crazy. The woman had locked her in the garage and pushed her into the pool, and was now pointing a gun at her heart, but she couldn't squash a tug of sympathy as she watched the woman fade back to the miserable, detached shadow who'd drifted through the Willows for the past three decades.

"What happened to Manny?" Livia asked.

"My father fired him, of course. And then he tried to run him out of town."

Ah, yes. The Benoit answer to any trouble. First try throwing money at the problem and if that didn't work, then bully them into compliance.

The question now was, what was the third option? Livia's stomach twisted with a strange sense of dread.

"But he wouldn't go?"

"No." Helene's eyes darkened with a long-held resentment. "We were determined to be together. Even after I lost the baby."

Livia found it absurdly easy to imagine a young Helene frantically attempting to escape her father and find happiness with someone who treated her as more than an asset to be bartered off.

"True love," she murmured.

"Yes. Just like Romeo and Juliet."

Helene's voice was distracted, as if she was lost in memories of happier times. Livia took a step closer.

"So where is Manny?" Livia demanded. "And why didn't you go with him?"

Helene winced, as if her pleasant daydream had been shattered. "Where do you think he is?" she hissed. "With Giselle."

It took a second for Livia understand what her aunt was implying. "He's dead?"

"He took him from me."

"Who took him?"

"My father. Who else?"

Livia stared at Helene. She wasn't shocked that Manny was dead. Somehow she'd sensed that his ghost was haunting the Willows. Or at least haunting poor Helene. But her brain rebelled against the implication that her grandfather was somehow responsible for his death.

"Are you saying he . . . killed him?" she finally forced herself to ask, making sure she didn't mistake what her aunt was suggesting.

Helene hunched a shoulder. "He said it was an accident. Manny came for me early one morning. I had my bags packed and I was about to escape this place. Then I heard it."

"Heard what?"

"That terrible scream."

A chill swirled through the room, sweeping past Livia with a brush of unseen fingers. Fear speared through her heart. The icy touch felt like a warning.

"What happened?" she demanded,

"I ran outside and Manny was lying in the middle of the driveway." Helene's eyes filled with tears. "My father had run him over."

Livia's memory of her grandfather was of an aging tyrant with a thickening paunch and perpetually bitter expression. It took no effort to imagine him using a vehicle to run down someone who'd pissed him off. Wait. Not just any vehicle. It had to be the one currently decomposing in the swamps.

"He ran him over with the limo," she rasped.

Helene gave a jerky nod. "He said he was just trying to scare Manny away, but I didn't believe him. Why would he put his body in the trunk of the limo and drive it to the swamp if he had nothing to hide?"

"No." Livia slapped her hand over her mouth as a rush of nausea threatened to bring up the contents of her stomach. She'd been standing just inches from the limo. She'd actually touched the rusty metal frame. "Oh my God. My grandfather killed a man and hid his body in the swamp. He must have been out of his mind."

"No, not crazy. Henri Benoit simply believed he was above the law."

Livia stared at the woman in horror. "So did you, obviously. Why didn't you call the cops when you'd seen what he'd done?"

Helene glared at her in frustration. "Because no one would have listened to me. The local officials were all on the payroll of the Benoits."

"Then you should have contacted someone . . ." Another shocking revelation slammed into Livia. "Wait. That's it. My mother found out about Manny, didn't she?"

"I told her to let it go, but she thought she was impervious to our father's rage." Helene's lips twisted into a humorless smile. "After all, she managed to run wild her whole life. She even had a baby with no condemnation from the family."

Livia resisted the urge to demand to know the identity of her father. The confession time was about her mother and what had happened after Manny had been murdered.

"She called the FBI. That's the note I found with the date and time she was supposed to meet with the agent."

"So foolish," Helene muttered.

Livia shook her head, her stomach still heaving with a sick sense of disbelief. She'd known her family were a bunch of arrogant asses, but now she realized they were genuine monsters.

"What did you do to her?" she demanded, stepping close enough to glare into Helene's wide blue eyes.

The woman flinched back. "Nothing."

"Helene?"

"It wasn't my fault."

Fury blasted through Livia and, without giving herself time to think of the danger, she reached to wrestle the weapon from Helene's hand. The older woman stumbled back, her tangled hair half hiding her flushed face. She looked like a wild animal. As if the civilized behavior she'd once possessed had been stripped away to expose a raw, savage bitterness.

With a shake of her head, Livia dismissed the ugly knowledge that her mother had been murdered. Probably by her own father. Eventually the truth would be revealed.

Right now, nothing mattered but getting to the phone and calling for help.

Launching toward the desk, Livia had managed to grab the receiver of the phone when a sharp voice froze her in place.

"Drop the gun, Livia, and turn around."

CHAPTER 24

Bryce forced open her heavy lids, briefly assuming she was in the middle of a nightmare. What else could explain the slimy, stinky mud beneath her face and the weird buzzing in her ears?

Only the throbbing headache and searing pain on the side of her neck assured her that this was horrifyingly real. With a groan, she managed to roll onto her back, gazing up at the clouds that hung low enough she felt she could touch them.

She knew she was in the swamps. She even had a foggy memory of walking through the darkness with Livia. And then what? Oh yeah, they'd found the boxes under the tarp. And there'd been another tarp that was covering a rusty old limo. After that it was blank . . .

No. She remembered. Someone had hunted them through the swamps and started shooting at them. With a hiss, Bryce shoved herself off the muddy ground, ignoring the dizziness that threatened to send her toppling back on her ass.

"Argh." She pressed a hand against her neck. It hurt like hell, but there was no blood pouring out. That had to mean she was going to survive, right? Sucking in deep breaths, Bryce glanced around the clearing, her gaze frantically searching for some sign of her friend. "Livia?" she at last called out, her voice soft.

Bryce cursed as there was the sound of heavy boots snapping the rotting branches buried beneath the slime. Pulling out her phone, she held it in her hand like a weapon. It was dark enough she might fool someone into believing she had a gun.

"Show yourself or I'll shoot," she called in a loud, commanding tone.

The footsteps halted and a male voice floated on the air from behind a clump of swamp grass.

"Bryce, it's Finn."

A strangled sob escaped Bryce's throat before she could squash it. She'd never been so happy to see anyone in her entire life.

"Thank goodness." She struggled to remain upright. Her knees were annoyingly weak. Just like some ridiculous damsel in distress. "What are you doing here?"

Finn cautiously stepped forward, his gaze sweeping the area for any signs of trouble. In the murky light it was hard to make out more than the fact that he was wearing jeans and a T-shirt and his dark hair was left loose to brush his shoulders. If she wasn't terrified for Livia, she might have taken a moment to simply appreciate the sight of his raw male beauty as he walked toward her.

"Looking for you," Finn said. "I got your text and I was worried. Why are you out here at this time of night?"

"It's a long story." Bryce glanced toward the spot where she'd pushed her friend, not sure whether to be relieved or alarmed that she was missing. Without a body she could still hope that she was alive. "Right now we have to find Livia."

"Is she lost? Is that why you came out here?"

"No. We were looking for evidence against her family."

"Evidence?" Finn repeated in confusion. "What evidence?"

"Another long story." Bryce waved a vague hand toward the rusty vehicle behind her. "Anyway, we managed to find what we were looking for, or least I guess it's what we were looking for, and then someone snuck up and took shots at us."

"What the hell?" With long strides, Finn was abruptly standing in front of her, his breath hissing between his clenched teeth as he caught sight of the blood splattered across her face and coating her neck. "You're injured."

"It's a flesh wound," she assured him, relieved he couldn't see the egg-size lump on the back of her head. It was possible she was suffering from a concussion after being knocked out. A worry for later. "I'll be fine."

"Not if it gets infected," he growled, his voice rough. As if he was angered by the thought she'd been hurt. "A one hundred percent likelihood if you don't get it cleaned and stitched up. Immediately."

"We find Livia and then I will happily get scrubbed and stitched." She impulsively reached out to grab his hand. "She's in danger, Finn. Someone wants her dead."

Livia reluctantly dropped the gun and turned to face Adrian Benoit. He was wearing his usual black slacks and white shirt, but they were splattered with mud and torn in several places. There was even mud in his dark hair that was mussed from the wind, and specks sprinkled over his grim face.

She should have been shocked to see him standing in the doorway pointing a gun at her. This was a man she'd known her entire life. A man who pretended that she was a member of his family. And even if he'd never been affectionate, he hadn't actively hated her. But she wasn't shocked.

Instead, she was resigned.

She glanced toward Helene, who was cowering on the floor next to the bookshelves. Her head was bowed and her hair had fallen forward to hide her face, but any sympathy that Livia had felt was destroyed by her cowardly refusal to stand up to her family.

"Did you know he was out there shooting at me?"

"He told me I had to stop you from leaving if you returned to the Willows," the woman whimpered. "I had no choice."

Livia made a sound of disgust, turning back to her uncle. "I knew it was you out there. You were the one who shot Bryce. Where is she?"

"Dead."

Horror exploded through Livia at the blunt revelation, along with an instinctive urge to launch herself toward the bastard and beat him bloody. If he'd truly killed Bryce, then . . .

No. Livia balled her hands into tight fists. This man had spent years weaving lies to protect the Benoit name. The disappearance of the chauffeur, her mother's death, even the failing family business. She wasn't sure he'd ever told the truth in his miserable life. She wasn't going to let herself lose hope. Not until she could see Bryce with her own eyes.

Until then, it was her job to make sure that Adrian and Helene paid for their crimes.

"You've lost your mind," she rasped. "Bryce is a deputy. You're going to jail for this."

"No one will find her. But don't worry." Adrian stepped forward, his expression grim. "You'll soon be joining her."

Livia tilted her chin, even as her stomach twisted with dread. She might have been able to overpower her aunt, but there was no way she could physically wrestle the gun away from Adrian. Not before he could shoot her.

Time for another distraction. She had to keep him talking long enough to get to the French doors. There was a tiny chance she could dart outside and make her escape before he could put a bullet through her heart.

"How did you know we were in the swamp?" She asked the question that had been troubling her since she realized they'd been followed.

Adrian shrugged. "I have a trail camera that alerts me if anyone is trespassing in that area. No one is supposed to be there. Especially you." His jaw muscles bulged, as if he was clenching his teeth. "But you never listen, do you? Always poking your nose where it doesn't belong."

Livia tossed her hair, folding her arms over her chest as she took a step backward.

"I'm not surprised you're involved in this, Adrian. You were always Grandfather's spineless toady."

Surprisingly, he flushed at her accusation, as if she'd struck a nerve. "My only involvement is cleaning up other people's messes. The story of my life."

He sounded like a whiny brat, as if threatening his niece with a gun was just another annoying task.

"What did you do to my mother?" she abruptly demanded, inching another step back. If she was going to die, she could at least get some answers first.

Adrian frowned. "Nothing."

"I don't believe you. I know that she called to meet with Special Agent Rice to confess that there was a dead body hidden in the swamp, didn't she? I talked to the agent and he said that she never showed up. Because she was already dead." Livia shuddered, trying not to think of how close she'd been standing to the limo. And the horrific secret hidden in the trunk. It was just so awful. "You had to stop her."

"How did you. . . ? Never mind. It doesn't matter." Adrian shook his head. "Okay, it's true. I overheard her calling the FBI."

Livia curled her lips in disgust. "You were spying on her."

"I knew she was upset and suspected she intended to do something stupid." Adrian's tone was defensive as he continued his role as the aggrieved victim. "So yes, I was watching her."

"And then you threw her off the balcony."

Her stark accusation resonated through the room. Helene

whimpered in fear, but Adrian ignored his sister as he stepped forward to glare at Livia.

"No one threw her," he snapped. "It was an accident."

Livia pretended to cower at his sharp retort, stumbling back a few steps before straightening to send him a glare. She wasn't close enough to make a run for it yet, but every inch was a victory.

"Just like running over poor Manny was an accident?" she demanded.

Adrian clicked his tongue, sending Helene an impatient frown. "My father had an explosive temper. Manny was an idiot if he thought for a second that Henri Benoit would allow his daughter to run off with the chauffeur."

"Because the Benoits are so superior?" Livia made a gagging sound. "You people make me sick."

Adrian's gaze snapped back to glare at her. "They were superior in his mind. He'd been raised to believe that nothing was more important than taking pride in the Benoit name."

"He was an aging relic with a bloated ego," Livia corrected before returning the conversation back to the only thing that mattered to her. "What happened to my mother?"

Adrian's lips snapped together, as if he was going to refuse to answer. Fear bubbled through Livia. She wasn't sure what was worse: the thought he was about to shoot her, or the terror she might die without ever knowing the truth.

Surprisingly, Adrian visibly forced himself to respond. "After I overheard Giselle on the phone with the FBI, I went to my father to warn him."

"Traitor," she hissed.

Adrian grimaced. "You might not believe me, but I regret that now."

"No, I don't believe you," she said in an icy voice. Between Helene's cowardly refusal to stand up for herself and Adrian's bootlicking, her poor mother was the only child with a spine.

It was no wonder she was Henri's favorite. "Just tell me what happened."

"No one really knows," Adrian reluctantly admitted. "My father said that he confronted Giselle in her room. There was an argument and she stormed onto the balcony. When he followed her to pull her back into the bedroom, she supposedly stumbled backward and fell over the railing."

"You don't believe that, do you?" she scoffed. "That railing must have come up to her waist. She wasn't going over the top unless someone picked her up and tossed her over."

"I don't know. And in the end it didn't matter," he insisted in a bleak voice. "Whatever happened up there that night destroyed the family. Helene turned to the bottle. My father became a recluse, and the business started to fall apart. I did my best to keep things from a complete collapse."

Livia released a sharp laugh. "Your best? You are . . ." Words nearly failed her. "Unbelievable," she finally hissed. "Henri Benoit sold off his daughter to the highest bidder, then went mental when she chose a chauffeur instead of her abusive husband, demanding she abort her child. And even after she lost the baby, he wasn't satisfied. He had to murder the poor man and stuff him in the trunk of his limo and drive it into the middle of the swamp to rot." Livia was trembling as a lifetime of pent-up fury cascaded through her. "And instead of confronting him—or better yet, calling the authorities—you spied and tattled on your own sister. Her blood is on your hands."

Helene gasped and Adrian's fingers tightened on the grip of the gun, as if he was struggling against the urge to pull the trigger. She wasn't really sure why he didn't. Maybe he hoped he could gaslight her into offering her forgiveness?

Hell would freeze over first.

"I told you," he rasped. "I did my best."

Livia edged another inch backward. She didn't dare glance

over her shoulder to see how far she was from the doors. All she could do was keep her uncle distracted until she reached her goal.

"Did your best include sending me to live with complete strangers?" she loudly demanded.

He didn't bother to pretend it hadn't been his decision to get rid of her. "What else could I do? Your presence was a constant reminder to my father of what he'd lost."

"Lost? He didn't lose anything." Her voice was shrill with a furious disbelief. "He deliberately murdered his chauffeur along with my mother."

"Whatever. I thought it was safer for both of you if you went to live in New Orleans."

"Right." Livia rolled her eyes. "And I suppose you also hoped that getting me away from the Willows would mean I'd also be cut out of the will?"

His dark flush revealed the truth. He'd fully intended to take her share of the money. "I needed every penny just to keep a roof over our heads."

"You mean a roof over *your* head, not mine," she reminded him. "Along with a closet full of designer clothes for your wife and daughter."

He shrugged. "The Benoits have an image to maintain."

"Here's a hint: We don't live in the Dark Ages anymore. No one cares about the Benoits or how they dress."

"You might not, but other people do," Adrian stubbornly insisted.

"Other snobs like you."

"Don't act so innocent." Adrian abruptly went on the offensive. "You were eager enough to come every year and take a handout from the family."

Livia smiled, ridiculously pleased to know that her visits to the Willows year after year had been a constant source of annoyance to this man.

"The money belongs to me." Her smile widened. "And I certainly wasn't going to let you have it."

"I always suspected you were going to be a pain in the ass. One of many aggravations I've had to deal with over the years."

He sounded harassed, reminding Livia that the secret they'd been trying to hide hadn't been entirely secret.

"Was Stella Gates one of those problems?"

Genuine hatred tightened his features at the mention of Livia's former nanny.

"The greedy bitch," he hissed. "I'm glad she's dead."

Livia no longer had to wonder how Stella Gates managed to squeeze so much money from the Benoits. She shared a suite with Giselle. How could she not have known what was happening?

"I assume she witnessed my mother being pushed off the balcony?"

Adrian's lips twisted, looking like he'd swallowed a lemon. "She claimed to have been there when it happened, but that wouldn't have bothered me. She was just a nanny. I could have convinced everyone she was lying to try and make an easy buck off my sister's tragic death."

The sheer arrogance stole her breath. Adrian pretended to be a better man than his ruthless father, but at heart he was still a conceited narcissist who was willing to use his power as a Benoit to destroy others. With an effort, Livia shook off her disgust.

"So how was she blackmailing you?"

"She had Giselle's diary. It revealed everything about our family. Every dirty secret written in my sister's hand. It would have destroyed us."

"A diary, of course." Livia released a harsh sigh as she recalled the note that she'd found hidden in her mother's scrapbook. She'd noticed the date stamped at the top of the paper. It was obvious that it had been torn out of a diary or daily calendar. Her mother's personal journal. That's what everyone had been looking for all along. "God, I've been so stupid."

"What are you talking about?"

"It doesn't matter." She concentrated on scooting back. How much farther to the doors? "That's why you hired Larry Sutton, isn't it? To find the diary?"

"I searched Stella's house and couldn't find the stupid thing," Adrian admitted. "I even loaded up her stuff and had it brought here. There was nothing. At last I got desperate enough to hire a private investigator to look for it."

Yet another mystery explained, she wryly acknowledged, but there was still one more. The mystery that had started everything.

"So how did I get involved in any of this?"

"While he was investigating, Sutton talked to one of the home health nurses who was taking care of Stella during her last months. She told him that Stella had given her a large envelope and asked her to mail it. The nurse hadn't paid much attention, but she did recall that the address was in New Orleans and she thought the last name was Benoit." Adrian shrugged. "I assumed she must have sent you the diary."

"To me?" Livia asked. "Why? I don't even remember her."

"Because it belonged to your mother. Once she'd used it to bleed me dry it was useless to her. My guess was that she wanted to make sure it ended up in your hands since it probably had a lot of stuff in there about Giselle's early days as a mother."

Regret stabbed Livia in the heart. She would have treasured something as personal as her mother's diary. But even that had been stolen from her.

She sent her uncle a look of pure loathing. "That's why Larry Sutton was searching my house."

"He convinced me that he could charm the information out of you. He had an inflated opinion that he was irresistible to women. When that didn't work he decided to search your house for it." Adrian made a sound of disgust. "He swore he couldn't find anything."

Livia suddenly felt like an idiot. When she'd been dating Jacob Pearson he had often discussed old books and diaries he'd bought in secondhand shops. He'd even asked her if she had any diaries that she'd collected from her family or old stories that had been passed down. At the time, she'd just thought that it was his hobby, and tried to act interested when he discussed his latest find. Now she realized he was waiting for her to pull out her mother's diary to show him.

When that didn't happen, he'd instead tricked her into giving him a key to search her house.

She'd been so stupidly naïve. She hadn't had one suspicion. Not until she caught him pawing through her underwear drawer.

"There was nothing to find. I never got a package from Stella Gates. Or anyone else."

"It doesn't matter." Adrian waved his gun, bringing an end to her questions. "I didn't want it to be this way, but there's no going back now."

Livia pressed a hand against her chest, taking another step. She sensed it was getting to the point of do or die.

And for once that wasn't just a cliché.

"What do you intend to do to me?"

"You have to disappear."

"Like Manny and Larry Sutton?"

He scowled, as if caught off guard by the question, but before he could speak, a shadow fell across the doorway and a slender form stepped into the room.

Livia felt a surge of hope as she watched Delilah glance around the office, her brows pulling together at the sight of Helene crouched against the bookcase and Adrian pointing a gun at his niece. The older woman might be a selfish bitch, but she surely wouldn't allow her husband to commit cold-blooded murder?

A second later, Livia's hopes were crushed as Delilah stepped toward Adrian and handed him a key fob.

"The SUV is parked out front."

"You too?" Livia breathed in shock. "Is there something in the air at the Willows that turns everyone into a homicidal maniac?"

The older couple ignored her as Adrian pocketed the key fob with a frown. "It's about time. What took you so long?"

Livia belatedly understood why her uncle hadn't shot her the minute he'd entered the office. Clearly he intended to do the deed somewhere else and had been waiting for his vehicle to be delivered to the front door.

Delilah clicked her tongue. She was wearing a silk caftan and matching slippers that made her look like she'd been enjoying a drink by the pool, not plotting murder.

"I not only had to get the SUV for you, but I had to turn off the security system and get rid of the earlier footage. You don't think someone will want to review them when we report Livia missing?"

Adrian flinched, easily intimidated by his formidable wife. "Sorry, I didn't think about that."

"It's good one of has the brains to take care of the little details."

"Fine." Struggling to regain command of the situation, Adrian pointed his hand toward the silently sobbing woman across the office. "Take Helene back to her room and make sure she's sedated. *Heavily* sedated. I don't want her blurting out anything that's going to send us to the gas chamber." He waved the gun toward Livia. "You, come with me."

Livia tensed her muscles, preparing to leap toward the French doors. "And if I don't?"

He shrugged. "I'll shoot you here and dump your body with your friend in the swamp."

"Helene?" Livia glanced toward her aunt, who was being hauled to her feet by an impatient Delilah.

She didn't expect the older woman to help her, but it gave reason to turn away from Adrian.

"I'm sorry," Helene whispered, not even glancing toward Livia.

Adrian stepped forward, his expression hard, although there was a dread in his eyes that he couldn't hide. As if he was afraid of what he was going to have to do.

Odd considering she wasn't the first person he'd killed.

"Let's go," he commanded.

Glancing toward the French doors, Livia was preparing to make her life-or-death leap when, without warning, they burst open. She blinked in shock. Had she somehow managed to open them with the force of her frantic need to escape?

Then reality returned with a painful explosion of sound as Adrian wildly began shooting toward the dark opening.

Slapping her hands over her ears, Livia scurried behind a nearby chair, instinctively trying to avoid the bullets that her uncle was spraying indiscriminately in her direction. The idiot was going to kill all of them. Delilah and Helene seemed to agree as they screamed and knocked over furniture in a wild dash to get out of the room.

Then abruptly, the crazy melee came to an end as the sound of a male voice boomed through the air.

"Drop the gun, Benoit, and put your hands behind your back, you're under arrest for attempted murder."

The shooting stopped, but Livia remained behind the chair as she peeked around the edge to see Sheriff Finn Maxwell slapping a pair of cuffs on her uncle, who was hanging his head, his shoulders hunched in defeat.

Still not sure if it was safe to come out, Livia was distracted as a second person entered the room. This one from the open French doors.

Joy blasted through Livia as she leaped to her feet, all thoughts of her monstrous family forgotten as she ran toward her bedraggled friend.

"Bryce! You're alive."

Bryce managed a wry smile despite the mud that covered her from head to toe and the deep gash that was leaking blood from her neck.

"It takes more than a gunshot wound, a few alligators, and a grumpy sheriff to keep me away," she assured Livia.

Then, still smiling, Bryce toppled forward, fainting into Livia's outstretched arms.

CHAPTER 25

New Orleans, LA
Wednesday, July 9th

It was midmorning the next day before Livia managed to make it to the hospital to visit her friend.

She'd spent a couple hours after being rescued at the sheriff's office in Rushville giving her statement before returning to her home in New Orleans, where she showered and managed to choke down some breakfast despite her lingering queasiness. There was no point in trying to sleep. She would only toss and turn, reliving each horrific moment of the past few days: finding Larry Sutton's body, slogging through the swamp only to be threatened by her crazy uncle, discovering her mother had been murdered by her grandfather.

For the next day or two, she was simply going to concentrate on the fact that she was alive and that Bryce was on her way to recovery.

Changing into fresh clothing, Livia took the time to style her hair and put on some makeup before driving across town to the hospital. She wanted to appear calm and composed for her friend, even if she felt rubbed raw on the inside. Bryce was the sort of person to be more concerned about Livia's mental state than her own injuries. She didn't want to give her any reason to worry.

Entering the hospital, she took the stairs to the upper floor. She wasn't ready to be trapped in a confined space. Not yet. Wandering down the long hallway, she grimaced at the sharp tang of antiseptic and freshly waxed floors. It was a universal smell of hospitals everywhere.

Turning a corner, she at last found Bryce's room and poked her head through the open door. She frowned, confused by the deep shadows.

"Bryce?" she whispered. "Are you awake?"

"Awake and ready to get out of here," an annoyed voice snapped.

Entering the room, Livia realized there was a long curtain suspended from the ceiling that divided the space in half. Brushing past the barrier, she discovered Bryce propped up in bed, fully dressed and obviously champing at the bit to leave.

Relief slammed into her with an unexpected force. When she'd seen her friend collapse, she'd been terrified that she'd been fatally injured. And even after Finn had assured her that Bryce was at the hospital, comfortably recovering from her gunshot wound and potential concussion, she'd worried that things were worse than he was willing to admit.

She would never, ever forgive herself if Bryce died. Or even if she was seriously wounded.

Now she happily studied her friend's flushed cheeks and sparkle of irritation in her eyes. The awful pallor of her skin was gone, along with the splatters of blood. Only the gauze taped to the side of her neck revealed she'd recently been injured.

"Don't be in such a rush," Livia teased, moving to stand next to her friend. "How often do you get to lie in bed and be pampered?"

"Pampered?" The hazel eyes widened. "I've been poked and prodded and X-rayed until I want to punch someone. Not to mention the fact that they wouldn't even let me go to the bathroom in privacy. They made me call for a nurse every time I wanted to pee until the doctor finally decided I didn't have a concussion."

"That is unacceptable," Livia commiserated, thankful that her friend had been cleared of any head injuries. It was weird to think that they'd been lucky after the trauma they'd gone through, but it was true. Things could have ended up so different. She shook her head, dismissing the morbid thought. Today was a day for counting her blessings, not dwelling on what might have been. "Do you know when you get out?"

"As soon as the doctor signs the paperwork."

"Good. I'll wait around with you and drive you back to Rushville."

Bryce cleared her throat, looking oddly embarrassed. "No need. Finn just called and he's on his way to pick me up."

Livia smiled. She hadn't missed the sheriff's frantic reaction when Bryce had collapsed. Or his determined expression as he'd warned the paramedics to take special care of her on the way to the hospital.

He wasn't going to let Bryce slip through his fingers.

Smart man.

"Lucky girl," Livia murmured, meaning it with her whole heart. Every woman deserved a man who cared so deeply.

"You're right," Bryce agreed in soft tones. "I am lucky."

"So am I." Livia reached out to lightly touch the gauze covering her friend's neck. "If you hadn't burst into the office when you did—"

"It's my job," Bryce interrupted.

"I don't care," Livia insisted. "You were shot, concussed, and on the edge of collapse, but you still waded through the swamps to save me."

"You forgot the alligators," Bryce teased.

"Were there really alligators?"

"There might have been."

They shared a weary smile. "You're my hero," Livia said quietly.

"Enough of that nonsense," Bryce said gruffly, visibly uncomfortable. "Are you staying in New Orleans?"

With a sigh, Livia resisted the urge to insist that her friend accept her gratitude.

"I am," she said. "I couldn't bear the thought of staying alone at the Willows. The whole family is in jail. Well, everyone but Celeste, who I think went to stay with her fiancé. And it's not like anyone cares about the rules of my grandfather's trust fund right now. We'll have to deal with that stuff later."

"So the house is empty?"

"It officially belongs to the ghosts." Livia's lips twisted with a bitter amusement. "Eventually it will be sold or left to rot. Either way, I never plan to set foot in that place again. I no longer have to deal with the Benoits. It's like a weight has been lifted off my shoulders."

Bryce clicked her tongue. "I still can't believe your grandfather killed your mother."

"And don't forget running down the poor chauffeur and stuffing his body in the trunk of the limo," Livia added. Manny had been allowed to disappear because he was a mere servant. She intended to make sure at some point his family was notified and his body returned to them to be properly buried. "Nothing mattered more to Henri Benoit than his reputation. He wasn't going to let anyone tarnish it. Not even his own child."

"Such a waste."

"Yes."

Bryce studied her with a blatant curiosity. "So now what?"

"I'm going to stop by the office and make sure the repairs are done," she said, firmly dismissing her clinging connection to the Benoits and their dark legacy. Time to concentrate on the future. "If everything is ready to go, I'll be back to work tomorrow."

"You don't think you deserve a vacation?"

Livia arched a brow. "Are you taking a vacation or going back to work?"

"Touché."

They shared a smile, but before Livia could speak, a tall, gorgeous man in jeans and casual T-shirt strolled into the room with a small suitcase and a bakery bag that smelled like heaven.

"Okay, I brought the clean clothes that your father dropped by the office and some beignets fresh out of the deep fryer. Is there anything else you need?" Finn abruptly noticed Bryce wasn't alone. "Sorry, Livia. I didn't mean to interrupt."

"You're not," Livia assured him, suddenly feeling like a third wheel. Time to move on. "I just wanted to stop by and check on Bryce." She sent the sheriff a smile. "And to say thank you."

"Just doing our—"

"Job. Yes, I know," Livia interrupted, wondering if law officials practiced that line. With a shrug, she leaned down to give her friend a gentle hug. "I'll see you later. It looks like you're in good hands for now," she whispered in Bryce's ear. "Enjoy them."

"I think I will," Bryce agreed.

Pretending she didn't feel a pang of envy at the knowledge her friend was going to be thoroughly spoiled by her handsome, sexy companion, Livia left the hospital and drove to her office.

She parked at the corner to make sure she didn't get blocked in, then used the side entrance that led to her office. The new front window was in, but she didn't want to risk joggling it until she had confirmation everything was dried and painted and ready to go.

Once inside, she flipped on the lights and headed toward the hallway that led to the front lobby. She would take a quick peek to make sure the recently shampooed rugs were dry and the holes in the wall repaired. Then she would go home and try to rest.

She was passing by the storage room when she came to an abrupt halt. She'd heard a rustling sound. Did they have a mouse? Aggravated by the thought of vermin chewing on her expensive supplies, she pushed the door open and flicked on the overhead light.

Her heart ricocheted against her ribs as she caught sight of the familiar male profile and broad shoulders visible beneath an expensive silk shirt that was tucked into a pair of black slacks.

Winston Durand.

"You," she breathed. "What are you doing here?"

Winston slowly turned, and for the second time in the span of twenty-four hours, Livia discovered herself on the wrong side of a gun.

"Christ, you're determined to get yourself killed, aren't you?" Winston snapped, his handsome features tight with a smoldering anger. "I hoped Adrian would take care of you, but once again I'm left dealing with a Benoit mess." His brows snapped together as Livia giggled. "Why is that funny?"

Livia felt weirdly lightheaded as she stared at the intruder. Was she hysterical? Maybe. Another giggle escaped her lips. Yes, definitely hysterical.

"That's exactly what Adrian claimed as he was hauled away by the sheriff last night. He said he was cleaning up a Benoit mess."

Winston curled his lips in disgust. "That's not going to happen to me. Adrian is an idiot. I'm too smart to get caught."

Livia ignored his boast. "Why are you here?"

"Looking for the diary, obviously." He held up his hand, revealing a slender book with pink flowers imprinted on the cover. Her mother's diary. "It occurred to me last night that we've been searching in the wrong place. It was doubtful your old nanny would know your home address, but it would be easy to locate your new business. Especially after you had your ribbon-cutting splashed across the front page. And I was right."

Livia's gaze moved to the stack of packages piled in the corner. She was constantly receiving promo items from various office supply chains and marketing firms. She pulled them out to look through them when she was getting ready to create a new order. Stella's package must have ended up there.

She shook her head, a wave of sadness rolling through her. How much tragedy could have been avoided if she'd just opened the envelope when it arrived? Then she desperately pushed aside her regret.

The past didn't matter. She was once again fighting for her future.

"What do you care about the diary?" she demanded, genuinely baffled. "My grandfather's crimes and the fact that the family covered them up have already been exposed. There's no way you can protect Celeste from the scandal now."

"You think I give a shit about Celeste?"

She blinked at the revulsion in his tone. "Why wouldn't I? You asked her to be your wife."

"No, I was forced to ask her."

Livia recalled Remy's suggestion that there was something sketchy about the relationship, and her own suspicions when she'd met Tara, the too-pretty nurse.

"Forced by who?"

"Adrian, of course."

"Why would he do that?"

"Because he was running out of money. He was desperate to get his hands on my bank account."

She stared at him in confusion, not sure whether to feel

sorry for her bitchy cousin or not. "That sounds like something Adrian would do, but why did you agree?"

He glared at the book he held in his hand. As if it personally offended him. "Because your family's homicidal tendencies aren't the only thing revealed in this diary."

Livia licked her dry lips. "My mother knew something about you?" she guessed, then she shook her head. Winston was too young to have a secret before Giselle had died. "No, not you. Your father?"

A strange emotion rippled over his face. "*Our* father."

"What?"

"I said . . . our father. You're my sister. Or more specifically, my half sister."

"Sister?" Shocked, Livia stumbled back, her breath squeezed painfully from her lungs. "I don't believe you."

"You want proof?" Winston waved the diary in her direction. "Your mother writes at nauseating length about her affair with my father and the inevitable consequences."

"Oh my God." Livia struggled to make sense of what he was telling her. Something that would be easier if her brain wasn't buzzing with a combination of adrenaline and pure terror. "My father is Gerald Durand," she managed to mutter, easily able to imagine her rebellious mother sneaking out to meet with the older, no doubt charming neighbor. She would have been intoxicated by the secrecy, and knowing she was defying her father with someone he couldn't bully or intimidate. Not when the Durands were as rich and powerful as the Benoits. "That's why no one would tell me."

"He denied everything, of course, after your mother revealed she was pregnant. He couldn't risk an expensive divorce." Winston shrugged. "And your grandfather wasn't willing to make an enemy of his wealthy neighbor."

Livia shuddered. It wasn't just the thought that Gerald had cheated on his wife, but that he'd seduced a minor and gotten her pregnant without concern for what would happen to her or the baby.

Her father was clearly a selfish asshat.

Thank God she hadn't been obligated to have a relationship with him.

"So what do you care if the truth comes out now?" Her voice was hoarse, as if she were sick. And she was. But it was a sickness in her soul, not her body. "Both our mothers are dead and I doubt your dad is in any condition to care about local gossip."

"I care about my inheritance, you bitch," Winston snapped. "In the past, my dad could deny you are a Durand. Now a simple DNA test would prove the truth."

Livia sent him a glare of sheer loathing. "You think I want your money?"

"That's exactly what I think."

"I don't." She held up her hands. "I swear on my mother's grave I wouldn't take anything from you or the bastard who seduced a child. Not even if you offered it to me on a silver platter."

"Easy to say when you're doing well," Winston sneered, clearly incapable of conceiving of anyone who wasn't equally greedy and selfish. "One medical emergency or downturn in the market and you would be at my door demanding a handout."

Livia bit back her words. There was no use arguing with someone who was obsessed with his wealth.

"So you agreed to marry Celeste to keep the truth from me?" She instead returned the conversation to Winston's connection to the nightmare she'd endured the past month.

"Yes. I gave Adrian the money he needed to keep the nanny quiet and then he announced that the old woman had died."

"You knew he hired Larry Sutton?"

"Adrian?" Winston laughed, as if she'd made a joke. "That incompetent coward didn't do anything but wring his hands and complain when the nanny died and he couldn't find the diary. *I* was the one to hire Sutton."

Livia frowned. "Larry Sutton worked for you?"

Winston nodded. "I assured Adrian I would hire a private investigator to find the diary, but he didn't know that I had every intention of having Sutton locate the stupid thing and put it directly in my hands. That way I could get rid of my annoying fiancée and any ties to your family for good."

Of course. Livia shook her head. It made sense now.

"It *was* you I saw in my house with Sutton."

"I went there to tell him that he was running out of time. If he didn't find the diary I was going to fire him." His expression hardened. "Unfortunately, I didn't realize you were there until Sutton sent me a text saying you'd seen us. I knew in that moment he had to go."

"Go where?" Livia sucked in a horrified breath, remembering the bloated, decaying corpse of Larry Sutton. "Oh my God. You killed him."

"What choice did I have?" Winston demanded. "You were a woman who'd been betrayed by her lover. You were eventually going to go looking for information on who he was and why he'd been sneaking into your house. Besides, he'd already learned that Stella Gates had sent you the diary. I could look for it as easy as him. And a lot cheaper." Winston's jaw tightened, as if he was battling a surge of anger. "Not that he made it easy. The bastard simply vanished after you caught him in your house. It took me forever to convince him to meet me in person so I could pay what I owed him. We met up at a bar and I followed him back to his cabin. It was isolated enough I didn't have to worry about any witnesses, so I shot him as soon as he got out of his car."

"Why tear up the cabin?"

"To make it look like a robbery." Winston looked smug. As if he was proud of shooting a man in cold blood. And maybe he was. Livia was starting to think there was something toxic in the bayous around Rushville that made people go crazy. Or maybe the swamps really were cursed. "Plus there was a chance he had something in there that would tie him to me," Winston continued. "As I said, I'm too smart to get caught."

"You . . . wait." Livia was suddenly confused. "When did you kill him?"

Winston gave a casual wave of the gun. "I don't remember the exact date. It was a day or two before you arrived at the Willows."

All this time she'd thought it was Sutton spying on her. Now she realized he'd been dead since she left New Orleans.

"It was you who tried to break into my house, wasn't it?"

Winston still looked smug. "I found the key at the cabin. It was worth a try. I didn't think you would have gone to the effort of changing your locks."

"And you shot out my window here at the office."

"A meaningless gesture, but Adrian kept demanding that I do something to distract you until Sutton found the diary."

"He didn't know you'd killed the man?"

"He didn't know a lot of things." He stared at her with an unnerving intensity, the space suddenly feeling way too small for both of them. "It's a pity really."

"What is?"

"That you're the only Benoit to inherit your grandfather's intelligence. He should have given you everything." Winston aimed the gun at her head. "Too late now."

Livia didn't think, she just let instinct take over as she whipped her arm to the side, hitting the wall behind her with enough force to send shock waves of pain through her. She barely noticed as the faulty alarm was triggered by the vibrations, the shrill beep deafening in the cramped space.

Winston hissed, thankfully distracted by the unexpected noise. Livia didn't hesitate. Bending low, she darted through the opening and slammed the door shut behind her. Then, saying a prayer of thanks that she still held her keys in her hands, she shoved the smallest one into the lock and turned it.

Inside the closet, Winston shouted in fury, banging his shoulder against the door. Livia raced out the back of the building, pulling her phone from her purse, and for what felt like the hundredth time in the past week, dialed 911.

Epilogue

New Orleans, LA
Mid-August

After weeks spent dealing with police reports, family lawyers, and persistent reporters, Livia at last pulled on her black A-line skirt and a sleeveless sweater before driving to her office.

It was a relief to know she would spend the day doing the things she loved: showing homes, meeting with potential clients, negotiating with contractors. She was ready to get back into a routine. Soon she would have to testify at her family's trial, along with the one for Winston Durand. He'd been arrested for burglary and attempted murder. Neither of them would be easy to get through, but today the sun was shining and she intended to live in the moment.

Entering the front door, she glanced around the lobby, appreciating the recently painted wall and the large window that had her name painted in bold letters. It looked better than the old one.

"It's about time," Marcel drawled as he rose from his desk and crossed the room to make himself a cappuccino. He looked as handsome as ever in his gold-and-ivory–striped shirt that brought out the golden flecks in his dark eyes. "The phone hasn't stopped ringing since we reopened. You are in fashion, my love. Everyone wants Livia Benoit as their real estate agent."

Livia shuddered, but she refused to let the thought of the gossip ruin her mood. Her family was too famous not to be the source of avid fascination as they endured their spectacular downfall.

"They do say any publicity is good publicity."

He turned back to her, genuine concern on his face. "I'm really glad you're back. How are you feeling?"

"For the first time in a long time I feel good," she assured him. "I've started sleeping through the night and the Willows is officially on the market. I never have to go back there again."

Marcel reached out to grab her hand. Although Livia hadn't been to the office since she'd found Winston in the storage room, they'd talked on a daily basis. Marcel knew everything that had been happening.

"And what about the request from your real father?" he asked in soft tones.

Livia shrugged. It'd been a shock when she'd received a voice message from Tara the nurse, claiming that Gerald Durand wanted to speak with her, and had even left a date and time she was expected to drive to his estate and meet with him.

Arrogant ass.

"I have no intention of visiting a man who denied my existence for my entire life. I'm cutting my ties to the past." She squeezed her friend's hand. "From today forward, I'm living in the moment."

"*Laissez les bons temps rouler?*" he teased.

"Exactly." With her first genuine smile in days, Livia headed for her office. "Let the good times roll."